UNBINDING DESIRE

Unbinding Trilogy
Book One

MAELANA NIGHTINGALE

Fated Love Publishing

UNBINDING DESIRE

Note from the Author:

Please take a moment to review the trigger warnings. While some TWs do not appear in this book, they may be present in future installments of the trilogy.

This series proudly features representation of neurodivergent characters. With personal experience with ASD and ADHD, along with clinical knowledge, I aim to portray these characters authentically. It's important to remember that neurodivergence exists on a spectrum and looks different for everyone. Nothing written or implied is intended as a blanket statement or generalization of any member of the neurodivergent community.

Trigger Warnings For Complete Trilogy
(may or may not be present in each book)

- Alcohol
- Anxiety
- BDSM
- Blindfolds
- Blood
- Breath Play (Sexual Asphyxiation)
- Car Accident
- Cheating
- Coma
- Depiction of Death of a Child / Significant Other /Parents
- Depression
- Divorce
- Drugs
- Dubious Consent
- Grief
- Hospitalization
- Injury
- Molestation (Historical False Accusation)
- Orphan
- Physical Injury
- Polyamory (Consensual)
- Profanity
- Post Traumatic Stress Disorder
- Severe Illness
- Rough Sex (Consensual)
- Sexually Explicit Scenes (Including Anal, Oral, & DVP/TVP)
- Slut Shaming
- Suicide (Historical Depiction)
- Toxic Parental Relationships

Dedicated to the friends and family who, from this day forward, will have to look me in the eye knowing I write smut, and to the women who want their own harem, please enjoy living vicariously through Alexis ♥

In shadows deep, where sorrows sigh,
Loved souls lost, beneath the sky.
Betrayal's cut, a jagged knife,
Yet love's embrace brings back to life.

From shattered pasts, new futures rise,
In love's embrace, beneath bright skies.
From tragedy, love finds its way,
In its embrace, we choose to stay.

Though family ties may break and bend,
New bonds of love, they surely mend.
Within the wreckage, love does gleam,
A gentle ray, a hopeful dream.

In sunlight's kiss, love's fire burns bright,
A beacon through the darkest night.
Through trials faced and battles won,
Love's journey has just begun.

PROLOGUE

ALEXIS

Caught between the memories of the past and the excitement of the future, I find myself waltzing the intricate dance of love and loss.

"Jake would be happy to know you're happy," Maryanne, my would-have-been mother-in-law, whispers softly after I place blue forget-me-nots on her son's snow-covered grave.

Her words carry both empathy and a touch of sadness as she envelops me in a gentle embrace. I appreciate her attempt to uplift me, but deep down, I can't shake the feeling of betraying the memory of the man fate took from me six years ago.

Maryanne has been a pillar of support, more of a mother to me than my own ever was. When I revealed my recent engagement to Brody, I felt like I was betraying her too, but her unwavering encouragement means everything. Her response, brimmed with grace, love, and acceptance, alleviated some of the guilt burdening my heart.

She is twenty years my senior, her hair dyed auburn over the years to mask the gray. A bit stout, she bears a resemblance to the actress who portrays Mrs. Weasley. Most importantly, I don't know what I would do without her.

Her brown eyes fall to the other bouquet in my hand. "Are the other flowers for Toby?" she inquires gently.

Tears well up in my eyes, cascading down my cheeks as I nod in response.

"Oh, honey," she embraces me once more, "It will be alright. Toby would be happy that you're happy, too."

Toby's grave lies a mere thirty yards from Jake's. These two men, who loved me deeply, departed from this world far too soon. As I place flowers on Toby's grave, I read the inscription on his headstone, penned with meticulous thoughtfulness by his mother, Eleanor.

In loving memory of a cherished son, devoted brother, faithful friend, and passionate lover.
The fire of love within him filled his whole heart.
Eventually it burned so fiercely it consumed him.
The flames of his love will forever glow in our hearts.

"Did you talk to Eleanor?" Maryanne asks gently as my sobs relent to more quiet cries.

I nod, meeting Maryanne's soft brown eyes. "Yeah, I did. She cried. But she cried when I told her about Jake, too."

Eleanor struggled a lot with losing Toby so young, more so than Maryanne struggled with losing Jake. Every milestone I have accomplished over the years made Eleanor so proud and happy, but they also left her so incredibly sad. They are milestones that Toby should also be reaching. Jake should be, too, but Maryanne is more at peace than Eleanor ever will be.

The snow crunches under our feet as we walk back to the car. Maryanne gently asks about the engagement. "You never told me the engagement story," she prompts.

I laugh softly, still sniffling from tears. "Are you sure you want to hear it?" I tease.

"I do," she insists.

Leaning against her car, the cold air nipping at us, this January day in Baltimore, I recount my history with Brody leading up to the engagement.

"It was New Year's Eve, at midnight," I begin with a smile. "He took me to this fancy, black-tie party. At the countdown, when I turned to kiss him, he dropped to one knee and said, 'I've been waiting my entire life to find a woman like you, and I hope you're willing to spend your entire life with me.' And then he opened the box." I pause, holding up my left hand.

"And you love him?" Maryanne asks, her gaze warm with understanding.

"I do," I affirm. "I'm a little worried because we haven't lived together, but that's part of why I'm moving out there now," I explain. "Our relationship has been short bursts, often in hotels in cities all over the country. It might be different when we live together, and I'd rather know that before we get married than after."

"And you don't have a job or anything, right?" Maryanne inquires, her concern evident.

Shaking my head, I reply, "I know it's crazy, but I gave my job here two weeks' notice. I have some money left from the trust, and the condo is on the market. Plus," I add, meeting her gaze meaningfully, "I need to move away from my parents, and this gives me the perfect opportunity to do that."

Maryanne nods in understanding. "I want you to know that if you ever need anything, please call me. But I hope that you are happy and that you keep me updated."

"I will; thank you for being the mother I never knew I needed," I say, a genuine smile on my face as I hug her tightly.

"Well, you are the daughter I didn't know I needed either," she replies with a warm smile.

* * *

Walking through my condo one final time, I'm thankful for the professional movers I enlisted. It's a weight off my shoulders knowing that my belongings are organized—some tucked away in my parents' basement, others entrusted to my friend Georgia, and the remainder making their way to suburban Denver on a truck that is also hauling my car on a trailer.

With my flight departing in just six hours, I anticipate Brody picking me up from the airport on the other end.

"You ready?" Georgia asks with a smile.

"As ready as I'll ever be," I reply, returning her smile.

For over fifteen years, Georgia has been my unwavering rock, a constant presence in my life, especially during times when family dynamics have proven challenging. We forged our bond on the softball field, spending countless hours together, forming a connection that has more than stood the test of time. I've had other girlfriends, but none that I was extremely close to, besides her.

Georgia's beauty is striking—smooth, dark ochre skin that seems to defy the passage of time. Gone are the days of small braids she wore under her batting helmets; now, she wears her hair natural, a perfect match to her effortless allure.

Like me, Georgia maintains her athletic physique, a testament to the years we spent competing at a high level. Despite being considered short within our athletic circles, standing at five feet seven inches, we're not exactly short in the grand scheme of things.

In the airport drop-off zone, I know we can't linger, but I hug her tightly and say, "I'm going to miss you so much. Once I feel se[...] come visit me?"

"Absolutely." She smiles back, her tone teasing. "Don't forget about me, bitch."

"I won't, and I'll come visit you too," I assure her with a short laugh.

Less than two hours later, I am boarding a plane to start my new life.

I

ALEXIS

Super Bowl Sunday falls just two weeks into living with Brody. And we're headed to a party hosted by one of his coworkers—or rather, her boyfriend. Apparently, they throw fantastic gatherings; Brody insists they're amazing.

He has mentioned a few times how he enjoys showcasing me, especially in front of his coworkers. I don't mind being his arm candy for the occasion, especially since it's really the first social event I've been to with him, outside of work. I'm well aware of my attractiveness; the constant catcalls and unwanted advances from strangers serve as a reminder if I were to forget. I had hoped wearing my engagement ring would fend off some of the attention, but it seems to have little effect.

For the party, I slip into a pair of cute jeans, strategically ripped at the thighs, and team them with a stylish Baltimore Ravens shirt. The shirt nonchalantly drapes off one shoulder, revealing peek-a-boo slits on the sides and back, adding just the right amount of allure. Underneath, a lacy purple bralette peeks out, adding a hint of flirtation to the ensemble.

With my hometown team making it to the Super Bowl this year, I'm prepared to represent as possibly the lone true Ravens fan at a party in Denver. Fortunately and obviously, the Broncos aren't playing, so I doubt it'll lead to any major issues.

I treated myself to a salon visit, indulging in long, coffin-shaped nails painted in a vibrant purple hue with intricate black designs. A matching purple pedicure completes the look, even if it means braving the snow-covered ground in cute, strappy black sandals to showcase my freshly done toes.

My makeup is relatively natural, with just a touch of dark purple eyeliner on my upper lids, perfectly aligning with the Ravens theme and subtly enhancing my blue eyes. I leave my long, cinnamon-colored hair cascading down in soft waves, and I keep a hair tie on my wrist just in case.

To accessorize, I wear dangle diamond earrings, a glitzy band on my smartwatch, and, of course, my engagement ring. Stepping out of the bedroom to meet Brody, his gaze sweeps over me like a predator assessing its prey, sending a shiver of anticipation down my spine.

"That'll do, babe," he murmurs, letting out a low whistle.

Returning his smile, I take in Brody's undeniable attractiveness. His tall, athletic physique likely garners as much attention from women as I do from men. He epitomizes tall, dark, and handsome.

Dressed in a simple yet striking ensemble—a dark black, tight, long-sleeve henley paired with dark jeans—he exudes quiet confidence. His defined muscles accentuate his rugged appeal, making him utterly irresistible.

I have a little social anxiety. Over the years, I've learned that women don't generally take to me well at first, or maybe it's me who doesn't take well to them. It feels like a self-fulfilling prophecy now—expecting this issue only makes it come true.

"So, remind me again, whose party is this?" I inquire as I open the door to his sleek silver sports car.

"It's my coworker Ellie's boyfriend's house. His name is Holden, and he shares it with four roommates. They've all lived together for ages, and it's a really nice, spacious place. I'm not sure if one of them is wealthy or if they manage because they split the expenses five ways, but they throw a lot of parties and always provide plenty of alcohol," Brody explains with a laugh, reaching over the console to grasp my hand.

"How many parties have you been to before?" I ask.

"I went to their Halloween party and a couple random birthday parties. Ellie mentioned their New Year's bash was spectacular, but I was with you in Maryland at the time." He smiles, lifting my hand to his lips for a gentle kiss.

"Okay, sounds like it should be fun," I reply.

Pulling up to the house, the door is wide open on this cold February Sunday, signaling it's a come-and-go-as-you-please affair. The exterior appears spacious, but the feeling of vastness intensifies dramatically once we step inside. The sheer number of people over-whelms and almost immediately overstimulates me; there must be at least fifty visible from the front door alone.

Brody's hand rests on the small of my back, offering either com-fort or protection; I'm not entirely sure which. The gender ratio is noticeably skewed, with far more men than women present. The air buzzes with conversation and laughter, but I can't shake the uneasy feeling settling in my chest. I glance around, trying to find at least a corner where I can catch my breath if I need to.

"Brody!" a woman's excited, high-pitched voice rings out from our left. She rushes over, her blonde hair bouncing as she sports short shorts and a Broncos tank top. With both hands on Brody's cheeks, she plants a kiss on his cheek before turning to me.

"You must be Alexis. I've heard so much about you," she chirps. "I'm Ellie. I'm glad you could make it."

Her words seem harmless enough, but her actions undeniably cross a line for me. I make a conscious decision to bring this up with Brody later, not wanting to make a scene now. I offer her a polite smile and possessively intertwine my fingers with his.

Ellie's voice attracts the attention of others as a couple of men join her. One of them possessively pulls her close, wrapping an arm around her waist, causing a subtle tension in the atmosphere.

"Brody," the man with his arm around Ellie greets, nodding at my fiancé.

"Hey, Holden," Brody responds, "this is Alexis, my fiancée." Three sets of eyes turn to me, and I offer a warm smile.

"Holden," he introduces himself, extending his right hand to me, his left hand still secured around Ellie; I shake it without hesitation.

Holden is undeniably attractive and tall, standing easily at six feet with sandy blonde hair and piercing blue eyes. His clean-shaven face features sharp cheekbones, and he's dressed in a black T-shirt emblazoned with a brewery logo, paired with dark jeans.

The other man standing to Holden's left is equally striking. With dark hair and impeccably groomed facial hair, he exudes an air of confidence without cockiness. Slightly shorter than Holden, he possesses chocolate brown eyes and an infectious smile. His attire consists of a green polo shirt paired with worn jeans.

"Ethan," he introduces himself, extending his hand as well. I shake it, and he charismatically adds, "Are you truly a Ravens fan or jumping on the Super Bowl bandwagon?"

"Maryland native, born and raised," I answer with a smile. "I only moved here a few weeks ago, actually."

"Well, you'll probably want to actually watch the game then and not just do shots with Brody and me," Ellie interjects with a giggle.

Instantly, Holden's brow knits as he seems uncomfortable, and as the air grows thick around me, I'm not particularly pleased with the interaction either.

"Ellie," Holden shakes his head. "Maybe you should drink some water and grab some appetizers." He gently takes her wrist, preparing to lead her away. Then, almost as an afterthought, he adds, "It was nice meeting you, Alexis."

"She's already had a few shots," Ethan chimes in. Laughing, he continues, "Brody, I know you've been here before, but Alexis, whatever you need, feel free to ask."

As Ethan gestures around the house, pointing out key areas like the kitchen, bathrooms, and prime spots for catching the game, I can't help but be drawn to his charm. There's an undeniable magnetism about him, the kind that could captivate anyone's attention. In a different universe, under different circumstances, he might be exactly the type of guy I'd be interested in.

"Enjoy yourselves," he adds before walking away.

The foyer exudes grandeur, offering glimpses into other rooms beyond. To the left, a cozy dinette area beckons with an archway leading to the spacious kitchen, though I can only catch a glimpse of its seemingly impressive layout.

Directly ahead, a grand staircase commands attention, while an opening to the left of the stairs appears to lead through a sitting room to a sliding glass door, likely opening to the patio area. To the right, a large living room awaits, featuring the largest television I've ever seen in a house, broadcasting the pre-game show.

Brody's hand shifts to wrap around my waist, pulling me closer. "Come on, let's see what we've got for food and drinks, and then we'll find a spot to watch the game," he suggests.

Planting a soft kiss on my temple, he laces his fingers with mine and guides me to the kitchen. I'm slightly awestruck; the expansive kitchen island is laden with an array of liquors, juices, and soda mixers, accompanied by the ubiquitous red solo cups in both regular and shot sizes. A fridge labeled "Beer and Water Fridge" is constantly being raided for bottles and cans. Across the kitchen, a giant Sub-Zero fridge presumably houses their household food.

Taking in the scene, I'm struck by the seamless blend of casual comfort and refined elegance. The dining room, just beyond the kitchen, exudes a similar atmosphere. A grand stone-slab, gray table, surrounded by wooden chairs and adorned with an assortment of delectable appetizers and desserts, dominates the space, offering ample seating for a large gathering. Along the far wall, the back of the house, expansive windows flood the room with natural light, while to the right, the grand staircase is definitely grand. To the left, a spacious area boasts a china cabinet and additional seating, creating an inviting, potentially intimate space for mingling and conversation.

Brody and I navigate through the bustling crowd, helping ourselves to drinks and appetizers along the way. Beyond the dining room, we discover a sitting room adorned with the continuing wall of windows and sliding glass doors leading to a patio where others are engaged in conversation.

"They even have a television out on the patio," Brody mentions. "It's a bit chilly, but it looks like they've got a couple of fire pits going, too."

"Definitely a spacious place," I remark with a chuckle as we make our way back toward the main room to catch the game.

With most people standing and socializing, there are plenty of seating options available. I settle at the end of a couch, tucking my legs beneath me and balancing my plate on the armrest. Brody joins me, resting his hand on my thigh.

Just before the game kicks off, another couple approaches us.

"Brody, hey, man," the man greets, "this must be the beautiful Alexis."

Brody nods in confirmation and proceeds to introduce me, "Yes, Alexis, this is Jeremiah and his girlfriend, Carrie. Jeremiah lives here along with Holden and Ethan."

"And Shawn and Carter," Carrie interjects with a laugh, teasingly glancing at me. "They tend to get a bit miffed if you forget one of them."

I smile and laugh along. "It's a pleasure to meet you both."

My eyes scan up Jeremiah's tall form. With his dark blonde, almost red hair, hazel eyes, and a well-groomed short beard, he is as attractive as his other two roommates I met earlier. Carrie exudes beauty, her light blonde, curly hair cascading around her shoulders, complemented by piercing light blue eyes. She stands a little shorter than me but possesses an enviable figure, clad in jeans and a fitted Broncos shirt. Jeremiah is wearing a long-sleeve gray henley paired with khaki pants. Much like on Brody, the henley does a perfect job of accentuating his clearly muscular physique underneath. His presence is commanding yet approachable, a combination that makes it hard to look away.

"Please don't hesitate to let us know if you need anything," Jeremiah offers before guiding Carrie away.

"They seem like nice people," I comment to Brody.

"Yeah, everyone here seems pretty decent, honestly," he agrees, taking a sip of his drink.

2

HOLDEN

"I should've told Ellie to leave him off the guest list," I mutter to Carter as we busy ourselves restocking the fridge out on the back patio during halftime.

"I get that Brody gets under your skin, but he's Ellie's coworker. Party or not, you're just gonna have to deal with them interacting," Carter replies with a nonchalant shrug.

Carter is more than just a friend; he's like a brother, even though we don't share blood. We click on a different wavelength, him and me. People often mistake us for siblings with our similar heights , hair, and eye colors. But while my hair is straight, his is a mass of light blonde curls. He's also covered in more ink than I have thoughts in my head most of the time.

"He brought a cute date, though," Carter remarks with a sly grin.

"His fiancée," I clarify pointedly. "Thank goodness he's tying the knot. Maybe that'll put a damper on the way he and Ellie carry on."

"I reckon Ellie's more the issue there, but Brody doesn't exactly put a lid on it," Carter adds with a knowing nod.

Before I can respond, Shawn saunters over, grabbing a drink from the fridge instead of stocking it. "Let me guess what has you upset, Brody and Ellie?" he interjects.

I shoot him a glare.

"Hey, I'm sorry," Shawn says, lifting his hands in surrender.

I release an exasperated sigh. "I'm just fed up. Hopefully, his fiancée can do what I seem incapable of. It's only when Brody's around that I feel this way about her."

Glancing back at Shawn. He is a bit shorter than me, with a mop of dark hair that falls a bit too long over his brow and deep brown eyes that always seem to see right through me even though he says very little most off the time. He usually has some stubble, but today, he's sporting a clean shave.

His face reflects understanding, but then he drops a truth bomb. "Honestly, man, I don't think you're happy with her at all. But I've got your back for as long as you want to stick it out."

He may be right. We've been dating for just under six months, and it hasn't been great, but she is a soft place to fall sometimes.

Shawn raises his beer bottle in a salute. "But damn, that fiancée of his is smoking hot, way hotter than Ellie. So, there's that."

Rolling my eyes, I rise from my seat, signaling it's time to head back inside.

Carter and I shuffle into the main viewing room, and there she is, Alexis, stationed in her claimed spot, actually watching the entire game. It's kind of endearing, maybe even a little sexy, how invested she is in the game.

I've witnessed her cheer and tense up at all the right moments. But Brody is nowhere in sight, and the realization that I haven't seen Ellie since before halftime sets off alarm bells in my head.

Finding myself on the other side of the couch, standing right next to Alexis; I wait for the current play to conclude before turning to her. "Hey, Alexis, I hope you're enjoying yourself. At least the Ravens are holding up their end of the bargain right now."

"Yeah, it's been fun. Thanks for hosting," she says, her smile beaming at me.

I have to admit, her smile adds another layer of allure to her already attractive features; her eyes, a captivating shade of blue, sparkle with joy.

"Did Brody ditch you?" I quip, trying to lighten the mood.

"He said he needed to take a call, but yeah, I haven't seen him since halftime," she shrugs.

My intuition, which I don't have much of, is practically screaming now, but I keep up the facade. "Hopefully, he finds his way back here soon."

She flashes me another smile before I start scanning the party for any sign of them. After a brief search, I grab Ethan, and we make our way toward the back rooms of the house on the main floor and then upstairs, where the bedrooms are. I hope I'm wrong, but where else could they be?

Upstairs, down the hallway to the left of the grand staircase, primarily guest rooms, Ethan checks the doors on the right while I handle the left. The second door Ethan tries is occupied, and I catch a muffled sound, a stifled shriek, as he opens the door. I shoot Ethan a look, and he holds his hand up in a stop signal, asking me to hold back while he reaches for his phone. My jaw tightens, and I shake my head in disbelief.

Whoever's inside that room, Ethan is giving them a look that screams, *"fuck around and find out."* I have no idea who Ethan is texting, but within about thirty seconds, Jeremiah and Carrie emerge at the top of the stairs, with Alexis trailing right behind them.

Fuck.

Carter and Shawn are only about ten seconds behind Alexis.

Ethan extends his arm silently, indicating that whoever's inside the room can come out now. He doesn't utter a word. As Brody and Ellie emerge, I doubt they realize the audience they're walking into.

Just before I react, I lock eyes with Brody's fiancée, and her widened gaze tells me she's piecing things together.

"It's not what you think, Holden," Ellie rushes to explain as she approaches me, but I remain a statue, arms crossed tightly over my chest.

I step around her, fixating on Brody, and without a second thought, I swing a punch at his jaw. He moves to retaliate, but Carter and Jeremiah quickly intervene, each grabbing one of his arms. Despite my rage, I restrain myself from hitting a defenseless man. My anger burns hotter towards Ellie anyway.

"You both need to get the fuck out of our house," Ethan commands, glaring between Brody and Ellie.

Carter and Jeremiah release Brody at his words. Ellie looks at me, but I only shake my head in refusal before nodding towards the exit, signaling her to leave.

Then, seemingly premeditated, Ethan turns to Alexis and says, "You can stay."

Carrie wraps a comforting arm around Alexis's shoulders, and she appears stunned. Brody approaches her, reaching out, but she flinches away from his touch, her bottom lip starting to quiver.

"Babe, come on, we'll talk about it," Brody pleads, but Alexis shakes her head, and her eyes start to well with tears.

Ethan positions himself protectively between Alexis and Brody. It's uncharted territory for us, but I'm impressed by Ethan's stance, especially considering we barely know this girl.

Brody starts to reach for Alexis; Ethan grabs his arm. "What do you not understand about 'get the fuck out of our house?'"

Tears begin to stream down Alexis's cheeks, her emotions raw and overwhelming. With trembling hands, she removes her engagement ring, flinging it toward Brody in a gesture of finality. He retrieves it with a fleeting glance back at her before Ethan steers him away down the stairs. As Brody and Ellie make their descent, Alexis collapses into Carrie's arms, her sobs echoing through the hall. In that moment, I feel a surge of gratitude for Carrie's presence, providing comfort amidst the chaos.

Turning to me with a look of remorse, Ethan expresses his apology, his regret evident in his furrowed brow. I offer a resigned shrug, acknowledging the inevitability of the situation. The signs were there, but I had chosen not to fully see them.

Feeling a sense of responsibility toward Alexis, I approach her, mindful of Carrie's supportive presence. Placing a gentle hand on Alexis's arm, I coax her attention away from Carrie. "Are you going to be alright?" I inquire softly.

In response, she shakes her head, a mixture of pain and confusion evident in her eyes. Meeting her gaze in a gesture that is relatively out of character for me, I wordlessly open my arms, offering solace and support. Without hesitation, she buries her face against my chest, her anguish pouring out in heart-wrenching sobs.

Meanwhile, Carter and Shawn take charge downstairs, ensuring that Brody and Ellie leave the premises. Jeremiah and Carrie depart shortly after, leaving Ethan and me to console Alexis in the aftermath of the emotional turmoil.

3

ETHAN

As I pushed the door open, a surge of urgency hit me like a ton of bricks. Holden couldn't see what I was witnessing, but I knew both he and Alexis should be involved. She needed to know too, and needed to be in on this.

Quickly, I fired off a message in our group chat, summoning everyone upstairs pronto. And I made sure to request Carrie and Alexis in the call-out to the guys. I had a gut feeling Alexis would prefer some female support when reality came crashing down on her.

It was evident they'd been caught off guard, fucking, when I opened the door, and now their clothes were thrown on haphazardly. Brody and Ellie were lucky I granted them even thirty seconds to compose themselves before Holden's eyes landed on them.

Now, here we are. Holden, empathetic, but awkward, holding onto Brody's ex-fiancée as she crumbles in his arms. And I am left here, mulling over our next steps with a houseful of guests downstairs, oblivious to the drama unfolding above.

Holden is likely doing his best to keep his head together, with the weight of the situation bearing down on him. Maybe having Alexis in his arms is a blessing in disguise, providing him with a much-needed distraction amidst the chaos.

As her tears subside, she pulls away from Holden and glances at me, a soft laugh escaping her lips. "Is there a bathroom where I can freshen up?" she asks, her voice barely above a whisper.

"Sure, come with me," I reply, guiding her across to the hall on the other side of the stairs.

My goal in that is to steer her away from the scene of the crime. Entering one of two guest bedrooms in that corridor, I direct her to the ensuite bathroom.

"We'll wait for you out here." I smile.

Finally, after what feels like an eternity of silence, Holden breaks it. "What the fuck, Ethan?" he demands, his frustration evident.

"Dude, I don't know, your instincts were right, but seriously," I turn toward the door Alexis is behind, "if he had *that* at home, why the fuck would he be fucking around with someone else's girl?"

Holden's expression tells me I need to shut the fuck up now.

"Fuck," he says and then crouches against the wall. "I'm not even all that upset about losing Ellie, just about the way it happened."

"I get it," I offer in understanding.

Alexis opens the door, and both our heads snap toward her as Holden stands up, regaining his composure. Despite having washed her face, Alexis's eyes remain swollen, and her cheeks and nose are slightly red. However, she appears much better than when she went into the bedroom.

"You okay?" I ask gently.

"Not really," she lightly scoffs, but she is much more composed now as she continues, directing her words to both of us. "Fucking Brody, I should have known it was all too good to be true. I literally left my entire life in Maryland, my job, my condo, my friends, everything, to move out here to be with him. All my shit is at his apartment, like literally everything I own outside of a few things I left at my parents' house in Baltimore. I have almost no money because I'm still looking for a job here and waiting for my condo to sell," she sighs and shakes her head. "In fucking around on me, he literally fucked me over completely."

I look at Holden, and our eyes meet for a second before I look back at Alexis. "You can stay here tonight for sure. If Carrie can't get you some extra clothes, we can get you something of ours. We can probably find whatever else you'll need. Tomorrow, Carter and I can take you to get your stuff, and we'll go from there."

"I think the only other thing I *need* is a phone charger," she sniffles.

"We have those too," I'm quick to offer.

"Are you sure? You guys don't even know me," she inquires warily.

"I'm sure," I answer quickly. "In case you didn't notice, we're not hurting for space here."

She laughs and nods, then turns to Holden to ask, "Are you okay?"

He nods, "As okay as I can be. I'm just pissed because I had suspected it for a long time, and," he pauses, swallows, and looks between me and Alexis, "I'm pretty pissed Brody would do that to you too."

Alexis looks at me. "I think I need to get drunk now."

Holden and I both laugh in earnest. I wrap my arm around Alexis and say, "I think that can be arranged."

When we get downstairs, Carter is in the kitchen, at the island, pouring himself a drink. "Hey, Carter, Alexis here needs a bartender for the night," I laugh. "Maybe make her forget Brody. Also, I volunteered you and me to go get her shit from his apartment tomorrow."

"Alexis?" Carter asks, looking at her, and I realize they haven't met yet, even though I know he saw her. "I saw you earlier, but we haven't been formally introduced. I'm Carter," he says, extending his hand to her.

She smiles at him and shakes his hand but doesn't say anything.

"What's your pleasure?" Carter asks, gesturing across the bar. "I used to be a bartender, so whatever you want."

"Can you make a long island out of this?"

"Sure can," Carter says with a wink and starts pouring.

After Alexis has a drink in hand, she, Carter, and I all head to the big screen to catch the end of the game. The Ravens win, providing Alexis with at least one positive moment on the day. Eventually, all the guests begin to leave, including Carrie. Soon, it's just the six of us.

Holden finds a phone charger and some clothes for Alexis to sleep in. I ensure she has towels and anything else she might need in the bathroom. Once she's settled in the guest room upstairs, the five of us guys convene in the kitchen for a roommate meeting, speaking in hushed voices to avoid her overhearing or disturbing her.

Shawn starts us off. "So what the fuck are we going to do with her?"

"Well, we sure as hell can't kick her out. She has nowhere to go," I reply, and it's a declaration, not a suggestion.

"Maybe we can help her find a job," Holden suggests with a shrug.

"Do you even know what she does?" Carter asks.

"No," I admit, "but we can find out. Carter and I will take her to Brody's tomorrow to get her stuff. She has the code to the door, so it doesn't matter whether he's there or not."

"I can go too," Holden volunteers.

"No," Carter and I protest in unison; the last fucking thing we need is for Holden to assault him on his own property.

"Sorry, man," I continue, "I don't want to risk you getting in an altercation, and even though Ellie has her own place, there's a chance she'll be there."

"Well, I can go with you," Jeremiah offers.

"And me," Shawn adds.

"You really think she needs four of us?" Carter asks, laughing.

"Well, if Brody wants to be an ass, I don't think he'd want to deal with all four of us," Shawn answers.

"What positions do you all have open at Laugherty, Jer?" Holden inquires.

We all look at Holden, sensing where he is heading with this, and I think we're a little apprehensive. But then we turn to Jeremiah, wondering what the answer is.

"Entry-level accountant, marketing director, graphic designer, and an executive assistant for Ethan," Jeremiah answers hesitantly.

"I'm pretty sure she could fill one of those roles, at least temporarily," Holden replies. "Long enough to get her on her feet, anyway."

Jeremiah sighs and rakes his hand through his hair. "Probably, but let's see what her background is. Maybe she's an elementary school teacher or some shit," he laughs.

"I'd be a'ight with her being my assistant," I joke and shrug; Carter smacks me in the chest.

"In all seriousness, guys. Don't be dicks. She just broke up from an engagement because he fucked around on her. I know she's hot, but don't be trying to be the rebound guy," Holden warns.

"Well, there's an expiration date on that, though," Carter jokes with a wink.

Holden rolls his eyes, but we all laugh.

4

ALEXIS

Laying in the extremely comfortable bed in this giant house, trying to figure out my life, is definitely not what I thought I'd be doing tonight when I left Brody's apartment this afternoon.

I think I'm going to have to move back to Maryland, with my tail tucked between my legs, to my parents, who said that Brody wasn't going to last—that he was too good for me. Maybe I can pull the condo off the market.

Fuck.

I am grateful that Holden and Ethan have been so cool about this. I have no clue what their dynamic is. Who owns this place? Are any of them brothers? I have no freaking idea, but I'll have to unravel that mystery.

The guest room feels like entering a small studio apartment or a luxurious hotel suite. The spaciousness immediately captured my attention. The walls are painted in a soothing light slate gray, accented by crisp white trim along the floorboards, door frames, and crown molding.

A king-size bed with a grand, square-post, slatted headboard dominates the space to the right from the hallway door, yet there's still ample room for an entire living room set between the door and the bed. Soft gray bedding adorns the bed, along with an array of plush pillows that call to me.

Past the bed, a large picture window offers a picturesque view of the back patio, its sheer white curtains filtering in soft, natural light from the moon. A desk that matches the headboard is positioned in front of the window, creating a cozy workspace, which I imagine becomes bathed in sunlight.

The room boasts not one but two closets—a smaller one with shelves located on the same wall as the headboard and a larger walk-in closet to the left of the desk.

The ensuite bathroom is a true retreat in gray and white. It features a luxurious five-piece layout complete with a spacious soaking tub, a dual-head walk-in shower, and two elegant sinks.

After I climb into bed, I take a few minutes to text my best friend, Georgia. She's really my only friend, but she is the best.

(Me) *I will need to call you tomorrow, but you will never believe the shit that happened today*

(Georgia) *Spill the mother fucking tea, I am riding the super bowl winning high*

(Me) *lol - well, one of the hosts of the party caught Brody fucking his girlfriend in the middle of the fucking party*

(Georgia) *Shut the fuck up - what are you going to do?*

(Me) *I don't know*

(Me) *I threw my ring at Brody, they gave me a guest room here, where the party was*

(Georgia) *What about all your stuff?*

(Me) *A couple of the guys that live here are going to help me get my stuff tomorrow*

(Georgia) *Lex, you vixen, are you in a house with a bunch of guys?*

(Me) *lol, five I think, I don't even know, I'll find out tomorrow*

(Georgia) *I'm sorry - keep me posted - sorry if I'm not a great friend right now*

(Me) *I will - and you deserve your party time, I'll be alright*

It takes me a while but eventually, I lay down in this oversized T-shirt Holden gave me. It smells like him—clean and crisp—like how he smelled when I buried my face in his chest, crying.

How fucking embarrassing was that?

I cry a little more as I lie there alone, thinking about the day. But it dawns on me relatively quickly that I don't feel broken-hearted, just betrayed. Maybe Brody was more convenience than love. The tears taper off, replaced by a strange sense of clarity. I realize that what I had with Brody was built more on routine than passion, more on habit than genuine connection. As I think about this new understanding, the sting of betrayal starts to fade. Maybe Brody did me a favor—I probably shouldn't have been engaged to him in the first place.

* * *

When I wake up in the morning, I'm not sure exactly what I should do, but I slip back into my jeans and knot Holden's t-shirt around my waist, just above my tailbone. I decide to venture to the kitchen, as I assume that's where people are likely to congregate.

When I get there, I find Carter and Ethan already in the kitchen with coffee hot and waiting.

"Hey, how are you this morning?" Carter asks with genuine interest.

I caught a glimpse of Carter last night, even talked to him, but my thoughts were scattered, and I didn't fully register all of him. He's certainly attractive, like all the men in this house, as if they've all been drinking from a fountain of sexiness. He and Holden definitely look alike enough to be brothers. Carter has the same chiseled jawline and piercing eyes as Holden, their resemblance uncanny which brings back the question of how they all came to be living together. It's hard not to wonder about the bond that ties them together and what led them to share this space.

Sporting basketball shorts and a simple white T-shirt, Carter exudes a toned physique. His arm muscles are defined even during mundane tasks, like putting dishes in the sink. Those arms are also adorned with vibrant tattoos, extending beneath the fabric to his chest, barely visible through the thin white material he's wearing. His blonde curls remind me of a few celebrities, but it's the eyes that really get me; they're sky blue and mesmerizing.

"Better," I sigh. "Probably better after coffee." I wrinkle my nose.

"That I can do," Carter offers, "How do you take it?"

"You have any flavored creamers? Otherwise, milk and sugar is fine."

Ethan, already dressed in jeans and a green polo shirt, opens the fridge. "We have these two," he says, placing a vanilla and caramel creamer on the counter.

"Oh, I love you guys," I exclaim with probably too much enthusiasm, "Caramel is my favorite."

"Love Holden then because it's his favorite too," Carter teases.

I feel the heat of my blush as Ethan pulls out his phone and starts typing.

"Alexis, we're going to have a little roommate meeting here with you," Ethan warns. "We're just trying to figure out how best to help you."

"You guys have already done too much," I acknowledge. "I'm probably just going to move back to Maryland."

"You don't have to necessarily do that if you don't want to," Carter says.

As soon as he finishes speaking, voices draw my attention, and Jeremiah, Holden, and Shawn enter the kitchen. Holden's sandy blonde hair, tousled from sleep, gives him a casual charm as he enters clad in basketball shorts, a hint of his boxer briefs peeking out. Shirtless, his sculpted muscles draw my gaze, and I find myself swallowing hard as I admire his physique. The 'v' leading down toward his shorts leaves me biting my bottom lip involuntarily, and his piercing blue eyes hold me captive.

Jeremiah, on the other hand, presents a more polished appearance. He is dressed in khaki pants and a red polo shirt that hints at his readiness for a work day ahead, like Ethan. His neatly styled, dark blonde hair shows hints of red and complements his light brown eyes, bordering on gold, which hold a captivating allure of their own.

They introduce me to Shawn, whom I hadn't met, but had seen the night before. Shawn's attire is more relaxed, sporting gray sweatpants and a black t-shirt with Squirtle on it. His long hair pulled back into a small man-bun gives him a laid-back vibe, while his dark eyes seem to hold a hint of mystery. When he smiles, revealing adorable dimples, all that sense of mystery melts away.

Despite their varying appearances, all five men clearly show signs of fatigue from the night before, yet each possesses a unique charm that draws me in. Part of me thinks maybe I should be more anxious or nervous surrounded by these five tall, built, and sexy men, but I feel at ease, almost at home.

I position myself next to Ethan on one side of the island while Jeremiah takes his place across from me. Carter settles across from Ethan, and Holden and Shawn stand side by side at the end of the island to my right, between Ethan and Carter.

"Okay," Ethan starts, "we all talked last night. Holden and I filled the other guys in on your situation, and we have some solutions if you want them."

"Okay?" I say tentatively, my voice laced with uncertainty and trying my best to avert my gaze from the sight of Holden's bare torso.

"First, you can stay here as long as you need to or want," Ethan proposes. "All of us, except Holden, are going to help you get all your stuff from Brody's today."

My eyes meet Holden's. He smiles softly at me.

"Next," Carter continues, "what kind of job are you looking for? What is your experience or degree or whatever?"

"My degree is in marketing with a minor in graphic design. I was a marketing executive for a tech company in Baltimore," I answer immediately and confidently.

They all laugh, and then Jeremiah looks at me. "You're kidding, right? Did Holden or Ethan tell you to say that?"

I shake my head. "Uh, no. You want to see my resume?"

"Probably," Jeremiah responds, pushing buttons on a tablet that had been resting on the kitchen counter before I had come downstairs and swiveling it in my direction, then asking, "Think you can handle that?"

The tablet screen displays a posting for a marketing director position at a small software company. As I skim through the job responsibilities, I realize they're all tasks I've handled before.

Swallowing nervously, I respond, "Uh, yeah, I've done all of that before." Ethan and Jeremiah exchange glances. "Do you know which company this is for? Is it someone you're familiar with?" I inquire.

Jeremiah takes the lead, explaining, "It's actually my—our company. I'm the CEO, Ethan serves as the CFO, Shawn leads IT and software development, and Carter is sales."

My eyes meet each one of theirs while he talks about their job titles. Then Jeremiah says, "Our current open positions are for a marketing director, graphic designer, accountant, and executive assistant to work under Ethan."

I swallow again, processing this newfound information. "So, you all work together?"

"Except for Holden," Ethan interjects with a grin. "He's the weird one who decided to pursue medical school."

My attention immediately shifts to Holden. "You're a doctor?"

He responds with a smile, "Yes, nearly there. I'm in my final year of residency."

Jeremiah clears his throat, breaking our eye contact. "Alexis, if you feel confident about taking on that job, we can get you started this week. It can be temporary if you prefer, just to ease into things. Working with us isn't a requirement for living here," he adds, shrugging, "We simply want to help."

I glance around, meeting the gaze of each guy in the room, and then the emotions overwhelm me, and tears involuntarily fill and fall from my eyes. Ethan and Carter laugh uncomfortably, while Jeremiah, Holden, and Shawn seem uncertain about how to react.

Ethan, right next to me and clearly impacted by my distress, puts his arm around me. I naturally turn into him and cry against his shoulder. Finally, I regain my composure.

"I'm sorry, I'm such a mess," I say, wiping my eyes.

"It's understandable," Ethan empathizes.

I take a deep breath and look at Jeremiah. "I would love to take the job. Can we start it like an on-the-job interview, make sure I'm a good fit and all that?"

"Absolutely," he replies and smiles.

***

A couple of hours later, I find myself standing outside Brody's apartment door. He opens the door, and there's a flicker of surprise on his face when he notices all four men standing behind me. I'm relieved I have them with me when I walk in and Ellie is sitting on the couch. I shoot him a glare that could pierce steel with my eyes.

"I'm here to get my shit, and then I never want to hear from you again," I announce.

"Lexi, Babe," he pleads, and I hear Carter tell him to stop.

Ethan and Shawn stand inside the master bedroom doorway as I pack all of my stuff in suitcases and trash bags. Carter and Jeremiah stay by the front door with Brody to make sure he doesn't do anything stupid.

Once all of my stuff is outside the front door of the apartment, I turn to Brody, hand him the key, and say, "Fuck you very much; I hope you have the life you deserve."

Carter and Ethan laugh, and then all four of them help me carry my stuff to Ethan's 4Runner. I follow them in my A8 back to the house. When I park in the driveway, the guys look at my car with its Maryland plates. Jeremiah playfully quips about the car, offering a lighthearted jab that dispels any notion of me being a freeloader.

As we return to the house, Ethan informs me that I have the option to choose from five different bedrooms. The bedroom I was in last night is in the same hallway as all the guys, but if I opt for a room on the opposite side of the stairs, I'll have a little more privacy.

"It's entirely up to you, wherever you feel most comfortable," Ethan assures me.

"I'm a bit of a creature of habit, so I think I'll stick to where I am," I reply with a smile.

Ethan chuckles softly, and the guys take charge of bringing all my belongings upstairs, refusing to let me lift a finger. In the background, I catch snippets of Carter and Ethan updating Holden on Ellie's presence at Brody's and filling him in on the details.

As I start setting up my new room—placing clothes in the closet, arranging items in drawers, and setting up my laptop on the desk—a knock interrupts my quickly moving brain.

"Come in," I invite, and I'm a little relieved when Holden enters, quietly shutting the door behind him.

"Are you settling in okay?" he asks, perching on the edge of my bed.

I offer him a reassuring smile. "Yeah, I think so. It's just a lot to take in," I admit.

He watches quietly as I connect my monitors and arrange my computer setup. "That's quite the fancy setup you've got there," he remarks with a chuckle.

"It's for graphic design," I explain briefly before turning to him, wrinkling my nose in concern. "And how about you? How are you holding up?"

Holden seems taken aback by my question. His face contorts a little before he smooths it out again, but he responds nonetheless. "I'm okay. I'm heading back to the hospital tonight for ninety-six hours, so that'll keep me occupied," he says with a hint of resignation in his voice.

"I bet it will. That sounds exhausting, though," I comment, closing the distance between us with two steps.

Holden chuckles, nodding in agreement. "It is, especially in my area."

Curious, I inquire, "What's your specialty?"

"ICU, intensivist," he replies.

"You sleep in the call room instead of coming home?" I ask, and he nods but looks at me questioningly, which makes me laugh.

"My dad is an emergency room physician, and my mom's an ICU nurse," I share, "and my brothers are both physicians; I understand better than most."

A small smile plays on his lips. "You probably do. I'm the chief resident until I'm done, so it's rewarding, but it's pressure."

I join him on the bed, sitting beside him. "I'm sure it is rewarding. People like to think being a doctor is all about the money; they miss all the sacrifices."

Holden meets my gaze, and there's a fleeting moment of silence that isn't uncomfortable. He swallows and then glances down at the bags I still need to unpack.

"It looks like you still have a lot to do," he remarks, rising to his feet. "I'll leave you to it."

I hesitate, not wanting him to leave.

Without thinking, I blurt out, "Wait, Holden."

He turns back, and I find myself at a loss for words; finally, I manage, "Thank you."

"You're welcome, Alexis. I just hope you're comfortable here," he replies before slipping out of my door.

5

ETHAN

Alexis has been holed up in her room for a while. Jeremiah and I both have some things we want to talk to her about. Realizing none of us have her phone number, I hesitantly knock on her door, hoping I've picked a decent time to disturb her. When she opens the door a few moments later, my jaw falls slack for a moment and I fight the urge to blatantly ogle her.

Her hair is still damp from a recent shower, cascading in loose waves over her shoulders. Droplets of water are trailing down her skin from her hair.

Sporting a royal blue crop tank top that showcases her toned stomach and a glinting navel piercing, I can't help but notice her figure. Her cleavage is anything but discreet. And those black shorts? They border on scandalously short, leaving little to the imagination. The contrast of her blue top against her piercing eyes is mesmerizing, almost hypnotic.

After what feels like an eternity of awkward silence, I manage to find my voice. "Hey, Alexis. I wanted to go over some more logistics about the house, just to make sure you're fully comfortable and in the loop."

"Sure," she responds with a smile. "Now?"

"How about in the kitchen in about ten minutes? I need to find Jeremiah and probably Carter as well," I counter.

"Sounds good; see you downstairs," she replies before flashing me that dazzling smile and shutting the door.

Fuck me.

As I walk away, a gnawing sense of doubt creeps in. Having someone as distractingly attractive as Alexis living under the same roof as all five of us may not be the brightest idea after all. And the way she looks right now—effortless and natural, probably in the kind of clothes she sleeps in, with no makeup—she's still stunning. We're already waist-deep in this situation, but I can't shake the feeling that this might've been a colossal mistake.

Then, I immediately chastise myself for even entertaining the victim-blaming thoughts. We're all adults here; we need to exercise self-control. It's not fair to blame Alexis for simply being herself, radiating that undeniable allure that draws us in like moths to a flame.

I text the group and let them know we'll be meeting.

> (Me) *Hey guys, another meeting with Alexis in the kitchen in five or ten minutes - I need Carter and Jeremiah, the other two are optional*
>
> (Me) *Also, if she doesn't change before she comes downstairs, just be prepared to not blatantly check her out, please, lol*
>
> (Carter) *I make no promises*
>
> (Holden) *Carter - seriously *eyeroll emoji* I'll be there*
>
> (Shawn) *Middle of a workout, I'll miss this one*

(Jeremiah) *Well, now I'm curious, your warning might have done more harm than good*
(Me) *Jer -one word - Carrie*
(Jeremiah) *I can look, I just can't touch*
(Me) *Y'all are infuriating*
(Holden) *You can exclude me from that statement - I agree with you Ethan - she's a guest*
(Shawn) *Now you all are making me want to ditch my workout to see what Ethan is talking about*
(Me) **facepalm emoji* I shouldn't have said anything*
(Holden) *It seems that way*
(Me) *Lesson learned*

Five minutes later, with Jeremiah, Carter, and Holden already in the kitchen, Alexis joins us, donning a short zip-up hoodie that now covers her stomach, but the allure of cleavage, ass, curves, and legs remains undeniable. Those shorts are *so* short.

"Hey, guys," she greets us with a glance around the room.

"Hey," I respond, clearing my throat. "I just wanted to touch base on a few house matters and give you a full tour—security system, basement, the works. Plus, Carter and Jeremiah have been diving into the employment situation, so they'll fill you in on that."

"Okay," she says, smiling. "Where's Shawn?"

"In the middle of a workout," Carter says. "He might be on his way, but probably not."

"Mind if I grab a water while we talk?" she asks.

"No, and groceries are on the list to talk about, too," I reply with a smile.

She strides over to the fridge, grabbing a water bottle, and I can't help but notice how the other three men's gazes follow her every move once her back is turned. I silently pray they'll adjust to having her around and this won't become a recurring issue—or she'll decide to move out sooner rather than later.

After she opens the water bottle and takes a sip, she returns to the center of our group, casually leaning on the island between Carter and Jeremiah, straight across from me. Holden is at the end of the island on her left and my right. I make a conscious effort to focus on her face as she leans in, ignoring the magnetic pull of her cleavage pressed against the counter.

Carter takes an intentional step back and leans against the counter behind her, leaving nothing to the imagination about where his attention lies. I'm sure with her bent over the counter like that, in those shorts, well...

He shoots a quick glance at me and then at Holden, mouthing the words *"Fuck me."*

Holden shoots him a warning glare, silently urging him to cut it out. This is all new territory for us; we've had Carrie, Ellie, and plenty of other women spend time in this house, but I've never seen my roommates act so feral.

I clear my throat, trying to shift the focus back to the task at hand. "Okay, first things first, we need your phone number to add you to the group chat. Do you have your phone on you?"

She reaches into her bra and retrieves her phone with a grin. Of course, she has her phone in her bra.

I hold my hand out, silently signaling for her to hand it over. She unlocks it and pulls up a blank text message as if she's already anticipating my next move. I quickly shoot myself a text and then hand it back to her.

"I'll send a group text with all of us, and then you and the guys can exchange contact information," I explain. "Next, groceries. We all chip in for groceries and then take turns ordering from the list. You don't have to worry about contributing until you've got a steady income, but there's a tablet over there," I nod towards the one on the island, "with a 'shopping list' icon on the home screen. Just add whatever you want or need, and we'll order twice a week."

Her response catches us all off guard. "*Whatever* I want or need?" she asks with a mischievous grin, her tone dripping with what sounds like sin; we all freeze a little before she continues, "Like lobster, filet mignon, champagne?"

Laughter, some of it uncomfortable, erupts around the room.

"Well, you can certainly try," I reply with a smile, trying to regain control of the situation. "It depends on who is doing the ordering at the time," I add, shooting her a playful glance.

She looks at me hesitantly, her brows knitted together with curiosity. "Can I ask a question?"

"Sure," I reply, giving her my full attention.

"What's the deal here?" she begins, her tone cautious. "Like, who actually owns the house? Are you all brothers? I don't know; maybe that's too much to ask. Maybe I'm being nosey, but I'm just trying to wrap my head around it."

"It's okay; it's a fair question, especially since you'll be here for a while," I start to explain. "I own the house, or rather, my trust does. The other guys all contribute a small amount for rent, except for Holden. We've decided he shouldn't contribute until he finishes his residency."

I pause, glancing at Holden and then Jeremiah. "You might think it's a bit childish or silly, but no, we're not brothers—we're friends. We've been friends since elementary school, and back in high school, we made a pact that we'd always stick together. Aside from Holden's decision to pursue medical school, we've pretty much kept that promise. We even planned our degrees around it. Mine in finance with a minor in accounting and economics, Jeremiah in business— he's got his MBA, Shawn in information technology, and Carter in psychology with a minor in marketing to help with sales."

"Jeremiah and Shawn came up with a brilliant software idea when we were seniors in high school, and a few years ago, we brought it to life. Now, we're working on other software projects," I continue, stealing another glance at Holden. "And Holden isn't completely out of the loop because we're involved in medical and healthcare software, and his expertise as a consultant is invaluable to us."

"Well, okay then," she says, her tone reflecting her gratitude for the clarity. "It makes a lot more sense now."

She pauses, hesitating for a moment before continuing, "Has it always just been the five of you here?"

I glance at Carter, silently deferring to him to decide whether or not to delve into that topic.

Carter steps forward, turning and leaning against the island with his back to me and facing Alexis. "Uh, no," he begins, his voice taking on a somber tone. "So, I think you'll be here for a while, and since we'll be working closely together, I'll fill you in. I was married. My ex-wife lived here with us, and we have a daughter. She's six years old, and she spends about forty percent of her time here. I try to make it closer to fifty, but with her school schedule now, it's a bit challenging."

"You're a dad?" Alexis's voice carries a hint of admiration as if she finds it incredibly endearing.

"Yeah, a divorced dad," Carter chuckles, though there's a touch of sadness in his laughter.

Alexis looks down at her hands briefly before meeting Carter's gaze again. "How long ago was that?"

"I've been divorced for four years, ironically the same amount of time we were married," Carter replies with a wry smile.

"What's your daughter's name?" Alexis inquires.

"Anastasia, but we call her Ana," he answers proudly.

She turns to the rest of us with a playful grin. "Any of the rest of you have kids?"

"No," I interject quickly, shaking my head. "Just Carter. But to answer your question, his wife did live here with us for a while. And Shawn had a girlfriend who stayed here for just under two years. But besides Ana, we haven't had anyone else here on a regular basis for a few years."

"Not even Carrie?" Alexis directs her question to Jeremiah.

He shakes his head. "No, we only spend a few nights together each week, alternating between her place and here. So, she's usually only here one or two nights a week at most."

Alexis looks back at me, so I go on, "I'm going to let Jeremiah and Carter talk to you about the employment side of things, and then I can give you the tour."

She turns so she can focus on Jeremiah and Carter.

6

❧

CARTER

I let Jeremiah take the lead, even though I can't help but feel a surge of curiosity about her reaction. I'm honestly not sure how Holden and Ethan will respond to what is coming, either.

"Hey," Jeremiah says, flashing a charming smile. "So, if you're game, Carter and I can give you the grand tour of our office tomorrow. We do plenty of remote work, but we've got brick-and-mortar space too. My assistant will sort out all the I-9 paperwork for you and get it to HR; just make sure you've got your docs handy. We'll also dive into the nitty-gritty of your salary and benefits." His eyes twinkle with enthusiasm. "Trust me, it's worth it, you won't be disappointed. Carter has been juggling marketing and sales for a while now. He'll walk you through everything we've got in the pipe-line, from brand logos to the latest strategies. Although, I will be honest, our marketing is in shambles right now."

"That sounds good," Alexis answers with a laugh. "What's the dress code?"

Ethan struggles to contain a laugh, and suddenly, all of our eyes are on him. Now, it's his turn to receive a glare from Holden, who clearly isn't amused.

"Business casual," Jeremiah replies smoothly, "unless we've got client meetings, then it's all business formal."

Jeremiah pauses, his gaze shifting to me, hesitant, and a thoughtful expression crosses his face. "Here's the kicker, Alexis. You can totally pass if you're not up for it, but in about a week, we've got a major sales pitch followed by a business dinner in Chicago. I'd love for you to tag along with Carter, if only for the learning experience."

With her back turned to them, Alexis remains oblivious, but both Jeremiah and I catch Holden and Ethan's subtle exchange of glances. It's a silent communication that speaks volumes; they don't like the idea of me being alone in another city with her.

Alexis looks from Jeremiah to me and then back at him; I can read the apprehension in her voice as she knits her brow. "I mean, that is fast, but I'm okay with it. As long as you think I wouldn't be any kind of burden in the process."

"I don't think so," Jeremiah responds, his tone reassuring. "Carter can handle the bulk of the talking, and he'll be more than happy to give you a crash course between now and then. Plus, you both can always preface with the disclaimer that you're new to the company."

"Okay, sounds good. When is this?" Alexis asks.

"I can handle that information," I interject, and those beautiful blue eyes meet mine. "The presentation and dinner are scheduled for February thirteenth, followed by a meeting with their chief information officer on the fourteenth. I'm planning to travel out there on the twelfth and return on the fifteenth."

She scoffs and then laughs, "So, Valentine's Day? I guess that's a distraction I can roll with."

The laughter ripples through the room, but deep down, I'm not certain any of us truly find it all that funny. Although, I'm on cloud nine, ecstatic at the prospect of being out of state, in a bustling tourist city, and spending Valentine's Day with this stunning woman.

"Alright, I think that covers everything Carter and I needed to discuss, aside from getting your phone number," Jeremiah says with a smile. "Just be ready to roll with us tomorrow around seven, okay?"

"Yeah, sounds good," Alexis responds.

Jeremiah excuses himself, mentioning he needs to make a work call, and leaves Holden, Ethan, and me with Alexis.

"You forgot to talk about meals," I say to Ethan.

"Fuck. Yeah, I did," he replies, pausing, probably trying to ensure he doesn't come across as pretentious. "So, we actually have someone who prepares and delivers our dinners most nights. It's something we decided to splurge on a while back. Do you have any allergies or anything?"

"Fancy, but okay." Alexis shakes her head no and adds, "No allergies; if there's something I won't eat, I'll figure it out."

Ethan nods, "Anyway, dinner is always ready around half past six. If we're on our own, we usually order out, but sometimes one of us will cook. Breakfast and lunch are pretty much a free-for-all, so feel free to help yourself."

Alexis looks around the kitchen and nods.

"You ready for the tour?" Ethan asks.

Alexis laughs, "Why not? I'm already thoroughly overwhelmed; more information won't hurt."

And, fuck, do I love this woman's sense of humor and optimism.

* * *

ALEXIS

For a moment, I half-expect the others to join Ethan as he

offers me a tour, but they scatter, leaving just the two of us. Ethan emanates this incredibly soothing aura, though I can't quite put my finger on what it is exactly. Being around him feels safe and secure.

Carter, on the other hand, exudes a vibe of excitement, danger, and unpredictability—it's not just the tattoos that give him that edge, it's his whole personality.

And Holden? He's got that silent, brooding demeanor, contrasting with Ethan's reassuring presence, but I still feel very safe with him. The brooding may just be a result of our recent shared trauma.

Jeremiah seems authoritative, but strangely enough, not in a way that sets off alarms, it's almost paternal. He's confident—definitely the kind of guy who knows what he wants and usually gets it.

As for Shawn, I haven't had enough time with him to form an impression, but he seems quiet, sweet, and genuine.

Of all the guys here, Ethan is the one who makes me feel the safest, like a gentle guardian watching over me. So, if I have to spend time alone with any of them, he's definitely the best option. The idea of heading to Chicago with Carter does stir up a hint of nerves, but I reassure myself that I can handle it.

Ethan's enthusiasm radiates off of him as he leads me through the house. We kick off our tour in the basement, the stairs conveniently tucked behind the kitchen. He jokes about starting from the bottom and working our way up.

As we descend, I'm greeted by another cozy living space, complete with a sprawling, inviting couch, a massive screen television, and an array of game consoles. Despite being underground, it doesn't have that typical basement vibe; instead, outside of the egress windows, it seamlessly blends with the rest of the house.

"Do you all game, or is it just some of you?" I inquire, curious about the gaming systems.

Ethan chuckles. "Well, all of us have been gamers in some

capacity, although much less so now than when we were younger, mostly Shawn now," he responds. "You don't strike me as a gamer."

"I played some pretty good Halo and Call of Duty back in high school and college," I say with a casual shrug.

Ethan's gaze narrows, fixing on me with a playful intensity. "You're full of surprises, Alexis," he muses, a flicker of intrigue dancing in his tone. "And I have a feeling we've only just begun to uncover them."

I chuckle, "Well, considering you don't really know me at all, that's probably true."

His smile softens as he motions for me to walk ahead of him, his hand lightly resting on the small of my back. It's a simple gesture, perhaps innocent, yet it sends a rush of warmth through me. Together, we veer right from the gaming room and enter a hallway.

"This," Ethan begins, "is the gym. Feel free to use it anytime."

As we step inside, my eyes widen a little at the sight of a shirtless and glistening Shawn.

"Hey, Shawn," Ethan says. "I'm just showing her around; sorry for interrupting."

"I know I missed the meeting," Shawn replies, walking over to us. I can't help but steal a glance at his impressive physique. "Ethan gave me your number. I'll text you mine once I'm done here."

"No worries," I respond, trying to keep my focus despite the distracting view of this utterly captivating man with his sweat-kissed skin.

Seriously, *did* they all drink from the magical, sexy spring around here? That is a recurring question I think I'll be asking myself.

"I was actually just finishing up," Shawn says, glancing between Ethan and me. "I'll see you both at dinner."

I smile as he heads out, and Ethan and I step aside to let him pass. The gym looks promising—plenty of mirrors, free weights, and a variety of cardio equipment. I could definitely see myself using this space.

Opposite the gym, Ethan opens another door. "This is the theater," he announces. "We don't use it much, but sometimes if there's a movie or a pay-per-view fight a few of us are interested in, we'll gather here instead of having a party."

Rows of recliners and a sizable projection screen greet us. "During parties, we keep people out of the basement," Ethan adds with a chuckle. "Let's just say cleanup hasn't been the most enjoyable task a few times."

I laugh, instantly catching on to the suggestive yet slightly gross undertone of his remark.

As we continue down the hallway, Ethan points out a bathroom and a steam room. I glance at him with a grin. "I think I might be in heaven."

"Just be careful," Ethan warns with a smirk. "Because most of us go in with no clothes on. So, maybe shoot a text ahead of time."

"Yeah, I think you all are going to have to get used to living with a girl," I tease, wrinkling my nose playfully.

"That is a *huge* understatement," Ethan agrees with a laugh. "It may not look like a stereotypical bachelor pad, but we're definitely used to living that way."

As we backtrack down the hallway, there's a door directly ahead. Ethan doesn't open it but gestures towards it. "That's Ana's playroom, filled with toys, puzzles, games, and coloring books. Carter spends a lot of time with her here on weekends when she's around. And that is really it for the basement."

He motions for me to walk ahead, his hand resting reassuringly on the small of my back until we reach the base of the stairs. From there, we ascend back to the kitchen, where Ethan begins the tour of the main level.

To the left of the stairs lies the kitchen, while the door to the right leads to the garage. Ethan opens it, revealing a typical four-car garage. I've already seen most of the main level, but he points out a couple of bathrooms I hadn't noticed before. Stepping out onto the patio, he shows me the outdoor kitchen, the outdoor television setup, and the hot tub and pool and teaches me how to use everything.

"Seriously, Alexis, I want you to feel at home here," Ethan proclaims earnestly. "Don't hesitate to use anything or do anything or feel like you have to ask for permission. I know it must feel strange for you to be here, in this environment, under these circumstances." His tone is empathetic, his expression sincere.

"You have no idea," I manage to reply, offering him a grateful smile.

Once we're back inside, he teaches me about the security system. There are panels by the front door, the garage door, and the sliding glass door.

"We don't fully arm it very often because it's pretty rare that we are all gone at once," Ethan shrugs.

It's time to ascend the stairs to what I assume are just bedrooms. I'm mostly correct. At the top of the stairs, we turn right. The first door on the left is mine. Ethan points out that the door across from mine belongs to Holden. Then he indicates Carter's room on the left, Shawn's on the right, Jeremiah's next to Carter's, another empty room next to Shawn's, and his own at the end of the hallway.

"I won't take you into any of their bedrooms because that's just weird," Ethan laughs. "But I do want to show you the balcony off mine."

He swings open his bedroom door, revealing a vast space that could easily accommodate two of my already sizable bedroom. A full living room setup, complete with a fireplace, occupies one corner. However, he leads me straight through to the balcony—it's large, adorned with patio furniture, and offers an incredible view of the Rocky Mountains. The crisp air greets us and the majestic peaks stand silhouetted against the twilight sky. It's breathtaking, and for a moment, I forget everything else, lost in the serene beauty of the scene.

"This must be breathtaking at sunset," I remark, gazing out at the majestic scenery.

"It is," Ethan responds, his gaze lingering on me as we both lean against the railing.

A subtle crackle of chemistry fills the air between us, and I meet his gaze. His chocolate-brown eyes feel deep. I instinctively moisten my bottom lip, and I can feel his eyes tracking the movement. He takes a step back, clearing his throat—a very gentlemanly gesture, though I can't help but wonder where his thoughts were headed.

"Even though you have to pass through my bedroom to get here, I'm usually fine with any of the guys—or you—using the balcony. It's a good escape when stress levels are high," he explains, pausing for a moment. "Now, let me show you the other side of the second floor." With a gesture toward his bedroom door, he lets me lead the way.

As we traverse the top of the grand staircase, I peer over the edge, taking in the view of both main floor sitting areas and the dining room table. I make a mental note, realizing that privacy might not be guaranteed in those spaces.

Down the other hallway, the first door on the right leads to Ana's bedroom, while the other four remain vacant. There is one more door in that hallway which is the laundry room, and who doesn't love an upstairs laundry room?

At the end of the hall, there's another bedroom that is setup as a living room area with a balcony. Though not as spectacular as Ethan's, the view is still soothing, and I can easily picture myself curled up there with my Kindle.

"There aren't any bathrooms upstairs outside of the bedrooms?" I inquire.

"No, because every single bedroom has its own bathroom. It's kind of ridiculous, but with all the roommates, it's also incredibly convenient," Ethan explains with a smile.

"You all must have a maid, right? I mean, you don't clean all of this yourselves," I laugh.

"That we do. She comes on Fridays and Tuesdays, sometimes on other days if there is a particularly wild party. And when I say 'she,' I mean the consistent one—Maria, but she brings three others with her," Ethan says, wrinkling his nose and narrowing his eyes. "I know it's a bit pretentious."

"I mean, I think most people would do it if they could afford it," I reply with a shrug.

Later that afternoon, I take the time to call Georgia and tell her everything that has happened.

"Girl, I need to get out there to visit you asap. Maybe I can bring some of that sexy man spring water with me back to Maryland," she teases.

"Maybe," I joke. "I miss you."

"Miss you too, call me tomorrow," she says and I agree.

7

CARTER

As we gather for our first dinner with Alexis, I sense a collective curiosity and a touch of apprehension lingering in the air. We all have countless questions, yet we're equally wary of coming across as intrusive or insensitive. So, as we feast on lasagna, garlic bread, broccoli, and wine, I decide to take the plunge.

"Alright, Alexis, let's address the elephant in the room," I say, flashing her a flirtatious smile. "Tell us your life story. We've known each other since before we had pubic hair, but we know next to nothing about you."

Her laughter fills the room, so infectious, and she nearly spills wine out of her nose. It's endearing, and I can't help but find myself drawn to her even more.

She is sitting almost across from me, next to Ethan. Shawn is to my left, with Jeremiah across from him and Ethan across from me. Holden normally takes the head of the table, between Shawn and Jeremiah, but when he's not here, it's just open.

"My life story might be a bit lengthy, but I'll do my best to give you the Reader's Digest version," she begins, "My name is Alexis Branthwaite, by the way, since I don't think any of you knew my last name so far. I've gone by a lot of names and I answer to a variety of them—Lexi, Lex, Alex, Allie, Lexis—the list goes on. My family calls me Lex. I was born in Baltimore to my healthcare worker parents—my dad's a physician, and my mom's a nurse."

Ethan interjects, "Holden would get a kick out of that. Too bad he's not here."

"I actually already told him. We had that conversation," she confesses with a smile, and I'm pretty sure I'm not the only one wondering when that conversation took place.

"I graduated with a degree in marketing and a minor in graphic design from the University of Maryland, UMBC," she shares with a mischievous glint in her eye. "My parents were a bit disappointed when I didn't follow in their footsteps into medicine and healthcare to Johns Hopkins, where they both attended. But I've always been the wild child, the black sheep, so they probably weren't surprised."

That "wild child" comment definitely caught my attention, especially seeing the playful smirk and glint in her eye.

"I have two older brothers, both doctors," she says, pointing at herself with a playful smirk. "Black sheep," she adds before continuing. "I'm twenty-nine, and they're thirty-one and thirty-five. They're both married, and I have four nieces and two nephews. I do not get along with my parents at all, especially my mom. I have a best friend, her name is Georgia, you will hear me talk about her, but otherwise, I don't have many girlfriends. My standard fun fact for work icebreakers and such—I played varsity softball and lacrosse all four years of high school and then travel softball from age ten to eighteen. In college, I played lacrosse all four years."

"Wait," Jeremiah interrupts. "You played serious softball?"

"Uh, yeah," she responds flippantly as if it were a silly question, bringing a smile to my face.

"So, not only do we have a company softball team," Jeremiah informs her, pausing to glance at the rest of us. "But Carter, Ethan, and I also coach Ana's softball team."

"It's been a while, but I'm sure it's like riding a bike," she beams.

"Well, we'll take all the help we can get," I chime in, flashing her a wink.

"Okay, we'll see what happens when softball season comes around." She pauses. "Let's see, the rest of my life story. Before I moved out here, I actually owned a condo. It's still on the market in Maryland, so when that sells, it will be financially helpful," she explains, glancing around the table. "And just so I don't have to answer these questions," she adds with a small smile, "I met Brody at a sales conference in Nashville. We spent a little over a year and a half flying back and forth to see each other or meeting in other cities. He proposed to me on New Year's, and well, now I'm here.

"The rest of the uncomfortable things I'm willing to share right now," she begins, pausing to take a sip of wine. "I have ADHD, unmedicated. My mom tried to therapy it out of me, which did help my executive function skills and my ability to mask, but it's still there. Sometimes, I hyper-fixate, and sometimes that's to my or other people's benefit, but sometimes it's not. I also can have weird sleep patterns. I usually just read when I have insomnia, but it doesn't help me sleep, just occupies my brain." She almost giggles, lifting her wine glass. "I drink," she continues, "but I don't smoke, vape, or do any drugs, not even weed. My favorite color is blue. I have four tattoos and one piercing besides my ears. I've had four serious relationships since I was sixteen, two engagements, no marriages, no kids. And that's pretty much everything y'all could need to know about me."

I take a moment to digest the fact that Brody was her second fiancé, and I'm not sure if I want to delve into what happened with the first one. The room falls silent for a moment, absorbing her candid revelations. There's a sense of admiration mixed with curiosity in the air. The openness with which she shares her story draws everyone in, creating a space for genuine connection and understanding.

"That," Ethan starts before pausing dramatically, "was a lot of information." We all chuckle. "But I do feel like we know you better now."

"I'm not going to make you all do that," she teases. "But now you know a lot more about me than I know about any of you."

"We'll get there," I promise with another wink.

After our meal, Alexis and I team up to tackle the aftermath, clearing the dishes. As we rinse and load the dishwasher, I seize the moment to connect.

"You holding up alright?" I ask, my tone gentle yet genuinely concerned. "I can only imagine how overwhelming this must be for you."

Her eyes meet mine, a soft smile playing on her lips. "It's a lot to take in," she admits, her voice carrying a mix of vulnerability and resilience. "But all of you guys, your kindness—it's been a lifeline. I thought my only option was to move back to Maryland, but now—now I might be able to carve out a new beginning."

I nod, understanding the weight of her words. "I may not have walked in your shoes, but I'm here to lend an ear or a helping hand whenever you need it." Pausing, I choose my words carefully, wanting to convey both support and sincerity. "I hope I didn't overstep with my question earlier. We just want to understand you better, that's all."

"No, it was fine; sometimes it's good to spill one's soul," she laughs.

* * *

The next morning, Jeremiah, Ethan, and I are in the kitchen about thirty minutes before we need to leave for the office when Alexis joins us for coffee. I'm a little taken aback by how this woman, who was downright captivating in her short shorts and tank top, is equally so in gray slacks and a blue oxford, carrying a small purse.

Her makeup is subtle, and her cinnamon-colored hair is down and straight, she must have spent time making it that straight. She greets us and then heads to make a cup of coffee.

Shawn joins us in the kitchen a few minutes later. It's a bit unusual for all of us to be heading to the office together, and it might throw off the people who are always in the office, but it's important to show Alexis around and get her acquainted with everything before our trip to Chicago. I have to keep reminding myself that this is purely business, even though I'm fighting the strong urge to reach out and touch her.

"We should take two cars," I suggest. "In case Alexis and I need to stay later than the rest of you."

"That's a good idea," Jeremiah agrees.

I glance at Alexis. "You can ride with me."

Her response is a bright smile, and damn, that makes me happy.

Once we're in the car, I seize the opportunity to learn more about her. "What kind of music do you listen to?"

Smiling, she responds, "Um, I like a lot of music, but mostly alternative and punk."

"If you tell me you're a Blink girl, I may not be able to control my actions," I joke in response.

"Then I won't say it out loud," she teases.

Turning on my playlist, I'm delighted when she knows all of the songs. That sets off our day together on a great note.

Twenty minutes later, we're pulling up outside the twelve-story building in the Denver Tech Center that houses Laugherty Software. I glance at Alexis and ask if she's ready.

"As ready as I'll ever be," she replies with a hint of determination, and we join the others at the elevator bank.

When we arrive at the office, I let Jeremiah take the lead, introducing her to various staff members. Then he and his assistant disappear with her behind closed doors to handle her paperwork. I know Ethan will have access to her salary details, but they consider that information "need to know," so Shawn and I are shooed away.

I take the opportunity to tidy up my office a bit. Alexis and I will be sharing an office, and although we won't be here often, I want her to feel like it's her space, too. As I'm finishing clearing off what will be her desk, Shawn brings in her computer and starts getting her set up. Until we hire a graphic designer, she'll be helping out with that, so she gets the drawing tablet and everything. Shawn normally wouldn't be doing this himself—he has people for that. I'm sure he's a little charmed by her as well, but I choose not to comment on it.

Shawn is just about finished setting Alexis up when Jeremiah and Ethan escort her into the office. She pauses to take in her surroundings. It's a pleasant office space, a corner spot with ample windows offering views of the mountains—and the freeway, but that can be easily overlooked. Shawn takes a moment to explain the system to her and get her logged in to everything. Jeremiah and Ethan simply stand there, observing, for reasons unknown but completely known to me.

In just two days, this woman has certainly thrown a wrench into our lives in some unexpected ways.

Once Shawn wraps up the setup, a moment of collective un-certainty hangs in the air, reflected in the silent exchange of glances between my colleagues and me. It's as if we're all silently asking, "What's next?"

A smirk plays at the corners of my lips as I break the silence.

"Looks like we've reached the point where it's all about diving into the sales and marketing strategies."

Jeremiah nods in agreement. "Yeah, I suppose that's the next logical step. How about we grab lunch later?"

My gaze shifts to Alexis, deferring to her for the final call. It's almost comical how Ethan, Jeremiah, and Shawn all turn to her simultaneously. In that moment, she holds the power.

"Uh, sure, sounds good," she agrees.

"Noon?" I confirm.

Jeremiah nods, and with no other reason to linger, they finally trickle out of our office.

Turning to Alexis, I ask, "Did the paperwork go okay?"

"Yeah, just standard stuff. And he was right. I was pleasantly surprised by the salary," she replies with a smile.

"Good. Do you mind if I call you Lex? I have a habit of shortening people's names, giving them nicknames, whatever," I chuckle.

"It's fine with me," she says enthusiastically.

"Alright, Lex, I'll walk you through where to locate all our existing files, and you can take it from there," I suggest, to which she nods in agreement.

I can't help but notice our dangerous proximity as I lean over, pointing out the intricacies of her screen and the resources we use. I'm acutely aware of how close we are—too close. I shouldn't be invading her personal space like this.

But then, there's her scent. It's intoxicating, a blend of cinnamon and caramel that wraps around me, pulling me in. I can't quite put my finger on it, but there's something undeniably unique about it, and it fans the flames of desire that are already burning.

8

ALEXIS

As Carter leans in behind me, his sculpted, tattooed arms flexing as he points out details on my screen, I feel a rush of heat cascade through me. I can smell his cologne; it's musky, covered in spice, almost like black licorice. His breath brushes against my neck, my hair, and my ear, sending a tingling sensation down my spine. I fight to suppress the shivers that threaten to betray the effect he has on me. It's like an electric dance through my nerves from the base of my skull down to the apex of my thighs.

I'm struck by the realization that this wasn't what I was expecting with Carter. I had envisioned this scenario with Holden or maybe even Ethan, but Carter has taken me by surprise. There's something about his presence, his proximity, that ignites a burning fire within me I truly hadn't anticipated. The feelings coursing through me also cement the fact that I am not really missing Brody—not that upset that he is no longer part of my life.

Instead, I'm caught in this moment with Carter, his closeness stirring emotions I didn't know I was capable of feeling so soon. It's exhilarating and terrifying all at once, and I find myself wanting to explore where this unexpected connection might lead.

Keeping my focus on his words proves to be daunting. As he straightens up, stepping away after guiding me through the intricacies of my screen, I find myself missing the warmth of his proximity almost instantly. There's an ache to have him close again, to feel the subtle electricity that seemed to hum between us.

Somewhat desperate for his return, I grasp at any excuse to prolong our interaction, urging him to retrace his steps and show me once more. As he obliges, I relish the chance to bask in his presence just a little while longer, secretly craving more of those fleeting moments with him.

I remind myself I am going to have days with him in Chicago and it sends a thrill coursing through me. The mere thought of it feels like a rush of adrenaline.

Once we've tackled the logistics of navigating my computer, I ask him to go over his sales pitch with me. "Could you run through your sales pitch with me? I really want to understand the software better and see how you're pitching it."

In response, Carter's eyes spark and he flashes me a grin that could melt glaciers. "You want me to perform for you, princess?" His words are laced with a teasing edge that sends a flush creeping up my cheeks.

Where did "princess" come from? And that tone—it's dripping with suggestion, maybe even sin, stirring something within me that I can't quite put into words.

I swiftly regain my composure, meeting Carter's tone and gaze with a teasing grin. "Yeah, Carter, I think I do want you to perform for me."

A flush creeps up his neck at the returned words, and he looks at me with a look that screams, *"What the hell am I going to do with you?"*

He manages to gather himself, swiveling his monitor to face me as if we're in the midst of a high-stakes presentation. Somehow, he manages to make this impromptu sales pitch erotic, and it's completely intentional. But by the time he wraps up, I'm not only better informed about their business but also understand better what they need from me and how I can help them.

"Do any of Shawn's team handle SEO for you guys?" I inquire with genuine curiosity.

Carter chuckles, his confusion mingled with amusement. "I don't even know how they would do that."

I smile sympathetically. "Alright, I'll check with him. My brain's already buzzing with ideas to boost your online presence. And what about social media? Does your company utilize it?" I press, already foreseeing the challenge ahead.

"We've got it, but it's honestly gathering virtual dust," he confesses with a sheepish grin.

"Well, looks like I've got my work cut out for me," I quip, shooting him an encouraging smile just as Ethan breezes in, interrupting, letting us know it's time for lunch.

Lunch with the whole crew proves fruitful. Shawn fills me in on the social media and SEO fronts, promising to loop me into their accounts' logins to breathe some life back into them.

Back at the office, I dive headfirst into mapping out my strategies for the future, eager to make my mark in this new role. Meanwhile, Carter is tied up with a string of sales calls, his focus unwavering as he navigates through potential leads. I try to pay attention to him, to his verbiage and how he conducts the calls.

As the afternoon wears on, we settle into the rhythm of a typical workday, the hum of productivity filling the air around us. It's mundane in the best way possible, a comforting routine already settling over us like a cozy blanket. For a first day, it's very promising.

As the day winds down, Carter shifts our focus from work to planning our upcoming trip to Chicago. I move closer to him, leaning casually against the wall beside his desk, enjoying the conversation.

"I've been a few times, but have you ever been to Chicago?" Carter inquires, his tone laced with curiosity.

I nod, a smile tugging at the corners of my lips. "Yeah, I've been a few times also. I played lacrosse there in college and attended a couple of sales conferences. It's an incredible and *huge* city. And the pizza? Absolutely unbeatable. My favorite pizza place in the country is in Chicago."

His blue eyes dance, and he grins mischievously. "Maybe that's where we'll have our Valentine's dinner."

I roll my eyes playfully, but his suggestion manages to coax a smile from me nonetheless. After Carter takes charge of booking our flights and accommodations, I can't help but pry into his plans prior to my joining him.

"Were you planning to go alone before?" I inquire, genuinely curious.

He hesitates before answering, revealing that Jeremiah and Ethan had contemplated joining him.

"Tell me about the prospective clients," I urge, still leaning against the wall near him, and he does.

As he divulges details about the prospective clients and the significance of our software to them, I formulate my own ideas about why our software would be beneficial to them.

"So, it's a boardroom pitch?" I confirm, wanting to ensure I have a clear picture.

Carter nods, and the conversation takes a playful turn as I tease him about his attire for the meeting.

"You gonna wear a suit?" I question with a hint of mischief.

"Of course," he responds, almost offended by the suggestion that he wouldn't. "And I hope you've got a power suit or two," he adds.

Carter's gaze takes me in from head to toe and back. He lingers shamelessly, intentionally making sure I know he is checking me out. It's the first time any of these guys I just met have made themselves so obvious, and I almost hate to admit that I'm not even a little bothered by it.

I laugh, enjoying the banter. "Don't worry, I've got it covered. Just make sure you and the prospective clients keep the focus on the presentation," I tease back, a playful glint in my eye.

Carter chuckles, his eyes twinkling with amusement. "I guess that depends on how tight the power suit is," he replies, punctuating his words with a wink that sends a rush of warmth through me.

Over the next few days, Carter and I work side by side on the couch in the main sitting area of the house on our laptops, mostly doing our own things, but I am grateful he is close to bounce ideas off of.

Jeremiah is incredibly impressed at the web presence I have been able to build in just a few days. He and Ethan even approved a short contract with a developer to revamp the website.

Friday night at dinner, Jeremiah says, "I think you're not allowed to leave now, Alexis; the on-the-job interview has been passed with flying colors in just four days."

I smile at him, and Carter winks at me. I shift the conversation to Holden because he has been gone.

"How were your hospital days?" I ask him.

Holden shares a few anecdotes, mentioning that despite the long hours, he managed to steal some moments of rest and sleep when he should have been able to—small victory amidst the chaos.

Ethan interjects with a playful jab, nudging me, "Holden missed your life story, Alexis. You should give him a recap."

I chuckle. "Maybe another time," I reply with a tired smile.

Just then, the doorbell interrupts our conversation, and Carter springs up with excitement. "That must be Ana," he announces before disappearing briefly.

Sure enough, when he returns to the dining room, his little girl is in his arms, clutching a stuffed cat while Carter sports a pink backpack slung over his shoulder.

Carter looks at me and says, "Ana, this is Alexis. She's staying with us for a while."

I smile at her. "It's nice to meet you, Ana."

She buries her face in Carter's chest but then looks up at me and smiles. It's adorable—she's adorable, he's adorable. I guess I discovered I now have a thing for single dads, or maybe it's just Carter.

9

CARTER

Watching Alexis interact with Ana over the weekend is a heart-warming sight. From coloring sessions to nail painting escapades, they form an instant bond. Even discussing Ana's school crush becomes a topic of giggles and shared secrets. Witnessing their playful antics of tag and hide and seek on the patio, I can't deny the softening of my heart. I realize quickly that I am falling for Alexis—hard.

Sure, I know she is on the rebound, probably not quite ready to dive into another relationship. Yet, the chemistry between us is undeniable. Even the other guys in the house seem to recognize it, giving us our space. Or maybe they just know we're working closely together, but it feels like more than that.

As we gear up for our trip to Chicago, I can't shake the conflicting emotions swirling within me. Yes, she's sexy and I want her, but more than that, I crave a deeper connection—a bond that transcends mere physical attraction and sex.

* * *

Before I know it, we're navigating a TSA line. Alexis remains her usual flirty self, which makes the mundane airport routine more bearable. Our flight passes swiftly, and we find a quick dinner at the hotel restaurant. Securing adjoining rooms may seem like a casual decision, but deep down, I just want her close.

Aware of the importance of a good night's sleep before our upcoming sales pitch, I tell her goodnight like a proper gentleman, setting our meeting time for the following morning.

And then comes the moment in the morning when she emerges from her room—a vision of elegance in a navy blue fitted skirt suit that she has paired with killer heels. My jaw nearly hit the floor at the sight of her, her makeup flawlessly understated, her attire exuding confidence with just a hint of allure with the proper business amount of cleavage.

Is that a thing? The proper business amount of cleavage? It feels like a thing, and it's a thing she seems to have perfected.

"Lex, you're going to have them all swooning." I can't help but grin; she laughs, a melodic sound that echoes through the hallway.

She takes a moment to appraise me, her gaze lingering as if pondering something. "You clean up pretty good, Carter. There might be women in the room. You never know."

I chuckle at her observation. "This is true, Lex," I agree, returning her smile.

Our presentation goes off without a hitch, fueled by Alexis's timely contributions and unwavering confidence. Despite being new to the company, she commands the room effortlessly. I can't help but marvel at her potential. Mentally noting I need to inform Jeremiah of her impact, I silently acknowledge that Alexis might just be the best thing to happen to our company in a while.

As we bid farewell to the executives and finalize dinner plans, we're reminded of the cocktail attire for the evening. Alexis and I exchange glances, already prepared for the occasion.

Once inside the elevator, the tension of the day eases, and I turn to Alexis with an admiring grin. "You were fucking amazing in there. You blew my mind."

Returning my smile, she proposes lunch, and I eagerly agree, suggesting we debrief over a meal.

We're seated in a cozy corner booth at a nearby café, shedding our jackets, and I rid myself of my tie and roll up my sleeves, instantly feeling more at ease. Despite our polished appearances, neither of us is truly comfortable in such formal garb.

As we're perusing the menu, Alexis goes off work topics and asks me about my tattoos. I tell her a lot of them were just ink therapy, but I point out one that I got for Ana; it's a daddy shark and a baby shark—they're realistic, not the cartoon version. The larger shark is protecting the smaller shark, and then the rest of that forearm is filled with other various ocean scene images.

"You said you have tattoos?" I ask her.

"I do," she replies. "I have four of them."

"I don't mean this the way it's going to sound, but occasionally, you walk around the house in very revealing clothes, and I've never seen any of them," I tease.

"If you're lucky and play your cards right, maybe you'll get to see them," she says salaciously.

"Is that a challenge, princess?" I query, matching her tone.

She doesn't answer but shrugs and goes back to looking at her menu.

"Woman, I swear to—" I stop myself before I say something I'll regret.

With a quick glance, a mischievous glint in her eyes, she offers no verbal reply, instead retreating behind her menu with a sly grin. I catch the telltale signs of her suppressed laughter. Biting back a flirtatious remark, I decide it's best to let the moment linger, savoring the easy banter between us.

After lunch, we head back to the hotel. Alexis says she is going to try to nap before dinner. I ask her if she's sure she's ready for cocktail attire, and she reassures me she is with unwavering confidence, her hand resting lightly on my forearm. And then, in a moment that completely catches me off guard, she leans in and plants a kiss on my cheek.

I stand there, momentarily stunned, as her hotel room door swings shut, leaving me rooted to the spot, a whirlwind of emotions swirling within me.

About thirty minutes before we're supposed to leave for dinner, I get a text from Alexis.

> (Lex) *So, I have a problem*
> (Me) *Oh yeah?*
> (Lex) *Yeah, I need help, but you can't make this about anything more than it is*
> (Me) *Color me intrigued*
> (Lex) *I need you to help me zip up my dress*

Fuuucck me.

> (Me) *Okay, unlock your adjoining door. I'll come help you*

I hear the click of her door just before I open mine. The scene unfolding is not as steamy as I had imagined, but still hot. She's almost completely dressed, but there are about six inches left on her zipper that she can't quite reach. The black lace dress hugs her ass and hips in a way that makes me hungry for her. My gaze lingers on the soft ivory skin of her back below her bra, and an overwhelming desire to touch her consumes me. I want to unzip the rest of the dress instead of zipping it up.

Without a word, she pulls her hair to the side, silently asking for assistance with her zipper. I step closer and zip her up, but as she starts to turn around, I place my hands gently on her hips, stopping her.

"Princess," I sigh, the word slipping out almost like a purr.

I watch as goosebumps rise on her upper back and neck, and that's all the encouragement I need. I wrap my arms around her waist, pulling her back into me. My lips trail gently along the side of her neck, then under her ear, igniting a spark between us that I can't ignore, and she doesn't stop me. Again, she smells like cinnamon and caramel, her scent invading my nostrils.

"You're fucking irresistible, you know that, Lex?" I whisper against her ear, and her head rolls back into my shoulder.

"Carter," she whispers, her voice barely audible, "we need to go to dinner soon, but when we get back, I'll probably need help un-zipping my dress, too."

Fuck, this woman is going to be the death of me.

I loosen my grip on her waist, allowing her to turn toward me. As I study her, I'm captivated by the fire in her blue eyes and her staggering beauty. She moistens her bottom lip with her tongue, and the glistening wetness invites me in. I'm overwhelmed by the desire to take her, to fuck her, right then and there, but simultaneously, I want to savor every moment. I want to seduce her slowly, to make her crave me as much as I crave her.

Raising my hand to her face, I gently cradle her jaw and run the pad of my thumb over her soft, lush bottom lip. Her lip quivers, her eyes close, and I move toward her slowly, deliberately, not wanting to rush or be aggressive. Her eyes flutter open just as our lips are about to meet. I steal one last glance into those beautiful blue pools, pupils dilated with lust before I gently press my lips to hers.

Our kiss is soft, sensual, unhurried, a tender exploration of each other's mouths and tongues. My hand tangles lightly in her hair, conveying my desire without forcefulness.

After a minute, I break the kiss and gently rest my forehead against hers, listening to her ragged breaths. "I don't want to rush this, Lex. I like you. I like you a lot."

Alexis places her hands on my chest. "We need to go to dinner anyway, but, Carter, I like you too."

Leaning up, she lands a gentle kiss on the corner of my mouth and then backs away from me.

10

ALEXIS

That kiss—it's like fireworks exploding in my mind, toe-curling and mind-numbing. Carter is incredible. I repeat it like a mantra, reminding myself over and over—I'm not going to sleep with him, I'm not going to sleep with him. Not yet, at least. We're going to enjoy our time together on this trip, but we need to talk, to figure things out.

We work side by side, we live under the same roof, and I refuse to let our actions jeopardize either our professional relationship or my living arrangements. But most importantly, I don't want to jeopardize Carter's friendships with his childhood buddies—I can't bear the thought of being the cause of any strain between them. Sure, they've probably been drawn to the same woman before, but I won't be the one to unravel their bonds of friendship. That's a line I don't want to cross.

Carter's hand rests on the small of my back as we step into the elegant steakhouse in downtown Chicago. We're meeting board members and executives from a major healthcare corporation, and from the moment we enter, we both switch into full-on business mode.

As dinner progresses, conversations become more personal. Carter shares anecdotes about Ana, and we delve into reminiscing about my college lacrosse years. One of the executives expresses curiosity about collegiate-level lacrosse, especially with his daughter playing in high school.

I limit myself to one glass of wine, not wanting to feel even a hint of a buzz tonight. By the time we leave, several others at the dinner are visibly intoxicated. Overall, the dinner feels successful, though the true verdict will come during our final meeting to-morrow morning.

The atmosphere in the rideshare back to the hotel and even in the elevator is unusually quiet. Both Carter and I typically have outgoing personalities, so the silence speaks volumes. Tension hangs heavy in the air, laden with unspoken words and actions not taken.

Wrapping my arms around myself protectively as we approach our rooms, I finally break the silence.

"Listen, Carter." I clear my throat. "I do like you a lot—"

"Here comes the but," he interrupts, sounding defeated.

"Yes, but no." I smile softly at him. "The 'but' is that I just think we need to slow down and think about this; it's not a 'but' saying I don't want you."

I scan the key to my lock and grab his hand, pulling him into my room. His pupils dilate a little, and I realize that may have been a mistake, but we're here now.

Kicking off my heels, I start talking. "Carter, you said you don't want to rush this, and I don't either. There's a lot for us to think about, at least for me to think about; this very short new life I am building could disappear if we do this and it doesn't work."

He doesn't say anything, but he keeps his hands in his pockets and stares at his shoes. I move closer to him and cradle his jaw with my hand, feeling the hint of stubble under my gentle fingers. Finally, his gaze meets mine, and there is hunger in his sky-blue eyes that he can't hide. I wonder how much of that is reflected in my own eyes.

"All I'm saying, Carter, is I agree, I don't want to rush this. I want every step we take to be thoughtful and deliberate. There are other people that could be impacted by our actions, Ana, mainly." As I finish saying that, it feels like the air between us becomes headier—like his fire is burning hotter.

I drop my hand from his face, and his voice is gravelly as he speaks. "Lex, the fact that you're thinking about how my daughter could be impacted by us makes me want you even more. But I have never brought a woman into her life in that capacity, and if I did, I would make sure that I knew it was worth it."

The backs of his fingers graze over my cheek, and he continues, "I know there are a lot of complications here. I know you're not even two weeks out of a broken engagement, and you probably aren't ready for it either." He swallows. "But I do like you, I want you, and I don't think any amount of talking or acknowledging all those issues will change that."

His hand moves to the back of my neck, gentle fingers moving across my skin, sending electricity through my body, down my spine. I ache for him almost instantly. Then he slowly moves his mouth to mine again, kissing me deeply, but it's not aggressive; he is trying to savor it, to actually feel the connection between us.

When he breaks the kiss, he smiles at me, a little cocky, but then he asks, "Alexis Branthwaite, will you be my Valentine?"

I laugh more at the look on his face than the question itself. I gently kiss him and then answer, "Carter Larkspur, I will be your Valentine, but I'm not going to sleep with you."

"Can we make out like teenagers, at least?" he jests, a sparkle in his eye.

"I think that can be arranged." I smile, and his mouth covers mine again.

We indulge in a glorious make out session; his hands wander a little, but for the most part, we keep it tame and under control.

* * *

The next morning, Carter likes my red suit even more than the blue one I wore the day before.

"It's Valentine's Day. It seemed fitting to wear red," I explain with a casual shrug.

His own choice of a red tie confirms that he had similar thoughts. I feel like he almost has two different personalities, when his tattoos are visible and when they're not, but I like them both.

As we settle into the rideshare, his hand finds its place on my thigh, and instinctively, I cover it with my own. The touch feels natural and comforting, but beneath it all, if I'm honest, it also feels confusing.

"Are you ready for this?" I ask, glancing over at him as we stride into the sleek, modern building.

"Always," he replies, his smile oozing confidence.

Our meeting with the chief information officer couldn't have gone better. They want our software, but naturally, they want to delve into the nitty-gritty of the financials. Carter assures them that he'll arrange a virtual sit-down with Ethan to iron out all the details. Despite the need for further discussions, the firm handshake exchanged tells us we've struck gold and sealed the deal.

As we step into the elevator, Carter puffs out his cheeks and exhales deeply, his shoulders relaxing; he turns to me, his eyes sparkling with excitement. "Okay, now we can call Jeremiah, and then it's time to celebrate."

Back at the hotel, we find ourselves sitting on the end of Carter's bed while he calls Jeremiah on speakerphone. Jeremiah patches in Ethan, and the call is positive and celebratory.

"We'll have to have a real celebration when you two get back," Jeremiah says.

I can feel the heat and blush on my cheeks as Carter sings my praises about how well I did. Jeremiah and Ethan offer their compliments as well and then Jeremiah changes subjects completely.

"So, while I have your attention," he begins. "Carrie's birthday is Friday. We're throwing a shindig at the house on Saturday. She's inviting a bunch of folks—still not sure how many. But, Carter, I figured you'd need someone to look after Ana, so I thought I'd give you the heads up."

"What time?" Carter inquires.

"Kicks off at eight, going until who fucking knows," Jeremiah chuckles.

After Carter ends the call, I can't help but laugh. "How many parties do you guys throw?"

"Sometimes too many," he admits with a smirk. "It's just one of those houses, I guess. And with the five of us," he nudges me playfully, "now six, we've got quite the network."

"So, Ethan mentioned something about the basement being off-limits. Are there any other forbidden zones?" I inquire, genuinely curious.

"Upstairs is technically off-limits, too, but we're not exactly running a tight ship. We trust people to be respectful. It's usually not an issue," he explains, his expression sympathetic; I'm sure he's remembering Brody and Ellie.

"When Ana's around, though, I make sure there's a babysitter holed up in her room. She doesn't need to be around a bunch of intoxicated adults. If someone does happen to wander upstairs, at least I know there's someone looking out for her."

"That sounds like a good plan," I reply, eager to shift the topic. "So, what do you want to do now?"

"That, princess, is a loaded question," he teases, his voice tinged with desire, but he sighs and concedes, "Maybe lunch, perhaps find something to do, or we could just come back here and chill. Then dinner," he laughs, shaking his head. "Seems like a lot of eating, but hey, that's all that is on our agenda. Tell me about this pizza place."

I excitedly share the details of my favorite pizza joint with Carter, telling him about the chain conveniently located just a few blocks from the hotel. It's settled; that's where we'll have dinner. Carter surprises me with a suggestion for a local gem for lunch. We both agree that casual attire is the way to go, so I head back to my room to change into jeans.

But as I step into the room, I'm utterly floored. On the dresser, two *enormous* bouquets of roses catch my eye—one red, the other white. I make my way over, my heart fluttering with curiosity, and pick up the card nestled amidst the scarlet blooms.

Alexis - I wanted to make sure you felt remembered this Valentine's Day. These past weeks may have been hard and despite our brief time together, your presence has left an indelible mark on me, captivating me completely. It's undeniable, and I find myself unable to shake the thought of you. - Holden

I take a deep breath and then move to the card on the white roses.

Lexi,

I hope this makes you smile. I've been hearing nothing but praise about you from Carter, and I wanted to take a moment to acknowledge the impact you've had on me, personally, as well. I understand that life may have thrown you a curveball recently, but I wanted to ensure you didn't feel forgotten on Valentine's Day. Looking forward to your return.

See you soon, Ethan

I put the cards down and pick up my phone to thank them; I start with Holden.

> (Me) *Hey, the roses are beautiful, the note is too, thank you, how are you holding up today?*
> (Holden) *I'm glad you like them, and better now that I've heard from you*
> (Me) *Are you home tomorrow or at the hospital?*
> (Holden) *I'm home until Sunday night*
> (Me) *Okay, I'll see you then*
> (Holden) *Happy Valentine's Day*

Then I move on to Ethan. I don't want to lead anyone on, but I'm not going to let the gestures go unacknowledged.

> (Me) *Hey, the roses are beautiful, thank you*
> (Ethan) *You're beautiful*

(Me) *lol thank you for that too*

(Ethan) *I'll be happy to have you back here tomorrow*

(Me) *It will be nice to be home; thank you for giving me a home*

(Ethan) *It was the least I could do*

I take pictures of the flowers and notes and send them to Georgia and then set down my phone and begin to change, my mind swirling with conflicting thoughts. Should I tell Carter about the unexpected attention from others?

I mean, I haven't done anything to encourage them, have I? All I've done is be myself.

If I'm honest, Carter is the only one I've allowed myself to even flirt with. So why does this gnawing guilt persist, twisting knots in my stomach?

My phone dings and I pick it up as I'm slipping on my shoes.

(Georgia) *Girl! They must think your pussy is made of gold, what are you going to do?*

(Me) *IDK honestly - but for now I'm going to enjoy the rest of my time in Chicago with Carter*

11

CARTER

I have butterflies in my stomach as I wait for Alexis to text me, letting me know she's ready for lunch. Why does she make me so nervous?

When I finally receive her text, I practically bolt out my door, unable to contain my excitement and anxiety. I greet her with a gentle kiss on the cheek as she emerges from her door. She looks adorable in ripped jeans and a black sweater.

I had made plans and reservations for us a few days ago, hoping she'd be willing to spend time with me. But I also hope she doesn't think I'm just trying to impress her with money; that's not my intention at all. I just want to create an unforgettable day with her for both of us.

Throughout lunch, I try not to be too handsy, but I find myself touching her frequently. Then, the nerves hit me harder.

"I have a surprise for you," I say with a smile as I open the door to our rideshare.

Her expression reflects a mix of apprehension and curiosity. Ten minutes later, we arrive at our destination, and Alexis looks around, puzzled; the building in front of us looks like a warehouse.

"What is this, Carter?" she asks skeptically.

"Lex, princess, we're going to take a helicopter tour of Chicago," I say, attempting to beam at her despite my nerves.

Her natural smile instantly calms my nerves. "Are you serious?"

"Very serious," I reply, taking her hand and leading her to the building.

Thirty minutes later, we're soaring through the air, and she still hasn't stopped smiling. I feel proud of myself, but more than anything, I feel a sense of peace and happiness wash over me. It feels a lot like the emotions I have when I do something that makes Ana happy.

After a forty-five-minute flight, we're back on solid ground. Knowing we have some time to kill before dinner, I lead Alexis to my next surprise.

As soon as we step out of the rideshare and start walking down the street, she slides her hand from my bicep down to my hand, intertwining our fingers. Electric sensations surge through me, coursing from my fingers, up my arm, and down my spine. Then, she doubles down and wraps her other hand around my forearm, drawing her body closer to mine.

Though it's a bit chilly, it's not too bad for a February day by Lake Michigan. We're only outside for a few minutes before I open the door to Willis Tower. We spend time on the Skydeck, which is a little less impressive after the helicopter ride. Throughout our exploration, she keeps her hand firmly in mine, and I find myself unable to imagine not touching her once we get home. It feels so natural, so genuine.

Finally, it's time to take her to her favorite pizza place. I have to admit, she's right; it's exceptionally good pizza. The crust is unique in a way I've never experienced before. She indulges in a few glasses of wine, and I can see the pink tint in her cheeks from the alcohol.

We linger at the restaurant, delving into conversations about our pasts and getting to know each other better. The more she reacts to my stories and the more I learn about her, the more I am drawn to her and the more I want her. I want her deep, down to the marrow in my bones.

The walk back to the hotel is only three blocks, and she resumes her previous position, her fingers laced with mine and her other hand resting on my forearm. Her hair dances in the breeze, somehow making her even more beautiful.

By the time we reach the hotel lobby, the alcohol and the wind have left her cheeks flushed with color. I pause for a moment just inside the doors, gently brushing her hair out of her face. Her eyes close in response to my touch, sending a surge of desire through me.

As we step into the elevator, her body language shifts slightly, her tone becoming more serious, but her hand stays firmly intertwined with mine.

"Carter, thank you so much for today and tonight," she begins, "This has been one of the best dates of my life, nonetheless, Valentine's Days. I appreciate you."

"Am I sensing another 'but' coming?" I tease, a smile playing on my lips.

Her voice rises a little. "Kind of," she admits, and I can tell she's not telling me something. "I'll just show you. That's easiest; I didn't want to cast a shadow over today, which is why I didn't show you earlier."

She scans the key on the lock to her room and then pulls me inside. But before she does anything else, her hand slips around the back of my neck, pulling me into a passionate kiss. In this moment, I'll take what she's willing to give, savoring every second.

As Alexis draws back from the kiss, she says, "I want you to know that I really do like you a lot. I enjoy this chemistry we have, and I don't want to walk away." She takes a deep breath and then says probably one of the last things I expect. "But I think you need to have some conversations with your friends."

I look at her quizzically, and she takes my hand, leading me further into the room. That's when I notice the roses, and she hands me the cards. I read them once, then sit on the end of her bed, scrubbing my face and running my hand through my hair, reading them again.

She stands in front of me, leaning against the dresser, and adorably says, "I don't want to be a homewrecker."

I chuckle, understanding her sentiment, though it's a funny way of putting it.

"What was it you said," she continues, "you've known each other since before you had pubic hair? I can't knowingly cause problems there, Carter."

I put the notes down, not saying anything, but I reach forward and grab the belt loops on her jeans, pulling her closer to me. Resting my forehead on her belly, she starts gently scraping her nails on my scalp, sending waves of pleasant sensations through my body.

"Lex, I told you, you're fucking irresistible, and that's not only to me," I say. "But you're right, I need to have those conversations with them because clearly, they didn't even talk to each other, let alone me."

She laughs, "I think it's weird that I would be the subject of some kind of friend meeting like you're deciding who is allowed to play with the new toy."

"Oh, you *are* the new toy, but you're so, so much more than that," I say, looking up and meeting her eyes.

Then she bends down and kisses me. I pull her between my thighs and then back onto the bed. I know she won't have sex with me, but again, I'll take what I can in the form of another intense make out session. Especially since everything will change tomorrow.

On the flight home, I treasure those last free moments with Alexis in ways I know I'll have to hold back on once we're home. I find I like her ripped jeans because I can slip my hand into the rips and feel her soft, silky, bare skin. She lifts the armrest and leans into me for most of the flight, giving me the opportunity to press soft kisses on top of her head.

My brain spins the whole time, thinking about how I'm going to approach this with my friends. Ethan will probably be okay, but Holden, Holden is a whole different story. He's a sensitive soul, almost empathetic to a fault, and sometimes he struggles with social situations. He would fall on the sword and sacrifice himself for me, but in the end, he'd be miserable for it.

12

ALEXIS

I can't deny that I'll miss the effortless connection I share with Carter, but he needs to sort things out with his friends on his own. It's not something I can do for him, at least not right now.

In the garage, his fingers wrap around my wrist, pulling me close to him. We share a tight embrace, his warmth comforting yet tinged with a hint of sadness. As he pulls back, I see the pain in his eyes, and he leaves me with the gentlest, tenderest kiss on my lips.

Then, he's off, retrieving our luggage from the trunk, refusing to let me carry my own, earning an eye roll from me in response. A playful smirk dances on his lips as he catches my gaze.

As we walk through the door into the kitchen, Carter yells, "Hey honey, we're home."

I laugh, and Carter shoots me a playful wink. But his call-out works. Shawn and Ethan are in the kitchen very quickly, and Jeremiah is right behind them.

Carter looks at me. "I'm going to take the luggage upstairs. I'll be right back."

I nod, and he leaves with both of our bags.

As soon as Carter disappears around the corner, Ethan catches my attention. "Sounds like you and Carter gave us a reason to break out the champagne."

"I believe so," I reply with a grin. "But I think you're the final piece of the puzzle."

Ethan chuckles and shrugs. "That piece is easy."

Returning his smile, I inquire, "Is Holden around?"

Shawn pipes up, a playful glint in his eyes. "He's down in the gym. He probably missed Carter's grand entrance."

"I'll go say hi then. I'll be back in a minute," I excuse myself, turning towards the basement stairs.

"Hurry back," Ethan teases, his voice trailing after me.

My response to Ethan is merely a smile as I descend the basement stairs. Standing at the gym's entrance, I observe Holden on the treadmill, waiting for him to notice my presence in the mirror. His shirtless, sculpted physique glistens with sweat, and I can't help but admire him. I run the charm of my necklace over my lips, secretly reveling in his impressive body and his obvious attraction to me.

After a moment, his gaze meets mine in the mirror, and he slows the treadmill, removing his earbuds as he approaches. "Hey, Alexis," he greets me with a dazzling smile. "Just got back?"

I straighten up, stepping away from the doorframe and dropping my necklace. "Yeah, just a couple of minutes ago," I reply, gathering my thoughts. "I wanted to thank you in person for the roses and the note. It was sweet. I wish I could've brought them back with me."

I make a conscious effort to maintain eye contact with him despite the distracting sight of sweat trickling down his chiseled chest and abs. Holden takes a step closer, his hand reaching up to brush the back of his fingers against my cheek. A shiver runs down my spine at the touch of his unusually cold fingers, and my eyes flutter shut for a moment.

When I open them again, I find him staring at me with an intensity and hunger that sends a rush of heat through me. "I can always get you more for here," he offers, his voice husky with desire.

"There's no need for that," I reply with a soft smile. "But I did want to express my gratitude. I didn't mean to interrupt your workout."

"It's fine," he reassures me, glancing back at the treadmill. "I was almost done anyway. I should probably go check in with Carter."

When we get back to the kitchen, I am quick to notice Carter's gaze shoot between me and Holden. I hold his eyes for a little too long as reassurance. Holden is right, though—he does need to check in with Carter.

I hop into the shower before dinner, and just as I'm wrapped in nothing but a towel, there's a knock on my bedroom door.

"Come back in ten minutes!" I call out playfully, hearing Carter's laughter in response.

Sure enough, almost exactly ten minutes later, there's another knock. I open the door, and before I know it, Carter's pushing me into the room, locking the door behind him. His hand is in my hair, his lips on mine so fast that it takes a moment for my brain to catch up. But when it does, I melt into him, wrapping my arms around him, tangling my fingers in his hair. We kiss for what feels like an eternity.

"I don't know how I'm going to keep my hands off of you," he whispers against my lips when we finally break apart.

"Carter," I protest with a whine. "That's something you'll have to figure out. I can't do it for you."

"I know," he murmurs, pressing a gentle kiss to my forehead. "Dinner's in about ten minutes. I'll see you down there."

"Okay," I reply softly, returning his kiss.

As he leaves my room, I can hear him interacting with Holden in the hallway. Well, that's cool; it looks like Holden definitely saw him leaving my bedroom.

When I join everyone at the dinner table, Shawn is the first to speak up. "Is that a Baby Yoda shirt?"

Glancing down at my attire, even though I didn't forget what I was wearing, I feign offense. "No, that's not Baby Yoda, it's Grogu."

Shawn dramatically puts his hand to his chest. "I think you just melted my entire nerd heart."

"She told me she plays first-person shooters, too," Ethan chimes in with a smile.

"No, no," I correct with a laugh. "I said I *used* to play first-person shooters."

"But you could again," Shawn suggests with a grin.

"GLHF," I say, and Shawn puts his hand over his heart again, playfully sighing.

* * *

A few days later, the afternoon before Carrie's party, there's an undeniable tension lingering in the air. Carter had conversations with both Ethan and Holden, but Carter said they weren't exactly receptive, especially Holden. Despite the less-than-ideal outcomes, those discussions seem to embolden Carter. His touches become bolder, though still subtle enough to pass off as friendly gestures.

While the caterer sets up a taco, burrito, and nacho bar, and the guys haul in an excessive amount of alcohol, I spend time with Ana. About thirty minutes before the party is set to start, I hand over Ana duties to her sitter, Hadley.

Dressing for the party in dark jeans and a royal blue cropped, wide-necked sweater, it's casual but cute. I wear a black bra with lacy straps since they will show. I go a little heavier on the eye makeup, and use a lip stain and lip gloss, but otherwise leave my face natural, along with my hair.

As the evening progresses, the house fills with twenty-two people, which honestly doesn't seem like a lot, given the size of the house. Along with my five roommates, myself, and Carrie, there's a diverse mix of guests—men and women, singles and couples—drawn from Carrie's life beyond our circle. Most of them, the guys seem to have met before.

Everyone dives into the food and socializes. I start to unwind, my social anxiety calming.

But just as I begin to relax, Carrie's loud and excited voice cuts through the chatter, "Let's play Never Have I Ever!"

Fuck me sideways.

For a minute, I seriously consider just going to my room. As everyone enthusiastically responds to Carrie's suggestion, they start reaching for solo cups, eager to fill them with their drink of choice. Carter extends a cup to me, but I shake my head and decline.

Looking at me quizzically, Carter watches as I reach for a full bottle of Jack Daniels, declaring, "I'm going to need more than a cup for this."

He laughs; I roll my eyes and then add, "I hate this fucking game."

"It can't be that bad," he reassures me.

I tilt my head at him with a challenging expression. "We'll see, but you may change your opinion of me after this," I respond. Sensing his growing intrigue despite my warning, I smile and then add, "Although for you, possibly for the better."

He cocks his head sideways with genuine curiosity.

The last time I played this game was at my friend Sasha's combined bachelor and bachelorette party. It quickly turned into a challenge of "let's see if there's anything Alexis hasn't done." The party ended with most of the women giving me dirty looks and even openly calling me a slut, while half the men tried to hit on me—even some of the ones that were not single.

Given the current vibe in the house, I have a feeling tonight could go in a similar direction. I've never played this game where the questions didn't turn all sexual, even when I was in high school. It's as if the game itself has a magnetic pull towards the most intimate and revealing aspects of our lives, and I can't help but feel a knot of apprehension tighten in my stomach as I brace for what's to come.

Carter and I return to the main living room, only to find all the seats taken. We end up leaning against the fireplace, joining a few others standing around. Ethan catches my eye and then glances down at the bottle in my hand before meeting my gaze again with a smirk. I simply smile back and shrug, ready for whatever happens at this point.

It starts out simple—I drink for some things, not for others.

"Never have I ever been skinny dipping," — I drink.

"—been arrested, —flashed someone,—shoplifted, —ghosted someone," — I don't drink.

" —danced in the rain," — I drink.

My first turn, I am innocent, even though the statement has meaning for me. "Never have I ever been in a car accident."

Carter looks at me like he is expecting more, but I know where this is going—this game always goes in one direction; it doesn't need any help from me. And a few people later, it starts.

"—had sex in a car," —I drink.

"— faked an orgasm," —I drink.

"— played strip poker," —I drink.

"Never have I ever had a threesome," Carrie says.

I interject, "You have to define that —an angel's three-way, devil's three-way, an all-same-gender threesome?"

"I don't even know what that means," Carrie replies, laughing.

Holding the whiskey bottle by the neck, I talk with my hands.

"Angel's is two girls, one guy. Devil's is two guys, one girl, or three of the same gender is a same-gender threesome," I explain like I'm teaching the quadratic equation to a bunch of teenagers; several people, including Carter and Jeremiah, snicker a little.

"Uh, angel's, I guess," Carrie says—I drink.

The next person goes with devil's, and I drink. Surprisingly, so does Carter, and I narrow my eyes at him. He smiles and shrugs.

"—had a same-gender threesome," —I don't drink.

"—called someone mommy or daddy during sex," —I don't drink.

"—had sex in a public bathroom," —I drink.

"—used handcuffs during sex," —I drink.

"—watched porn during sex," —I drink.

"—bitten someone during sex," —I drink.

"—had sex in a shower," —I drink.

"—had sex in public," —I drink.

"—had anal sex," —I drink.

"—had food eaten off my body," —I drink.

"—eaten food off someone else's body," —I drink.

We're back to me, and this is intentional for Holden and Ethan. "Never have I ever had sex with anyone in this room." Interestingly, Shawn and a few others drink in addition to Jeremiah and Carrie.

"—had a dream about sex with anyone in this room." Touché, Carter, you would throw that in there after mine—I drink.

"—given someone a lap dance," —I drink.

"—received a lap dance," —I drink.

"—been choked during sex," —I drink.

"—been fisted," —I drink.

"—had sex in a pool," —I drink.

"—had sex in a hot tub," —I drink.

"—been paid for sex." I start to raise the bottle to my lips, and then I say, "Just kidding."

"—masturbated during phone sex," —I drink.

"—had a friends-with-benefits arrangement," —I don't drink.

"—kissed someone of the same gender," —I drink.

"—had a sexual encounter on an elevator," —I drink.

"—had sex on a beach," —I drink.

"—had sex with a stranger," —I don't drink.

"—acted out someone else's fantasy," —I drink.

"—knowingly hit on someone in a committed relationship," —I don't drink.

"—made a sex video," —I drink.

"—had sex in the workplace," —I drink.

"—bought sex toys," —I drink.

"—cheated on a partner," —I don't drink.

"—Googled sex positions," —I drink.

Then we're back to me, and after all of that, I think everyone is stunned when I say, "Never have I ever had a one-night stand." All my guys, all five of my roommates, drink.

"—woken someone up with sex," —I drink.

"—had a pearl necklace," —I drink.

"—been tied to a bed," —I drink.

"—tied someone to a bed," —I drink.

"—been blindfolded during sex," —I drink.

"—been whipped during sex," —I drink.

"—whipped someone else during sex," —I drink.

The game is back to Carrie, who started it. She glares at me and she decides she is done. "I think it's weed time," she says. Several of Carrie's friends whisper to each other while one or the other of them looks at me.

My fifth of Jack is more than half gone, and I feel Carter's hand possessively resting on the back of my neck. My eyes scan the room, and each of my roommates seems momentarily frozen; their eyes fixate on me with a hunger that sends a chill down my spine.

Even Shawn, usually so laid-back, is caught in the grip of the moment, his gaze locking onto me with an intensity I've never seen before. Surprisingly, Jeremiah is affected. His attention momentarily diverts from Carrie as she grabs his arm, her eyes darting between us with a hint of uncertainty. The moment feels heady, charged, and transformative.

As the spell is broken, and people start to get up to head outside to add marijuana to their alcohol, Carter turns to me, facing the fireplace to hide his mouth and mute his voice from the rest of the room. "Princess, if I did what I wanted to, I would throw you over my shoulder and take you to my bed right now because you answering those questions was fucking erotic as hell."

"No, Carter, you wouldn't." He looks at me confused but still with fire in his eyes. "Because one thing I do know is that when I fuck you the first time, I want to be sober."

His eyes widen, and he almost growls, sending heat through my core. "If that is a 'when,' it needs to be soon."

Taking another sip out of my bottle, I smile at him before I walk away. He heads upstairs to check on Ana.

13

ALEXIS

I slip away, taking my bottle of Jack, seeking refuge and solace on the patio, in the outdoor kitchen where the scent of pot isn't so overpowering. The cold air nips at my skin as light snowflakes dance around me, providing a refreshing contrast to the warmth and chaos of the house and the party. I lean my back against the bar, facing the house, away from the rest of the party, pulling out my phone to text Georgia. I need to vent about the way Carrie and her friends are looking at me and I need to do it with someone who really knows me.

Ethan joins me, casually leaning against the counter beside me, a playful glint in his chocolate-brown eyes. "I guess I understand why you needed that bottle," he teases, a smirk playing at the corners of his lips.

I let out a grumble, taking a long swig from the bottle of Jack in my hand and pocketing my phone. "I hate that fucking game," I mutter, the bitterness evident in my tone.

"I'm pretty sure all the other women here hate you playing it, too," Ethan chuckles.

"Oh, they'll slut-shame me to high hell, but they have no clue. Just because I'm adventurous doesn't mean I'm promiscuous. My body count is probably lower than everyone else here," I retort sharply, taking another sip of Jack to wash down the bitterness.

"I'm not trying to be the bad guy here," Ethan says, his voice gentle and conciliatory.

"Sorry," I reply, meeting his gaze and offering him a small smile.

Ethan's hand rests lightly on my stomach as he leans in closer, his voice low and intimate. "I know Carter's all but claimed you, but just so you know, every single man here found you attractive before that game, and they probably feel it even stronger now. So who the hell cares what a bunch of catty women say?"

"Does Jeremiah know you call his girl catty?" I tease, trying to lighten the mood and putting the bottle of Jack back to my mouth.

"She's fine when it's just her, but when she's with a bunch of girl-friends, she can be a bit much." Ethan smirks. "For some reason, I don't think you'd be like that."

"Don't put me too high on that pedestal, Ethan," I reply with a smile, "I'm not perfect—I have plenty of faults. I'm not the fantasy you all have made me out to be."

I don't know where that came from. Apparently, the alcohol has made me braver than usual. His eyes narrow, and he smiles at me.

"Maybe, but I'm pretty sure I'd like to fuck around and find out," Ethan murmurs into my ear, his breath warm against my neck, his facial hair tickling my cheek. There's a surge of electricity and heat in the air, but the chemistry doesn't feel as potent as it does with Carter and Holden—either that or I'm just too drunk to fully sense it, which is entirely possible.

As Ethan leans back, I give him a warning look. "Remember, Carter called dibs," I say with a smile. "But in all seriousness, Ethan,

I don't want to cause problems for you guys—your friendships, your business, any of it. I won't even 'fuck around and find out' with Carter if it's going to cause issues."

"Lexi, people don't surprise me very often, but you surprise me every fucking day. I respect you even more for saying that," Ethan responds, pulling his hand away from my stomach. "But, just so you know, we'll be okay, whatever happens. Don't worry too much about that. We've been through a lot and we're all still here. Honestly, it will cause just as many issues if you deny Carter because of us as it will otherwise."

I contemplate those words as I take another sip of Jack and glance up to meet Carter's eyes as he approaches us.

I lift my chin at Carter. "How's Ana?"

He grins. "Sleeping like an angel. What are you two up to?"

"Avoiding the pot smoke," I reply with a smile, "and discussing how women tend to slut-shame each other."

Carter leans against the counter on my other side, effectively sandwiching me between him and Ethan.

"Apparently," Ethan chimes in, "Lexi here claims that despite her answers, she probably has the lowest body count of all of us."

"I believe it, actually," Carter responds, chuckling. "She's a 'go big or go home' kind of girl, so I think she's either all in or all out."

"Guys, I'm right fucking here," I interject with a laugh. "Don't talk about me like I'm not."

Carter's curiosity gets the better of him. "Since you made that statement, what's your count?"

I look at him incredulously. "Seriously?"

"You made the claim," he laughs.

"Seven," I answer.

"Does that include all those threesomes?" Carter jokes.

"*All* those?" I laugh. "But yes, it does."

"That actually is pretty low," Ethan remarks with a smile.

"Like I said, I'm not promiscuous, just adventurous," I retort, taking another sip of Jack. "People like to confuse the two, especially women, or at least that's my experience."

"I'm going to go out on a limb here and say that's not the first time that game went that way for you," Carter remarks with a smile.

"Hence the bottle," I joke, holding it up for emphasis.

"You actually don't seem that drunk for drinking that much whiskey," Ethan observes.

"Meh, I can hold my liquor. I won't be hungover, but I'll still be drunk in the morning," I assert nonchalantly.

"Hey, you three!" Jeremiah's voice booms from across the patio, drawing our attention. We turn to face him as he continues, "You all having a group make out session over there or what? Come back and join the party."

"Are they done smoking pot?" I yell back.

Jeremiah strolls over to us, and I turn to lean on the counter so I can fully face him; Ethan and Carter mirror my movement.

"They're still smoking," he confirms with a smile.

"In that case, I'm staying right here, or maybe inside. I hate the smell." I shrug. "I don't care that anyone else does it; it's just not my thing."

Jeremiah eyes the bottle in my hand. "You gonna finish that?"

"Maybe, depends on how long it is until I go to bed," I laugh.

"I can't believe you're still standing," Jeremiah remarks, a hint of admiration in his tone. "You're so... tiny. That much alcohol would have had me on my ass."

I shrug. "Get better, scrub."

All three of them laugh, and Jeremiah responds with a mock, hurt expression. I glance past him and catch Carrie and a couple of her friends looking our way.

"Jer, you should get back to your girl. She's going to be pissed you're over here talking to me," I suggest, pointing between him and Carrie with the opening of the liquor bottle.

Jeremiah turns to look and then back at me. "You're right. And that, Alexis, is because you're a siren, and most women hate sirens." He twirls a tendril of my hair before walking back to Carrie.

"Cool, I've been upgraded to a mythological creature now," I quip, taking another sip of Jack.

"He's not wrong," Carter murmurs quietly, his gaze intense; I catch the hunger and fire in his eyes, and I start to reconsider what I said to him earlier about needing to be sober.

I hold Carter's gaze steadily and say, "I think I need to go to bed now. Well, I think I need to drink water, then go to bed."

Ethan seems to pick up on the atmosphere and the tension between Carter and me. He announces, "I'm going to go find Holden and Shawn."

"Okay," Carter responds, briefly glancing past me before meeting my eyes again.

Once Ethan is out of earshot, Carter leans in closer to me. "Let me come to bed with you."

"No sex," I clarify firmly, "of any kind," I add with a smile. "But you can come to bed with me."

"You better move, princess, or I'm going to take you right here." Carter's voice drips with temptation.

"I said no sex," I laugh, playfully pushing against his chest.

"You're torturing me." He smiles, his fingers brushing over my cheek.

"I know, and I'm sorry," I say, offering him my bottle of Jack. "If it makes you feel better, I'm torturing myself too."

He takes a swig before looking back at me. I loop my fingers through one of his belt loops, pulling him closer. His lips hovering inches from mine.

"Lex, what are you doing?" he asks, his voice husky with desire.

"Claiming you," I whisper before closing the small gap between us in a deep, passionate kiss.

Our chemistry ignites, sending shivers down my spine and fire through my veins. Carter sets the bottle on the counter and wraps his arms around me, lifting me up slightly. I let out a small shriek of surprise, then laughter, as he seats me on the counter in front of him.

"Princess, if this is a public claiming, it's definitely me who's claiming you," he growls, moving closer between my thighs, his lips tantalizingly close to mine.

He pulls me closer by my hips, until I'm on the edge of the counter. Then his hand tangles in my hair as our mouths meet once more in a long, heated kiss.

"Are you sure you're not going to let me fuck you tonight?" Carter asks, a playful glint in his eyes as he breaks the kiss.

"I'm sure," I reply softly, kissing him gently. "I want to be sober; I want to feel all of you without a filter. But Carter?"

"Yes, princess?"

"It's definitely a when, and if you want to come with me to bed, you can."

He pulls me off the counter, a mischievous grin on his face. He says, "Let's go," giving my ass a playful smack, eliciting another shriek from me as we head inside.

14

CARTER

Alexis let me claim her publicly, and I am completely fucking here for it.

I think it might have had something to do with Ethan, something he said to her, but I catch Holden's and Shawn's somewhat shocked expressions on the way into the house.

Taking a gold, permanent marker, she writes "Lex's Whiskey" on the bottle of Jack, puts it in the fridge, and grabs several bottles of water. It's another one of those quirky things she does that is unique and a little surprising.

I hold out my hands, silently asking her to let me carry her water, and she acquiesces easily.

"Lex?" I ask quietly.

"Carter?" she replies sarcastically.

"Because of Ana, come to my room." She looks at me questioningly. "If she wakes up and comes looking for me, I want her to be able to find me."

Her expression softens.

"Of course, Carter, let me go get ready for bed, and then I'll come snuggle with you," she adds with a playful smirk.

About twenty minutes later, Alexis enters my room. She doesn't bother to knock, and honestly, I'm okay with that. Her natural face, free of makeup, is absolutely stunning.

She's wearing one of those crop tank tops that barely cover anything, paired with those short shorts, and when I hug her, I can feel the top of her thong peeking out over the waistband of her shorts.

I swear, she's seriously going to be the death of me.

Plugging in her phone by the side of the bed, she looks at home while climbing into my bed.

"It smells like you," she purrs.

I chuckle, "Well, I hope it wouldn't smell like anyone else."

"Maybe me soon." She smiles.

"Yeah, it can smell like you," I pause, "Lex, just so you know, as much as I want you, I absolutely believe you're worth the wait."

"Okay, so I can string you along for months?" She wrinkles her nose.

"Could *you* last for months?" I retort.

"Maybe," she says with a shrug. "Come snuggle with me."

And who would I be to say no to that?

I slide into bed next to her, my hand tangling in her hair as our lips meet. Despite our conversations, despite my words, I find myself eager once I'm that close to her—covering her body with mine while holding my weight off of her with my elbows. I know she can feel my very stiff cock against her center.

She laughs. "Carter, don't make me go back to my room."

I move off of her and pull her close, her back against me.

"What about if I just dry hump your ass?" I jest.

She facepalms, laughs, and then adorably asks, "Is that what you want the memory of your first orgasm with me to be?"

She's right; I don't, although I've been jerking off to images of her in my mind for days, so there's that. I manage to breathe my way out of the hard-on and to spoon her or have her in the crook of my arm all night.

I stir awake in the morning before Alexis, planting a soft kiss on her cheek before slipping out of bed and making my way down to the kitchen; gotta get that coffee brewing before Ana opens her eyes.

As I shuffle to the coffee pot, I find Holden and Jeremiah already in the kitchen, probably brewing up their own caffeine fix. I offer up a lazy "good morning" and reach for a mug.

"It looks like you're the winner," Holden remarks, a smirk playing on his lips but jealousy written all over his face.

I shoot him a half-hearted glare. "Oh, come on, don't start with that—she's a person, not a trophy," I chuckle, pouring myself a cup. "And for the record, nothing even happened."

"What went down on the patio didn't seem like nothing," Jeremiah remarks, shooting me a knowing glance.

"Okay, nothing *else* happened," I counter, shooting Holden a pointed look. "It's not like I planned for it or wanted it to turn into some kind of competition. We just clicked, you know? We ended up spending a lot of time together for work."

"Like I said," Jeremiah begins, his tone thoughtful, "she's a siren, and you boys are going to have to figure out how to share or be cool with whatever decision she makes among all of you."

"Share?" Holden inquires, confused at the mere idea.

Jeremiah chuckles. "Yeah, sharing is caring, right?"

It takes a few moments for Jeremiah's words to sink in. Part of me feels possessive, thinking he's out of his mind, while another part of me finds the idea strangely intriguing and hot. But it leaves me with lingering questions about whether or not it would be a real possibility.

"What are you guys sharing?" Ethan asks, appearing around the corner with his trademark grin.

"The siren," Jeremiah remarks with a knowing smile.

"I'm pretty sure that's more up to her than anyone else," Ethan remarks, his tone light but observant.

Ethan took that as a completely normal statement. He didn't even flinch at the suggestion.

Holden interjects, "Are we seriously discussing this?"

Jeremiah shrugs nonchalantly. "I'm just saying it's a possibility. Ethan's got a point, though; ultimately, it's up to her. At the moment, she's got her eyes on Carter, and there's not much the rest of you can do without stirring up drama. So, my advice? Just accept it for what it is."

"Why Carter, though?" Ethan jests, throwing a playful jab my way. "I mean, she could have all of this." He gestures up and down his own body with a grin. "And she chooses that?" He nods in my direction.

I can't help but swat him lightly on the shoulder. "Watch it, man," I chuckle.

Ethan's expression turns serious. "But seriously," he continues, looking back at Jeremiah and Holden. "She's actually upset at the idea of causing any issues between us, so I think we need to do our best to make sure it doesn't cause any. I tried to give her some reassurance about that last night."

"I'm with you," Jeremiah nods. "I might not know her as intimately as you two do, but she strikes me as empathetic. I doubt she'd want to hurt anyone intentionally."

"Did Carrie not stay last night?" I inquire, turning to Jeremiah, wanting to change the subject.

"Nah, she was pissed I was talking to the siren," he chortles—so much for changing the subject.

"Seriously?" Ethan raises an eyebrow in disbelief.

"Yep, completely serious," Jeremiah confirms with a grin.

"You were there for like thirty seconds," I counter with a chuckle.

"Oh, I know," Jeremiah responds with a grin.

Just then, I hear Ana's voice, and I turn the corner to see her coming down the stairs with Alexis, who looks effortlessly beautiful despite her disheveled hair.

"Ana came looking for you," Alexis says with a warm smile. "So, I figured I would bring her to you."

A pang of guilt goes through me that Ana found Alexis in my bed, but it's fleeting.

"Hey, sweetheart," I greet Ana, squatting down to her level for a hug.

"Hi, Daddy, can we go to McDonald's today?" Ana asks, her eyes sparkling with anticipation.

I can't help but laugh. "A Happy Meal for lunch, huh?"

Ana nods eagerly.

"I think we can make that happen."

I glance up at Alexis, gratitude evident in my expression. "Thank you."

She smiles softly in return.

"Are you good, or do you need more rest?" I inquire, standing and looking at Alexis.

"I'm okay, actually. I just need coffee," Alexis replies.

"Come on, we've got that," I assure her, leading the way to the kitchen.

She seems a bit surprised to find everyone gathered, but friendly greetings are exchanged all around. She's still wearing almost no clothes, and I can't help but notice how all their eyes follow her every move. When she leans up on her toes and bends over the counter to grab a mug from the cabinet, I feel a surge of possessiveness. I rake my hand through my hair and then over my face, trying to mask my reaction. I'm surprised they're all not actually drooling.

"Is Carrie still sleeping?" Alexis inquires as she turns around.

They all share a laugh. "Okay, apparently, I missed something," Alexis remarks with a smile.

"You were right," Jeremiah confesses. "She was upset I was talking to you."

Alexis simply shrugs, a silent "told you so" in her gesture.

* * *

A few hours later, sitting at a table in the McDonald's PlayPlace with Alexis while Ana plays and runs around with the other kids, I enjoy some relatively quiet time with Alexis.

"Ana goes back to her mom's tonight?" Alexis asks.

"Yeah, I'll drop her off around six before dinner," I confirm.

"You're a good dad, Carter. I think it's important that you know that," she says, and my heart melts a little at her words.

"Thank you, Lex. I appreciate that," I reply, genuinely touched.

"Do you think you'd want more kids someday?" she asks.

"That's a really good question, Lex. If the situation was right, yes, but I have her, so it's not like a big thing where I feel like I *need* more kids," I explain with a shrug. "If that makes sense."

"It does," she nods understandingly. "I was just curious."

"Do you want kids?" I inquire.

"I *think* so," she answers thoughtfully. "I know that's not a typical answer. I should know, right? Like yes or no?" Alexis laughs.

"Not necessarily. It could depend on so many factors," I re-assure her.

"Yeah, I guess so," she says with a smile, then adds, "Besides, I have an IUD, so I don't have to worry about that for a while."

I smile back, appreciating her openness, and glad to know I don't have to ask that question later.

* * *

Ana is back at her mom's, and Holden is off at the hospital, so it's just the five of us for dinner, and it's quiet and drama-free.

After dinner, Alexis and I load the dishwasher together. Then she tells me she's going to take a shower and get ready for bed. It's early, but she did drink a lot last night.

"Okay," I say with a sigh, and she smiles mischievously at me. "What?" I ask, narrowing my eyes at her suspiciously.

She grabs my hand. "Come find me in like twenty minutes," she says, walking backward and dragging my fingers along with hers.

"Wait," I call after her, trying to process what she just said, but she just grins playfully and heads toward the stairs.

Waiting those twenty minutes feels like torture, but when they finally pass, I knock softly on her door.

She opens it wearing only a towel, her dry hair pulled up in a clip. Once she lets me in, she locks the door behind me, pulls the clip out of her hair, and drops the towel to the floor.

I stand there stunned for a little too long.

"Carter?" She smiles flirtatiously. "You okay?"

"I am now," I say, gathering my composure. "I'm pretty sure that's the fastest my cock has ever turned to concrete."

"Carter," she whispers, "I want you."

And, fuck me, I will give her what she wants.

15

ALEXIS

Carter wraps his arms around me, enveloping me in his warmth and the smell of his cologne, and asks, "Are you sure?"

His asking for consent when I just presented my naked body to him makes me want him even more.

"Yes, Carter, I want you—in every way. You said I was a new toy, I think you should treat me like one," I answer, my voice filled with desire and a hint of playfulness.

And the man fucking growls as he picks me up and tosses me on the bed.

"You might regret that, princess," he whispers against my lips.

"I really don't think I will," I counter playfully. "But you are wearing entirely too many clothes."

With a fluid motion, he pulls his shirt off over his head with one hand, revealing a sight I hadn't witnessed before—Carter, shirtless. My eyes widen as I take in the intricate tattoos that adorn his muscular frame, accentuating every contour of his arms, shoulders, and chest. In that moment, he becomes an even more perfect specimen of a man in my eyes.

"You're so fucking hot," I say to him as he looms over me from between my legs, and he is shameless in the way he is studying my naked body in front of him.

"You're fucking beautiful," he says as he pulls down his shorts and boxer briefs, and when his cock is freed, I'm more than impressed.

He is thick and long, and I can tell he really is as hard as concrete. I take a little pride in knowing that is all for me. There is a clear bead of precum on his tip and I reach up and brush it with my finger and put it on my tongue. His head falls back as he groans at the action.

"Fuck, princess," he groans.

"Carter?" I ask.

He looks at me and raises his eyebrows, and I continue, "How quiet do we need to be?"

He chuckles. "Well, if it were up to me, I wouldn't care who heard us, but yeah, pretty quiet, Lex. They can hear everything in the hall."

"Okay, just curious."

"Show me your tattoos," he demands.

I point to the one below my right breast, the script reading "What's past is prologue."

"Shakespeare?" he asks, and I'm impressed by his recognition.

"Impressive, Mr. Larkspur," I say, and a cocky grin turns the corners of his lips.

Then, under my left breast, in the same font, is "Carpe Noctem."

"Seize the night," he chuckles. "I like it."

I guide his fingers to a small tattoo inside my bikini line, two parallel squiggly lines. Carter looks puzzled by that one.

I laugh, "It's the symbol for slippery when wet."

He cocks his head and snickers. "I don't think I need a sign to know that, princess. You have one more. Where is it?"

I spread my thighs, revealing two black diamonds just inches from my pussy on my left interior thigh.

"Damn, Lex," he laughs again, "Experts only?"

I smirk at him. "Do you qualify?"

"Fuck yes, I qualify. Trust me, I will treat your pretty pussy well," he says, and his hands and mouth meet my tits aggressively.

I weave one hand into his hair, and the other one grazes up and down his upper arm. After he works my nipples over thoroughly with his mouth, he trails kisses down my body, his hands travel with him, and as I feel his hands on my inner thighs, electricity waltzes from his hand to my aching cunt.

His mouth, lips, and teeth find their way to my inner thigh as he pushes my legs open even further. My skin turns electric under his touch.

"That's a good girl, open wide for me," he growls, and then he licks my entire slit, from taint up, causing my hips to rise into him. "Fuck, Lex, you taste so fucking good, and you're so fucking wet."

Somehow, I knew he'd have a filthy mouth, and from him, it's perfect. He will fulfill my praise kink in ways I probably don't even realize yet. And oh my fuck, does everything he is doing to me feel so good.

He dips two fingers inside me and then runs them up my stomach, leaving a trail of fluid. "Feel how fucking wet you are, how much you want me."

Moaning, I grab his fingers, bringing them up to my mouth, tasting my arousal off his fingers.

Carter's voice is primal as he says, "That is so fucking hot."

Strong and confident, those fingers move back to my wet center, and he pushes three fingers in before hooking them up while my hips naturally rise and grind into him in response to him finding that sweet spot.

"That's it, princess, fuck my fingers," he says, and then he uses his other hand to pull the hood back, and his mouth closes down on my clit.

He licks and sucks, and I start to unabashedly grind against his hand and his mouth until I feel the spring tightening in my core, and my toes start to curl while my fingers look for purchase on the sheets, on his skin, anywhere they can find it.

In the seconds before I reach that apex, I still my body and let him work, and then I pull at his hair as I come undone.

"Fuck, Carter," I moan quietly as I convulse around his fingers.

"Good girl," he swoons, "now give me another one," and like an expert, he keeps doing exactly the same thing with his fingers and his mouth.

I'm so sensitive, so turned on, and I'm on the edge so fast. "Carter," I moan again as I convulse around his fingers.

My legs start shaking from the intensity of the orgasms, and I'm positive there will be more. I'll be lucky if I can walk when he's done with me.

"Lex, I fucking love the way you come for me," he says and then moves quickly up my body, his mouth colliding with mine; I can taste myself on his tongue, and it's fucking hot.

Three of his fingers keep working inside me while his thumb puts pressure on my clit; I grind into him while he kisses me so passionately, fucking my mouth with his tongue.

He breaks the kiss and whispers against my lips, "I love how needy you are, fucking grinding into my hand; I think I need you to ride me," and then his mouth overtakes mine again.

As I come again, my head tilts back, and his mouth drops to my neck. I claw at his arm, and I'm almost positive I am leaving marks on him.

He rolls over and sits up against the pillows before pulling me over on top of him. I grind over his hard cock, rubbing it between my wet folds.

"Fuck," Carter groans, and then he grabs my hips and stills me. I fight him and then whimper; he chuckles softly. "Patience, princess, we have business to take care of."

I look at him questioningly, my hips still trying to roll on their own, loving the feel of his hardness in my slick, wet heat.

"Lex," he says, trying to draw my attention to his face, and then his fingers guide my chin up so he can look at me; he has a huge grin on his face. "I love how much you want me, but talk to me about testing."

"Look at you, the responsible one," I joke and then kiss him.

He breaks the kiss. "Lex, princess." His voice is a warning but still has humor in it.

Oh, this man.

Stilling my body, raising my hands to his cheeks, I meet his gaze. "Thank you for being responsible." I smile softly. "And negative, a week after I moved in, just before we left for Chicago. You?"

He kisses me softly. "Negative after my last relationship, which was a while ago."

"We good?" I inquire, knitting my eyebrows together.

"Yeah, Lex, we're good; I trust you, so as long as you trust me," he whispers.

"I trust you," I agree, and then his hands fall gently on my waist while his mouth meets mine again.

"Carter, I need you buried inside me," I whisper, and it sounds like I'm begging.

"Well, we should give you what you need, princess." His hand reaches between us, and he positions himself under me.

Slowly, I sink him into me; he's so thick and so long. "Fuck," I moan. "You feel so good."

Carter answers me with his own filthy words, "You are so fucking tight, fuck, Lex."

Laughing for a second, I reply, "I think part of that is you are so thick." He smiles and kisses me.

"But look at how well you take me," he approves and thrusts up into me for emphasis. "You're doing so good, princess." His voice drops to a whisper. "Now ride me, grind on me just like you were grinding on my hand."

And I do, rolling my hips and grinding, spreading my legs further apart to take him even deeper.

"Fuck, yeah," Carter groans, his hands on my hips, not guiding me but feeling me rock against him.

Sweat beads on my chest and drips down my cleavage as I build myself back up to a breaking point.

My head falls back as I start to fall over the edge again, and encouragement leaves his lips. "Yes, baby, come on my cock, fuck." His mouth takes one of my nipples and sucks hard as I convulse around him.

When my body stills, he pushes me sideways and ends up on top of me impressively without letting his cock leave me.

Carter puts a wide, pussy eating grin on his face and leans down next to my ear to whisper, "I'm going to fuck you into oblivion now."

I whimper, and he gets up on his knees, my legs wrap around him, and then he fucks me hard, harder than I've been fucked in a really long time. He moves me up the bed with each thrust until I brace myself—us—with my hands on the headboard.

Carter's muscles flexing over the top of me is erotic and hot on its own. His unique smell, that spiciness with a hint of black licorice, is amazing; the skin on his chest is glistening with sweat, and my senses feel absolutely overwhelmed by the sheer presence of him. Every thrust brings me closer to another climax, the head of his cock hitting me just right. As my muscles start to tighten, I grab his arm, feeling his muscles flex and ripple, and I convulse around him again.

Shortly after I come, he thrusts and then holds still. I feel him throbbing and pulsing inside me as he lets out a guttural sound. It's feral, and I feel the vibration of it through my whole body.

Breathing heavily, his forehead drops to mine. "Fuck, Lex," he manages to say, his voice strained.

Feeling the dampness of the sweat on his skin, I trail my fingers down his biceps and then up and over his chest. His breathing begins to steady, and he places a soft kiss on my lips before rolling off to my side, but not without pulling me close to him.

Gentle kisses rain down on my temple and forehead as his tender hands explore my body. Despite the intensity of our encounter, he remains quiet, and I find peace in the shared moment.

After laying there together for what feels like an eternity, he finally speaks, his words still coated with breathiness and gravelly tones. "Princess?"

"Carter?" I whisper back.

"You were absolutely worth the wait." I feel his lips curve into a smile against the skin near my temple, sending a warm wave of contentment through me. The tenderness in his voice, the sincerity of his words, all blend to create a moment so intimate, it feels almost surreal. I snuggle closer, feeling a deep sense of belonging I hadn't felt in a long time. This moment, with Carter, feels like the beginning of something beautiful and a little unexpected.

16

ALEXIS

My alarm disrupts the morning silence, and I hear Carter groan, but he pulls me closer, showering my neck with soft kisses.

"Good morning," I greet him, turning toward him and meeting his lips with mine.

"I like waking up next to you," he murmurs, his hand tracing down my still-naked body.

"I like you, but we have a sales meeting in an hour," I remind him.

"Now who's the responsible one?" Carter teases.

"I need sustenance and coffee to ensure my brain works during the meeting," I pout.

"Me too," he agrees, planting a gentle kiss on my lips before slipping out of bed. "Meet me downstairs when you're ready."

He throws on his shirt and boxers and exits my room, closing the door softly behind him.

After a refreshing shower, I dress in leggings and a nice shirt suitable for the virtual sales call. Holden is at the hospital, but the other roommates are in the kitchen when I arrive. Everything seems normal, so I assume Carter didn't kiss and tell.

Carter hands me a cup of coffee and slides a plate of food in front of me.

"Thank you," I say gratefully.

"You're welcome," he replies softly, brushing a tendril of hair away from my face; the gesture conveys an intimacy that likely doesn't go unnoticed by the others.

"Are you guys ready for this call?" Jeremiah asks, drawing our attention, and I pick up my fork.

"Yeah," Carter confirms. "It's pretty much a mini version of what we did in Chicago."

Jeremiah nods. "You doing it from the dining room?"

"That's the plan," Carter agrees.

"I might eavesdrop on you if that won't make you nervous," Jeremiah directs the last comment to me.

"I'll be fine," I reassure him.

Two hours later, after Jeremiah, Ethan, and Shawn have all eavesdropped on us, they sing our praises.

"I thought Carter was exaggerating," Jeremiah admits. "You are impressive, and the amount of knowledge you already seem to have about our products is also impressive."

"Carter is responsible for that part." I smile.

"Not for the retention of the information," Jeremiah teases.

"Also, our internet engagement between the website and social media is up over three hundred percent," Shawn adds. "You literally have breathed life into the company in a very, very short amount of time."

I feel a blush creep up my cheeks. "Honestly, you guys," I start, looking around at all of them, "I appreciate all the compliments and kind words, but," I pause, trying to find the right words, "Laugherty is small. I came from a very large corporation that had a lot more products. A lot of what I've done is very basic marketing strategy. I'm glad it helped, but there is a lot more we can do."

"Did you just tell us we didn't know what we were doing, and you fixed little things?" Ethan observes, chuckling.

I wrinkle my nose playfully, my pitch getting higher. "Maaayyybe."

"Yeah, you're not allowed to leave," Jeremiah teases. "I think you're one of us now."

Carter nudges me playfully as Ethan adds, "Seriously, Lexi, you've already proven yourself very valuable. This whole thing happened through such shitty circumstances, but I think we," he pauses and glances at the other guys, "are all happy it did."

"Geez, cut it out," I utter playfully, waving them off. "But seriously, thank you. Performing well at my job is the least I can do after everything you all have done for me."

"I think it's lunchtime," Carter exclaims, and everyone agrees.

* * *

Later in the afternoon, I'm in the midst of putting away laundry in my room when a knock interrupts my task.

"It's open," I call out.

As I expected, it's Carter. He strides in, closing the distance between us swiftly, but then he gently places his hand on my waist and plants a tender kiss on my forehead.

"We good?" he asks, his tone tinged with uncertainty.

"Yeah," I reply, furrowing my brow in confusion. "Why wouldn't we be good?"

"I just wanted to make sure you didn't have any regrets," he explains with a shrug and then sits on the end of my bed.

"Carter, where is this coming from?" I inquire, absolutely puzzled.

Running his hand down my arm, from my elbow to my fingers,

he intertwines our hands. "Because I know you had reservations about how you and I would impact other people, and I don't know why you let that go, but you did, and I just want to make sure you don't regret it."

I move closer to him, my thighs between his, as he sits on the bed. "Ethan set that straight. I have no regrets; we're good."

"Ethan?" Carter echoes, a little surprised.

"Yeah, he pointed out that it would cause just as much drama if you couldn't have me because of them. He basically said it would be the same amount of drama either way."

"On the patio? After Carrie's party?"

"Yeah," I answer and then scrape my nails along his scalp and down his neck.

"Well, the timing of your public claiming makes a little more sense to me now. I thought it was just the alcohol," he teases, delivering a playful smack to the side of my ass.

"No, that was real, Carter. I know I had a lot to drink that night, but I was very in control of my actions," I assure him.

"Maybe we should look up the characteristics of sirens; I think they have higher alcohol tolerances than the rest of us," he jokes.

"Shut up," I laugh.

"Oh, I think I can find better things to do with my mouth, and yours for that matter, than speak anyway," he murmurs, pulling me closer.

Lifting my shirt, his mouth and tongue explore my belly button. As he indulges in his playful exploration, I continue to run my nails through his hair and along the back of his neck. He pulls me even closer, but our intimate moment is interrupted by another knock on my door.

I put my hands on either side of Carter's face, give him a quick kiss, and flash a smile before walking over to open the door, revealing Jeremiah on the other side.

"Hey, Jeremiah, what's up?" I greet him.

He smiles. "You have a minute?"

"Uh, yeah, join the party unless you need to talk to me without Carter," I offer, gesturing to invite him into the room.

They nod at each other, and I'm grateful it's obvious I was folding clothes, so it doesn't look like he interrupted an intimate moment, even though he did.

"No, Carter is fine, maybe better, actually," Jeremiah considers with a laugh.

"Carrie is coming for dinner. I know that I probably don't have to tell you that she feels all kinds of threatened by you now. I understand part of it, but she's also never had to deal with another woman being around the house this regularly—it's new territory for us. I don't know exactly what I want to ask you to do or not do, but I guess try not to be less threatening." He falters, stumbling over his words as he realizes how ridiculous they sound.

I laugh, and Carter rolls his eyes.

"I know it's a stupid request," Jeremiah adds.

"I'll wear baggy sweats and a hoodie, no makeup, and a messy bun," I reply with a smile and a shrug.

"And you'll still look hot," Carter interjects, wrapping his fingers around my wrist and pulling me toward him.

"If that's the case, I can't do anything about that, but I'll be on my best behavior, Jer. I'll try," I assure him. "As long as she doesn't choose to play that stupid game, we'll be fine."

Carter and Jeremiah laugh, and then Jeremiah turns to Carter. "And I don't know; I mean, I know that you're still trying to be re-spectful, but maybe a little normal couple behavior wouldn't hurt."

Carter looks at me and then back to Jeremiah, laughing as he replies, "Whatever you say, boss."

17

CARTER

Lex, true to her word, is wearing the baggiest clothes I've ever seen her in—gray sweatpants, bulky, fuzzy socks, and a baggy, black and yellow UMBC Lacrosse pullover hoodie. Not a spot of makeup on her face, and her hair is in a very messy bun.

She is fucking adorable.

As a creature of habit, Lex had been sitting next to Ethan at the dinner table since her first night here, but tonight she moves over next to me, which also allows Ethan to move down and Carrie to sit between him and Jeremiah.

As we eat and talk, Lex is oddly quiet, but I know it's intentional. I ask Carrie questions about her job and such, letting her take some of the spotlight. Carrie then turns the conversation to Alexis, and at that point, there's not much Jeremiah or I can do about it, but Carrie doesn't start out on a great note.

"Did you date someone who played lacrosse at UMBC?" Carrie asks.

Ethan and I brace ourselves for a smartass remark from Alexis, but she surprises us with a simple smile and says, "No, I played lacrosse there."

Carrie persists, "It's a smaller school, right? So is it NAIA?"

I can feel the tension emanating from Alexis, but she maintains her composure and sweetly responds, "Uh, no, it's NCAA Division I."

"You were a DI athlete?" Carrie says, sounding a bit stunned.

Alexis shrugs casually. "Yeah, it paid for some of my degree, so that was a benefit."

And then we're all a little stunned when Carrie just starts laughing uncontrollably. None of us say anything. I lean toward Lex, resting my elbow on the back of her chair, and graze my fingers over her neck.

Finally, Carrie calms down and breathily says, "I'm sorry, I am, but seriously, is there anything you haven't done?"

Lex smiles gently. "Oh, there is plenty I haven't done."

"I'm really not trying to be a bitch," Carrie adds, her tone sincere. "Honestly, I'm trying to figure out why anyone would choose Ellie over you. She was so shallow and so... dense." She looks at Jeremiah and continues, "I would not be saying this if Holden was here. But seriously."

Lex swallows hard, and I move my hand down to cover hers on her thigh. Nobody says anything. Carrie can read the awkwardness of everyone's reaction to what she just said.

"I don't think he chose Ellie over her," I interject, breaking the long silence. "Because if that's what he was doing, he would have left her in Maryland. He just wanted a side piece. And Ellie *is* shallow and dense, so maybe she was easy to manipulate."

"You sound like you're speaking from experience," Carrie jokes.

"I am," I hiss, "but from the same side Lex and Holden were on."

Carrie looks at me and then at Alexis. "I'm sorry. I was trying to make it better, and I made it worse." She glances at Jeremiah and then back at Alexis. "Alexis, I *do* want to be friends with you. You just continually surprise me; you're so unpredictable and intriguing, and I am not good at this, all my friends are from college, I haven't made a new girlfriend in a while."

"Surprising, unpredictable, intriguing," Ethan says with a chuckle. "Yeah, I'm pretty sure those are words we've all used, too." Then he nudges Carrie with his elbow. "Maybe don't try so hard."

Carrie looks a little defeated but then says, "I think you're right, Ethan."

Alexis takes a sip of her water and sits up, putting her forearms on the table. As she leans forward, my hand settles on her thigh. "Look, Carrie, I'm not that complicated, I'm really not; I like coffee and music, I like reading and running, I like my job." She smiles at Jeremiah. "I am a little spontaneous and adventurous because I've found over time—and a lot from past trauma—that I would rather have regrets over things I did, than things I haven't done. But when I do something, I'm all in; maybe that's my ADHD, maybe it's just my personality and the ADHD has nothing to do with it, but what did you say it was?" Lex looks at me.

I grin. "Go big or go home? Is that what you're referring to?"

"Yeah, that *is* me. I go big, or I don't do it at all. So if I'm going to do something like play lacrosse, I'm going to hyper-fixate and practice eight hours a day for months so I can play varsity and then DI; if I decide to be a marketing director, I'm going to hyper-fixate on that so I can be the absolute best one I can be." She takes a quick glance at Shawn and then back to Carrie. "If I decide to play a video game or Dungeons and Dragons or something like that, I'm going to hyper-fixate on it and learn every single little detail. If I decide to love someone or be in a relationship with someone, I am in it for pretty much anything they are, or they want, as long as they are." I feel my heart melt into a puddle at her feet, and I squeeze her thigh. "Sometimes it's a bad thing; I stay in jobs, relationships, hobbies, whatever, I shouldn't stay in. But all that passion sometimes comes off as something negative to other people, especially women, and I am not sure exactly why, but I've dealt with it my whole life. I am absolutely not opposed to being your friend. In fact, it would be really fucking nice to actually have a girlfriend here because I don't have any."

Ethan locks eyes with me, conveying the same thing I'm thinking —that was *a lot* of information, but it makes her even more appealing. There is silence for a few beats, and then Carrie breaks it.

"Alexis, I think we should go do something this weekend. Is it time for your rebase? Or we can just go grab lunch or something." Carrie offers a soft smile.

Lex smiles. "Absolutely will need a rebase by Saturday."

Carrie takes a deep breath and exhales, and then Shawn interjects, "Did you seriously just say 'Dungeons and Dragons?'"

The whole table laughs, and then Lex smiles. "Yeah, I've been down that road, too."

"More important question," Jeremiah says. "What the fuck is a rebase?"

Carrie and Alexis laugh, and then Alexis explains, "It's just another way of saying we need to get our nails done because they've grown out too much."

"Learn something new every day," Jeremiah replies.

There's a hockey game on, so we all make our way to the main living room after dinner, except Shawn, who disappears downstairs to game with some other friends. Alexis tucks her legs to the side and snuggles up right next to me; my arm naturally finds its place around her, her hand resting gently on my thigh, and here in the most public room in the house, I like it.

Halfway through the third period of the game, Holden walks in, and he looks ragged—like he has been through hell.

"Hey, man," Ethan says, noticing Holden's appearance. "Rough shift?"

Holden lets out a small scoff. "That obvious?" he replies, glancing at Alexis and me, then walking to the kitchen without another word.

I squeeze Lex to me, kiss her softly on the temple, and then get up to follow him.

I'm not far from the living room, so I keep my voice down. "Hey, you okay?"

He slams the cabinet he had been looking in and leans back against the counter, his thumb and forefinger squeezing the bridge of his nose. "Not really," he says.

"What happened?" I ask.

"We lost a young patient today; she was only twenty." He pauses, his voice heavy with emotion. "I don't know why this one hits so hard. We fought so hard, and we thought she was improving." He shrugs before running his hands over his face. "I'll be okay; I just really need some sleep."

"I think you need food, too," I counter. "Do you want me to heat up some dinner for you?"

"That would actually be nice. I'm going to take a hot shower, and I'll be back in about twenty minutes if that's okay?" Holden asks.

"Yeah, man, do what you need to do; text me about five minutes before you want food, and I'll heat it up." I gently squeeze his upper arm. "I'm sorry."

"No worries, thank you," he says and heads upstairs.

I find my place, back next to Lex, and when the game is over, I still haven't heard from Holden, so I text him.

(Me) *Hey, man, did you pass out?*
(Holden) *No, but can you just bring me something up here?*
(Me) *Absolutely*

I let Lex know what's happening, and she suggests that she take him his dinner. It stirs up a twinge of jealousy in me—I know there is chemistry between them. But deep down, I know she's probably better equipped to handle whatever's eating at Holden right now than I am.

18

HOLDEN

Assuming it's Carter, I call for him to enter when I hear a knock at my door. When the door swings open, revealing Alexis, a rush of unexpected emotions floods over me. The turmoil I'm already grappling with intensifies exponentially.

"Hey," she says softly. "I brought you some food; I thought you might want some company, too."

I suddenly realize, caught off guard by her presence, that I'm standing there in nothing but my boxers. She doesn't comment or seem fazed, but I swiftly grab a pair of sweatpants and pull them on while I respond.

"Hey, thanks. You don't have to stay."

She chuckles gently. "It's not about 'have to,' Holden. Do you need to talk? Want to tell me what happened?"

I accept the plate from her and settle at my desk to eat. She gracefully perches her petite and cute ass on the edge of my desk, her gaze fixed on me. And I feel an unexpected surge of absolute resentment towards Carter.

"What happened, Holden?" she prompts, her concern evident in her voice.

"I guess I forgot for a moment that you grew up with an ICU nurse and an ED physician for parents," I confess with a small smile.

"Yeah," she responds, empathy lacing her words. "I've heard my fair share of stories," she laughs, but it lacks any real humor.

Sighing, I start the tale, "It was a motor vehicle accident. She was only twenty and came in my first night there with severe brain trauma and internal bleeding. This afternoon, she was conscious and talking to us. We were discussing discharging her to the regular med-surg floor, and then suddenly, she wasn't okay," I explain, running a hand through my hair. "She had a sudden hemorrhage in her brain, and now she's technically alive on life support, but she's brain dead."

"Holden," Alexis breathes my name softly.

"I had to have the conversation with her parents and her boyfriend right before I left the hospital. It was just... a lot," I finish, the weight of the situation still like a ton of bricks on my shoulders.

"Holden, I'm so sorry," she says, taking a deep breath while I take a bite of my food. "I know they say you should be able to compartmentalize, but you're only human. My mom, even being the heartless person she is, would talk about it sometimes, saying that it was the surprise ones that were the hardest. Some you know don't have much of a chance, and it's easier to accept, but something like that, where you really thought she was better, and she was so young." She swallows. "I get it. That would be upsetting to most people."

"It doesn't help that I've had almost no sleep in four days," I admit, pausing briefly. "And we lost other people in that timeframe, too. It's just been a rough few days."

"No sleep makes everything worse," she affirms with a gentle laugh.

I clear my throat, attempting to steer the conversation away from heavier topics. "Looks like Carrie and Jeremiah are back on good terms," I remark.

Alexis chuckles, "There was a bit of drama at dinner, but now, apparently, we're friends and planning to get our nails done together on Saturday."

"Are you okay with that?" I inquire, genuinely uncertain about her feelings.

"If you had asked me yesterday, I might have said no. But honestly, yeah, I don't have many friends here aside from you guys. And when I say 'here,' I mean this entire city, state, who knows," she laughs. "It'll be nice to do something with another woman for a change."

"Well, then, I'm glad you have plans to hang out with her." I offer a sleepy smile.

"Carrie brought up Ellie at the dinner table," Alexis begins, her voice trailing off as she swallows.

"Why would she feel the need to do that?" I ask, my concern shifting from my own feelings to a protective instinct for Alexis.

"I think she was trying to compliment me by comparing me to her, but it didn't quite come off that way," Alexis explains with a shrug. "Ethan and Carter both got a little defensive in their own ways."

"What exactly was she comparing?" I inquire as my curiosity piques.

"Everything," Alexis replies, rolling her eyes. "Our entire person- alities. She basically said Ellie was shallow and dense." She stifles a laugh, but when she genuinely smiles like that, she's absolutely beautiful.

I chuckle, "Ellie was shallow and dense." I pause for a moment. "But it's weird because I'm surrounded by all these brilliant, beauti- ful minds all the time. I think I actually appreciated not having to be so cerebral around her." I shake my head. "But saying that out loud makes me sound like a jerk, I know."

Alexis laughs, but then she adds, "No, not really. I understand what you're getting at. Sometimes you just need a place where you don't have to be 'on,' and with her, you didn't."

"Very insightful," I reply, and then we lapse into silence for a few moments.

For some reason, I muster up some courage and pose the question that's been on my mind for a while now. "Hey, Alexis, I hope I'm saying this in a way that doesn't offend you, but I'm curious." I pause, my nerves creeping in.

Alexis's voice takes on a slightly mischievous tone as she asks, "Curious about what?"

"Why Carter?" I continue, feeling the weight of the question hanging in the air. "Were you completely attracted to him from day one? Was he the first to make a move? I'm just curious."

She takes a deep breath, and for a moment, I'm not sure if she'll answer.

But then she does; her voice is slightly high-pitched, her inflection almost like a question. "Yes," she begins, pausing briefly. "Yes to both."

"So you were both attracted to him from the beginning, and he was the first one to make a move?" I inquire, seeking clarification.

She nods and shrugs. "Pretty much."

I swallow, trying to gather some courage to express what's on my mind. "You should know that all the rest of us basically decided to give you space, let you deal with whatever you needed to after Brody, and intentionally didn't go there," I admit, unable to maintain eye contact as I lower my gaze to my plate.

"*All* the rest of you?" Alexis playfully queries.

"At least me and Ethan," I respond, more seriousness in my tone than she anticipated.

"Holden." Her voice is coated in empathy. "Carter and I spent a lot of time together in the week leading up to Chicago, and then we had Chicago. He didn't cross a line or push me before I was ready; it simply felt like a natural progression."

There's another knock at the door, and I glance at Alexis before inviting them in, too. It's Carter, as expected. Alexis has been in here for a while now. He was bound to want to check on her.

"Speak of the devil," I quip. "Were your ears burning?"

Carter laughs. "No, just making sure everything is okay. I can leave," he offers, sounding genuinely sincere.

"No," I chuckle. "Actually, if Alexis doesn't mind, I'd like to talk to you for a few minutes, Carter."

Alexis looks between us and hops down from the desk. She gives my shoulder a supportive squeeze, and then, as she walks by Carter, she trails her hand from his bicep down to his fingers, dragging them along with her as she makes her way to the door. His eyes follow her in an expression I've rarely seen on Carter.

"Let me know if you need to talk more, Holden, and get some rest," she instructs before closing the door behind her.

"What's up, man?" Carter asks, his tone casual.

"First off, sending her was actually helpful, so thank you," I begin.

"It wasn't so much that I sent her as she volunteered, but I figured she would be more helpful than I would be," he admits with a sheepish smile.

"Secondly, I've been grappling with jealousy a lot lately, and I apologize for that. I just wanted to check in with you, see how things are going, and if you're happy—you know, all the same stuff I'd ask if it were a different girl than Alexis," I suggest, genuine concern evident in my voice.

Carter's lips curl into a small smile. "It's going really well, Holden, honestly. I'm happy. I wasn't trying to cause any rifts between us or with Ethan or anything like that, truly. There was a moment in

Chicago where I think we both just decided to cross that line at the same time."

"I believe you, Carter, I really do. And I know you recognize how unique and special she is. I can't promise that I won't ever have jealous moments," I say earnestly. "Just don't fuck this up."

"She and Ana have already formed a bond. Messing this up is the last thing I want to do for a whole lot of reasons," Carter responds with sincerity.

"Alexis mentioned that Carrie brought up Ellie at dinner," I remark.

"Yeah," he nods, shaking his head. "Carrie put her foot in her mouth a few times tonight."

He pauses, collecting his thoughts. "Holden, I feel a little bad that you missed both of Lex's big moments of getting to know her better, but she had a good one tonight."

"Really?" I inquire.

"Yeah, she basically explained her entire personality to Carrie, but it was insightful for us, too. You weren't there that first night she dove into all that either, but did you know she's neurodivergent?" he reveals.

Well, that's a revelation I wasn't expecting. Maybe deep down, I already knew it, but it just hadn't fully registered.

"She's on the spectrum?" I ask, genuinely intrigued.

"No, she has ADHD, but some of it is similar," he explains, leaning in slightly. "She hyper-fixates on things, you know? It's like she's either all in or all out; there's nothing in between. But she brought it up the first night we had dinner here; you were at the hospital. And then tonight, she really dove into it, defending herself to Carrie."

He pauses, running a hand through his hair. "She mentioned how her hyper-fixation helped her with playing college-level lacrosse and in her job. Even explained how it impacts her relationships," he continues, shrugging. "I think it was her way of defending against the slut-shaming she felt like Carrie tried to put on her after the other night. But the way Alexis said it was much more eloquent."

"That actually makes a lot of sense," I agree, a smirk playing on my lips. "'Never Have I Ever' was insightful. In all the times I've seen people play that game, I don't think I've ever seen someone drink that much. But it was also interesting to see the things she didn't drink for—like all the things that had the potential to hurt someone else."

"I noticed that too," Carter replies.

"I'm sure you did," I say knowingly, meeting his gaze. "You're lucky, Carter. Don't take that for granted."

"After Katie, I think I'll always appreciate good women and not take them for granted," he states, taking a step closer to me. "Holden, I'm sorry. I'm sorry about Ellie, I'm sorry about Lex, I'm sorry that it just hasn't gone that way for you, I really am."

I narrow my eyes at him teasingly. "But you're not sorry that you benefited from it," I jest.

"I have to admit, that is true." He smirks. "We good?"

"Yeah, Carter, we're good," I hedge. "At least for now."

19

ALEXIS

I'm trying to be patient, but I'm just not, so I text Carter.

(Me) *You still talking to Holden?*

It's a few minutes later when he answers.

(Carter) *No, where are you? Lol*
(Me) *In your bed ... waiting*
(Carter) *You dirty girl*
(Me) *Not yet, I need you for that*
(Carter) *Five minutes ... and I will ravage you*
(Me) *That better be a promise*
(Carter) *I think it's a threat*
(Me) *Even better*

It's only about two minutes later when he finds his way to

his room; he immediately locks the door behind him and pulls off his shirt.

"Lex, I don't think I've ever been so turned on by a text message," he laughs as he climbs on the bed.

"Maybe you've been texting the wrong people," I tease.

He pulls back the blanket to discover I am completely naked and groans. "You can wait for me like this anytime."

"You haven't even discovered how wet I am yet," I tease seductively.

The noise he makes in response to that is feral and guttural. And then his fingers run through my wet folds, and he makes the sound again.

"Princess, how long have you been like this? Waiting for me to do something about it?"

"All night, Carter," I say and then wrap my hand around the back of his neck pulling his mouth to mine.

Kissing me slowly, sensually, I feel the emotion in the kiss, not just lust; I even feel tears prick my eyes because it's so intense. Without breaking the kiss, he dips two fingers inside me, immediately curling them and finding that sweet spot inside that makes me writhe under him.

When my head tilts back, his mouth falls to my neck, and he kisses along my collarbone before moving his mouth down to my taut and waiting nipple. Biting my nipple gently, he draws a groan from me and sends shockwaves through my body. Lava fills my veins as the rush of hormones and chemicals Carter brings out in me erupts.

I feel my body building toward its climax, the muscles tightening, my toes curling, my hips naturally wanting to push into his hand, wanting more.

"Carter, fuck," I bite out the gasp, and he keeps his same speed and angle with his fingers, but he increases the pressure, and in seconds I fall over that edge, convulsing around his fingers and my body vibrating underneath him.

"I love how responsive your body is to me, princess, fuck, it turns me on so much," he murmurs as his tongue slides along my pulse point, up to my ear. "What do you want?" he asks.

"Everything, all of you," I groan.

"Not specific enough, princess."

His lips ghost over mine, teasing my bottom lip with his tongue. It feels like fireworks going off, stirring the electricity in my core as his tongue teases my lips.

"What do you want?" he repeats.

"I want you to kiss me," I say, my voice breathy and needy. "And then I want you to go down on me and make me come and then kiss me again so I can taste myself on your tongue." I pause, and his tongue runs over my bottom lip again. "And then I want you in my mouth so I can taste you when you come."

I thought the noise he made before was feral and guttural, but the one he releases when I finish talking is so primal that it's terrifying and erotic all at the same time.

"Fuck, Lex, you're all my fantasies come to life," he proclaims and then kisses me deeply and passionately.

Carter's tongue exploring my mouth with such enthusiasm and want makes my hips lift into him. I feel my cunt getting needier, wetter, and aching for him as his mouth is hungrier on mine.

Breaking the kiss, he licks my lips again, saying, "I need to taste your needy, pink pussy now, but don't worry, I want to kiss you after too."

Using his mouth, his tongue, and his teeth, he moves down my body, stopping at my nipples, sucking and nipping them to the point I almost scream with pleasure, but I grip his hair and bite my lip instead; his tongue finds my belly button and then finally, fucking finally he finds my needy cunt.

Deft fingers spread me open, and he spears me with his tongue, over and over and fucking over again.

I feel his breath and the vibration of his words against my pussy as he whispers, "You are so fucking wet, and you taste so fucking good," and then his tongue travels from taint to clit, and he stops, sucking my swollen clit into his mouth.

I feel at least two fingers enter me and start massaging and exploring me as his tongue expertly sucks on and licks my clit. As my moans get sharper and he feels my climax coming, he plunges a finger into my ass, and I come completely undone.

My hands grip at his hair, my thighs clench around his head, and I moan loudly. As I convulse and throb around his fingers, he doesn't stop his ministrations. I grind into him, his mouth on my clit, his fingers in my cunt and my ass, and it feels so good; everything about him feels so fucking good. It's euphoric, and I feel lightheaded and boneless; the pleasure is so intense my stomach feels like I am falling out of the sky.

I keep grinding into him, using him unabashedly for my pleasure, as he sucks hard on my clit, until I come one more time, and as the convulsions end, he climbs up my body, and his mouth meets mine.

"You are such a good, dirty girl," he whispers against my lips and then plunges his tongue between them, kissing me deeply, before pausing to whisper again, "Your body coming for me is fucking ecstasy for me too."

I break the kiss, and his piercing blue eyes meet mine. "Roll over for me," I request in a soft whisper, and he does, pulling me with him.

Starting a trail of kisses from his neck down his body, when my tongue finds his abs, he inhales sharply.

"Fuck, Lex," escapes his lips in a groan.

I continue the trail of licks, nips, and kisses until I get to his thick cock. The thought of tasting him excites me and turns me on, but his reaction to it excites me even more.

Carter is positioned against the headboard so he can see everything I am doing to him, and that is exactly what I want for him. As my hair falls in curtains around my face, he quickly wraps it in his hand, unblocking his view.

I cup his balls in my hand and then run the entire flat part of my tongue from his scrotum to his head; I meet his eyes as I lick the bead of precum of the tip of his cock.

"Fuck, Lex," he growls, and he closes his eyes as his head tips back.

I make sure he is looking again before I wrap my lips around his head and take him slowly into my mouth. Wrapping my fingers around the bottom of his shaft, making sure his entire cock is almost always completely surrounded by me, I work him to the back of my throat, twisting and sliding my hand outside of my lips.

The hand clutching my hair gets more forceful; I feel the prick and pull of tiny hairs on my scalp as the strands are pulled tighter. My mouth works diligently, sucking and sliding, my tongue circling the head of his concrete cock. The tang of beads of precum encourage me to take more, to work toward his release, to taste all of him on my tongue.

I start bobbing my head faster as I feel his thighs clench and his hand in my hair gets needier. Suddenly, I feel his hand over the top of mine, guiding the rhythm he wants and needs, and fuck, that turns me on too.

"Lex, I'm going to fucking fill your mouth with so much of me," he grunts, just before I start to feel the throb of his cock under my hand and then against my lips, as a very short warning, before he explodes inside me.

The salty fruits of my labor are swallowed in three swallows, and then I make sure that I suck him clean before I let him leave my mouth, even as he is shaking and his cock is softening.

When I finally let him go, I trail my tongue up his abs and his chest. I stop to kiss, bite, and suck his neck, leaving a small hickey between his tattoos near his collarbone before I straddle him, and my lips finally collide with his again. One of his hands weaves into my hair while the other finds purchase around my waist.

Carter breaks the kiss and gently grazes fingers over my cheekbone as he looks deeply into my eyes.

"Lex, I am so lucky to have you," he whispers reverently, and then his mouth meets mine again.

After a while, I find myself nestled in the curve of his arm, his fingers tracing gentle paths through my hair and along my spine. With each tender touch, a wave of contentment washes over me, and I drift off to sleep in Carter's embrace, feeling sated and blissfully happy.

20

ALEXIS

"Alexis, I'm so glad we're doing this," Carrie exclaims excitedly as we walk into the salon.

I smile at her, maybe not quite as excited as she is, but I do need a girlfriend. Also, I want to make this work for Jeremiah and the general peace of the house—the house I've lived in for only a few weeks now.

"I think I'm going to do something St. Patrick's Day themed, even though I know I'll have to rebase before then and before the party," she says as we're looking at color choices.

She's referring to the St. Patrick's Day party that my roommates are throwing. I've been told they throw four really big parties every year—New Year's, St. Patrick's Day, Fourth of July, and Halloween. Carter has told me that hundreds of people often are there for those —their alcohol bill is in the several thousands of dollars, which was astounding to me until I realized everyone except Holden makes six figures, and they have almost no housing or utility payments.

Smiling at Carrie, I suggest something I've never done, but I have a feeling it will make her happy. "Carrie! Let's get matching nails." I can't believe those ridiculous words left my mouth, but I am right; she is elated.

"We are going to be such good friends, Alexis," she exclaims with a smile.

During our pedicure time, feet soaking and then gently being massaged, I learn more about Carrie. She is in high-level retail management and travels for work sometimes. She has three sisters, which actually makes her personality make sense to me a little more. Before Jeremiah, she had a boyfriend she lived with for four years, and he royally fucked her over on a financial level, along with an emotional one, and that's why she has no interest in living with Jeremiah.

I can't help but wonder how much they really care about each other, given that they're both so flippant about their relationship.

After the salon, we find a place to have a nice dinner, and the conversation continues. Then she turns the conversation to subjects I thought I knew she wanted to broach with me, the alcohol likely making her bolder.

"So, Alexis," she starts while running her finger around the rim of her margarita glass. "I wanted to apologize for my reaction to you the night of my birthday party; I think I was just surprised."

"I think a lot of people were surprised, and I hate that fucking game," I proclaim with a smile.

Smiling, she looks down at her glass before looking back up at me. "So, you've been with a girl?"

I'm very leery of where she is going with this. "Um, yeah," I respond. "A few times, with an ex-boyfriend, all three times the same woman."

"I'm not trying to pry; I'm genuinely curious. Are you, like, bisexual?"

I laugh a little. "Carrie, I think a lot of women, and even men, are bisexual, or at least bi-curious."

"What do you mean? I have no interest in being in a relationship with a woman," she replies.

"There's a difference between sexual and romantic relationships, Carrie," I say gently. "I think a lot of women are sexually attracted to or at least curious about other women. I would describe myself as heteroromantic but bisexual. *However*, because I tend to be in monogamous relationships, it's just in the one situation that I actually explored that or did anything about it."

"Interesting," she wonders and then takes a sip of her drink.

We eat and drink in silence for a few minutes, the air feeling a little tense and awkward between us.

"I was a little surprised that you were able to rope in Carter," she breaks the silence with a shrug. "I've watched a lot of girls try, even just to have a one-night stand or whatever, with him at various parties over the last couple of years. He just never seemed very interested."

Realizing my truth before I speak it out loud to Carrie, I swallow. "Honestly, outside of Ana's mom, we haven't talked much about his history, and even that wasn't much. He said it had been a while, but that's all he has said, and I haven't pushed for that kind of information."

"Yeah, I don't think there have been very many since then, and none in the last two years that I know of." She shrugs. "It just surprised me. At the Super Bowl party, I just thought you and Holden would hook up for revenge sex," she laughs.

"I'm pretty sure Holden thought that might happen too, but he was a gentleman, and so was Ethan." I smile, taking a sip of my own margarita.

"Ethan is *such* a good guy, generous to a fault," Carrie says.

"Holden is, too, but he tends to be harder to read. Ethan wears his heart on his sleeve."

I nod at her. "I can see that for both of them."

* * *

Later that night, I lay completely sated and weak in Carter's arms when Carrie's words again occupy space at the forefront of my mind.

"Hey, Carter?" I ask, tracing the designs of his tattoos on his chest.

His reply is raspy and tired. "Princess?"

"Carrie said something today and it made me wonder," I continue my gentle traces of his tattoos. "What happened with Ana's mom?"

Carter shifts me in his arm to turn toward me and pull me closer at the same time; he kisses my temple and then responds, "She changed after Ana was born. I don't know if it was becoming a mom or if she had postpartum depression issues, but she changed."

Running his hand gently down the ladder of my ribs, he continues, "She decided she wanted something that wasn't me, but she went and found it before she told me that. Jeremiah found her and another guy in the hot tub when he came home early from a business trip."

Another gentle kiss finds my temple. "I probably could have gotten over and dealt with the cheating, but the relationship was so far gone it wasn't worth salvaging. My only hesitation was Ana. I really didn't want that for her, but now we're here."

"I'm sorry, Carter," I say gently.

Letting out a soft, short laugh, he brushes his lips over my cheekbone. "It is definitely not your fault, Lex. I'm pretty sure you're the most therapeutic thing that has happened to me since, though."

Nuzzling into the crook of his neck, inhaling that unique scent that is Carter, I reply, "Carrie said that too; she said she had never seen you date anyone or whatever."

Carter sighs a little exasperatedly, maybe at Carrie gossiping about him, I don't know. "After Katie, Ana's mom, I went a little crazy for about a year, but since then, there was nobody until you."

I lightly scoff, "Hasn't that been like three years, Carter?"

"Yeah," he says and softly kisses the top of my head. "And yet something about you made me want to jump right in. I think that Monday morning after the Super Bowl, I was hooked. You were under my skin, and all I could think about was Chicago; the timing of that trip was just luck. It had been on the books since before Christmas."

"Was it your idea to take me to Chicago?" I ask, my voice carrying accusatory undertones.

"Actually, no, but when Jeremiah suggested it, I definitely wasn't going to argue with it," he laughs.

"Well, Carter, I loved Chicago with you, everything about it. The success for Laugherty, but you blew my mind with everything else," I laugh softly. "If your friends hadn't sent me roses, you might have gotten lucky that night."

"Yeah," he sighs. "That was an unexpected and new cockblock for me."

I laugh and then kiss his neck where my face is nuzzled against him. He moves to meet my mouth with his, and as I feel his hard cock press into my hip, I know we're done talking for the night.

* * *

"Georgia, it's so good," I sigh, my phone on speaker, sitting on my bed.

"I'm so glad, Lex, you deserve that. What about the other guys, still drama?" Georgia asks, sincerely wanting to know.

"Not really. I don't think they're happy, but there isn't any drama."

"Hopefully, it stays that way," she replies. "I was thinking about coming out around your birthday for a week or two. Do you think that would work?"

"Yeah, I can talk to Ethan to make sure, but I'm sure it will be fine. Apparently, they throw a huge Fourth of July party; if you came early enough, you could experience that," I suggest.

"That sounds fun. Let me look at my calendar, but it should be fine."

"I'm just excited for you to meet all these guys," I almost giggle.

"Maybe I can take one or two of them off your hands," she teases.

"Oh geez," I laugh, but envy hits me harder than I expected, leaving me confused about my own feelings. I wasn't prepared for the surge of jealousy, and it makes me question what I really want.

I can't put a claim on all of them.

21

JEREMIAH

Sitting in my corner office at Laugherty with Alexis, I realize something; this is probably the first time we've been alone together, and definitely the first time we've been alone behind a closed door.

Poring over the marketing budget and strategy details, she's perched on the rolling office chair beside me. I'm finding it hard to focus because her sweet perfume fills the air, reminiscent of candy. The draw of her soft skin as she points to various things on my monitor and her smile when she looks at me is substantial. Her movements ooze professional confidence with a subtle allure, and nothing comes off as too bold or vain.

It's not lost on me that she's dating one of my closest friends, and she's also my employee. Plus, I'm in a committed relationship with Carrie; we're approaching our two-year mark.

Is it perfect? No, but we complement each other in many ways, including our mutual appreciation for maintaining our independence outside of the relationship.

None of that diminishes the intense attraction I feel toward the woman sitting next to me, nor does it dampen my desire to explore that attraction.

The siren flips her hair, and her neck is there on full display, so pretty and inviting. Resisting the urge to brush the rest of her hair off her neck and bite that soft skin takes more self-control than I would have predicted before this moment.

Perhaps my subconscious arranged this alone time with her for a reason. There's no practical reason why we couldn't have discussed these matters at home or with Carter or Ethan present. I think I simply wanted this time alone with her.

She's impressive. The amount of knowledge she has, her business and marketing planning—all of it floors me professionally. We conclude our business discussions by forwarding budget information and proposals to allocate more funds to marketing to Ethan, and I suggest we grab lunch together.

Despite my familiarity with her professional persona and the things we've learned as a group at the house, I realize I haven't invested much effort in getting to know her on a personal level. And I'm certain she knows very little about me. It's refreshing to have this opportunity to converse with her outside the confines of business.

As we settle into seats at the café down the block from the office, I begin with a simple question, "What drew you to marketing? Clearly, it's been a successful choice for you, but what inspired you to pursue this path?"

A radiant smile lights up her face as she talks about her passion, and it's utterly endearing. "To be honest, I was drawn to graphic design for its creativity, but the stability and higher pay of a marketing career ultimately won me over. Having skills in both fields made me marketable, opening the way for my first career opportunities."

I offer her a soft smile. "I'm sure it did. I have a feeling you were quite the diligent student."

Blushing slightly, she returns the smile. "Absolutely, I tend to dive deep into school and grades; I can get competitive and obsessive about them."

"Artsy, academic, athletic, and attractive," I remark, noticing her blush deepen. I enjoy her reaction; it makes me wonder how much she would blush if I talked dirty to her.

Then I seriously wonder what the fuck is wrong with me.

After the server takes our order, she dives into her own questions. "So, Jer, how long have you and Carrie been together?"

"Almost two years," I answer with a sigh, hearing the hint of resignation in my voice.

She smirks a little. "You don't sound thrilled about it. Why's that?"

I shrug. "It's fine, fulfilling enough. But it's more about convenience for both of us." I pause, searching for the right words. "Neither of us has any desire to get married or even live together. So, it works out that we have a couple of nights a week of companionship, or whatever you want to call it, and then we go our separate ways again."

"And that's what you want?" Alexis asks, her tone laced with concern.

I don't do personal conversations. Usually, I find my way out of them, but Alexis has me opening up in ways that are a little foreign to me.

I can feel the cracks in my walls.

"Honestly, yeah," I reply with another shrug. "At least for now. I'm not really keen on feeling completely accountable to someone." I clear my throat. "Even the night of her party, when she stormed off angry, I didn't really care. I don't feel like I owe her explanations for my actions unless it's something really serious. I just don't want that level of accountability with anyone."

"Do you not *want* that level of accountability, or are you *scared* of it?" she challenges, catching me off guard.

It takes me a moment to gather my thoughts. "Probably both, if I'm being honest. I cherish my independence, and I guess I'm afraid of losing it. But it's also a conscious decision not to pursue that kind of relationship."

She presses further. "Do you love her?"

Feeling like the interrogation isn't going to end, her question hits me like a ton of bricks. "Honestly, I don't think so. But I've told her I do."

She takes a bite of her food, and seizing the opportunity to change the subject, I raise my eyebrows suggestively and ask, "How are things with Carter?"

Her cheeks flush once again before she replies, "They're good. We're good."

"I'm relieved to hear that. Would've hated for all that drama at the house to be for nothing," I say, flashing her a smile and a wink.

She swallows, her expression turning somber. "I know they say they're okay with it, but Holden and Ethan still aren't exactly thrilled."

"Yeah, they're not," I acknowledge before adding, "And just so you're aware, Shawn isn't thrilled either. He's just different from the others, more introverted. So, we don't always know what's going on in his head."

"Seriously?" she asks incredulously.

"Seriously. Remember how you melted his little nerd heart?" I chuckle.

She smiles that natural, gorgeous smile at the memory. "That wasn't intentional; none of it was intentional."

I offer her a soft smile and conciliatory reassurance, "I know, siren. I know."

* * *

ETHAN

Doing laundry isn't really how I want to spend my Saturday, but with my clothes dwindling, it's become a necessity. As I push open the laundry room door, balancing a giant basket of clothes, I'm taken aback to find Alexis already there, pulling clothes out of the dryer. I try my best not to pay too much attention to the several lacy thongs sitting at the top of her basket.

She startles slightly as I enter the room.

"Sorry, I didn't mean to startle you; I didn't know you were here," I chuckle.

"It's okay," she shrugs with a soft smile.

"Are you done with the washer?" I inquire.

"Yeah, I'm good," she confirms.

Inadvertently, I block her exit from the laundry room. When she bends to pick up her basket, it puts her cleavage on full display before she places it on top of the dryer. In a rush of realization, I begin to load my own clothes into the washer, a feeble attempt to both busy myself and clear the way for her departure.

As I go through the motions, a strange sense of contentment washes over me, and I realize I am really enjoying this moment of proximity and privacy with her. It is rare that I am behind a closed door with her.

She doesn't pick up her basket, and she doesn't appear eager to leave either, so I smile and check in with her. "How are you, Lexi? I haven't really checked in with you lately."

"I'm good," she says, swallowing slightly. "Jeremiah and Carter are keeping me busy with work, but I'm good."

"And everything here is good? Nothing I can do to make you more comfortable at home?"

"No, Ethan." She takes a step toward me, and I catch the enticing scent of her perfume as those mesmerizing blue eyes meet mine under dark lashes, causing me to swallow. She places her hand on my upper arm as she speaks. "You've been great; the house is great. I'm very appreciative of everything you have done."

I make a point of looking at her hand on my arm; she grazes her thumb in a few swipes. The touch sends a surge of heat through my veins and static through my nerves. My gaze travels up to her face, but she doesn't drop her hand.

"I'm glad, Lexi, but be careful, love," I say softly, my voice barely above a whisper, looking down at her hand on my arm once more before I meet her eyes again.

Reaching out, placing my hand on her waist, I lean in close to speak more intimately. "I know Carter called dibs, but I can't help the way my body reacts to you."

Withdrawing from her, I can't help but brush my thumb over her jawline, feeling the tension between us.

"Ethan," she responds, her voice quiet and breathy. "I'm not trying to lead you on."

"That's the problem, love; you don't even have to try," I confess, hearing the heat in my own voice and twirling a tendril of her hair between my fingers.

She drops her hand and I step aside, silently granting her the space to leave. But to my surprise, she remains rooted in place; she doesn't move. She is a magnetic force that draws me in. We stand there, suspended in a moment of unspoken, forbidden understanding, locked in each other's gaze.

The tension between us is palpable, a tangible force of heady air that seems to envelop us both. It's an uncomfortable sensation, yet beneath it lies an undeniable familiarity. There's no refuting the electricity that crackles between us, igniting the air with a charged energy that makes me forget how to breathe. Time stands still, the world around us fading into insignificance as we remain locked in this silent exchange.

A torrent of desires races through my mind, each thought more intoxicating than the last. I envision tangling my fingers in her hair, drawing her close until our lips meet in a fervent kiss. That sweet, pouty, sometimes sassy mouth of hers beckons to me, inviting exploration and passion.

I picture tracing the contours of her curves, reveling in the sensation of her softness beneath my touch, and dipping my fingers into her wet heat. In my imagination, she tastes of sweetness and feels like pure heaven. The mere thought of sinking myself inside her or my mouth exploring the taste of her arousal sends a shiver down my spine.

And then, a more daring image takes shape. Envisioning effortlessly lifting her and seating her on the washer, our bodies pressed together in perfect alignment. The height difference suddenly becomes an advantage. The perfect height to fuck her, and that ignites the flames of desire even further. The lucid daydream causes reactions in my body that I've rarely felt.

Finally, breaking the potent silence that envelops us, I muster the words, my voice barely above a whisper, "You should go, Lexi, before I do something I'll regret."

Smiling softly, she grabs her basket and sincerely murmurs, "I'm sorry, Ethan," before quietly exiting the laundry room.

Exhaling deeply, I lean against the dryer, the cool metal providing a brief reprieve from the storm raging within me. Taking a moment to gather my thoughts and steady the racing beat of my heart, I finally kick the machine in frustration before venturing out into the quiet hallway, the echoes of the fleeting moment lingering in the air.

22

CARTER

After finishing a great workout and an interesting conversation with Ethan, I feel recharged and refreshed, heading back to my room for a shower. As soon as I open my bedroom door, I am greeted by Alexis—naked.

Perfect tits, hard nipples just waiting to be expertly handled. That perfect, hairless pussy wanting to be filled and all the other flawless curves just waiting for me.

Fuck, she is so hot.

"Well, hi," I say, feeling my cock respond to her almost as fast as my eyes.

"I need you, Carter," she states seductively. "Now."

Smiling, I move toward her, my hands finding her hips. I have a funny feeling that something got her all hot and bothered, but I am happy to quench her thirst.

"Shower with me?" I propose. "I'm all post-workout sweaty."

"If you want to fuck me in the shower, I'm okay with that," she says flippantly and then wraps her arms around my neck and kisses me with a passion I have felt from her, but not all the time.

"Woman, what got into you?"

"Nothing yet, but hopefully you soon." She smiles.

Fuck, now she has me so turned on, so fucking hard.

I drop my mouth down right next to her ear. "Where do you want me, princess? Because I'd really like a chance to fuck that ass."

And this woman, this absolutely fucking perfect woman, says, "Make my pussy happy, and you can have any other part of me you want."

My mouth crashes into hers, and I can feel her wanton desire in the movements of her tongue. She is so fucking needy right now.

Breaking the kiss, I take each of her hands in mine, backing into the bathroom and taking her with me. After turning on the water, I take my clothes off, and as soon as I free my cock, this woman drops to her mother fucking knees and takes me in her mouth like she has never tasted anything more wonderful in her life.

"Lex, princess, fuck," I growl.

I'm tempted to just let her finish, to swallow me, but no, I am on a mission this afternoon. I wrap my hand in her hair and gently pull until she listens and looks up at me.

"Your turn, then my turn," I dictate, flashing a smile at her.

After she stands, I pull her into the shower with me. Then, much to her frustration, I legitimately soap my body before I do anything else. She's adorable—pouting, whining, and begging—while she's waiting for me. I love the giant showers in this house. She has her own shower head, and there's a small bench, so at least she can stay warm.

Finally, I put an end to her pouting, ordering her, "Put your hands on the bench, baby, and bend over. I want to finger fuck you from behind." She obeys like the good fucking girl that she is.

"Such a good girl," I whisper, and then I cup her pussy from behind.

Entering that sweet wet cunt with my thumb, my fingers find her clit, and I work both of them until she is mindlessly grinding against me, working toward her own climax, and it's so fucking hot.

With my other hand, I fist my cock up and down, root to tip and back. It's so hard, it doesn't need the stimulation, but it is aching to be touched, and I can't control myself. Her moaning is so loud there is no way that the others in the house can't hear it, and that makes me both a little embarrassed and a lot proud.

"Fuck, Lex, I like you like this, so fucking needy," and then I feel her convulse around my fingers, the orgasm wracking her body in waves.

She gasps when I dip two of my fingers from my other hand into her wet pussy, joining my thumb, filling her more. I know she loves it because when I pull them out, she whines over their absence.

"Don't worry, princess, you're about to be so full of me, you won't know what to do," I whisper and then take my fingers and run them, covered in her fluids, up to her ass, circling that puckered tight hole.

Leaving my other hand in place, thumb in her cunt and fingers on her clit, I slowly push my cock into her ass, gauging her reaction. She gasps but continues to make noises of pleasure and she grinds into me, letting me know she enjoys every second of it.

Once I'm buried in her ass to the hilt, I move my thumb and my fingers, making sure she is fully aware that I am everywhere in her.

"Look at you, such a good fucking girl taking me like this," I praise in a groan. "This ass was made for me, fuck."

As I pull back and thrust, she moans loud again. "Fuck, Carter, you feel so good."

That is all the permission I need from her; I sink hard into her again and again and again. I fuck her ass like is the last lay I will ever get. She grinds into my hand while bracing herself with her hands on the tile bench and wall.

Feeling the channels of her cunt and ass convulse around my thumb and cock, I'm done. I let her milk me through her climax, my own orgasm one of the hardest I've ever had in my life.

I'm pretty sure I fall in love with her in this moment, as my body stills from the orgasm. Even though I'd never tell her that. Love should be all about emotional connection, but, fuck, I realize in this carnal moment that I love her now. I'm addicted to her soul and mind, but this fucking body, I'm addicted to that, too.

"Such a fucking good girl," are the words that come out of my mouth instead of "I love you."

My hand and my cock leave her at the same time before I turn her around so I can kiss her. And kiss her, I do, deeply, passionately, like every unspoken feeling I have can be transferred to her through my tongue.

Then, I help her clean up, and I let her help me. My mouth frequently finds hers, along with her neck, ears, and other parts of her face.

"You're so fucking perfect, princess," I say to her as I wrap her in a towel.

"You're pretty perfect yourself," she replies and gently kisses me.

"Hopefully that satiated you," I tease.

"For now," she answers with a coy smile.

"Good, because it's almost dinner time." I kiss her on the forehead and then leave the bathroom to go get dressed.

She follows me and puts on the clothes she must have taken off when she came in here; I don't think I saw anything in the room except her when I walked in.

I study her for a moment and then address her, "Can I ask you something, Lex?"

She looks at me and raises her eyebrows, challenging me to just ask the question.

"The 'Never Have I Ever' night." She scoffs and rolls her eyes; I laugh. "I'm just curious, don't kill me," I add in a conciliatory tone.

"What do you want to know, Carter?" Lex almost snaps at me.

"Hey," I say softly, making my way toward her and softly brushing my lips on her forehead. "I'm not the enemy, Lex."

She looks at me but doesn't say anything.

"When you were in threesomes, what were the circumstances around those?" I try to make it sound as peaceful and inquisitive as possible.

"Why don't you tell me yours first?" Alexis challenges.

"Okay," I concede, crossing my arms. "With Katie, my ex-wife. Toward the end of our marriage, she thought that maybe she just needed some spice, some variety." I pause. "I refused to have another girl because I didn't need it, and that felt like cheating to me. She was excited at the prospect of having another guy. It was fun, I liked it." I study her reaction to my words. "I liked watching her be pleasured by someone else. I didn't expect that at the beginning, but it was hot to me, a turn-on."

"Obviously, it didn't save the marriage, though, right?" Alexis asks, her voice thoughtful.

"No, but it didn't hurt it either," I reply honestly, and then I look at her.

She clears her throat and sits on the end of my bed; I lean against it next to her.

"The boyfriend I had before Brody, my fourth boyfriend ever," she laughs like that is embarrassing, "was a little adventurous. He had been the extra guy in situations like you are describing, but he'd never been the guy in the relationship, and he'd never had an angel's three-way."

Lex is looking down as she plays with her fingernails and cuticles.

"So, we decided to do both. I learned I'm a little selfish when it comes to those things," she laughs.

"Selfish, how?" I ask, genuinely curious.

"I really, really liked more people touching me; I didn't like touching other people as much," she laughs. "I know that sounds awful."

"No." I smile. "Not awful, but maybe extrapolate on that for me for a minute."

"Having a girl all up on me was nice, and honestly, there were things I enjoyed doing to her, but I just felt selfish. I wanted all the attention on me." She pauses and looks at me with a smirk. "Which made the devil's three-way a lot more fun for me. Because a lot of the attention was on me."

"Was it a one-time thing?" I ask.

"No, but it was a one-guy thing, like just one other guy, not multiples," she answers.

"I figured, from your body count." I smirk.

Smiling, she responds, "Yeah, it was probably about a dozen times over a few weeks."

"What happened with that boyfriend?" I ask.

"He was cheating on me; in that same timeframe, I caught him red-handed. Very similar to Brody." Looking at me, she shrugs and then looks back at the floor.

"I'm sorry, Lex."

"It's not your fault," she replies with a smile.

"I know," and then I pause. "If he hadn't cheated on you, do you think you would have kept going with the other guy, like a consistent thing?"

"Maybe," she shrugs. "I don't know, really. It was all about sex; there were no feelings there, not even *real* attraction. There was a camaraderie; what we did was hot, but we didn't hang out outside the bedroom."

"So it wasn't like a polyamorous, throuple, type thing, it was just sex?" I clarify.

"Yeah, pretty much." She looks at me like she is trying to read the questions I'm not asking. Then she adds, "I think a lot of those things can work as long as there's no lying; the dishonesty makes it feel like cheating to me anyway."

I nod at her and I'm glad she was willing to be that open in talking about it with me.

23

ALEXIS

"Alexis," Ethan playfully growls at me.

It's the fourth time he has warned or teased me that I am torturing him as we're setting up for the St. Patrick's Day party.

"You're the one that put me on a ladder," I laugh.

"Yeah, well, I didn't think through you wearing those damn shorts," he snickers at me.

"Just hand me the garland; we're almost done," I chuckle.

Ethan has been more relaxed with me the last couple of days. There used to be so much tension between us, but something has changed, and it's nice. I finish placing the garland along the railing of the grand staircase and then start to climb down the ladder.

When my foot hits the third rung from the bottom, Ethan wraps his arms around my waist from behind, pulling me off the ladder. He swings me around to face the other direction. It pulls a playful shriek out of me as I feel like I'm falling. Both of us laughing, he sets me down, and I like this playful side of Ethan. I had seen hints of it before, but not like this.

I turn toward him, and I see the hunger in his eyes, but he doesn't look tortured like he has before. There is still something playful to his expression even though I see the longing there, the fire that sparks in his eyes when his gaze meets mine. He's smiling, and I've always thought Ethan was attractive, but when he genuinely smiles, he's even more so.

"Ethan," Jeremiah calls out as we hear the door between the garage and the house open.

We find Jeremiah, Carter, and Shawn carrying in cases of alcohol; Ethan starts to help them. I make myself useful in setting things up in the kitchen, pulling bottles out of boxes, setting some on the kitchen island and some in the pantry we're using for backup. After they're done carrying things in, Carter and I fill the beer and water fridge.

"Okay, all that's left is the catering delivery," Ethan says.

"We have two hours, right?" I ask.

Ethan looks at his watch. "Yeah, just about."

Grabbing Carter's hand, I kiss him on the cheek before saying, "I'm going to take a shower and make myself pretty."

Smiling at me, Carter almost gushes, "Princess, you don't have to *make* that happen."

I roll my eyes and then smile at the other guys before I find my way upstairs.

After showering, I work on my makeup. I'm Irish on my mom's side of the family, so St. Patrick's Day has always been a big day for my family. In the Northeast, I've always felt like it's a bigger deal than the Western states, but I will feel right at home at a St. Patrick's Day Party.

I expertly highlight my eyes with dark green eyeliner, wings and all. I think about drawing clovers on my cheek but decide against it. However, I do dab gold glitter on my cheekbones near my temple.

Then, I decide I'll add it to my cleavage and other places once I'm dressed.

After curling my hair, I add green and gold extensions in layers so they peek through my natural hair. Then, it's time to get dressed. I had debated what I was going to wear, but I decide to go with exactly what I would have worn to a St. Patrick's Day party back in Baltimore. Looking in the mirror, I check my outfit, even taking a couple of mirror selfies for social media before I take a deep breath and leave my bedroom to go downstairs.

I send my selfies to Georgia; she had already sent me hers for barhopping in Baltimore.

> (Georgia) *JFC girl, you are fucking smoking*
> (Me) **hairflip* thank you*
> (Georgia) *How are all your boy toys going to react?*
> (Me) *That's a good question*
> (Georgia) *Well you better update me with the answer*
> (Me) *I will, but when you're sober lol*
> (Georgia) *Fair lol - have fun bitch*

I do know how they're going to react, though. These guys, all five of them, are going to kill me.

* * *

CARTER

Fuck me, this goddamn woman.

We're in the dining room setting up the catering trays when Alexis comes down the stairs looking like sex on a stick. I watch my roommates all try to hold their shit together. Ethan and I lock eyes for a brief second, and then he shakes his head and looks back at her.

She has green and gold streaks in her hair and perfect makeup. Her green shirt says "Irish Girl" across her perfect tits. It's off the shoulders and stops a couple of inches above her cute, little, pierced belly button. There are rips on the sides of what is already a short shirt, showing even more skin and hints of her ink.

It's the first time I've seen her in clothes where I can see her tattoos at all, and it's still not much. I'm grateful she is wearing a black bralette under it, like a sexy sports bra. Glitter adorns her cleavage and her flat stomach.

As my eyes work down her body, she just gets sexier. She's wearing a black and green plaid skirt that I'm sure barely covers her ass cheeks. But what really draws my attention are the garter belt straps that come down over her thighs, attaching to black fishnet thigh-high stockings. She has a garter on her left thigh with a button that says "Kiss Me I'm Irish," and she wraps it all up with short, black, strappy heels.

After my eyes reach her feet and I make my way back to her face, her eyes lock with mine. All I can do is smile at her—I'm sure as hell not going to tell her to go change.

After her eyes dart quickly to the faces of the other four guys, she walks straight up to me, her expression and movements coquettish and seductive.

"Alexis," I purr her name. "That's really not fair to all the other women who will be here." I smile, eliciting a laugh from Jeremiah and Ethan.

Holden and Shawn are oddly quiet and unreactive, almost like they're in shock.

All of us guys are wearing jeans and some kind of funny

St. Patrick's Day shirt, so in her current company, she definitely stands out.

The doorbell rings, announcing the arrival of Carrie and a few of her girlfriends. They are not dressed quite as scantily as Alexis, but they definitely make her stand out a little less. She's still the only one in fishnet. As Jeremiah and the other guys are greeting them, I take the opportunity to pull Alexis close to me.

"I don't need to tell you that you are sexy," I praise her quietly. "I'm pretty sure you are not ignorant at all about how you look tonight."

I brush some hair off her shoulder, then weave my hand through her hair at the base of her skull. Pulling her mouth to mine, I kiss her deeply. When we break the kiss, I press a soft kiss on her forehead.

Shortly, it's time to play host and bartender. Shawn starts a playlist of music that is mostly Flogging Molly and Dropkick Murphy's. Abstract images in green, white, and gold flash on the large-screen television, timed with the music. Less than twenty minutes later, there are over one hundred people at our house, both inside and outside, and I am grateful for the unusually warm weather we are having. However, the outdoor heaters and firepits are still glowing on the patio.

Alexis is by my side a lot at the beginning of the party, but she starts breaking off and socializing more as the night goes on. She's not really drinking. She made a couple of oatmeal cookie shots at the beginning of the night for herself and Carrie, but she's been drinking water since then.

A few hours into the party, I realize I haven't seen her in a while and I start looking around for her. As I turn the corner into the kitchen, a flicker of movement catches my eye in the dark recesses of the unused and unlit part of the dining room.

There, in the shadows, I see Alexis and Ethan; their proximity to each other is mere inches. His hand rests lightly on her arm while her own arm is draped across her waist like she is hugging herself, but her body language is not defensive.

I watch, transfixed, through the chaos of the people and music of the party as they lean toward each other, their eyes locked in an intimate exchange. Though I can't discern the words being spoken, the expression on Ethan's face is suggestive enough.

With determination, I take deliberate steps toward them; my gaze locks with Ethan's as I reach out to Alexis. My hand finds its place on her upper arm, trailing down to entwine our fingers, pulling her gently towards me.

As I pull her to the wall that separates the kitchen from the living room, I turn my attention from Ethan to Alexis. Studying her flushed complexion and dilated pupils, I recognize that she looks absolutely guilty.

Cupping her chin tenderly, I place a soft kiss on her forehead before tracing the soft, lush curve of her bottom lip with the pad of my thumb, savoring the electrifying connection between us. Finally, I lean in to capture her lips gently in a kiss, pouring all of my emotions into the confluence of our mouths.

Breaking the kiss, I look into her eyes and then feel her gasp beneath my touch as I swiftly and forcefully maneuver her so that her back presses against my chest, our bodies aligning in a primal embrace. With a firm hand placed flat against her stomach, I pull her close, ensuring she feels the undeniable hardness of my cock pressing against her, a voiceless testament to my arousal.

Her hands find purchase on my forearm, a silent acknowledgment of the intensity of my grasp on her and my erection pressing into her. Wrapping my other arm around her chest, I draw her closer still, my fingers tangling in her hair as I expose the sensitive skin of her neck and ear.

Positioning my mouth next to her ear, my lips ghosting the shell,

I whisper softly, each word laden with lust and urgency, ensuring she hears every syllable as I lay bare my salacious suggestions.

"Princess," I purr, feeling her shudder at the sensation of my breath against her skin; with a soft chuckle, I continue, my voice low and intimate, "Ethan wants you."

Locking eyes with Ethan, I hold his gaze through the crowd of people between us as I guide her through the tumultuous emotions I know are swirling within her. Her head rolls back into the crook of my shoulder, but I refuse to let her retreat into herself or me.

"No, princess, open your eyes," I urge, my voice a gentle coaxing. "Look at him."

I feel her hand tighten on my forearm, her uncertainty hangs heavy in the air, but I watch as Ethan's gaze moves from me to her as she lifts her head.

"He wants you. If you want him too, you should go to him." Her hand squeezes my forearm.

"Carter," she whispers, her tone uncertain.

"Alexis," I whisper, my voice a tender caress as I kiss her gently on the neck. "Go to him, and then find me so I can savagely reclaim you."

With deliberate slowness, I pose the question, my gaze still on Ethan. "Do you want him?"

"Carter," my name comes off her lips as a plea.

"Lex, answer me." I smile against her neck, and I'm positive she can hear the delight and humor conveyed in my voice as I repeat each word individually, "*Do. You. Want. Him?*"

My eyes meet Ethan's again, and her response is barely audible—a breathy "Yes" that sends a surge of hunger and lust coursing through me and ignites a primal response within me. The sound that comes from me, while quiet, is feral, something between a laugh, a purr, and a growl.

"Then go, princess," I murmur, loosening my grip on her. "I'll be waiting for you."

With a gentle push, my hands on her hips, I guide her toward Ethan, watching as she moves away from me without a backward glance. And in that insanely erotic moment, I'm consumed by a heady mix of arousal and anticipation, knowing that this is just the beginning of a new journey.

* * *

ETHAN

SIX DAYS EARLIER

Needing to burn off all the extra energy in my body after that laundry room encounter with Alexis, Carter finds me on the treadmill when he enters the gym for his own workout.

He senses the intensity immediately. "What are you running away from?" Carter teases.

Why does he have to know me so well?

I just shake my head at him. He takes the message and puts earbuds in his ears while he starts his own workout.

Four miles later, as I'm walking out of the room, he removes his earbuds and calls out to me again.

"Ethan," his voice stern, coated with concern, "what the fuck is wrong with you?"

I sigh, still breathing heavily from the run, and I can feel the sweat dripping off me.

I need a shower.

"Carter, I'm not going to have this conversation with you," I say as I turn toward him, meeting his eyes in the mirror, and I realize that is probably already too much information.

"You mad at me?" Carter inquires.

"Mad? No."

I can almost hear the gears working in his head before the switch flips. "Wait, Alexis? What happened?"

I laugh, but it's humorless, and shake my head, looking at the ceiling and then the ground.

"Ethan?" The worry and frustration coming from Carter is palpable.

"Nothing, Carter, nothing happened," I respond, his facial expression still asking an unspoken question. "Just remember, you're a lucky son of a bitch."

Carter laughs and responds like the asshole he is, "I *know* that, but I don't believe you that nothing happened. Something drove you down here."

I roll my eyes. "I ran into her in the laundry room, that's all. Nothing happened."

Carter studies me for a minute and then breaks the silence, his words surprising. "Do you remember the conversation we had in the kitchen? The one when Jeremiah suggested we share?"

I swallow—hard. Looking up and down the hall outside the gym for any of our other roommates first, I step fully back into the gym and close the door.

"What are you saying, Carter?" I ask a little apprehensively.

Turning so he is facing me instead of looking at me through the mirror, he explains, "I'm saying maybe that's a possibility. I mean, you're the one who said it would be up to her, and it would. But I think you and me, *we* could do it without drama. I think she could, too, if it's something she wants. And I don't think you'd be standing there looking at me like that if she completely shut you down with whatever *didn't* happen in the laundry room."

I take a moment, letting his words sink in. "Carter, I know I was flippant about it in the kitchen that day, but that's an insane, maybe fantastical idea."

"I don't think it is," Carter reasons. "And you didn't deny what I just said." The shit-eating grin that crosses his face is lascivious.

I pull the towel off my shoulder, wipe my face, and take a step toward him. "You're actually serious," I say and it's not a question.

"I am," he responds, and I let that hang in the air for a minute. I can feel my heart beating faster, and my dick starts to stiffen at the thought of it. In the kitchen that day, I was mostly joking, thinking they all were too—mostly.

"How would we even do that?" I laugh; it's crazy we're even having this conversation. "Separately or together?"

Carter shrugs, his face in a sober and earnest expression, while his voice remains nonchalant. "Either, both, whatever she wants, whatever happens."

I straddle the workout bench across from Carter and rake my fingers through my hair, trying to calm my brain and my hormones, which are rapidly firing at everything he suggests.

I cover my face with the towel in my hands before meeting his gaze again. "Carter, if this goes wrong, it could mess up everything, and not just for us; for the company, for the other guys."

"But what if it goes right?" he marvels.

I laugh uncomfortably, "How do we propose that idea to her? Do we hide it from everyone?"

Carter chuckles, "You just said 'we.'" I roll my eyes at him. "I can handle the conversation with her; it will be more about finding perfect timing. Obviously, you'd have to have a conversation with her, too. But I know I would need to go first because I need to give her permission or whatever you want to call it." He pauses, letting that sink in.

"As for everyone knowing, I think that's a decision between the three of us, where one 'no' is a full veto," he continues.

Uncomfortably laughing again, I ask, "How long have you been thinking about this?"

Carter shrugs one more time. "Honestly, since Jeremiah suggested it." He takes a moment to look at me. "You in?"

I shake my head, wondering how I found myself in this position and thinking Carter is crazy. But then I remember what it felt like on my balcony with her, in the laundry room with her, and in so many moments in between.

"I'm in," I concede.

24

ALEXIS

Carrie and her entourage of six single girlfriends—some of the same crew from her birthday bash—practically swarm me as they make their way past Jeremiah and the other guys.

"Alexis!" Carrie exclaims excitedly. "I'm thrilled to be partying with you tonight!"

I smile in return, but my gaze flickers past her to Jeremiah and Ethan, who share an unspoken understanding that Carrie might be a handful tonight.

"You should join us for some shots," Carrie insists, her friends nodding enthusiastically in agreement.

Their high-pitched voices grate on my nerves and I wonder if maybe this is why I don't have many girlfriends.

"I'll indulge in a couple of shots with you," I agree with a laugh. "I'll make you my favorite St. Patrick's Day shot, but then you're on your own."

"You have a favorite St. Patrick's Day shot?" Carter queries, a smirk playing on his lips.

"Of course," I retort playfully. "Doesn't everyone?"

"Woman," Carter warns with narrowed eyes, a hint of amusement dancing in his gaze.

I motion for Carrie and her friends to follow me, Carter trailing behind like my loyal sidekick. It's kind of endearing.

Turning to Carter, I tease, "You want in too?"

"Absolutely, if it's your favorite," he replies with a wink.

Rolling my eyes, I grab eight plastic shot glasses and locate my liquor bottles.

Carter catches on quickly. "Ah, I know what you're making. But you do realize only one of those bottles is Irish, right?"

"Oh, I'm aware," I quip, examining the cinnamon schnapps bottle. "This one's from the Netherlands, apparently, and the other two are from Germany."

I pour a mixture of Baileys, Jagermeister, butterscotch schnapps, and Hot Damn for an oatmeal cookie shot, toasting with the girls before pouring another round.

One of Carrie's friends exclaims, "That's the best shot I've ever had!"

Grinning, I warn, "You can turn it into a full drink, but be careful—it packs a punch."

"Come on, Alexis," Carrie pleads. "Let's have more fun together."

Chuckling, I decline, "No, it's a marathon, not a sprint. It's a long night, and I'm good for now."

Carrie persists, "But, Alexis, at the last party, you practically drank a whole bottle of whiskey."

"That was a different story," I counter. "You made me play that game."

"Fine, but I'm making you drink more tonight, too," Carrie challenges. "And by the way, you look fucking hot tonight."

The woman looks me up and down like she wants to eat me. For some reason, that makes me more uncomfortable than any of the guys doing it.

Teasing her, I ask, "Did you pre-game, Carrie?"

"Just a tad," she admits sheepishly.

Carter rolls his eyes discreetly, a silent conversation between us.

"Alright, we'll see," I concede as they move on to the appetizer table.

Jeremiah sidles up beside me, whispering, "You do realize you've taken yourself off the market for all of them, right? And now, Carrie's single squad bypassed all the available guys in the house just to find you."

Heat floods my cheeks as I reply, "Jer, you want me to be mean to her?"

"No, siren, only pointing out what just happened," he explains softly and sighs.

* * *

A few hours into the party, Ethan asks me to help refresh the appetizers in the dining room. While helping him maneuver through the crowd to bring trays in from the garage, I get side-tracked, dumping empty bottles off the bar into recycling bins and adding replacement bottles. Finally, I remember what I was doing and make my way back over to help Ethan in the dining room.

While I'm rearranging crackers across the table, Ethan catches me off guard, placing his hand on my hip; he leans into the opposite ear and whispers, "Don't bend over too far, love; otherwise, you leave nothing to the imagination in that skirt."

Part of me wants to counter that, informing him this skirt covers just as much as my lacrosse skirts in college did, but I feel the heat of the blush climbs my cheeks. Then he drops his hand and moves over to the side, fixing another appetizer tray. When he's done fixing up what he needs on the table, he turns and looks at me.

Our eyes lock for a few seconds too long. Before I realize what is happening, he moves toward me. I feel his fingers wrap around my wrist before he pulls me to the back corner of the dining room. He backs himself into the wall instead of pushing or caging me into it; *he* takes the more vulnerable position, and then he just talks to me.

"Lexi," he sighs and rakes a hand through his hair. "I just want you to know that I don't want things to be weird between us." His hand finds my upper arm and squeezes gently, a gesture of reassurance.

"Ethan, they don't need to be weird," I reply. "The other day, in the laundry room, I—I'm sorry."

Smiling softly, his chocolate-brown eyes dancing a little in the dark, he replies, "Don't be sorry, love. I respect you, whatever it is you want." He pauses. "I just—"

His voice breaks off as he looks past me—to Carter. I don't fully realize he's there until his hand is on my arm, tucking under my upper arm—opposite Ethan's hand that falls away as well.

For a second, I think Carter is angry, but his expression, looking at Ethan and then at me, is relaxed—determined maybe, but relaxed. Then he lays the gentlest kiss on my forehead, followed by kissing me with so much emotion it feels like a claim—maybe it is.

Suddenly, he turns me and pulls my back flush with him. Using a splayed hand on my waist, he pulls me even closer, emphasizing how turned on he is by rolling his hips into me. I start to block out the cacophony of sounds around us from the many partiers and music.

Carter's other arm crosses from my shoulder to the opposite side of my neck, his forearm almost around my throat. Moving my hair away from my ear, intentionally giving his mouth a clear path to my neck and my ear, the way he is holding me is savage and primal, and I am so here for it.

But then his words are the opposite of a possessive man—of a claiming. Apprehension and lust consume me at the same time.

"If you want him too, you should go to him." Carter's voice seems to contradict his words; his voice is seductive and warm—husky— the same one he would use to tell me to meet him in his room, but he's telling me to go to his friend, to Ethan.

I want Ethan; there is no denying that I want him, but telling Carter that and acting on that is much different than thinking it or knowing it. It is a decision none of us can take back. My mind tries to find logical paths of thought, wondering if it's a test. The spaghetti brain in my head is following the paths of multiple noodles at once, trying to find the end to this interaction that I want, the end that they want.

Have I had too much to drink to be making this decision? I haven't had anything to drink in hours, and then it wasn't much. Is this a trick? Is Carter trying to test me?

Nothing about the way his hands are moving, the tone of his voice, or the way he is trying to reassure me of how he feels about me, about this, is telling me this is a test or trap.

My eyes fall on Ethan across the room, and I see the hunger and longing there; he has barely moved from where Carter pulled me away from him. I watch Ethan's eyes drift between Carter and me, but then I lock his eyes with mine.

That is when I finally let the word "yes" slip off my tongue like a confession when Carter asks me if I want Ethan.

The sound that Carter makes at that moment is primal and the biggest reassurance of the entire interaction.

He gently pushes me toward Ethan. "Then go, princess. I'll be waiting for you," are the last words Carter speaks, and I never thought my man pushing me toward someone else could turn me on so much.

I think about looking back at Carter, but I worry that if I do,

I will lose my nerve. I walk straight to Ethan. I don't drop my gaze from his, and I watch his Adam's apple bob as I get closer to him. His eyes track mine as I move, and he doesn't look past me to Carter, either.

When I get close enough to touch him, I do. Grazing the fingers of my left hand along the inside of his left arm, from his bicep all the way to his wrist, and then I drag my fingers along the palm of his hand. His sharp inhale tells me what his lack of movement doesn't.

"Alexis." His voice is raspy, somewhere between a warning and a plea.

"Ethan," I reply, matching his raspiness but adding a seductive tone to mine.

My eyes drift from his eyes to his mouth and back, and then I lick my lips and bite my bottom lip. His eyes track it all.

When his eyes meet mine again, in a breathy whisper, I make my intentions crystal clear, "I think you should take me to your room."

Ethan's eyes widen as fire flashes in them, his jaw falls slack, and his features freeze. As the shock dissipates, his eyes trail down my scantily dressed body, and he nods. Strong hands find my waist and he turns me, guiding me. Confusion washes over me when he steers me out to the patio.

"Ethan, where are we going?" I whisper to him with a soft laugh.

An arm around my waist, pulling me closer to him, he whispers, "We're going the back way."

Ethan drops his hand to my arm and smiles and nods at a few people as we cross the outdoor kitchen, but then we fall into an area of the patio that isn't lit by the floodlights and turn a corner. There are stairs that lead to the balcony attached to his bedroom around the side of the house. I don't remember that from his tour, but as we climb the stairs, my steps just barely ahead of his, my anticipation grows.

Electricity courses through me like one of those static plasma lamps I played with in middle school. Everything that touches me —Ethan's guiding hand, the wind, my own hair—everything sends static and electricity through me.

Ethan opens the door from his balcony to his bedroom, letting me enter first. As soon as he closes it behind him, he cages me against it. All he gives me right away are his words. He doesn't touch me or kiss me; he just talks in a way that feels like he is pouring his heart out.

"Alexis," he breathes. "I need to know this is what *you* want, and it's not something you're doing because Carter asked you to or told you to. Is this something *you* want?"

I grab handfuls of his T-shirt over his ribs and pull him toward me.

"Ethan, I want *you*," I say confidently, trying to give him all the reassurance I can.

His eyes light up, the back of his fingers trail from my cheekbone to my jaw, and he brushes my hair behind my neck.

"Ethan?" I ask hesitantly.

"Yes, love?"

"Did you and Carter talk about this?" The visible movement of his swallow is an answer in itself.

"We did," Ethan replies, gliding his fingers back down across my jaw.

Now, it's my turn to swallow and hedge, "Is this just a one-time thing?"

My eyes involuntarily close as the pad of his thumb gently grazes over my lower lip. When they open again, his gaze is locked on mine.

"Lexi, love, I don't want it to be, but that is entirely up to you." His nerves betray him as he inhales deeply through his nose and then audibly exhales through his mouth. "But if you know you just want this to be a one-time thing, I'd rather know now."

It's devastating for me to think we'd connect like this and go back to how we were ten minutes ago—it's heartbreaking to even consider it. The flurry in my mind causes me to act. Reaching up to cradle his jaw, I run my thumb over his soft facial hair.

Meeting his chocolate-brown eyes, I effortlessly say with all the sincerity and desire I can put in my voice, "Ethan, I absolutely and undeniably do *not* want this to be a one-time thing."

25

ETHAN

The emotions that rush through me surprise me, but elation is among them. I don't think I knew how much I wanted to hear those words until they came off her tongue.

"Lexi, you have no clue how happy that makes me," I profess, and then I take a minute to look her up and down, appreciating the way she's dressed again. "Also, you look so adorably sexy tonight; I *almost* don't want to undress you."

"*Adorably* sexy?" she teases.

"Yes, which is better than just sexy," I clarify. "It's a fun kind of sexy," I laugh.

And she is. Her outfit is playful and adorable, a little schoolgirl, and way too sexy.

"I should probably make you sign some kind of waiver so you don't get mad at me over the amount of glitter you're going to be finding in your bed for the next week," Lexi teases.

"I think I'll live," I reply with a laugh, and then my fingers find their way to the back of her neck, tangling lightly in her hair.

I've thought about this moment, dreamed about it, and I almost don't believe I'm here. I gently pull her face toward me, leaving gentle kisses on her forehead, along her browline to her temple, and then down her cheekbone. Then I gently kiss the corner of her mouth. Her breathing is already ragged, and I've barely touched her. I'm a little intrigued by the amount of assurance and encouragement that gives me.

Pausing, I let Lexi's sweet scent invade my senses before I lightly press my lips to hers once, twice, and a third time, looking into her beautiful blue eyes between each one. On the fourth, I part her lips with my tongue and kiss her sensually and deeply.

I get lost in the kiss, in our tongues exploring one another, the intoxicating effect it has on me, and the chemical reaction it sets off in my body.

One of her hands finds its way to my back, her nails digging into my skin through my shirt, while the other anchors on the nape of my neck, playing with my hair.

Stepping toward me, she closes the little bit of distance left between us. Pulling her around the waist, my hand finding purchase on the bare skin of her lower back, I bring her almost impossibly closer. Flush against me, her soft body forms to mine, and it feels like perfection like she was made to fit in my arms flawlessly.

Pulling on the hem of my shirt, her hands start searching for bare skin. I break the kiss and pull my shirt off with one hand because I want her hands on my skin. I *need* her hands on my skin.

"I'm not even sure how to take all this off you," I joke while my hands gesture to her body.

The corners of her lips turn up just slightly, and then she keeps her eyes on mine while she unzips her skirt and lets it fall to the ground, leaving her in just a black lace thong and garter belt attached to those fishnet stockings.

Fuck me.

Placing my hands on her hips, I watch, fully enraptured as she draws her arms across her body, grabbing the sides of her shirt and pulling that off easily, too, leaving her in only a black lacy bralette. This gorgeous woman is now standing in front of me wearing only black lace and fishnet—and glitter; I can't ignore the glitter—she is beyond irresistible. She's a symphony of beauty, inside and out, each note pulling me into the harmony of her irresistible allure.

My eyes are drawn to the black scrolling script of the tattoos below her breasts. I knew she had ink on her body, and now I know where two of them are, although they're still slightly hidden by the bralette.

Splaying her hands on my abs, she runs them up my chest, across my shoulders, and down my biceps, leaving heat and static in the shadow of the path behind them. Leaning up, she kisses me again, and as she kicks off her heels, her height drops, bringing a soft laugh out of me.

Wrapping my arms around her waist, I pick her up gently. Her legs wrap around me like we've done this hundreds of times, and fuck, I hope it turns into hundreds of times. As she rolls her hips into me, grinding on me, I know she feels how stiff and turned on I am, her rolling and grinding making me even harder.

Fuck, this woman.

Turning, I carry her toward the bed, laying her down gently. I kiss her softly before I reluctantly leave her for a moment to lock the door.

"Just in case," I whisper when I return to her, as her eyes follow me back across the room. Her bottom lip is captured under her teeth in a way that I read as more seductive than it is probably meant to be.

"Ethan, you and Carter, did you talk about protection?" she asks.

"We did," I answer her. "I'm good, if you're good."

"I'm good," she agrees with a nod.

I drop my jeans before I move to cover her body with mine, kissing her deeply again. Her hands are hungry and needy, finding purchase on my arms, my back, my chest, wherever she can reach. At this point, I already have no doubt of how much she wants me, but those needy hands speak words her mouth never could.

Eventually, almost reluctantly, I break away from her soft lips, and my mouth trails down her jaw and then her neck. As I trail lower, I pull up her bralette, and she pulls it off over her head, revealing amazing tits. I knew they were amazing clothed, even barely clothed, as I've seen them so many times, but bare they are so much more so.

Trailing kisses over her soft, salty, glitter-covered flesh, I eventually take each of her rosy, hard peaks into my mouth, sucking them and working them with my tongue while she writhes underneath me.

And, fuck, I love how reactive and responsive she is. As her skin shivers at every slight movement and caress, it's a harmony of sensations that seem to orchestrate a dance of nerves beneath the surface. Each touch of my fingers is like a whispered sonnet, igniting dormant senses and awakening the unfulfilled longing in her soul.

Fingers wind in my hair as I move lower on her body, my tongue finding and playing with her pierced belly button, then trailing down to the elastic on her garter belt.

Her want and impatience win out as she pulls each of her thighs up, unclipping the garter from the fishnet. Reaching behind her, she unclasps the garter belt and tosses it to the side.

I trail kisses down to the top of her thong. I cross over her center and move down to her thigh. Rolling down one of her stockings, I dot kisses along her newly bare skin, following my hands down the length of her leg. When I pull the first one off her foot, I do the same with the other one, and I find myself immensely grateful I have the privilege of undressing her tonight, of all nights.

Once I've successfully removed both stockings, I trail kisses back up one of her legs. When I get to the lace of her thong, I hook my fingers on each hip and pull it off quickly. There is more ink that I will fully explore later, but I am not pausing to explore it now.

Flattening my hands over her thighs, I sweep them up over her hips and then the ladders of her ribs as my mouth follows, and I meet her lips with mine again.

Breaking the kiss, I look into her eyes and graze my thumb over her lips. "You're beautiful, Alexis." I kiss her softly. "Even if you do cover me and my bed in glitter." I smile, and she laughs a musical laugh.

One of my hands travels back down her body, grazing the inside of her thigh before I slide my fingers into her wet folds. Her hips arch into me, and I groan at how wet she is.

"Fuck, Lexi," I whisper against her lips as I dip two fingers inside the warm wetness of her.

She gasps and then arches into me as I find the sweet spot inside her. My name comes off her lips like a curse, and it's sweeter than all the fantasies I've had of her; I think I might lose my goddamn mind.

I kiss her deeply as my fingers work inside her, my thumb finding her clit. She shamelessly grinds against my hand while I continue working her body like a finely tuned instrument.

Her head tilts back, and she stills for a few seconds before I feel her convulse around my fingers; her body shakes under me. Watching Lexi come is so fucking hot. I don't know how she can make that experience hotter and surpass any other time, any other woman, but she does. Her body literally vibrates under me as the convulsions and throbbing inside her stop.

I quickly trail my mouth back down her body, leaving my fingers inside her. I use my other hand to spread her open, finding her clit with my mouth. My tongue circles it while my fingers work inside her. She starts grinding into me again, and I suck her clit into my mouth. She lets out a high-pitched moan, and I don't change anything I am doing until I feel her convulse around and under me again.

I pull my fingers from her and trail them up her body. As I graze them over her lips, she brings them into her tongue and sucks them clean before I cover her mouth with mine again.

Fuck me, she's perfect.

Her fingers slide into the waistband of my boxer briefs and starts to push them down. I oblige her and pull them off my feet. As soon as I am back in her reach, her fingers wrap around my shaft, pulling an involuntary gasp from me.

She glides from the root to the tip and then grazes her thumb over the head, and I let out a soft growl. My mouth lands on her neck, biting her gently. She pushes on my chest and rotates her hips, signaling me to roll over, and I happily oblige.

Once I'm on my back, she straddles me. She grinds on my dick outside the wet heat of her folds, along her clit. She is unabashedly using me for her own pleasure, and I don't fucking mind at all.

My hands are mostly on her hips, finding purchase on her perfect tits at times. As she comes again over the top of me, I feel her wetness coat me, and I am done; I need inside her now.

Her eyes widen in surprise as I wrap my arms around her waist and flip her. Settling between her thighs, I tease her entrance by hovering outside of it for just a moment; her hips tilt up into me, trying to pull me closer, and I thrust inside of her, inside her perfect pussy.

Lexi's legs wrap around me as she tilts her hips up more, letting me drive into her deeper. She's so tight and so wet, and she does feel like the heaven I imagined. She shifts her hips just slightly, and her breathing and moaning become less controlled.

"Fuck, you feel so good, Ethan," she moans, and then her nails dig into my shoulder while her other hand grips the sheets.

She stills for that few seconds I already recognize as a sign she's about to come undone, and then she does. She throbs around me, and I bury my face in her tits while she arches her back as the shockwaves wreck her body.

When her body has calmed, she lets out a raspy murmur, "Ethan." Her hand finds my jaw, getting me to look at her. "I want to taste you."

I cover her mouth with mine and roll us over moments later so Lexi is straddling me again. She leans over and kisses me, then trails kisses down my chest and my abs, and then takes my head in her mouth.

Fuck, her perfect fucking mouth.

Her lips, tongue, and hand work together in perfect harmony with each other and me. I know she can taste herself on me, and that is hot, too. I hold her hair out of the way and watch as she takes my full length to the back of her throat, and it's so fucking erotic, I'm ready to climax already.

Holding out, I enjoy her a while longer, her hands twisting on my shaft and cupping my balls, working in perfect tandem with her mouth. As I finish, she swallows, and she makes sure I am completely clean before she lets me fall from her mouth. Gently, I pull her hair, bringing her up to my mouth and kissing her deeply.

In the solace of the blissful aftermath, I just hold her for a while. I am in a state of both awe and disbelief, and I am so grateful.

We can still hear the music from downstairs, along with the sounds of revelry.

Eventually, I kiss the top of Lexi's head and say, "I hate to say it, love, but we—or at least I—should probably go back downstairs." I look at the clock on my nightstand. "People will probably be here for another few hours and, well, it *is* my house," I laugh.

Propping herself up on her elbows, she kisses me gently, her hand running over my beard. "Okay, I'm going to sneak to my room and try to make myself look like I haven't just been doing exactly what I've been doing," she laughs.

"You look beautiful," I breathe, smoothing her hair.

Lexi steals a shirt from me in case someone is in the upstairs hall, gathers all her clothes, and kisses me.

"I'll go back the way we came," I say. "You should be fine going back down the stairs when you're ready."

Right before I open the door for her, she leans up on her toes and kisses me one last time, and I let her slip out into the empty hall. The music and party noise echo from downstairs, grounding me back in reality.

I can already tell it's going to be tough to wipe this grin off my face. Taking that step with her has left me feeling over the moon. I'm happier and a lot less anxious.

After getting dressed again, I look in the mirror, making sure I don't look too disheveled or have too much glitter on me. When I make my way back downstairs, I make a point of socializing with people on the patio before making my way inside. It feels like I'm establishing an alibi, and I can't wait until we don't have to even think about hiding this.

26

ALEXIS

I call Georgia and put her on speakerphone in the bathroom while I'm putting myself back together.

"ALEXIS BRANTHWAITE," she screams. "Are you in a throuple now?"

"I don't know, Georgia," I laugh. "I'm in something, and everyone is okay with it."

"Are you happy?" Georgia asks.

"Perfectly and incandescently." I smile.

She shrieks a little. "Okay, I need to go take more shots now, but you better call me tomorrow," she giggles.

"I will," I promise and then we say goodbye.

It takes me about twenty minutes in my room to get myself put back together—garter belt, eyeliner, glitter, and all. The hardest part is my hair; pulling all the extensions out, combing them, brushing my hair, and then putting them back in took me more than half the time I used.

By the time I'm done, I look almost the same as when I left. I slip my heels back on and head downstairs.

Jeremiah sees me on the stairs and asks if I escaped for a few minutes. I tell him I just wanted to refresh my makeup and hair.

My mission is to find Carter, and it doesn't take long to spot him playing the role of bartender in the kitchen. Leaning against the corner of the wall that separates the kitchen from the living room, where he stood with his arms around me not that long ago, I simply watch him. I'm captivated by his outgoing, social demeanor, waiting for him to notice me.

Observing him in this element, I'm reminded of his sales persona —charming, flirtatious, and effortlessly charismatic. But beneath this surface lies a depth of emotion and complexity that few get to see. His love for his daughter, the scars left by past relationships and familial conflicts—he keeps these parts of himself hidden, reserving them for moments of intimacy and vulnerability.

As he hands off a red plastic cup to someone, his gaze meets mine, and I feel the heat emanating from him. Moving towards me, he closes the distance incredibly quickly, his hand finding its place behind my neck as he claims my lips in a possessive, hungry kiss. It's a public reclaiming, a silent reassurance that quiets the lingering doubts within me that this was some kind of test of loyalty.

Before releasing me, he presses a soft kiss to my forehead, his eyes finding mine as he asks, "You good?"

There's so much meaning in those two simple words. Cradling his face in my hand, I offer a reassuring smile.

"Yeah, Carter, I'm good," I reply before shifting the conversation to the chaos of the party.

He chuckles, the sound warm and familiar. "Drunken madness," he echoes, gesturing to the dwindling liquor supply. "I need to restock, wanna help?"

"Sure," I agree, stepping forward to assist him as we take inventory of the bottles scattered across the counter.

As we're finishing the restock, I hear Carrie's high-pitched, very inebriated voice. "Alexis, there you are; I've been looking for you."

"Hey, Carrie." I smile at her.

Now, *she* looks like she has been thoroughly fucked and well-used. Her hair is crazily disheveled, her mascara and eyeliner are smeared, and her clothes are cattywampus.

"I'm obviously not driving tonight," she declares, sloshing her drink in her cup and slurring her words.

"I hope not," I tease.

"*Anyway,*" she says like a little girl saying, "Pretty please!" And then she continues, "Jeremiah is mad at me. Can I stay with you?"

My eyes flash to Carter's for just a second, and I deflect before answering.

"Why is Jeremiah mad at you?" I laugh.

"I don't remember, honestly." She shrugs.

"Well, how about if you go find out and see if you can fix it, but if not, you can stay in one of the guest rooms, I'm sure."

"Okay," she says and then she sways a little before she walks away.

Carter wraps his arms around my waist from behind me and whispers, "If I never told you that I'm glad you can hold your liquor before, I'm saying it now." He softly chuckles against my neck.

"Am I not that annoying when I'm drunk?" I tease.

"No, fortunately or unfortunately, you're a pretty serious drunk." He laughs again and then kisses my neck.

Carter releases me just as Ethan turns the corner. There is an awkward moment where we all just look at each other, but it's fleeting.

Ethan addresses Carter to discuss the logistics of people who don't want to leave and have claimed guest rooms, those who do but can't drive, and the cars that will be left on the street by the number of people using rideshare services to get home.

"Can you tell Jeremiah to make up with his girlfriend?" I look at Ethan and jest, "Because she is under the impression she can't sleep in his room, and I don't want her to end up in mine," I laugh.

Ethan sighs, "I'll find out what's happening."

With one last glance at Carter, Ethan starts walking away to talk to Jeremiah. But as he crosses behind me, he runs his hand across my lower back, leaning into my ear to whisper, "I'm relatively certain your bed is going to be vacant tonight anyway, and if you're not in Carter's, you are more than welcome to add more glitter to mine." Then he drops his hand and walks away.

I feel the blush and heat in my cheeks from both his words and his breath on my neck. My gaze meets Carter's, and he laughs softly.

"You look cute, all flushed and turned on like that." He winks at me, and I grab an empty plastic cup and throw it at him.

Laughing again, he shares, "I definitely wasn't saying it's a bad thing."

Carter moves around the island, puts his hands on my waist, and gently kisses my forehead. I thread my arms under his and hug him around the waist, my head resting against his chest. I smell his licorice-esque cologne and listen to his heartbeat.

He kisses the top of my head and asks, "You sure you're okay?"

I push my fingers into his back reassuringly and say, "Yeah, I'm sure. A little tired, and we'll need to talk about all this, but not tonight."

"We do, I agree," he confirms. "Probably all three of us, and I hope you're not *too* tired."

I lean back and gently kiss him before assuring him, "I'm looking forward to this so-called reclaiming, so no, I'm not *too* tired."

He tilts his head, narrows his eyes, and opens his mouth to say something but then snaps it shut when he sees someone behind me and lifts his chin in acknowledgment.

I turn and look to find Jeremiah. His eyes are focused on Carter, though.

"Hey, man, can we talk for a minute?" Jeremiah asks Carter.

Carter steals a glance at me before answering, "Yeah, I guess."

Jeremiah gestures to the back door, taking Carter out onto the patio.

Ethan finds me just after they walk away, his hand on my back he leans into me to whisper in my ear.

"Did Jeremiah tell you what that's about?" Ethan inquires.

"Uh, no, he just wanted Carter," I answer, turning toward Ethan and locking eyes with him long enough to be turned on again.

Ethan cages me against the island for just a minute while he talks to me about Jeremiah and Carrie.

Leaning into me, his voice is a mere whisper next to my ear as he lets me in on the secret. "Jeremiah and Carrie fought because Carrie wanted him to try to arrange a threesome—with you."

My jaw drops, and my eyes meet Ethan's. His eyes spark a little with fire, but I roll mine, and he laughs.

"What, love?" Ethan teases. "You don't want in on that one?"

"With Carrie?" I question. "I don't think so."

"Interesting how you said Carrie but not Jeremiah." He winks.

I roll my eyes again and lightly smack his chest. "Ethan, no."

"I *want* your answer to be no, so that's okay. I'm just playing with you," he admits.

Carter and Jeremiah walk back into the kitchen as he finishes his words. He lifts one arm, uncaging me, as I turn toward the other two.

"You tell her?" Jeremiah laughs.

Ethan smiles and confirms, "Yeah, I told her."

I look at Jeremiah and smile. "No offense, but no."

188 ～ MAELANA NIGHTINGALE

He laughs but reaches up and twirls a tendril of my hair. "I wasn't going to ask, siren, which is why she is mad."

I feel the electric current from the small pull on my hair as his fingers twist the tendril, but then he drops his hand. Maybe everything that already happened tonight has my body on edge, but that current went straight down my spine to the apex of my thighs.

I slowly but instinctively back up into Ethan before I look at Jeremiah again. "You going to let her stay in your room, or is she going to need mine?" I laugh.

"She's not staying with me, siren." He pauses and looks up at Ethan. "Are all the other rooms taken?"

"Yeah, completely spoken for," Ethan answers, his fingers lightly tracing random patterns on the bare skin of my back between my shirt and my skirt, sending more electricity through my body.

Jeremiah looks back at me. "So, it's either your room, or I can try to make her take a rideshare," he shrugs.

I roll my eyes and concede, "Fine, but if she pukes in my room, I am *not* cleaning it up."

All three of them laugh before I add, "I can get what I need out of there, so she can crash whenever." I start walking toward the stairs but turn and look over my shoulder, catching all three of them watching me walk away. Only partly teasing, I continue, "Which should probably be sooner rather than later, or you might have to carry her."

Jeremiah smirks before I turn back toward the stairs.

27

ALEXIS

I don't know how long Carrie will be in my room, and knowing I'll need to shower off my glitter soon, I quickly gather my shower essentials along with clothes for tonight and tomorrow. With my arms laden, I make my way to Carter's room to drop things off.

Returning to the hallway, I spot Holden emerging from his room, realizing that I haven't crossed paths with him much tonight.

"Hey," I greet him. "You okay?"

Holden is surprised to see me but says, "Yeah, just a little crazy down there." He laughs softly, "I needed a minute or two of quiet."

I laugh, stopping in front of his door. "I understand that. I haven't seen you much tonight."

He shrugs. "I've been a bit of a wallflower. You look cute tonight; I'm sure you know that, though."

"Thank you." I smile. "St. Patrick's Day has always been a big deal for my family."

"You don't talk much about them," Holden observes as we start walking toward the staircase.

"Black sheep." I shrug and smile. "We're not really fans of each other. They would *love* you though."

He laughs, "Just because I went to medical school?"

"Pretty much," I answer, nudging him with my elbow.

As we descend the stairs together, it dawns on me that this is precisely the scenario Ethan had hoped to prevent, yet here I am, unwittingly portraying it with Holden.

Despite the lack of reaction from anyone around us, I can't shake the thought of how it might be perceived. I remind myself that we both live here, irrespective of our relationship status. Walking down a staircase together shouldn't feel taboo or wrong—it's simply a natural part of sharing a living space.

Carrie runs up to me at the bottom of the stairs. I cast a sideways glance at Holden, and he holds his hands up in a move that clearly says, "She's your problem, not mine," before he walks away.

"Alexith," Carrie slurs, "can I go tchu your room now?"

I laugh and nod my head. "Yeah, Carrie, you're good; just try to make it to the toilet when you puke."

"Thank you," she exclaims, her voice way too high-pitched.

I turn and watch her move up the stairs, and when I turn back, Shawn is standing next to me.

"Hey, you," I greet him. "Haven't seen you hardly all night."

"I've been around." He shrugs and gestures to Carrie. "That looks like fun."

I roll my eyes. "Jeremiah owes me."

"I'm sure he'll find a way to repay you," Shawn replies with all kinds of sexual overtone, the expression on his face matching his tone.

"Hey, now," I tease and nudge him with my shoulder.

"Well, you're the one that came dressed like that," Shawn jokes.

"Are you victim-blaming, Mr. Whittier?" I laugh.

"Never, Allie, but thinking about it and acting on it are two different things." He smiles and winks, and those sexy dimples come out.

I shake my head and smile at Shawn before he says, "I think Carter was looking for you to help him restock again."

I sigh, "So much alcohol."

Shawn nods in agreement, and I find my way to the kitchen.

"Hey," I say, sliding next to Carter by the island. "Shawn said you needed my help."

"Hey, beautiful. You get everything you need?"

"I did. You might think I'm trying to move in, though, but I wasn't sure how long she'd be in my room." I shrug.

"I'd probably be okay with you moving in, which is weird since we already live together," he jokes. "And yeah, you want to get rid of my empties for me? I'll grab the other bottles."

"I can do that," I say, scanning the island for empty or almost-empty bottles.

I make my way out to the garage, carrying what I can to the almost full recycling bin, and I find solace for a few extra moments in the cool, quiet space. It feels like a refuge from the chaos of the house.

As I reenter the house, I'm taken aback when I nearly collide with Holden, who's emerging from the basement hand-in-hand with a girl I don't recognize. He shuts the basement door behind them, and our eyes meet briefly. He couldn't have been down there long; I was talking to him fifteen minutes ago. The girl, clearly intoxicated, sports jeans and a "Kiss Me, I'm Not Irish" T-shirt, her disheveled chocolate brown hair and flushed cheeks betraying her state.

"Sorry," Holden apologizes and then moves out of my way.

As they're walking away, the unknown girl asks, "Who's she?"

"Don't worry about it," Holden answers and glances back at me one more time.

* * *

I'm so grateful when the party is deemed to be over, and Carter and I get to make our way upstairs.

Locking the bedroom door behind us, Carter moves quickly. With one hand on my stomach, he pushes me gently toward the bed. I feel the bedding with my calves first, and he pushes my back onto the bed.

"I think I want you to stay in the outfit," Carter teases as his fingers slide up under my skirt and between my thighs.

"Yeah?" I tease back.

"At least to start," he confirms with a seductive laugh. "I can get to half of what I want to without you taking off a single thing."

As if to prove his point, he moves my thong to the side and plunges two fingers inside of me. I gasp, making a high-pitched noise; Carter laughs and then covers my mouth with his.

Positioning his thumb to massage my clit, he moves with the expertise of a skilled painter moving their brush across a canvas. I feel the coil tightening in my core, my body on the very edge of release, and he stills.

"Carter," I whimper.

His mouth moves to my neck below my ear, and he growls his question, "How many times did he make you come?"

"Carter," I warn.

"Answer me, Lex," he demands and then kisses my neck.

I swallow and then whisper, "Four."

"Fuck, princess, how needy you must be to still want more," he teases lasciviously.

His fingers move again, pushing me right to the edge of release and then stopping again.

"Carter, please," I whisper, my voice raspy, his mouth on my neck again.

Wickedness coats his tone. "Are you begging, Lex?"

I match his wicked tone. "Do you want me to beg?"

"Do you want to come?" he counters.

"Carter." My voice is now a pure warning.

"One more question, then I will make you come so hard and so many times you won't even know what month it is," he growls.

The only response I give him is the grip of my nails on his arm.

"So aggressive, princess. Did he come inside you?" Carter asks, his tongue running down the soft part of my throat to my collarbone, then lifts his face to look at me, raising his eyebrows in a question.

"No," I answer, and then his mouth covers mine again, aggressively and passionately.

He then does exactly what he promised. Carter, with his expert fingers and mouth, drives me over the cliff to climax so many times I lose count.

After I am trembling and weak, he deftly and expertly unclips the garter from my stockings and rolls them down very similarly to what Ethan did earlier, his mouth trailing behind his skilled fingers. Carter strips me quickly and completely and then looks at me reverently before the corner of his mouth twitches up.

"That is *a lot* of glitter," he laughs.

"I know." My voice is barely a whisper. "I told Ethan I should have made him sign a waiver for the bed covered in glitter."

Carter laughs, kisses me, and then bites my lower lip before rocking my body with so much more pleasure and countless orgasms. I think I do forget what month it is. By the time I curl into his arms to sleep, I feel sated, lightheaded, and boneless.

When he insinuated the savageness of a reclaiming, he wasn't misleading me. As I'm drifting off to sleep, I decide that I am a fan of being reclaimed.

28

CARTER

I feel Lex stir in my arms before she slides out of the bed to use the restroom. Sunshine floods the room; I rub the sleep from my eyes with tired fingers before stretching and sitting up in bed.

"Hey, beautiful," I yawn as she finds her way back to my bed, still naked.

Snuggling up to me, she murmurs, "Good morning," her head resting on my shoulder and her hand tracing the ink on my chest, sending warm sensations straight to my spine and stiffening my cock.

I roll over her, covering her body with mine, and kiss her deeply.

"Last night not enough for you?" Lex snickers.

"Not even close, princess. Was it too much for you?" I counter.

"No, it was perfect, and I'm sure this will be, too." Her hand finds my nape, and she pulls my lips back to hers.

My hand travels down her body, grazing her perfect tits, sliding over her hip, and then moving to her perfect cunt, wet and waiting.

"Fuck, princess, you're so wet," I whisper against her lips.

"Well, that's what happens when you kiss me, Carter," she asserts with a soft smile.

I chuckle quietly and kiss her more. My fingers push inside her, hooking up in the come hither motion that makes her come, and my thumb finds her clit. I continue to fuck her mouth with my tongue while my fingers work her perfect cunt, and when she tries to break the kiss when she comes, I don't let her. I feel her moans on my lips and the vibration through my core.

Immediately I settle between her legs and get ready to replace my fingers with my cock. I pull off her lips, dragging her bottom lip with my teeth as I thrust inside her. The sound she makes is so erotic it turns me on so much more than I already am.

"This is gonna be a quick one, Lex," I softly laugh.

"I finished, so that's fine," she jokes back. Her breathing is ragged, and the fingernails digging into my arms tell me she wants me.

I drive into her hard until I fall over the edge and then kiss her lips gently before pulling her back into the crook of my arm.

We lie there for a few minutes when she looks up at me. "Carter?"

"Yeah, princess?"

"I think we need to talk," she proposes and wrinkles her nose.

"I agree. I think all three of us need to talk," I surmise and kiss her on the top of the head.

"How do you know that's what I want to talk about?" Lex teases.

"Well, am I wrong?" I ask, grazing my thumb down her back.

"No, you're right," she confesses. "Ethan and I kind of talked. I know you two have talked, but yeah, we probably need to have a conversation."

"What did you and Ethan talk about?" I inquire, genuinely curious.

She lies back down, her head on my chest; I don't know if this is intentional, as she doesn't have to look at me in that position, or just more comfortable. I trace abstract patterns on her back, enjoying her silken skin while she continues.

"He asked me if it was something I wanted and not just something I was doing to make you happy," she starts. "I asked him if you and he had a conversation about it, and then I asked him if it was a one-time thing; he said that was up to me."

"You did want to, right? It wasn't something you just did for me?" I worry for a moment that maybe that could have been a component.

"No, yes," she laughs. "Yes to the first question, no to the second question. I did want to; it was hotter because you wanted me to."

I squeeze her closer to me.

"What did he tell you we talked about?"

She laughs again. "He didn't. I think his answer was literally just, 'We did.'"

"And I feel like I'm safe in assuming that if you want to have a talk with both of us, that you didn't want it to be a one-time thing?" I clarify, already confident of the answer.

"That would be correct," she says and picks her head back up to look at me. "I've never done anything like this before, Carter. I'm good with it, but I just want to make sure we're all on the same page."

"Lex, none of us have done anything like this before, princess," I console her and brush a tendril of her hair behind her ear. "Some of it will be trial and error, but I think the main thing we have to have is total honesty and really good communication."

"I have one more question, Carter," she says and wrinkles her nose.

"What's that?"

"How in the hell did you two even end up in that conversation?" Lex's laugh is pure after she asks; there's no judgment; she simply wants to know.

"Jeremiah," I snicker.

"Okay, that was definitely not the answer I was expecting, not that I know what I was expecting," she says, sitting up, pulling the sheet up with her for modesty, even though I have memorized every square millimeter of her body at this point.

I sigh and sit up a little more against the headboard. "That goes back to just after Chicago, actually the morning after Carrie's birthday party. We, Jeremiah, Ethan, Holden, and I, were in the kitchen, and Holden said something smart ass about me winning. Jeremiah suggested we could share. I don't know if he meant it as a joke or if he was serious, honestly, but it planted a seed for me anyway."

I give her a minute to digest that. "Wait," she starts and shakes her head, "that conversation started because of something *Holden* said?"

She would hone in on that. I explain further, "Yeah, he thought Jeremiah was fucking crazy."

"Okay," she says, a little confused. "So how did that lead to you and Ethan actually talking about it?"

I come to the quick conclusion that honesty is the only way to go here. "I ran into Ethan in the gym about a week ago; he was on the treadmill, and it was like he was running away from something. I've known him since we were in the second grade, so I can read him. I knew something was wrong. It took more than asking. I had to basically beg him to tell me what was wrong."

I take a few beats to study her face before I go on. "He finally told me that he just needed me to know I was a lucky son of a bitch and something *didn't* happen in the laundry room."

There is an immediate flash of recognition on her face, and then she starts blushing.

"Why are you blushing, princess?" I chuckle. "Do you know what I'm talking about? Because I don't even know what I'm talking about."

"Uh, yeah, and nothing did happen, but I think we both wanted something to," she says guiltily and looks down at her hands.

My first two knuckles find her chin and bring it back up so I can meet her eyes. "It's okay, Lex, that's why we're here."

She looks at me, swallows, and nods.

"Anyway, I told him I had been thinking about what Jeremiah said, and I thought he and I could make it work if it was something you wanted, too."

"Why didn't y'all just talk to me about it?" Lex asks.

"That's a fair question," I answer with a nod. "I could have been wrong, but I thought you would need a situation like the one last night to believe that I was really okay with it. You needed to know on an emotional and physical level that I was good, that we were good." I pause. "And, honestly, I thought maybe having the heat in a moment like that would help too."

Alexis shrugs, her smile betraying anything she is trying to hide. "Maybe. It was pretty hot," she admits.

Chortling a little, I continue, "It wasn't planned, Lex. I told Ethan it was going to take a perfect, well-timed moment to make it 'hot' as you say." I grin at her. "When I turned that corner and saw the way you were looking at each other, I took a chance."

"No regrets?" Lex questions.

"None," I declare, then correct, "Well, maybe one."

She raises her eyebrows and lifts one corner of her mouth, a silent question.

"That I wasn't the first one to take that cute little St. Patrick's Day outfit off of you." I laugh and she snorts and then giggles.

"No, princess, I have no regrets," I emphasize. "Do you?"

She's still giggling, but she shakes her head no.

"Okay, we should get cleaned up and then we'll find Ethan and we can all talk; sound good?"

Lex nods and I kiss her before I get out of bed to shower.

29

ALEXIS

"Well, this isn't awkward at all," I proclaim sarcastically as Ethan, Carter, and I stand at the bar of the outdoor kitchen to talk about our relationship—relationships—I don't even know.

Ethan and Carter are standing next to each other on one side of the bar, and I'm on the other. I don't think that was intentional, but at least they can't really touch me while we have this conversation.

Ethan laughs, "It isn't that awkward, Lexi. I think most anything we need to talk about comes down to you, anyway. You're the boss."

Carter looks at Ethan before he shrugs and nods in agreement.

"Okay," I say, not knowing exactly where to start this conversation. "First question, do you, either of you, have an expectation of complete openness, like other women, other men, whatever, or just contained to the three of us? Because that brings all kinds of safety issues—"

Carter puts his hand on top of mine and interrupts, "Lex, I'm going to stop you right there; that is a no. No other women." He looks at Ethan.

"No," Ethan agrees. "I can share you, but I don't want anyone else."

I'm not sure what exactly my face does at that point, but I really hope it's expressing how much I appreciate that. I also realize it's a little hypocritical.

"As for other men," Ethan says and looks at Carter, who nods at him. "I think that the other men that live here wouldn't be out of the question, but that would need to be a conversation. Otherwise, I think that's a no too."

I snort and laugh. "Okay, so I'm limited to the three other guys who live here, but I have to talk to you about it first?"

"Pretty much," Carter says, and I facepalm as he adds, "At least before you sleep with them. I mean, there might be a moment like whatever the fuck happened in the laundry room, and that's one thing, but going beyond that is different"

"What?" Ethan snickers a little as I shake my head.

"This is just such a new concept for me," I say, taking a deep breath and blowing it out.

"In all reality, Lexi," Ethan says, "that really only means Shawn. Holden, maybe someday, but I don't think he could share. I might be wrong, but I'm just not sure he could do it. And Jeremiah has Carrie, so there's that."

"No, I get it," I say. "No sex with other roomies without a conversation," I scoff. "And, honestly, I'm still trying to wrap my mind around two, so let's not talk about three, four, or five right now." I wrinkle my nose, and they both laugh.

"Well, we answered your question," Carter jests.

"I know, and honestly, my ADHD, the part that gets bored of repetitive things, not the part that fixates on things, is really happy about this." I shrug, and all three of us laugh.

"You think you'll like the variety, princess?" Carter teases.

I reply by rolling my eyes and blushing again, then look down at my hand tracing patterns in the bricks of the bar. "That all leads to my next question. What about telling them—Jeremiah, Holden, Shawn?"

They look at each other, and then Carter says, "I honestly don't know. I don't want to hide anything from them. I think Jeremiah will be fine, probably Shawn too, but Holden, that's another wild card, but if we hide it from him, it might be worse."

"Alright, I'm just going to let you all lead on that." I look at Ethan, directing my next words at him. "But I just don't want to feel uncomfortable touching you. They're all used to me touching Carter; I just don't want it to feel like a secret." I shrug.

Ethan smiles knowingly at me. "I get that, but honestly, love, we've been touching each other a lot for the last week, ever since Carter and I talked. I let down my guard, and you followed my lead."

I look between them, and Carter arches his eyebrows and laughs.

"I didn't even realize," I respond.

"Okay, final question, I think," I laugh uncomfortably. "What is your expectation about this on a logistical level?"

Neither of them says anything; Carter raises his eyebrows at me. "You're going to have to get a little more specific there, princess."

I feel the heat rising in my face.

"Lexi, there is literally nothing to be blushing about at this point," Ethan reassures me with a smirk, steepling his fingers in front of his mouth.

"Okay." I take another deep breath. "So logistical expectations." I clear my throat. "Separate, together, or both? Should there be a schedule or something, or just whatever happens happens?"

They look at each other before either of them answers me.

Carter starts, "The first question, that is really up to you. Thanks to the game you hate," he winks at me, "we all know that both you and I have done it before; Ethan hasn't, but it's up to you."

I look at Ethan, and he nods in agreement, "Yeah, it's completely up to you, love, but," he looks at Carter and then back at me, "I definitely want separate time to be part of the equation."

"I would too," I agree.

"As for a schedule," Carter laughs. "I don't think that's necessary. If it becomes some kind of issue, we can talk about it, but I think a lot of that is up to you, too. Including if you want to sleep in your room and want us both to leave you the fuck alone."

Ethan looks at Carter and then at me. "Completely agreed."

"That's all my questions," I say. "Thanks for coming to my TED talk, I guess," I quip and we all laugh. "What do you guys have?"

"Well, princess," Carter starts. "You didn't answer that question; the one you asked us. We threw it back in your court, but you didn't answer it."

"Which question?" I ask a little too coyly.

Ethan narrows his eyes, smiles, and shakes his head at me. It's sexy, and I want to reach across the counter and kiss him.

I swallow and look between them as I reply, "I'm good with a balance of together and separate. But always only if everyone is feeling it."

"Okay," Ethan says, and then he looks between the two of us before asking, "What about hard limits?"

"I only have three that I know of," I assert almost instantly. "No bathroom play, like golden showers and such." I shudder, and Carter laughs. "And, along those same lines, nothing else after anal, like whatever body part was there doesn't go anywhere else."

Ethan looks at Carter. "Did she just say, '*whatever* body part?'" His smile is salacious.

I feel the heat rise in my cheeks as Carter smiles and answers, "She did."

"That's still only like two body parts," I retort, shaking my head and laughing.

"What's number three?" Carter saves me with that.

"No spitting in my mouth." I wrinkle my nose, and they both laugh at that one, too.

"That's it? Those are your only hard limits?" Ethan asks.

"That I know of, yeah." I shrug.

"So," Carter begins and then pauses, looking at Ethan and then back to me, "that leaves a lot on the table."

"It does," I agree with a nod.

I see the heat in Carter's eyes, the hunger, and I can tell that this conversation has him all sorts of turned on.

"What about you two? What are your limits?" I question, because their feelings matter too.

Carter speaks first. "There is only one that I think is a possibility, and that's," he pauses, trying to think of the words, "I don't really want to go down on you after someone else has finished there, which is why I asked last night."

My eyes flash between them, and I clear my throat. "I figured, which is part of why—" my eyes flash to Ethan's, and I cut myself off, "I just figured."

"What about you?" I ask Ethan, who has a playful smirk on his face.

Ethan nods, "Same for me."

"Nothing else?" I ask them both.

They both shake their heads no.

"Not on limits. I do have something to add," Carter asserts. "It's crucial that all three of us are completely honest with each other. Lack of communication could be disastrous, so if any of us is upset about something or needs something that isn't happening, we just need to talk to each other."

Ethan nods at Carter and then looks at me. "Lexi, you need to know, and I know Carter feels the same way; the fact that we're doing it this way doesn't mean either of us doesn't care about you just as much as we would in a traditional relationship. We recognize that we each have an individual relationship with you, both with and without the physical aspect." As he finishes, he looks at Carter.

Carter picks up where he left off, "Exactly, it's way beyond just a physical relationship, and we both appreciate and acknowledge we each have that with you and that it will look differently for each of us."

He pauses and looks at Ethan before looking back at me. "That also means that if one of us is worried about you for some reason, we're going to talk to each other."

Ethan nods, "I'm not sure what those circumstances could be, but if you're hurt or struggling in any way, we'll coordinate to ensure we're on the same page. And we don't want to compete with each other in any way. We've made it clear to each other that viewing it that way would only lead to you getting hurt. Secondly, by considering both of our perspectives, we can probably provide better support for you."

"That's actually really sweet," I admit.

"And that's why if you want to bring anyone else into this, we need to have a conversation because they need to understand that too," Carter says, and Ethan nods.

"I know you both had a few days on me, but *apparently*, you thought and talked a lot about all of this," I say, looking at both of them.

"Neither of us takes this lightly," Ethan declares. "We both understand that not taking it seriously could be devastating to all three of us."

I swallow and nod. We all stand there for a little while, none of us saying anything, when Carter breaks the silence.

"Okay, that was enough of the heavy for right now," he states. "Unless either of you has anything else."

"I don't," I respond.

"I'm good," Ethan agrees.

When we walk back into the house, Jeremiah and Holden are at the dining room table eating lunch.

"What were you three doing out there in the cold?" Jeremiah teases.

"Talking." Ethan smiles. "Do you have a minute, Jer?"

"I do," he answers. He looks between the other three of us and then back at Ethan. "Do you need me in private?"

"Carter and I do, yeah," Ethan answers, and they make their way back outside with Jeremiah.

I sit down at the table across from Holden. "How are you?" I ask.

"Tired, but okay." He smiles.

"Yeah, it was a late night." I narrow my eyes at him before asking, "Who was the girl?"

Holden sighs and shakes his head. "She was stress relief; that's all it was, Alexis."

"That surprises me from you," I rib a little.

"It maybe shouldn't," he warns. "I don't even know her last name; I'm not positive I remember her first name."

"You say that like you're proud of it," I contend, probably a little too much judgment in my tone.

"Not so much proud as factual," he compromises.

I decide not to push the subject any further. Instead I ask, "When do you go back to the hospital?"

"Tomorrow night," he offers. "For three days, seventy-two hours though, so not as long as usual."

"That's good," I hedge a little. "I was wondering—I'm sure people ask you all the time, but I've never asked—why you wanted to go into medicine."

Holden smiles softly at me, a nice change from the contention of the last subject. "People do ask me a lot. But my mom is chronically ill. She is on disability and can't work. My dad did a lot to try to help take things off her plate, but I always just wanted to fix it, you know?"

I nod, "I do know."

"I know I can't fix everything, but I want to be able to fix what I can." He shrugs.

"Did you always want to be an intensivist, to work in the intensive care unit?"

Holden laughs, "No, actually. When I first started, I wanted to be a rheumatologist, but when I got into intensive care, I liked it. It feeds my adrenaline junkie side, without being quite as crazy as emergency medicine."

I nod at him, reassurance that I understand. "Also, in emergency medicine, you get ear infections and strep throat; in the ICU, everyone is either really sick or really hurt." He shrugs.

I clear my throat. "It's honestly really noble work, Holden, if nobody has told you that. I don't think I could do it; it's part of why I didn't stick with the family tradition of going into healthcare."

"I think you could," he argues. "You're so empathetic, I think you'd be great in healthcare."

"That's the problem; I'd internalize all of it. I don't think I could successfully compartmentalize, especially somewhere like the ICU where you fight so hard to save people and still lose them." I shrug. "It takes someone special, Holden. Don't undervalue yourself. I've seen ICU doctors and nurses cry when I watched someone I cared about be pulled off life support; I know it's not easy."

"It's not easy; there are rewarding moments when we discharge someone we didn't think would make it." He studies me for a moment. "I feel like you've been through a lot more than any of us know about."

I offer him a soft smile and shrug. "Someday, you all can hear the tragedies that were my prologue to this part of my life."

Just then, the sound of Jeremiah, Carter, and Ethan's hearty laughter drifts in from the patio, echoing through the room with such intensity that it's hard to miss. They have to be laughing really loud to hear it in here.

"Do you know what that's about?" Holden asks, pointing at the back door with his fork.

"I could guess, but I don't know, no," I answer.

He shrugs. "It's not that unusual for the three of them to have a secret of some kind, just curious."

"They can be troublemakers, that's for sure," I laugh, looking back out the door.

As I turn back and our gazes lock once more, I'm captivated by the sudden fire burning in Holden's eyes, a palpable longing radiating from him. The surge of chemistry that courses through me in response is undeniable, a potent cocktail of emotions that leaves me reeling. Involuntarily, I bite my bottom lip.

Moments like these remind me of our undeniable connection, catching me off guard with its intensity. I feel a flush creeping up from my chest to my cheeks, but Holden shows no signs of looking away. Our silent exchange is charged with unspoken desire, each second stretching with tense anticipation.

Suddenly, the back door slides open, and Holden's attention shifts abruptly above my head as if the spell that enveloped us has been broken by the return of the other men. At that moment, the magnetic pull seems to dissipate with the sudden intrusion of reality.

I stand and look around at all four of them before settling on Jeremiah. "Do you know if Carrie is gone?"

"Gone from your room? Yes. Gone from the house? No." He looks a little sheepish.

"Can I use my own bedroom?" I ask, narrowing my eyes.

"You should be able to, yes," Jeremiah answers.

"I think I'm going to go take a shower and see if I can get the rest of this glitter off of me," I laugh.

"As cute as it was, glitter is a pain in the ass," Carter teases.

"Oh, I know," I joke back, looking between Carter and Ethan.

30

ALEXIS

I practically jump out of my skin as I step out of my bathroom, clad in only a towel, only to find Carter and Ethan lounging in my room, both dressed casually in the jeans and T-shirts they were wearing before. My surprise is magnified by the fact that I'm relatively sure I locked my door.

"Um, hi," I say after I gain some composure.

Neither of them says anything right away.

Ethan moves behind me, his arm enveloping my waist as he leans in close. His voice drops to a low whisper in my ear. "Since you covered both of our beds in glitter, we figured we could use yours."

The sensation of Ethan's breath tickling my neck sends a surge of electricity dancing through me, igniting a fiery sensation that travels straight to the core of my being. With Carter now standing just a foot in front of me, the intensity of the moment is palpable, stirring a potent desire that tingles at the very apex of my thighs. I feel my pussy vibrate in anticipation.

"Yeah?" I ask breathily.

"Unless you want us to leave." Carter smirks.

"I don't want you to leave," I rasp, dropping my head back against Ethan's shoulder.

Ethan pulls me tighter against him, leaving no doubt about his arousal as his stiff cock presses into my tailbone. Carter steps forward, swiftly closing the distance between us, sliding his hands inside my towel and pulling the edges apart. Ethan moves just long enough for the towel to fall in a puddle at my feet.

"Fuck, baby," Carter groans.

Ethan's hand moves up to my breast, pinching and rolling a nipple, while his mouth finds the sensitive spot on my neck beneath my ear, swirling his tongue in ways that make me weak. His other hand splays across my lower abdomen. Carter runs a hand up the inside of my thigh, then his middle finger glides through my wet slit, from taint to clit.

I jerk in Ethan's arms, drawing a quiet laugh from him.

"You're so fucking wet, princess," Carter says. "Feel how wet she is," he directs to Ethan.

Ethan obliges, his hand moving down to cup my pussy from the front, his middle finger slipping into my slit and finding my clit, teasing it briefly before pulling away, leaving me yearning for more.

"So fucking wet, so fucking needy," Ethan whispers in my ear, then he pulls my earlobe into his mouth.

Carter's fingers find me again, and he dips two fingers inside me before dropping to his knees in front of me. I gasp, my hips moving instinctively.

"You got her?" Carter asks.

"Yeah, I've got her," Ethan rasps against my neck, sending shivers down my spine. "Make her fucking come."

Ethan lifts me just enough for Carter to pull my leg over his shoulder. He holds me tightly, one hand cupping my breast and the other splayed over my lower abdomen. Carter adds a third finger inside me, quickly finding my G-spot. He uses his other hand to spread my folds, pulling the hood of my clit back so he can take it between his lips and brush it lightly with his teeth. Then he sucks hard while his tongue circles it.

"Fuck," I moan, my body trying to move, to grind into Carter or collapse against Ethan—I can't even tell.

Ethan tightens his grip on me, the hand on my abdomen pressing lower, intensifying Carter's ministrations inside me. His other hand travels up my body to my throat, tilting my head back. He leans over my shoulder to watch what Carter is doing.

"That's so fucking hot," he breathes against my neck, his fingers tightening around my throat.

My hands, resting on Ethan's forearm, move—one to Carter's hair and the other behind me to the back of Ethan's neck. The hand on my throat is firm enough to make breathing a challenge, but not impossible. I use my hands to signal to both of them when I'm about to come undone.

Ethan's grip on my throat tightens as I pull at Carter's blonde locks, my climax building with an overwhelming sensation. When it hits, my pussy convulses, and my whole body shakes as I feel the gush of fluids coat my thighs.

I've undeniably squirted before, but never standing, and the warm fluid dripping down my legs is intoxicatingly hot.

"Fuck, yeah, such a good fucking girl," Carter praises. Ethan loosens his grip on my throat, grabs my jaw to turn me toward him, and kisses me deeply. Carter gently sets my foot back on the ground before standing, wiping his hand off on my tits and belly. The wetness on me feels incredibly erotic. Carter then puts his fingers in his mouth, sucking off the remnants.

Ethan breaks the kiss and murmurs against my lips, "I want to taste you."

He quickly turns me in his arms so I'm chest-to-chest with him.

Still fully clothed, Ethan's hands find my hips, and he backs me toward the bed. My hands tangle in his dark hair, my nails scraping his scalp.

Pushing me back onto the bed and coming down on top of me, his mouth finds both my nipples briefly before his tongue and lips trail down my belly until he reaches my drenched pussy.

"Fuck, Lexi, you made a mess down here," Ethan chides, his breath hot against my skin. Then his tongue spears me, relentless and demanding, as his facial hair teases my most sensitive spots.

Carter moves behind me, sitting me up between his legs. His hands are on my tits, and his mouth is on my neck, opposite the side Ethan was showering with kisses. Ethan's fingers find their way inside me, locating that sensitive spot immediately. His other hand pushes my knee, spreading me wider. I feel the tickle of his facial hair on my inner thighs as he dives back in, his lips finding my swollen clit, sucking and swirling his tongue in perfect rhythm with his fingers.

Carter watches Ethan over my shoulder, his fingers rolling and pinching my nipples, whispering praises in my ear, just loud enough for me to hear over my breathy moans.

"You're such a good fucking dirty girl," Carter murmurs. "Come for him, drench him, and then we'll give you what you really want."

My head falls back into the crook of Carter's neck, my lip caught between my teeth to stifle the noises rising within me. My fingers loop through Ethan's hair before clutching Carter's arms as the coil of another orgasm tightens in my core. As it builds, my body moves involuntarily, and Carter's hands press down on my upper thighs, holding me still.

"Fuck, Ethan," I moan, barely audible as the coil releases, and I convulse around his fingers, gushing fluid over his hand.

"God, you're fucking perfect," Ethan exclaims, his tongue licking up every last drop.

"Such a good girl," Carter whispers against my neck. "You want to know what we want from our good dirty girl?"

As I recognize that he called me "our dirty girl," my heart and blood warm at the words.

"Hmmm," I manage, still shuddering as Ethan's tongue slides over my clit.

"You think you can take both of us at the same time, princess?" Carter's voice is a mix of question and challenge.

My clit pulses at the thought, my whole body aching and needy, craving exactly that.

"Fuck, yes," I whisper eagerly, and Carter groans against my neck.

"Such a good fucking girl," he croons louder. "She just gave us the green light, Ethan."

My mind races, curious about their conversations while I was in the shower, but those thoughts vanish as Ethan stands and strips off his shirt, unbuttoning his jeans and dropping them along with his boxers. His cock is hard and ready. He grabs my hands, pulling me up to him, our chests pressing together as he kisses me deeply, passionately. Behind me, I hear the rustle of Carter undressing. He wraps his arms around my waist, pulling me back into him as he sits on the edge of the bed.

Carter grinds his hard length through my wet folds. "Fuck, princess," he groans. "You're still so fucking wet, but I need you that way."

Carter's fingers slide between us, dipping into my pussy from behind. Then he drags his wet fingers back to my ass, teasing the rim.

"You good, princess?" Carter whispers in my ear.

"Yeah," I nod, reaching for Ethan. He's fisting himself with one hand but gives me the other.

Carter positions himself against my ass, slowly lowering me onto his cock, sinking into me to the hilt. The stretch is intense and the euphoria is immediate.

"Fuck, princess, such a good fucking girl," Carter whispers. "Look at you taking all of me."

My head falls back with a moan, my fingers looped with Ethan's. Carter's cock in my ass feels so fucking good. When I'm turned on enough, it's an incredible sensation—euphoric and intense. It's like a natural high, intoxicating, sending waves of pleasure straight to my brain, like the best kind of narcotic, heightening every sensation, including my inner walls and clit.

Carter pulls me back onto the bed, my back against his chest. He's braced on pillows, giving Ethan the access he needs. Carter thrusts into me twice, his hands on my tits, before Ethan settles between our legs.

"Fuck, Lexi, that's hot," Ethan says, looking at where Carter and I are joined. "You ready for me, baby?"

"Yes," I gasp as Carter pinches one of my nipples.

"Fuck," both Carter and I groan as Ethan drives into me.

Carter braces us on the bed, and my nails dig into Ethan's arms. I love being face-to-face with him.

"So fucking hot," Ethan marvels, watching us. He has the best view, but I can feel every inch of it, and it feels amazing. Everything Ethan does is intensified by Carter's small thrusts. When Ethan moves his thumb to my clit, I know I'm going to break.

Ethan feels it coming before Carter does, my nails digging into his arms.

"Fuck yeah, Lexi, come for us," Ethan commands.

My hips rise, but I don't want to lose either of them. I try to still my body as my hands dig into the mattress, and then I start convulsing around both of them.

"Holy fuck," Ethan groans, while Carter growls in my ear.

I feel Carter tense under me, then the unmistakable throb of his release. Ethan's climax follows a few thrusts later, his fingers digging into my thighs, I'm sure leaving bruises from his strong hands.

Ethan leans down to kiss me while Carter nibbles on my neck. Ethan pulls me off Carter as he collapses on the bed, leaving me sandwiched between them in post-orgasmic bliss.

Both of them graze gentle fingers over me, but Ethan holds my eyes, and there's so much depth in his. He looks like he is in a state of not only bliss but amazement.

"You good, princess?" Carter murmurs.

"I am *so* good," I sigh.

Ethan gently brushes my hair out of my face and grazes the pad of his thumb over my lower lip, and it feels wholly intimate between him and me, even though Carter's hands are all over me at the same time.

"I do need to go to the bathroom, though, and I'm pretty sure I'll need another shower," I jest and softly giggle.

Carter smacks my ass and then orders, "Get going then, so you can get back here."

31

ALEXIS

I clean up in the restroom, a quick whore bath style, and step back into my bedroom. Carter is fully dressed, and Ethan has his boxer briefs back on, making me the only naked one in the room.

As soon as I step out of the bathroom, Carter places a hand on my stomach and gently pushes me back in. He maneuvers me to the side wall, out of view from the bedroom, and confines me in his arms.

Kissing me passionately, his lips are searing against mine, his hand grazes down my arm before he drops his mouth to my ear.

"You're perfect, princess," he whispers and brushes my cheekbone with the back of his knuckles before kissing me again.

"I'm going to leave you with Ethan this afternoon and tonight," he says, kissing me on the forehead. "I know you two need more time, but let me know if you need me, okay?"

I nod and trail my fingers down his chest.

Pulling back from me, he says louder, "Plus, I beat him to the washing machine, so I don't have a glitter problem anymore, and Ethan does."

I laugh and lean against the bathroom door jam, out of view of my bedroom door, while Carter leaves the room. Still naked, I meet Ethan's gaze as soon as the door closes. I'm drawn to him like I've been hypnotized.

He's sitting on my bed, and I close the space between us quickly, climbing onto his lap. I straddle him, my knees on either side of his hips, and his eyes watch me carefully as I place the palms of my hands on either side of his face, relishing his soft, well-groomed facial hair before my mouth meets his.

One of Ethan's hands finds the small of my back, and the other finds my ass as he kisses me hard and sensually. Eventually, my hands move behind his neck, my arms wrap around him, and his face falls to my cleavage. As he finds my nipples with his mouth, I feel his cock stiff again under my core.

"You still needy?" Ethan teases in a whisper against my skin.

"For you? Always," I answer in earnest, my mouth near his ear.

He flips me over and peels off his boxer briefs before he fucks me again. This time, it isn't about it being hot or trying to outdo anyone or anything else. This is just about us. There's emotion behind it, no dirty talk, no talk at all. It's just Ethan and me, our mouths, hands, skin, and our need to feel connected.

In the afterglow, lying in his arms, trailing my fingers down his chest through his chest hair, I check in with him. "You good? Do you have any regrets?"

He laughs softly. "I'm good, absolutely no regrets." He pulls me closer. "It is a little weird that it was my second time with you, but I kind of anticipated it would go fast once it started." He laughs again. "It's kind of like ripping the bandaid off."

I look up so I can see his brown eyes. "I'm glad you stayed," I say softly before I kiss him again, and he strokes my hair.

"Well, if you hadn't gotten glitter in my bed," he jests.

"I'm sure that's the only reason you stayed." I smirk.

"You know it's not," he confesses. "I like having you to myself too."

"Yeah, I couldn't do this without having time with you by myself." I pause, looking into his brown pools. "Ethan, I want to tell you something," I hedge as he focuses on me. "Now that we're where we are, there was never a time when I didn't want you."

A flicker of surprise flashes across his eyes, and I notice a subtle swallow, betraying emotion behind his confident facade.

"From day one," I continue, "from the minute you introduced yourself to me. And then it was cemented by everything else that happened that day and the next. There was always chemistry; I just thought you should kn—"

Interrupting me, his mouth covers mine, kissing me hard.

"You know I always wanted you," he whispers against my lips. "But thank you for that, Lexi. I'm glad to know I wasn't a consolation prize."

I stifle a giggle. "You are definitely not a consolation prize."

"That's good because I'm pretty sure you've got me so far gone. I've fallen so hard, there's no going back," he admits with a soft smile.

"Ethan," I softly croon.

"I know, too much, too soon," he sighs.

"No, not at all," I assure him. "It makes me incredibly happy to know this isn't just physical for you."

"It's so far beyond physical, Lexi," Ethan confesses. "All of me needs all the parts of you. I mean, I like fucking you too." He laughs as I gently pinch him. "But, sunshine, it's so much more than that."

"Ethan, can I ask you a question?"

"You can ask me anything, love," he answers, brushing his knuckles across my cheek.

"Maybe it's not a question, but talk to me about your family, the house." I run my thumb over his lips, cradling the soft beard on his jaw. "I just want to understand you better."

Ethan kisses me softly and sits up more, his back against the headboard. I pull the soft sheet up around me and sit up as well—tucking my knees up under my chin and wrapping my arms around them—facing Ethan.

His jaw sets and he reaches out and takes my fingers in his before he starts talking.

"My parents are around," he explains to start. "My mom had family money, but she is a corporate attorney; she travels constantly, overseeing mergers and such. My dad is a CEO and board president —he has been over a lot of different corporations and companies. That's where the money comes from." He clears his throat.

"I have a few trusts, one I got when I turned twenty-one, that bought this house and started the company—even though it has Jeremiah's name on it, it was all my money to start. There are a lot of rules around the trusts I have already been granted access to and the next one I get when I turn thirty. But when I'm thirty-five, or when my parents die, a lot of those rules go away."

Ethan pulls me closer to him, and I oblige so he can wrap his arm around my legs.

"So, *I* don't actually own anything bought with the trust money outside of what I buy with what surmounts to an allowance; the trust owns it. If something happens to me, it reverts back to my parents as long as they're alive; even if I were married or had children, they locked it all down so well." His other hand crosses over and laces with mine.

"I don't have any brothers or sisters. I *do* have a few cousins." He pauses and swallows. "I have almost no relationship with my parents. I was raised by nannies. Funny and also not funny story: When Carter lost his parents, he lived with me and my nanny for seven months before my parents even knew he was there. That's how much I didn't interact with them as a child."

"Ethan," I empathize. "I'm sorry."

I also make a mental note to talk to Carter. I knew his parents weren't around, but I didn't realize he lost them so young.

Ethan shrugs. "It is what it is. I did have really good nannies; I only went through three of them growing up. But part of how I became so close to both Holden and Shawn is that they had—they *have*—amazing parents. It was nice to spend time at their houses, to sit down at a dinner table and eat as a family. To feel like they were a family."

"Is that why you all do dinner together now?" I smile.

He smiles back. "It is; it's important to me, it's important to Carter. I think it even means something to Jeremiah. Holden and Shawn grew up with it, so they know it's important to us, but they don't know what it's like to be without it so I don't think it means quite as much to them."

"I didn't have family dinners very often, but I did have two brothers," I respond. "They remember the nannies, I don't. By the time I was old enough to remember, they were old enough to take care of me, so there were no more nannies. But usually, one of my parents was home by the time I went to bed. I know you didn't ask, but," I gesture to myself, "ADHD, anecdotal communicator, relator, whatever you want to call it—I tend to share my own experiences in response to other people's stories," I explain with a shrug, acknowledging my tendency to respond to people through personal anecdotes, and then I laugh.

Ethan reaches up and brushes some loose hair out of my face. "Lexi, love, you can tell me all the stories you want, especially if they relate to what I'm saying."

I smile at him. "Well, in that case," I laugh, "you should know I'm also a trust funder." I look around the room. "Although definitely

UNBINDING DESIRE ~ 221

not your level of it, but I had part of it at twenty-five, another when I turn thirty, and then thirty-five."

"You buy your condo with the first one?" Ethan knowingly smiles.

"I did, and when I sell it, I can only keep the profit; the rest goes back into trust," I confirm, and Ethan nods; he clearly knows how these things work, probably better than me.

"Who took you to your softball and lacrosse stuff?" Ethan asks.

"It varied." I shrug. " Softball, I had Georgia. She's still my closest friend; her parents would take me a lot, and when I got older, sometimes my coaches. My parents never traveled with me when I played travel ball; they always paid for me to have my own hotel room and stuff. They barely came to any of my lacrosse games in college." I swallow. "My brothers did, though. There's a really long, horrible history with my parents. Honestly, I don't know why I have a relationship with them at all."

"It sounds like your relationship with your parents wasn't much, if any, better than mine, but you did see them a lot more," Ethan laughs, but there's no humor.

"Yeah," I agree. "I think that's part of why I'm not sure if I want kids. I wouldn't want to parent them like I was. I don't know."

He squeezes my hand. "I don't want kids," he asserts, and he sounds certain. "I like having Ana around, like a niece, but I don't want any of my own."

"Good to know," I reply with a smile.

"Speaking of dinner at the table, we have an hour," Ethan points out.

"Wanna shower with me?" I suggest.

"Uh, yeah, I do," Ethan almost growls at me.

32

JEREMIAH

The shift in Ethan is tangible. Even if they hadn't pulled me out onto the patio that day to fill me in, I would've sensed it. I can't recall seeing him wear a smile that seemed to stretch on for days like he does now. Carter has been with her for six weeks now and Ethan for over two, but in some ways, it feels like an eternity.

In just a few short weeks, Alexis—this siren—has wrought a remarkable transformation in our household dynamic, mostly for the better. Holden is struggling, but Shawn is managing. The company is in a stronger position, and there's a renewed sense of vitality in the house. Ana seems happier when she's around; this siren has become a beacon of positivity for almost everything under our roof.

She has a unique connection with each of us.

With Carter, their physical energy syncs perfectly; they play off each other in ways publicly that leave no doubt about their chemistry behind closed doors.

Emotionally, she and Ethan are on the same wavelength. They share similar backgrounds, both familiar with parents who only throw money at them without providing the emotional support they need, even as adults.

Alexis and Shawn bond over their nerdy inside jokes and discussions about upcoming shows that the rest of us aren't as interested in. In the past week, he's even convinced her to pick up a video game controller again, and the laughter echoing up the stairs from the basement tells me they are enjoying themselves immensely.

Holden sees her as both his personal heaven and hell. Having watched her brothers navigate medical school and residency and with her parents in high-stress healthcare jobs, she understands his academic and professional struggles better than any of us could, no matter how much he shares. The chemistry between him and Alexis is intense, we can all feel it; the air becomes palpable at times between them. I'm sure even Carter and Ethan can feel it, and in that she becomes his hell.

And then there's me; outwardly, I don't think anyone realizes how much impact she is having on me. I have Carrie, but Alexis is something else entirely—something more, so much more. Her business astuteness impresses me on a professional level, but it's the way she carries herself with confidence that truly captivates me. I've always recognized her allure, her siren-like charm since the first morning she woke up in our house. But I've managed to resist it.

Now, I'm not so certain.

She could offer me what I desire and need—physical intimacy and a connection with an extraordinary woman—while allowing me to maintain my independence. I'm also relatively certain that some of my less conventional desires and fantasies would be things she wouldn't shy away from.

The unconventional dynamic she shares with Carter and Ethan and the inevitability—whether they admit it or not—of the other two joining in some capacity or another would enable me to have precisely what I desire from a relationship.

I still struggle with the fact that she is my employee. It's a constant battle between my professional ethics and the undeniable chemistry I feel. Despite this internal conflict, I can't deny the comfort I find in my relationship with Carrie. Even though the intensity of feelings and attraction I have for her is less than what I feel for Alexis, Carrie fulfills my needs in a reliable and predictable way. In some ways, I'd rather stick with what is known and comfortable than risk everything by pursuing what I really want. It's a safer path, one that doesn't threaten to upend my carefully constructed life. Yet, every time I'm around her, I can't help but wonder what it would be like to let go and follow my heart.

Despite everything else going on, Ethan and I now need to coordinate everyone for a crucial investor meeting, which happens to coincide with the prediction of a major snowstorm. The dinner table seems like an appropriate place to do that, where we can make sure everyone is on the same page.

"Okay," Ethan begins. "We were supposed to have that big investor meeting on Tuesday downtown, but with the weather moving in, they moved it to virtual. I know Jeremiah, and I *have* to be on that; I would like to have all the rest of you." He looks at Holden. "Including you. I'd like you to be available if we need you."

"Tuesday morning?" Alexis confirms, and everyone nods in agreement.

"Yes, Tuesday morning," I answer. "And that brings us to our second issue. They're forecasting this storm from Monday afternoon into Wednesday to be a hundred-year event. The last time we saw over twenty inches of snow in April was in 1957, and this one is expected to be even more snow. So, make sure you all add anything you need to the shopping list, and we'll take care of it Saturday morning to hopefully avoid any issues."

Ethan looks at me and adds, "We have a lot of stuff in the pantry, but just in case. Also, sometimes they're wrong, but the way all the models are looking at this, they're probably not."

"Anyone have any questions about either?" I query.

Everyone shakes their heads, and I address Holden, "You're back from the hospital Sunday night, right?"

"Yeah," he confirms. "Until Wednesday night."

It's a relief that everyone seems to be on the same page. I need to schedule individual meetings with each of them to discuss expectations for the investor meeting. Ethan, in particular, understands the significance of this more than anyone else.

Meeting with Ethan first to discuss our game plan, one of the main questions I ask him is if he prefers to meet with Alexis individually or if he wants me to handle it. He defers to me, emphasizing the need for a clear professional boundary.

Shortly after, I meet with Alexis in the sitting room upstairs. Ethan and I joked about needing a room with a closed door for these meetings, and this seemed like the best option.

"Hey, Alexis," I greet her as she walks in, sporting those damn short shorts.

I wonder if she's aware of the effect they have on all the men in the house—whether she enjoys it, couldn't care less, or is simply oblivious.

"Hey, Jer, how are you?" she responds.

"I'll be better after Tuesday," I quip. "And you?"

"I'm good." She smiles.

We spend about two hours delving into marketing strategy and budget, approaching it from a perspective geared towards selling our strategies rather than our products to investors. As expected, Alexis is brimming with fantastic ideas and insights. I have no doubt she'll put together an amazing presentation over the next couple of days.

After wrapping up the business side of things, I shift the conversation to a more personal note, just wanting to check in with her.

"You good otherwise, siren?" I inquire.

"Outside of work?" she clarifies.

"Yeah," I chuckle.

"Yeah, Jer, I'm good," she assures me.

Then, her expression shifts to one of genuine concern. "I know they told you and Shawn, but did anyone tell Holden?"

"I haven't yet. I'm not sure about the timing on that, but he's still in the dark," I reply.

"I feel like maybe I should be the one to tell him," she suggests, running her fingers through her gorgeous hair.

Sighing, I weigh the options. "Alexis, siren, I think there are some advantages to that. If he hears it from you, it might dispel any thoughts that you were coerced or anything. But if he's upset about it, it might be best coming from Ethan."

She nods, understanding the complexities of the situation. Holden's closeness to both Ethan and Carter adds another layer of complexity to the whole situation—it's both a blessing and a curse. Holden and Carter do share a close bond, but Ethan has the emotional intelligence to handle a conversation like that, whereas Carter may not.

"Are things going how, I don't know, how you expected them to?" I ask with a small laugh.

Alexis blushes a little. "Yes and no, we're good. I think Carter and Ethan talk to each other more about the complexities than they talk to me. Usually, by the time they loop me in, they already have a game plan as far as logistics and whatnot." She pauses and sighs. "Surprisingly, it's not as complex or awkward as I initially thought it would be."

"I'm glad," I reply.

"Is your girlfriend still trying to convince you about that three-some?" Alexis asks, her eyes sparking with a challenge.

I laugh and shake my head. "She is, but her requests are probably not what you're thinking."

Curiosity dances in her eyes. "You going to explain that one, boss?"

I chuckle, noting the unintended heat in her calling me "boss" while discussing something as intimate as sex.

"No, I'm not," I chuckle. "Maybe someday, but not now."

The truth is, the conversation about a threesome started immediately after Carrie's birthday party. At first, Carrie was a little unsettled by some of Alexis's previous experiences, but I confided in Carrie that I found some of them intriguing and expressed a desire to explore some of them.

Carrie's suggestion of a threesome with Alexis, however, isn't what it seems. She wants me to act out my fantasies with Alexis while she watches. Essentially, she wants me to use Alexis as a toy while she observes and then take Carrie to bed and fuck her. But Alexis is not a toy, even if the idea is tempting. Moreover, if I were to pursue anything with Alexis, I'm pretty sure I wouldn't want Carrie involved at all—in fact, she'd probably need to be completely out of my life, or she'd remove herself quickly.

Carrie is playing with fire and she doesn't realize it.

33

ALEXIS

Monday morning, just before the impending snowstorm is set to hit, I meet up with Carrie for our salon date, followed by brunch. With the investor meeting looming the next day—even though it's virtual—I opt for a shorter French manicure. It ends up taking longer than my usual nail routine as they meticulously file down my nails, much shorter than I normally keep them. Despite the extra time, the fresh manicure makes me feel polished and ready for the important meeting ahead.

Sitting in the salon chair, I feel the corners of my lips turn up as the thought crosses my mind that Ethan will likely be upset about my decision for a shorter manicure, while Carter will probably be pleased. Carter worries I might accidentally mar his tattoos, but Ethan enjoys the marks left by my nails on his skin.

Carrie, already finished with her pampering session, sits nearby, engrossed in her phone. I'm caught off guard when she suddenly speaks up.

"Hey, Alexis, did Jeremiah tell you why we fought on St. Patrick's

Day?" Carrie's inquiry catches me off guard. Her tone is devoid of negative emotion, sounding more like she's casually asking about dinner plans.

"Um, no, but Ethan did," I respond with a coy smile, knowing full well the implications of my statement.

She sighs, "I figured someone would tell you, but it's not what you think."

My mind flashes back to the conversation I shared with Jeremiah just a couple of days prior.

"Carrie, you really don't have to tell me," I say with a smile, reassuring her that she doesn't need to divulge any further information because, in all honesty, I really don't want it.

"Well, I won't here, but maybe over brunch," she volunteers.

Then, over brunch, she follows through on that promise. Threat? I don't know.

"Here's the thing, Alexis," she confides in a quiet whisper. "There are things that you have done, that you're probably willing to do, that I am not, and Jeremiah wants to do. So, it was more the idea of a kitchen pass for him, but I'd have to be there."

I'm fairly certain my eyes widen to the size of saucers as I process what she's just revealed.

"Don't worry," she shakes her head. "He shut me down so fast, but if it was ever something you would be interested in, *you* could probably convince him."

She wiggles her eyebrows mischievously, and my jaw drops momentarily before I quickly snap it shut, trying to regain my composure.

"Carrie," I warn, my facial expression stern.

"What? You've done things," she remarks flippantly.

"I have, within the confines of a relationship," I retort sternly.

"Well, if you ever change your mind." She shrugs.

I'm left stunned by the audacity of Carrie's revelation. Taking a few more bites of my food in silence, I struggle to process her bombshell. Eventually, I excuse myself to the restroom, needing a moment to collect my thoughts in private.

I sit in the stall and open my text thread with Ethan and Carter.

(Me) *Did either of you know EXACTLY what Carrie was asking Jer for at the St Patrick's Day party?*

(Carter) *Yes*

(Ethan) *I plead the fifth, but my guess is since you're WITH her, she just told you*

(Me) *Y'all should have told me*

(Carter) *I figured since Jeremiah shut her down we didn't need to - I'm sorry*

(Ethan) *Do I get any points for telling you anything? Because Jeremiah didn't want me to tell you what I did*

(Me) *Points to be redeemed for what exactly? Lol*

(Ethan) *Okay - you're not too mad lol*

(Me) *No, just a little thrown by what she just told me*

(Carter) *You gonna do it? Lol*

(Me) *Carter!*

(Carter) *That wasn't an answer*

(Me) *Okay, Ethan earns points, Carter loses points*

(Ethan) *Lol*

(Carter) *Well, as long as I'm already in the dog house - you still didn't say no*

(Me) **facepalm emoji**

(Carter) *Still not a no*

(Ethan) *How long do you want to be in that dog house?*

(Carter) *Until she answers me*

(Me) *Just for that, I won't*

(Carter) *So much sass, princess*

(Me) *You're infuriating*

(Carter) *I know, that's why you have Ethan*

(Ethan) *Um, what?*

(Carter) *I piss her off, and then you calm her down*

(Ethan) *Is that how that works?*

(Carter) *Have you pissed her off yet?*

(Ethan) *No, but that's because I'm not an asshole*

(Me) *Boys - I have to get back to Carrie before she wonders where I am - you two can argue amongst yourselves*

(Carter) *No arguing, just playing - he's sitting right next to me, and he's right, I am an asshole*

(Ethan) *Hurry home, Lexi, the snow is starting*

(Carter) *Bring the sass with you lol*

"You okay?" Carrie asks when I get back to the table.

"Yeah, sorry. I made the mistake of checking my phone while peeing," I jest.

She laughs. "Okay. I didn't mean to make you uncomfortable, I just wanted to be honest."

"It's fine, Carrie, but honestly, it's not something I see happening," I reply, though I can't shake the feeling that Carter might have a point—I seem unable to definitively say no to the idea.

We continue eating in silence for a few moments until I glance out the window and notice the snow starting to intensify.

I gesture toward the window with my fork. "We should probably get going, Carrie. Looks like the snow's picking up."

Grateful that Ethan insisted I take his 4Runner today in

anticipation of the worsening weather, I feel relieved as I inch closer to home. The slush on the roads is rapidly accumulating.

I find Carter and Ethan seated on the couch in the living room, engrossed in a game on the television. They probably *were* sitting right next to each other during that text conversation.

"How was Carrie?" Carter mocks.

I narrow my eyes at Carter but playfully nudge his knee, silently coaxing him to make room for me between him and Ethan.

"How are the roads?" Ethan inquires, concern evident in his voice.

"They're getting pretty sketchy," I tell them. "I'm glad we left when we did."

Ethan's gaze flickers to me with more concern. "Did the car work okay for you?"

"Yeah, it was great, actually. I'm really glad I had it, so thank you," I express sincerely.

Carter shifts the conversation. "Where'd you go for lunch?"

"Some new brunch spot in Lone Tree," I reply. "It was okay, nothing special."

Ethan reaches for my hand, a smile tugging at the corners of his lips. "Well, the nails look nice, short but nice."

I chuckle, "I knew you'd notice they were shorter; I figured even though it's on video, I'd go as professional as possible for the meeting tomorrow."

Carter and Ethan both find subtle places to touch me, mostly out of respect for Holden if he walks in. Ethan's hand is under my forearm, his fingers gently tracing patterns on my thigh and arm. Carter's is on my thigh, under my arm. Both of them touching me, even so innocently, at the same time is hot, and I start to feel the ache at the juncture of my thighs.

I look up at the television. "Oh, shit, this is a close game."

"Yeah, so be a good girl, sit there, be quiet, and just look pretty," Carter nudges me.

"You *are* an asshole," Ethan laughs, but that ache moves a little deeper in my core.

* * *

A few hours later, all six of us gather around the dinner table; the atmosphere is filled with warmth and laughter. Surprisingly, even Holden seems to be enjoying himself, caught up in the fun and conversation. We sit there long after we're done eating. However, as the evening wears on, the realization dawns upon us that we do have an exceedingly important meeting in the morning, and the need for sleep begins to sink in.

Jeremiah shuts down our little party. "You know, guys, this has been a blast, the most fun we've had in a long time, but we need to call it a night," he says, glancing around at the group. "I want everyone fresh and ready to go in the morning."

As we're cleaning up the kitchen, Ethan leans into me, quietly speaking into my ear. "I still have some prep work to do for tomorrow. Go hang out with Carter. Hopefully, I'll be able to celebrate with you tomorrow afternoon."

I lean into him and tease, "Did you seriously just put that much breath on my neck and ear to not take me with you?"

Ethan laughs, "Lexi, sunshine, I'm sure you'll be fine."

I roll my eyes at Ethan's teasing and impulsively grab his forearm, tugging him into the garage. The cold air hits me like a wall; I just don't care.

"Lexi," Ethan almost growls, his voice tinged with amusement.

"Shhhh," I hush him. "Just kiss me for a minute."

"So needy," he whispers before covering my mouth with his.

After a few minutes of deep kisses, I confess, "I just needed *you* for a minute. You can go back to work now."

Laughing softly, he pulls me closer and plants a kiss on my forehead before we head back into the house.

Jokingly, I add, "You still have bonus points."

Ethan chuckles as he holds the door open for me. Inside, I find Carter engaged in conversation with Jeremiah in the dining room. I squeeze Carter's arm affectionately.

"I'm gonna go get ready for bed. See you upstairs," I murmur, kissing his cheek before smiling at Jeremiah and making my way upstairs.

However, as I start changing for bed, I begin to feel unwell. Clammy and nauseated, a sense of unease washes over me.

Suddenly, it hits me like a ton of bricks, and I find myself doubled over, losing my dinner into the toilet. Instantly, my mind races with worry, consumed by the thought that maybe I've made Ethan or Carter sick.

I'm still in the bathroom when Carter walks in, finding me curled up on the floor.

"Go away," I manage to order him, though a half-hearted smile tugs at my lips. "You don't want what I have."

"Lex, what happened? You were fine like ten minutes ago." Carter's voice is laced with concern.

"I don't know, it hit me all of a sudden," I explain, sitting up slightly. "I really hope you all don't get sick."

"What do you need, princess?" Carter asks, squatting down beside me.

"Water, probably," I reply, meeting his gaze. "And maybe help me get off this floor."

I chuckle weakly, and Carter rolls his eyes. "Come here, princess," he says gently, helping me to my feet and guiding me to my bed.

"You want a bucket?" he jokes, but there's a hint of seriousness in his tone.

"I don't think there's anything left, so no," I reply, managing a small smile. "But thank you."

Carter helps me settle in before filling up my trusty emotional support Stanley, and planting a gentle kiss on my forehead before preparing to leave.

"Let Ethan know?" I inquire softly.

"Already did," he assures me. "Let either of us know if you need anything."

"Thank you," I reply gratefully, reaching for the television remote on the nightstand and flicking it on to find something to help me drift off to sleep.

34

HOLDEN

I'm startled awake when Carter charges into my room. "Holden, I need you now," he snaps.

"What the fuck, Carter?" I counter, looking at my watch; it's three in the morning.

"It's Alexis." He's frantic, running both of his hands through his blonde hair and starting to pace. "I can't wake her up, she's so fucking hot, like so fucking hot, Hold, but she's also shivering."

Now that has my attention—I bolt out of bed and throw on sweatpants and a T-shirt. "Is she in your room?" I direct the question to Carter.

"No, she's in her own room," he corrects. "She threw up late last night, and I left her to lie down alone. I woke up, and I just had a feeling I had to check on her." His voice is amping up. "Fuck, Holden, there's like twenty inches of snow out there, and she won't wake up."

"Calm down, Carter," I insist, reaching for my medical bag in the closet. "You freaking out is not going to help."

The tension is palpable coming off of him, and I, somehow, have managed to put myself into business mode, hospital mode, doctor mode, whatever it needs to be called, but what he's saying doesn't sound good.

Carter leads me into her room. Her headboard is against the wall to the right, and she's lying on her right side, on the very edge of the far end of the bed. I can see the tremors of her rigors from the door, and my adrenaline kicks in.

Rushing in, I kneel by the bed and try to get her to respond to me. I can feel the heat radiating off of her. A lot of physicians blow off tactile fever reports, but when someone is this hot, there's no denying how real it is.

"Alexis," I yell, and she stirs and lets out a small moan, but she doesn't wake up.

I roll her to her back and sternal rub her, saying her name again, and her eyes flutter open before she looks at me and murmurs, "Holden?"

That's good enough for me, even though her eyes shutter closed again immediately after.

I scan her with the temporal thermometer: 104.9.

Fuck.

"Carter, listen to me," I command. "Go start a tepid bath for her."

"What the fuck is a tepid bath?" he snaps.

I take a deep breath so I don't snap back. "Lower than body temperature, but not cold, lukewarm."

"Okay," he says and starts toward the bathroom.

My fingers move to the pulse point on her wrist; she's so fucking tachy, her heart is beating so fast, and thoughts of sepsis go through my head.

This is so not good.

I can hear the bath water running and call out to Carter, "Let me know when the tub is half full."

I take her blood pressure and auscultate her lungs and heart. Outside of the tachycardia and the altered blood pressure to go with it, everything else is normal, which is good, but it also doesn't give me any answers. Moving the stethoscope to her abdomen, the sounds are hyperactive, which does tell me something, and Carter did say she vomited earlier.

"It's half full," he announces from the bathroom door.

I stand, scoop Alexis in my arms, and carry her to the bath, clothes and all. As I lower her into the bath, she moans again but otherwise doesn't react. I drop down to my knees in front of the tub while I'm lowering her and hold her neck up so she doesn't slip under the water.

I turn to Carter. "Do you have any liquid Tylenol, Motrin, or something fever-reducing around for Ana?"

"Yeah, which do you want?"

"Just bring me everything you have," I answer, pulling a wash-cloth off the rack, and Carter leaves.

Dipping the washcloth in the water, I place it on her forehead. She's almost submerged to her shoulders, and the rigors have stopped.

Carter comes in, puts four bottles of medicine on the counter, and then, seemingly out of the blue, announces, "I'm going to get Ethan."

I start to ask him why, but he is already gone; then I reach over and turn off the water. Grabbing the first bottle of ibuprofen off the counter, I make some quick calculations in my head, and luckily, Carter returns just then, with Ethan on his heels.

I hand Carter the bottle. "She's going to need fifty milliliters of this; the cup is for fifteen. Just fill it, and I'm hoping I can wake her up enough to drink it."

"What do you think is wrong with her?" Ethan asks, his tone quiet but anxious.

"Right now, I think it's probably food poisoning, but the biggest issue is the fever. Her temperature was almost to brain damage and seizure levels, so once we get her cooled off, then we'll worry about what is causing the fever." I deliver the information clinically, the same way I would to a family member in the hospital.

Carter holds out the full cup of opaque liquid; I hold Alexis' neck firmly with one hand, and I sternal rub her again. Her eyes shoot open this time, which is a good sign.

"Holden?" Alexis questions. "What's going on?"

"Hey, angel," I answer. "You're really sick; I need you to try to drink some medicine, okay?"

She nods, and I take the cup from Carter and gently put it to her lips, giving her small amounts at a time. When the cup is empty, I hand it back to Carter.

"Fill it again," I request and then look back at Alexis. "Alexis, angel, I'm going to need you to try to drink about five more cups of medicine; two of this one and then three of another. I know it's not fun, but we have to get your fever down."

Again, she nods, and I put the cup back to her lips. When she has all the ibuprofen in her, we do the same with the acetaminophen.

I look behind me, and this time, I address Ethan, "Can you grab the bag I left on her nightstand?"

Ethan nods, and then I look at Carter, asking him to hand me a dry towel. I use the towel to dry her forehead and then grab the temporal thermometer from my bag. I know it won't be perfect right now since her skin was wet, but I use it and I get a much better reading at 103.4.

I puff out my cheeks and blow it out, looking back at Carter. Alexis's eyes are open now, but she's still lethargic. Her eyes track my movements with the thermometer and follow mine when I look at Carter.

"Okay, we can probably put her back in the bed now, you want to see if you can find her some dry clothes? It's probably best if you help her change at this point." I shrug and smile at him.

"I'll get her some clothes," Carter says, slightly smiling and looking between Alexis and me before leaving the bathroom.

I look back at Alexis. " Do you think you can stand? Ethan and I can help you."

She pushes her feet against the end of the tub and then nods. "Yeah." Her voice is raspy and weak. "I think I can."

"Okay," I reply, looking at Ethan. "Can you grab her a towel?" I ask, pointing at the towel rack next to him.

Ethan doesn't say anything, but he pulls the towel off the rack and steps closer to me.

I look at Alexis. "Okay, angel, I'm going to lift you out of the tub, and then we'll see if you can walk to the bed."

"Okay," she nods.

I count to three and then lift her out of the tub. She is not as deadweight as she was the first time, and she wraps her arm around my neck, which helps. I gently place her feet on the floor outside the tub and look at Ethan.

He wraps the towel around her, and we both support her back to the bed. Carter is throwing her clothes on the bed right as we exit the bathroom. Ethan and I turn Alexis and help her sit on the end of the bed.

I squat down in front of Alexis so I am at eye level with her. "I'm going to let Carter help you put on dry clothes, and then I'll come back and check on you, okay?"

"Yeah, thank you, Holden," she replies weakly but with a small smile.

I stand to leave, expecting Ethan to follow me, but he doesn't. So, I pace the hall by myself, raking my fingers through my hair and massaging the back of my neck, waiting for them to let me know it's time to go back in.

The emotions going through me are contradictory and strong now that I'm out of doctor mode and back in the mode that is the torture I live in with this girl I want and can't have.

I am relieved to have gotten her this far because I was worried about her, too, and getting her to the hospital would be almost impossible right now. I also know she's not out of the woods yet. If she is septic or has some kind of major infection going on— appendicitis, pyelonephritis, or something else—she's still going to need a hospital.

"Holden," Ethan says as he opens the door. "We're good; you can come back in now."

I rake my hand through my hair one more time and then follow Ethan through the door. I get my bag from the bathroom and then sit on the edge of the bed next to Alexis.

"Hey," I greet her, and she offers me a soft smile.

Now I can't turn doctor mode fully back on. The adrenaline is gone, and I have to actually think about what it is I need to say and do besides just comfort her.

"Does anything hurt?" I ask.

"Everywhere," she laughs weakly and then shakes her head. "My joints ache like the flu."

"Okay, but nowhere specific?" I ask.

She shakes her head.

"Your fever was really, really high. You're lucky that Carter checked on you when he did." I pause, casting a glance in Carter's direction. "There are a lot of things that can cause a fever that high, most of them minor, some of them pretty serious. We just need to keep an eye on you for a while and make sure the fever doesn't get up that high again."

"Okay," she says, and I can tell she is lethargic and wants to go back to sleep.

"With that high of a fever, your heart was also beating super fast;

we call it tachy or tachycardic. That got better while we had you in the water, but I'll want to check that frequently, too." I pause and stroke her hair; it's a natural instinct, and I catch myself before I do it a second time. "You need to drink some water, even in small sips; you burned off a lot of fluid with the fever, and you're really dehydrated, so whenever you think about it, take a sip of water. There's also a cycle there; dehydration can make the tachycardia and fever worse."

"I can go get her some more water," Ethan volunteers. I don't turn to look at him, but I see Carter in my periphery nod at him and hand him her cup.

"I'm going to check you out here one more time, and then I can leave, and Carter or Ethan can get me if you need me," I suggest.

Alexis reaches up, covers my hand, and pleads, "Stay."

That one word pulls at all my heartstrings; I turn and look at Carter—he doesn't react or say anything, so I answer, "I can for a while, but let me get your temperature and check you out real quick, okay?"

She nods. Her temperature is still 103, and her heart rate is lower than it was but still high—both better but still worrisome. I listen to her again, and now that she can tell me if something hurts, I push on her belly and have her sit up so I can check her kidneys with percussion. All of that is mostly normal.

After I have her lie back down and Ethan is back in the room, I let them all know what I'm thinking.

"Carter said you threw up?" I ask, putting my stethoscope around my neck.

"I did," she responds. "Just once."

"Okay, your fever is still really pretty high for an adult, but it's not dangerous right now. Everything else that I can test for at home is okay, but there are still things we need to look out for." I look at Carter. "But I do want you both to know, you all to know," I say, turning to Ethan. "That even without the snow, with how high the fever was, I would have done the same thing, tried to get you cooled off at home and then see how it goes from there."

I look back at Alexis again and squeeze her hand. "My guess is that since none of the rest of us are sick and you threw up, it's food poisoning. It needs to work through your system, but it may be something else, so we need to keep an eye on you and make sure you're getting better. We probably will never know for sure what made you so sick."

"What else could it be?" Ethan asks, handing Alexis her full cup of ice water.

I shrug. "A lot of things, but with no other symptoms, the most likely serious things are appendicitis and pyelonephritis—a kidney infection, but typically, not always, she would have localized pain with those. They could both cause vomiting." I pause and look between all of them. "Regardless of what caused it, the big concern would be if she becomes septic, which is why we need to watch the fever."

Alexis puts her cup on the nightstand and then looks at me. "Am I allowed to sleep now, Dr. Ashford?"

It's adorable, and I don't know how she can have so much sass when I know she feels so weak.

I laugh and squeeze her hand. "Yeah, you can go to sleep. I'll put together a medication schedule; we'll alternate ibuprofen and acetaminophen, but as long as you can take the pills, you won't need to steal any more of Ana's medicine." Her eyes dart from me to Carter.

I clarify the unspoken question, "First, I wasn't sure if you'd be able to swallow pills. Second, if you threw up again, it's more likely you could have absorbed at least some of the liquid medicine. Third, the liquid is absorbed faster, and the faster I could get it into your system, the better."

"I knew we kept you around for a reason," Carter jests, checking me softly in the shoulder with his elbow.

"Thank you, Holden," Alexis groans sleepily as she lays down and pulls the blankets up.

"I'm going to put on a shirt and grab my phone," Ethan informs us, then leaves the room.

Carter rolls Alexis' desk chair over to the side of her bed, and I squeeze her hand one last time. Then, I stand up and head toward the door.

"You're not leaving, are you?" Carter asks.

"There's not much point in me staying at this point," I answer.

"Except that she wanted you to," Carter counters.

I sigh, rake my hand through my hair, and concede, "Okay, I'm going to change in to dry clothes and grab my phone too."

"Okay. Holden?" Carter asks.

"Yeah?"

"Can you grab my phone from my nightstand?"

I laugh at the fact that we all have to have our phones to sit around her room and then respond, "Sure, Carter."

I find Carter's phone on his nightstand before I go back to my room. I pull my phone off the charger and grab my desk chair to roll across the hall to Alexis' room. I'm surprised when I get back to her room to find Ethan on her bed, next to her, gently combing his fingers through her hair, and Carter is in the chair next to her, holding her hand. I had suspected some kind of throuple situation between them, but I thought I was paranoid or crazy or something.

So, now, not only did I not get the girl, but more than just Carter did.

The good news is Alexis seems to be comfortably sleeping. I text them a med schedule to stay on top of her fever and we all sit there in relative silence, staring at our phones until sunrise.

35

ALEXIS

The last thing I remember is Holden sitting on the bed and talking to me, so when I wake up, and Shawn is there, I'm very confused.

I blink away the sleep and swallow. "Hey, Shawn. What are you doing here?"

"Carter, Ethan, and Jeremiah are on that investor call; I was left to babysit," he says with a giant grin. "How are you feeling?"

I stretch a little and start to sit up. "I think a little better. Where's Holden?"

"He's around. He left me with instructions on when to wake you up and give you medicine," he informs me.

I pick up my phone and look at the time. It's only eight, so they probably haven't all been gone that long.

Looking at Shawn, I request, "Can you get Holden for me?"

He looks offended. "Uh, yeah."

As he is getting ready to leave my room, I stop him, "Shawn?"

"Yeah, cupcake?"

I laugh, "Cupcake?"

"Why not?" he rebuts.

"It caught me off guard, but it's fine." I smile. "You can come back and fulfill your babysitting; I just want to talk to Holden for a minute."

He smiles and nods before he steps into the hall.

Holden walks in a few minutes later. He looks ragged and tired, and I feel bad for making him come talk to me. Shawn is right behind him.

"Hey, Shawn, can you give us a minute? I promise it won't be long." I wrinkle my nose, acknowledging I'm a pain in the ass.

"Holden, could you just grab me from my room when you're done?" Shawn asks, and Holden nods at him.

My gaze falls on Holden. "Hey." My voice is soft and gentle. "You look like crap," I laugh.

Holden smiles. "I still probably look better than you," he teases.

"Come here," I plead, holding my hand out to him. I see the resistance on his face, but I don't change my mind or my body language.

I scoot over on the bed as he gets closer, inviting him to sit on the bed rather than the chair Shawn was in. He complies without any coaxing from me.

I sit up a little more and take his right hand in mine. "Holden, I wanted to say thank you. For everything." I put my left hand up on his jaw and he tries to cover the sharp inhale that comes with it.

Looking away from me at the floor next to my bed, his facial expression turns a little miserable. "Holden," I say, drawing his eyes back to mine and squeezing his hand. "I appreciate you. I need you to know that."

I see his Adam's apple bob as he swallows, and then he sighs. "How are you feeling?"

As soon as he's done speaking, he pulls his right hand out from under mine and then gently wraps his fingers around my left wrist, guiding that hand away from his face.

"Holden," I sigh his name.

A switch flips in him as he stands, crossing his arms over his chest and backing a few feet away from the bed behind the chair that Shawn was sitting in.

"Did I do something wrong?" I ask, seriously trying to understand.

"Seriously, Alexis?" Holden snaps, causing me to flinch.

Raking his hand through his hair before he rests his hands on the back of the chair, he lets out a long sigh, opens his mouth to speak, and then snaps it shut.

"Holden?" I almost beg.

"Alexis, it's too painful," he swallows. "You did nothing wrong. I can tolerate Carter, and I guess Ethan." He gestures toward the door like Ethan is right outside it. "I can tolerate it from a distance, but I can't be sitting here with you touching me."

"I'm sorry," I apologize, pulling my knees to my chest and wrapping my arms around them.

"It's not your fault, but I can't do it." Holden crosses his arms again. "I care about you, Alexis. I wish I could just get over it, but I can't, at least not yet."

I swallow, trying to keep the tears at the back of my eyes from spilling over and whisper, "I'm still sorry, Holden. You can go."

I tuck my forehead onto my knees, hiding the tears that are flowing down my cheeks.

"Alexis." His voice filled with desperation and pain. "I'm the one that should be sorry."

I don't move and don't say anything until I hear the door close, and then I release the sobs I had been holding in. I'm still sobbing uncontrollably when Shawn comes back in, and I almost leap into his arms when he offers them to me.

* * *

SHAWN

I'm completely out of my depth here. I mean, sure, I've had my fair share of interactions with women—I have sisters, had girl-friends—but when Jeremiah calls Alexis a siren, he's hitting the nail on the head. There's this intense energy swirling around her, some-thing we've never quite encountered. She has injected life into the house, no doubt, but along with it comes a whirlwind of chaos and tension.

Right now, it feels like we're all caught in some high-stakes first-person shooter, with Carter and Ethan teaming up while the rest of us are just trying to survive, maybe even Alexis herself.

I don't know what went down with Holden, but when he came to fetch me, he was far from happy. And now Alexis is a complete wreck, unable to articulate anything. Holding her should be some-thing nice for me, but holding her while she sobs uncontrollably isn't quite the scenario I'd envisioned.

Ethan was wrestling with something fierce until whatever de-cision the three of them made came to light. But Holden is taking it harder than anyone. Jeremiah might seem composed on the sur-face, but I catch the way he looks at her when he thinks nobody's watching. And as messed up as it sounds, I'm pretty sure he's using Carrie as his physical outlet for all the chaos we're trying to manage without an outlet.

I've always been the invisible one around here, even before Alexis showed up. Usually, I don't mind. I'm not one for the spotlight or being the center of attention. But being invisible also means I'm privy to more than anyone realizes. I'm an observant introvert—I pick up on the subtle shifts in facial expressions and the nuances in tone. We're all grappling with something. Alexis is struggling. I'm struggling. Even Carter and Ethan are struggling because they feel the weight of Holden's burden.

We're all just trying to keep our heads above water. But Holden... he's sinking fast. And judging by the tears streaming down Alexis's face as she clings to me, I'd say she's not okay with that either.

As her sobs begin to quiet, I attempt to lighten the mood or at least offer some small comfort.

"Hey, Alexis, Allie, cupcake," I chuckle, feeling her laughter ripple against me. "It's not your fault, whatever happened."

"You don't know that," she sighs.

"I'm pretty confident," I argue. "You can't control how other people feel about you or their reactions to how you feel about other people. And I'm pretty sure both of those things are at the root of why you're upset right now."

She laughs and shakes her head.

"What?" I ask.

"I'm pretty sure that was the longest thing you've ever said to me at once, and it was deep."

I feign offense, clutching my heart dramatically, "Did you not think I was capable of deep? I'm offended."

She shakes her head, laughing again. "Oh, I know you're capable of deep."

I raise my eyebrows at her, and she gasps before smacking me, realizing the unintentional double entendre in her words.

"You know what I meant," she chides.

"I do," I laugh. "I know I'm quiet, but that doesn't mean I'm not paying attention."

My phone alarm interrupts us, causing me to jump slightly before glancing at Alexis.

"That means it's time for your meds," I remind her, handing over the pills.

"I feel mostly normal, just tired," she says.

"Holden said we should keep you on them until tomorrow morning to stay ahead of the fever if it comes back," I explain.

"Well, if Holden says," she echoes sarcastically, rolling her eyes.

"So sassy," I tease.

She takes the pills and settles back down. I lean back in my chair, returning to my phone, which I'd been engrossed in before she stirred.

"What're you playing?" she asks, her voice thick with drowsiness.

"Oh, just Hearthstone," I reply casually, assuming she wouldn't be interested.

"From Blizzard, right? The World of Warcraft people?" she adds.

My mind feels like glass just shattered at the realization of how much this woman knows.

"Yeah, actually. I'm surprised you know that," I chuckle nervously.

"I played with some friends in high school, but mostly, I did a paper on Blizzard's marketing in college. They are incredibly successful at building and maintaining a customer base with almost no television advertisements," she explains as if it's common knowledge.

"Allie, cupcake, I think you just melted my little nerd heart again," I say genuinely.

She laughs, rolls her eyes, and retorts with a sarcastic, "Cupcake," followed by, "GLHF, I'm going to try to sleep now."

I smile and shake my head. "Sweet dreams." Then, teasingly, "Cupcake."

Her lips twitch upwards, though her eyes remain closed.

About an hour later, I receive a text from Carter.

(Carter) *She still sleeping?*

(Me) *She's sleeping ... again*

(Carter) *She woke up? She take her meds?*

> (Me) *She woke up and took her meds, yes, your presentation over?*

(Carter) *It is*

> (Me) *I'm going to text the group except Alexis and Holden*

(Carter) *Um, okay*

I open up that thread, which I don't use very often.

> (Me) *Hey, so I don't know what happened, but Alexis woke up earlier and asked to talk to Holden - he came and got me about ten minutes later all sorts of upset - and when I got back to her room, she was crying*
>
> (Me) *Just full disclosure, I thought you all should know*

(Jeremiah) *Fuck, okay, I'll see if I can deal with Holden, I don't think either Carter or Ethan will be helpful right now*

(Carter) *She didn't tell you what it was about?*

> (Me) *Nope, and neither did he*

(Ethan) *Well fuck, I think we can all guess to some extent, but someone needs to talk to one of them*

(Jeremiah) *I'll take Holden*

(Carter) *I'll talk to Alexis, but I'm not pushing it, and she needs to wake up and feel better first*

> (Me) *She did say she was feeling better, just tired, pushed back a little on taking her meds, but then she did*
>
> (Me) *How did the presentation go?*

(Jeremiah) *I think it went really well, we could have used both of you, but that's okay - we should know something in the next few days*

        (Me) *Well, I'm good here, just playing on my phone, I know Carter and Ethan didn't get much sleep so whatever you need*

(Ethan) *Thanks, man, I will go lie down, but wake me up if she wakes up again*

(Carter) *Me too*

        (Me) *Will do*

I prop my feet up on Allie's bed, recline in the chair, and lose myself in my phone while I wait for her to wake up once more.

36

JEREMIAH

I'm relatively certain Holden is sleeping. He had a long night, just like Carter and Ethan, but I knock softly on his door, and he immediately asks who it is.

"It's Jer, just wanted to talk for a sec," I answer.

A few seconds later he opens the door and gestures for me to come in. He does look tired, ragged, and like he hasn't slept.

"What's up?" Holden asks, his tone full of annoyance.

"I just wanted to see how you were doing after last night. I know that you deal with stuff like that all the time, but Alexis, in our home, is different." I try to keep my voice level.

"Let me guess; you were chosen because y'all knew Carter or Ethan couldn't come to talk to me?"

I snicker, "More like I volunteered than I was chosen."

Holden sits on the end of the bed, his knees wide and his elbows on his knees. Letting his head fall into his hands, he pulls at his hair. His jaw is clenched so tight he's going to give himself a headache.

"Look, Hold, I know this sucks for you, I get it. It's not like—"

"Why didn't anyone tell me about Ethan?" Holden interrupts, still looking at the floor between his feet.

Well, fuck.

I suck in air through my nose and exhale slowly. "Because I knew you wouldn't handle it well. I probably should have just ripped off the Band-Aid."

"Having to put the puzzle pieces together wouldn't have been bad if it hadn't been clear everyone else knew." His gaze meets mine.

"Carter, Ethan, and Alexis were kind of operating on a need-to-know basis. They talked to me because of that conversation back when she first moved in, but otherwise, I don't know that I would have known either."

Holden doesn't respond; he just drops his face back into his hands.

"You know, Holden, I'm pretty sure you could have her if you're willing to share. I know that's probably not something that appeals to you, at least not right now anyway, but I think it's important you know that." I walk past him and look out the window to the snow. We're both quiet for a long moment.

"I don't think I could do that," Holden finally mutters. "I don't even know how they're doing it."

I shrug. "It's not a competition for them. They both provide her with different things, things the other can't give, or at least not well."

"She's not a pet, like a dog or a cat that anyone in the house can just love on and give pets to," Holden scoffs.

I chuckle at that. "Yeah, I don't think Alexis would appreciate the comparison there either, but in all honesty, it's not a horrible one."

"So, next, are you going to tell me that you and Shawn are in on this too?"

"I have Carrie, so no for me. Shawn is his own person, and I don't know, it's a possibility," I answer.

"And are they out sleeping with other women too?"

His curiosity is good because it means he cares, he wants to understand, so I want to do my best to give him the information I have.

"My understanding is the three of them sat down and had a pretty serious discussion about expectations. At the very least, nobody else would enter the picture without them talking about it, but I'm pretty sure neither Carter nor Ethan has any interest in pursuing other women, at least not right now." I shrug, and Holden meets my eyes again.

I choose to add, "They're not the only people that are existing in a relationship like that, and it's sure a hell of a lot better than Ethan brooding around here like he was for weeks."

"Like me?" Holden snickers.

"A little different, but yes," I concede. "Also, I don't know what happened or what was said with you two earlier, but Shawn said Alexis was really upset after, so if you think she doesn't give a fuck, you're wrong. Knowing her, she really doesn't like the idea that anything she is doing is hurting you."

Holden sighs, debating whether or not to say what comes next. "I just couldn't deal with her touching me. She was thanking me for helping her last night, but she kept touching me." He pauses, raking his hand through his hair. "Jer, I just couldn't do it. For me, there is so much fucking chemistry there, I just—"

"I'm telling you, Holden, she's a siren, and living with her platonically is not easy for any of us, including me," I admit.

"You keep saying that, but I don't even really know what you mean by it," he almost pouts.

"Mythologically, sirens are irresistible women who are dangerous or even fatal, but when I say it, I just mean the irresistible part." I take a deep breath and sit next to him on the bed before I continue.

"In my life, I've only met a few. They're honestly not common, but they are the women who command a room just by walking into it, and it's not all about how attractive they are, not that they're not; Alexis certainly is. It's more about their presence, the way they carry themselves, and the extreme empathy they emit to other people. There's probably a pheromone component, but men are drawn to them; other women typically don't like them."

"Are you telling me the chemistry I feel, you all feel it? Because I'm not sure that is helpful," he questions.

"Probably not exactly the same. Shawn and I are obviously not hurting like you are, so I'm going to say no. Ethan, though, maybe, he was just as miserable as you are, so it's possible." I pause, shoulder checking him gently. "I think at some point, soon, you're going to have to decide whether you want to be part of it or just learn how to let go of it completely."

"I don't think that's helpful, Jer, but okay." He half smiles at me.

"If you need to talk, you know where to find me, but at some point you should probably talk to her. If you need to gently set boundaries with her about what you can and can't deal with, like her touching you, then do that. It's better than whatever happened today," I conclude and pat him on the shoulder as I stand.

When I get to his door, I hear a quick "Thank you" from him, and I leave him to his own thoughts.

When I leave his room, the hall is quiet. Knowing Carter and Ethan are both trying to sleep, I head to see how Shawn is doing in Alexis' room. I open the door softly and beckon Shawn to come to the hall.

"How is she doing?" I ask.

"Still sleeping." He looks at his watch. "She is due for meds in about thirty minutes."

"Are you good, or do you need a break?" I ask.

"Honestly, I could use a break to get some food," Shawn laughs.

"Okay, go." I gesture with a tilt of my head. "I'll sit with her, same med schedule as Holden texted earlier, right?"

"Yeah," Shawn replies before making his way downstairs.

I take the spot Shawn was in, in the chair next to her bed. Alexis is lying on her right side facing me, looking so peaceful but also so pretty. I spend the next twenty minutes just staring at her. I glance at my phone for the time now and then, but I don't scroll; I just watch her sleep.

When it's time to wake her up, I gently stroke her hair. "Siren," I croon softly.

Her eyes flutter open gently. "Hey there, siren," I whisper.

The corners of her lips turn up. "Hey, boss," she teases, bringing her hands to her eyes to wipe away the sleep.

"If you're going to try to be formal, maybe you should go with 'sir,'" I counter.

"Psssh," she laughs. "We'll see about that."

"I'm glad you seem to be feeling better." I smile.

"I'm assuming you woke me up for meds," she says, meeting my gaze and mirroring my smile.

"Yeah, it's med time," I concede, letting her sit up and then handing them to her.

"How'd the investor meeting go?"

"It went well, maybe it would have gone better with you and Shawn, but I think it still went really well," I answer.

"Good, I'm glad. I'm sorry I wasn't there." She wrinkles her nose, and it's adorable.

"You were really, really sick, Alexis. I'm glad that Holden was here, and there is no reason for you to be sorry for missing work over it," I console.

I watch her face fall at the mention of Holden's name, and I take a deep breath. "Listen, Alexis. Holden is struggling. Don't be too hard on him."

"I know," she snaps and then schools her expression and voice. "Sorry, it's not your fault either. I hate it, boss... sir," she snickers, and I like that word coming off her lips. "I don't want him to be hurting at all, least of all because of me."

"Just give him some time, and maybe don't touch him." I shrug. "Or try not to."

"Yes, sir," she says and grins.

Fuck me.

I don't know if I love or regret that I told her to call me that now. Because now all I want to do is tie her up and do really, really dirty things to her.

"Siren," I sigh. "You *are* trouble."

She grins again and takes a sip of water, and her lips around the straw pull more inappropriate thoughts and feelings out of me. I decide it's time to let Carter and Ethan know she's awake.

"You think you're going straight back to sleep again?" I ask.

"No, I think I need to try to find some food, actually," she answers.

"Food would probably be good for you. Carter and Ethan wanted to know when you were up, so I'll let them know, okay?" I ask.

"Yeah, thank you, Jer, I appreciate you," she says.

"Anything for you, siren." I smooth her hair and kiss the top of her head before leaving her to go find her boyfriends.

37

ALEXIS

Ethan, Carter, and I eat lunch in the kitchen while Jeremiah is working at the dining room table. Ethan asks him if he has a minute to chat, and I suddenly feel paranoid about whether it's about me—it could be about anything.

I meet Jeremiah's gaze before he and Ethan leave the room. "Do you know where Holden is?" I ask.

"I do," Jeremiah answers. "He's downstairs, in the gym."

"Okay, thanks," I answer with a smile.

Jeremiah casts me a warning look before I turn toward the stairs. I know he's telling me to be careful, not to push him, and that's not exactly my plan. But I do want to talk to him.

The basement is dark, except for the gym. He has music playing, blasting, really, and it's angry music. I stand in the doorway and watch him for a minute. I know that it's hard for him that I'm not available, not his, but I am insanely attracted to him, too.

He was my first sanctuary in the house; he loves hard, I know that even though I barely know him. Holden has walls built up that

I will need to scale or tear down, but I fully plan on doing one or the other.

I swallow hard, mustering courage before I press the button on the speaker system to turn down the music. I turn it down to a level at which we can talk, but I don't turn it off.

Holden meets my gaze in the mirror. We've been here before; the deja vous is real. He pulls the safety on the treadmill and steps off it before he turns to look at me, but he doesn't speak, and he doesn't step toward me.

"Hey," I say softly.

"Alexis," he replies and then sighs. "What do you want?"

I shut the gym door. "To talk."

"There's nothing to talk about," he contends; his voice is rough, and he doesn't look me in the eyes.

"Holden," I plea. "Don't shut me out. If you want to be angry with me, then be angry with me, but don't shut me out."

"I'm not angry with *you*. I'm angry with the situation, Alexis." He crosses his arms across his chest and takes a step out, widening his stance.

It's protective; his body language says he is protecting himself, but he can't physically protect himself from what he's feeling.

I swallow and then speak, "I am immensely grateful for you. I'm glad you were here; I'm glad you were able to help. I need you to know that I am so, so thankful."

"I just did my job." He shrugs.

"Don't do that. Don't minimize it. You and I both know this was different. You didn't have the resources you normally have, and I'm not some random patient in the hospital." My voice cracks, and his hard facial expression falters.

Holden swallows, but he doesn't say anything.

"I'm sorry," I say, trying to soften my voice. "I'm sorry nobody told you; I'm sorry *I* didn't tell you about Ethan."

He still doesn't react; he just holds my gaze, and I hold his for a moment. I take a step toward him, but my stance continues to be protective, too, my arms across my waist.

"Nobody told you because they didn't want to hurt you. *I* didn't want to hurt you, and in the end, not telling you hurt you more, and I'm sorry." I drop one of my arms, holding it by the elbow, and take another small step toward him.

Holden watches my movements carefully but still doesn't say anything. I take another step toward him, and he swallows. I decide to lay it all out there.

"Holden, I care about you. We have to figure out how to coexist without making each other miserable, so if you need to have it out with me or if you need to just bare your soul and get it all off your chest, then do it. What do you need from me? What can I do for you? How can I help you?"

I watch as he breaks—as he shatters. "Make the rest of them disappear," he snaps. "That's the only thing that will fix this. Fuck, Alexis," he explodes; he uncrosses his arms, making big hand gestures to emphasize his words. "I would have moved on you so fast if I had known, but I was trying to give you fucking space. The shit with Brody had just happened, Ethan and I both thought it would be a dick move to take advantage of that, but then Carter, he didn't give a shit, and now we're here."

I've never seen him truly angry, never heard him raise his voice, but I try to stay stoic, regardless of the river of emotions flowing through me. I watch him, still shirtless from being on the treadmill, his skin still glistening, beads of sweat dripping down his cut abs, and I feel the heat and desire growing in me, not just from his appearance but also from his words.

I look at him and wait for him to continue, to keep going; this is what I wanted from him: raw emotion. It's what I *need* from him.

"I don't know how Ethan can do it. I don't know how either of them can do it." Holden shakes his head, and the volume of his voice comes down a couple of notches. "I know there are other people who do it successfully; I just don't get it."

He is quiet for a while, and I decide to address what he said. "I want to acknowledge something because I think it's important for you to know. If you had moved first, I can't imagine a scenario where I would have denied you." I wait until his gaze meets mine, pain flashing in those blue pools. "I also can't imagine a scenario *now* where I would deny you." Something else flashes in his eyes. "I know that you're not comfortable with all of that right now, but I need you to know that."

I take another step toward him, and he watches me carefully. "Obviously, I can't make Carter and Ethan disappear, and honestly, I don't want to. As for how it works, I have two very different relationships with each of them, and all three of us communicate constantly, so we know we're on the same page."

"'*Communicate*,' is that what you're calling it?"

"Holden," I chide, tilting my head and taking another step toward him; two more steps, and there will be no more distance between us. "Yes, we talk. We have boundaries, rules, expectations; honestly, I think they talk to each other more about it than they talk to me about it."

Holden rakes his hand through his hair and then shakes his head.

I continue, "I care about you. I'm glad that you're in my life. I'm so, so sorry that this is so hard for all of us, not just for you." I add for emphasis, "They care about you too, but I don't need to tell you that; you should know that."

His Adam's apple bobs with his swallow. "I do know that." His voice is gravelly.

One more step. I don't say anything; I just hold his gaze, and he holds mine. Fire and hunger burn in his eyes, and maybe there's still some anger.

I'm not going to close the distance, that one more step, and I'm not going to initiate anything physical, not even a hug. Those balls are in his court.

"Alexis." My name comes off his tongue reverently, like a plea.

I offer a soft smile, swallow, and just hold his eyes.

"Fuck, why does this have to be so fucking hard?" Holden asks rhetorically and laces his fingers behind his head, looking at the ceiling, his jaw set tight.

"It doesn't have to be," I suggest.

His eyes pull down to mine from the ceiling, and he closes the distance between us with one small step. His hand weaves in the hair at the base of my skull.

Shockwaves go through me—his touch feeding a hunger and desire stronger than anything I've felt in a long time. I try to bury that, knowing it's not fair to Carter or Ethan for me to even acknowledge that comparison.

I know he is going to kiss me. I lick my lips and leave them slightly parted, but then—he doesn't.

Holden tilts my head up by pulling my hair back, an aggressive and possessive move that takes my breath away. He rests his forehead on mine, his lips so close to mine that we're sharing breath.

Moving his mouth next to my ear, he kisses my neck, and then he speaks.

"Alexis, I want you, but I can't share you," he murmurs, pressing a gentle kiss to my forehead before reluctantly releasing me.

Stepping back, he puts distance between us. His actions leave me feeling weak, lightheaded, utterly bewildered, and wet.

"That," he exclaims. "That right there; the way you're feeling right now is how I feel every time you touch me. I can live in this platonic hell that has been created for me, but I need you not to touch me, Alexis, angel, please."

I bite my lip until I taste copper and breathe through the

chemicals invading all my senses. Wrapping my arms around myself, I nod in agreement.

"Okay, Holden. Point proven, I'm sorry," I concede softly, acknowledging his sentiment.

"Alexis," Holden pleads a little apologetically. "I don't want to hurt you. I care about you so fucking much. And that's the problem, just please, don't make this harder."

My tears betray me, and I see the pain on Holden's face.

I shake my head in silent turmoil and turn to leave the gym. But just as my hand reaches for the door handle, I feel his firm grip on my forearm, pulling me back into his embrace.

My cheek ends up against his bare, sweaty chest as his strong arms envelop me. Tears stream down my face uncontrollably, my body yielding to the overwhelming flood of emotions. I keep my hands pressed against my face, unable to bring myself to wrap them around him or even touch him.

I sob, the sound muffled by his chest, and then my cries soften into quiet sobs that seem to stretch on for an eternity. Holden's lips brush gently, peppering kisses against my hair, a tender gesture of comfort, while his hands remain steadfast, just holding me tight.

"Alexis, angel," Holden breathes. "I don't know how to do this. I don't know how to make this okay for either of us."

"I don't either," I confess, my lip quivering. "I'm sorry."

"Don't be sorry." He pulls me in tighter. "It's hard for both of us. I see that now; it's not just me."

"I'm not trying to torture you," I admit. "I'm not trying to torture me. I can't—I *won't* change the other part of the equation, Holden."

"I know," he quietly concedes and slowly unwraps his arms from around me. "And I'm not mad at them either. Again, it's just the situation."

I wipe my eyes and sniffle before Holden continues, "I've known Ethan since kindergarten and Carter since second grade." He gently brushes my hair off my face. "We'll be okay, and I'll try harder to be okay with you to figure out how to do this in a way we can both live with."

I nod, wiping my eyes. "Me too, Holden," I murmur. "I'm sorry."

"Also," he reasons, "I know you're not at one hundred percent. It wasn't even eighteen hours ago that I was desperately trying to get your body temperature down. You need rest. I'm exhausted, and I'm sure Carter and Ethan are too. It probably isn't great timing to even try to have this conversation." I start to object, and he shakes his head. "But I appreciate you trying to make it better. I'm sorry, there's no magic wand here."

As soon as he finishes speaking, a sudden knock echoes through the room. Someone knocking on one of the doors in the house that is almost never closed. My gaze meets Holden's, and I hastily wipe my tear-stained face one last time before I turn to open the gym door.

I am quietly hoping it's Jeremiah, maybe Shawn, but on the other side stands Ethan. His eyes swiftly scan my expression before shooting a less-than-friendly glance in Holden's direction. His focus returns to me, and a concerned furrow knits his brow.

"You okay?" Ethan asks softly.

"Yeah," I assure him quietly and nod. "I'm good. I think I need to lie down, though."

"Yeah, you probably should," Ethan agrees. "Why don't you do that? Let me talk to Holden for a minute?"

I nod and look back at Holden and utter quietly, "Thank you."

Holden softly smiles at me. As I walk past Ethan, he grazes his hand down my arm and squeezes my hand before turning back to Holden. I find myself hoping that Ethan doesn't overreact.

38

ETHAN

I was definitely pissed off when Alexis first opened the door, all puffy-eyed and tear-stained, but then she thanked him, and now I'm just confused.

Closing the door before I glance at Holden, I try to keep my cool.

"What happened?" I ask, crossing my arms but keeping my tone casual—like I'm asking about the weather.

Holden shakes his head, looking conflicted. "Nothing... everything." He hedges and then sighs, "I don't know how to have this conversation with you, Ethan."

"Just start at the beginning," I suggest, taking a less intimidating position and straddling a bench.

Holden is probably the person I trust the most of all these guys I've known since childhood. I'm not angry at him; I just need to understand what's causing them both so much turmoil.

"I freaked out earlier," Holden admits, leaning back against one of the machines. "I just needed her to stop touching me." He rolls his eyes and gazes at the ceiling.

He must notice something on my face because he quickly laughs and clarifies, "Not like that, Ethan. Just normal, everyday friendly gestures." He swallows. "She was just trying to say thank you and put her hands on me the way a lot of people do. Fuck, the way even sometimes patients and family members at the hospital do."

I stay quiet and just look at him, giving him space to work through his thoughts. The irony doesn't go unnoticed by me that I was sitting on this very bench when Carter talked to me a few weeks ago.

Holden meets my gaze. "She tried to apologize, to make it better." He gestures toward the door. "I made it worse, and now I think it's okay—as okay as it can be."

"Are *we* good?" I ask, trying to keep my voice calm. "You and me? You and Carter?"

Holden inhales deeply. "Yeah, I'm not mad at any of you; I'm upset about the situation, but not at any of you."

"Look, Holden," I begin, my tone serious but soft. "I know that the whole situation probably doesn't make sense to you, at least not right now. I know, we *all* know, that you are struggling with this on multiple levels."

I pause, giving him a moment to absorb my words. He nods and takes another deep breath but doesn't say anything.

"I'm sorry we didn't tell you," I apologize sincerely. "*I* should have told you. I respect you so much, and I didn't want to hurt you, but this was clearly not the way to go about this."

He puffs out his cheeks and blows them out again, but he doesn't meet my eyes. He does, however, speak quietly.

"I just don't understand it," he confesses. "I have a million questions, but none of them are appropriate to ask."

I chuckle quietly. "We had and still have a lot of questions for each other, so you're not alone."

"I guess my biggest question is, what does a future look like in a relationship like that? I just feel like there is disaster written all over it from the start. Like it will all unravel when people decide they want to get married or have kids and all that 'normal' stuff," Holden confides, using air quotes at the end.

We haven't had this conversation outside of the three of us, and I feel like I need to be a little guarded to protect Alexis and Carter, but I also need to be honest.

"For the three of us, that's easy, and we've talked about it," I acknowledge.

Holden's expression flickers in surprise. Maybe he thought this was just a carnal thing or that we hadn't thought any of this through.

I extrapolate on the subject. "Carter is pretty sure he doesn't want more kids, I don't want kids, and Alexis is undecided on that, but she loves Ana." I pause for a long moment, letting Holden absorb that. "As for marriage, Carter doesn't want to get married again, and my only reasons would be financial and other logistical stuff. I can take care of that with paperwork other than a marriage license. Alexis has had two engagements that ended abruptly. She isn't sure she wants to get married, but she's not opposed to it."

Holden doesn't say anything, but he is looking at me. I can tell he's processing.

"Also, if she did want to get married, she could marry one of us, and it wouldn't need to change our dynamic." I swallow. "But honestly, Holden, we've had all those conversations, and we're weeks into this. How many relationships have you had where you have had those deep conversations so early?"

He scoffs, "Yeah, probably none. Maybe a casual conversation about children, but not in depth."

"Also, Hold, I think it's important for you to know that our relationships with her are not just physical." Swallowing, I hesitate, about to say something out loud I haven't even said to her yet. "We're not quite three weeks in, but it has already set a new standard for me. This is probably emotionally and psychologically the best relationship I've ever been in. With Alexis, everything feels refreshingly straightforward—no mind games, no manipulation, no hidden agendas, no saying one thing and meaning another. I have no concerns about her only being here for the money—it's a stark contrast to some of my past experiences. I find myself falling deeper every day, and, honestly, after last night, I'm pretty sure I love her; I'm *in* love with her."

"And that doesn't bother Carter?" Holden asks, almost interrogating.

"Carter has his own relationship with her, his own feelings. He and I are navigating uncharted territory together, recognizing the importance of having each other's backs and openly communicating with each other. We understand that the success or failure of one of us would undoubtedly have ripple effects on the other," I admit. "Still, it's important to remember that this is all still in its infancy. While we're optimistic about the future, we're also aware that uncertainties lie ahead; it *is* still uncharted territory, and we don't have a crystal ball."

I feel my phone vibrate in my pocket, and Holden looks like he is contemplating everything I just said, so I give him that minute and check my phone.

(Carter) *What the fuck happened?*

(Me) *Down boy, lol*

(Carter) *Ethan*

(Me) *I'll explain soon - trying to bring Holden down a few notches - Alexis was good with him when she left*

(Me) *She even told him thank you*

(Carter) *Fuck, okay - she asked Jeremiah to go sit with her,*
so I need you to fill me in
(Carter) *My anxiety is through the roof*
(Me) *I'll fill you in*

"Sorry." I clear my throat, pocket my phone, and look back at Holden.

It takes him another few heartbeats before he speaks. "She—she eluded to—" He stops himself and looks at the ceiling.

I know where he's going with this, and I have mixed feelings about it because he is so much more outwardly emotional than Carter or me.

"She eluded to you being able to be part of it?" I ask, and it's almost more of a statement than a question.

Holden nods and then scrubs his face with his hands.

I take a solid minute, making sure I choose my words carefully. It's a delicate situation, and saying the wrong thing could have con-sequences far beyond just Holden and me. Plus, I'm acutely aware that shutting him down without hurting Alexis is impossible now, especially after he's just confirmed she made that offer to him.

Fucking siren.

I laugh more at myself than anything else, and Holden looks at me.

"Holden, listen," I confirm, meeting his gaze directly, "That's def-initely a possibility. Carter and I have discussed it, and he'd be okay with it, too. It's a conversation we've already had."

"You talked about *me*?" Holden's skeptical expression and tone prompt me to elaborate further.

"Yes, we talked about several potential scenarios and possibilities, including you."

His surprise is evident, so I decide to reinforce my point. "Alexis does care about you, Holden. She's attracted to you, and while she has stopped only a little short of explicitly saying it, it's clear to us. Just like Carter knew the same about me."

I pause, allowing my words to sink in before continuing. "But here's the thing, Holden. If you're considering pursuing something with her, you need to be absolutely sure. You need to understand that it wouldn't just be you. There are complexities involved, the potential for ripple effects, and you have to be prepared for that. There's no half in; you need to be sure."

He replies almost instantly, "I don't think I could do it." Swallowing, he continues, "I have always envisioned and dreamed of a nuclear family and white picket fences, and in none of those scenarios and dreams is my wife off fucking other people."

I shrug one shoulder and shake my head. "Well, then that's your answer. And I respect it. But that means you have to figure out how to be okay with us." I meet his gaze. "Even if you were to move out, we've been friends forever, Holden, I don't see us walking away from each other."

He shakes his head. "No, I'm not walking away from you and Carter. Bros before, well, yeah," he laughs, and I laugh with him.

"I'm sorry, man. I know we're all sleep-deprived and coming down off the adrenaline high of last night; it's a lot right now," I acknowledge.

Holden nods, and I stand.

"I'll leave you to run off your feelings now," I suggest while opening the door.

"Thank you, Ethan," he says as I leave the room.

Upstairs in the kitchen, I find a pacing Carter. He immediately starts an interrogation.

"Ethan, what happened?"

"First, where's Alexis?" I counter, my hands in front of me in a placating gesture.

"In her room. Jeremiah is still with her." Carter is exasperated.

"I think she just needs to decompress with someone who isn't us." I swallow, thinking to myself that it really is just Carter, but saying that right now won't help.

The look he shoots me tells me he isn't happy with that response, and he continues pacing.

He's so wound up from the adrenaline crash from last night and the big meeting this morning. Carter operates by amplifying hard and then crashing hard in high-pressure situations, and I've watched him do it for years.

Right now, Carter needs sleep.

"She'll be okay, Carter. From what Holden said, it sounds like she just grabbed his arm or hugged him or something, trying to say thank you for helping, and he freaked out on her to not touch him," I explain, and Carter's gaze snaps up to mine.

I put my hands back up in concession. "That was earlier, what Shawn was talking about." I clear my throat. "Then it sounds like she tried to fix it. He made it worse again, but then he made it better. They were good when she left the basement, as good as they will be, anyway."

Carter doesn't say anything; his arms are spread wide, hands resting on the end of the island, and he drops his head.

"Holden was struggling with Alexis and you—we—knew that. Finding out about Alexis and me, well, it pushed him over the edge." I give Carter an opportunity to respond. "One of us should have told him, but we didn't, and this is the fallout. There may have been fallout anyway, but that's what this is."

Carter nods, and then I continue, "Also, probably should not be discussing this in the open, but you should know that she did put an offer on the table to Holden."

That gets his attention.

"Like—" He pauses and gestures between the two of us.

"Yeah," I nod in agreement. "At this point, it won't happen.

But she planted the seed and he had questions, questions that I answered. So, I thought you should know."

"How do you feel about that?" Carter asks me.

Shrugging, I answer, "I think it would be okay. I don't know if *he* can do it, but I'm good with it. What about you?"

"I'd be fine with it, especially if it saves drama," Carter responds as he crosses his arms over his chest and starts pacing again. "Honestly, I stand by the original conversation I had with you and then the one I had with the both of you. I think any of them Jer, Shawn, or Holden, I'd be okay with, but I compartmentalize better than you I think, so I need to make sure you're good. Alexis would need to make sure you were good."

I take a moment to decide whether or not that was an insult. "I think I'm good with anything she is good with."

Carter nods at me, and as we hear Holden on the basement stairs, we stop the conversation.

I look at the two of them, knowing Carter needs to have his own conversation here. "I'm going to head upstairs. I'm exhausted."

They both nod in agreement and I leave them to their own conversation.

39

JEREMIAH

Moments after Ethan went down to the basement, Alexis comes up the stairs. Her tear-stained face and swollen eyes instantly trigger Carter. I know Ethan never would have sent her back up alone if she was really still upset.

Carter is a little too aggressive as he asks, "Lex, what the fuck happened?"

She shakes her head, her voice cracking when she answers, "It'll be fine, Carter. I need to lie down, though." She pauses and looks at me, back at Carter, and then back at me. "Can you come talk to me?"

I nod yes, but I don't miss the tick and tightening of Carter's jaw. For being so open with her in so many ways, there is an extremely possessive element to him, too. I know he is going to be fuming and amping up until Ethan makes an appearance back upstairs or she invites him to her room, but that is going to be for him to work out.

Alexis and I are quiet as we ascend the stairs. When we get to her room, she smiles and asks me to give her a minute. While she is in the restroom, I take a minute to look at some of the personal touches she has added to the room. Earlier, my focus was different, and I hadn't really paid attention.

She put up a bookshelf near her desk, and while there are books, there are also pictures. There are a few of Alexis with another woman, and it looks like pictures of them when they were younger, too. There are also a few pictures with men, maybe brothers. I don't know; it's none of my business. I do notice, though, that there are no pictures of parents or big family pictures.

"Hey," I hear her voice behind me, "sorry."

"There's nothing to be sorry about," I answer, turning towards her.

"Please," she says, pointing to the chair still setup next to her bed, and she climbs in her bed, tucking her knees to her chest. I sit and wait for her to start because I'm not sure where she is going to go with this.

"Jer, do you think I should move out? I mean, you pay me enough." She steals a side glance at me. "I just think it's too much drama, me being here."

Well, fuck, that is not where I thought we'd go. I take a few moments to gather my thoughts.

"Alexis, siren, no." I lean forward and put my hand on the blanket over her foot, just seeking some connection. "I don't think that would fix this."

"Maybe if I walked away completely, it would." She shrugs. "From Carter, from Ethan, found another job."

Now, I feel my own anxiety ramping up. It's a litle unexpected and I'm not quite sure how to process my own feelings.

"Could you really do that, though? Could you walk away from them? From us?" I ask, and that last question brings a lump to my throat.

Sighing, she shakes her head and then leans her head back against the headboard. She is quiet for a few, long moments.

"I just feel like I've fucked up everything for all of you," she states quietly.

"No, you haven't. You have been amazing for all of us, professionally, personally, you have made so many positive impacts." I take a breath and lean closer to her. "The drama is because you have been amazing."

A tear falls down her cheek, and I want to wipe it away, but that feels too intimate.

"I think the dust will settle; I also think you need sleep. All of you; you, Holden, Ethan, Carter, all of you—you're all trying to deal with this sleep deprived and you probably still don't feel great." Her beautiful blue eyes meet mine. "Give it some time; recover from last night, see where everything lands."

Alexis surprises me by starting to laugh. She covers her face with both hands and just keeps laughing.

There's a knock on her door; she looks up and says, "Come in." And then continues laughing.

Ethan walks in, shuts the door behind him, and then smiles, looking between us. "What's so funny?"

"I have no idea," I answer.

"It's just—it's just—" Alexis starts and then laughs so hard she can't talk.

"I think she's slaphappy," I comment to Ethan.

She breathes for a minute and looks at Ethan. "Have you ever noticed how father-like Jeremiah sounds sometimes?"

"Hey," I say, feigning offense, and Ethan smiles at her.

"I have, actually," Ethan responds. "It's part of why I keep him around."

"Maybe I should call you 'daddy' instead of 'sir,'" she barely gets the words out and then falls over on the bed laughing.

Both Ethan and I start laughing, too. But if she starts calling me "daddy," I don't even know what I'll do with her.

"She is definitely slaphappy; she needs to sleep," I say, rolling my eyes at Ethan. "Is everything okay downstairs?"

Ethan shrugs. "Holden is good, Carter is good, they're figuring out now if they're good with each other."

That sobers Alexis a little as she looks at Ethan, but then she laughs again.

"I'm going to leave you two. I'm sure you've got her now," I assure Ethan with a smile. "I think she is due for meds soon."

* * *

ETHAN

"Hey, baby girl." I smile, taking the chair by Lexi's bed. "You okay?"

Nodding, she reaches for me, takes my hand, then asks, "Holden okay?"

"He is, mostly anyway," I answer and smooth her hair.

"Did you yell at him?" Lexi questions, wrinkling her nose.

"No, we just talked. He told what happened and asked some questions about us and our dynamics," I answer. "I didn't yell at him."

"Thank you," she replies, and then she smiles softly, and it lights up her face.

"So 'sir,' huh? That's what you're calling Jeremiah now?" I joke.

"Inside-ish joke from earlier today. He actually was being fatherly then, too," she laughs. "I said 'yes boss,' and he joked about if I was going to be formal, I should say 'sir.'"

I roll my eyes. "Oh, that's just what we need: a bigger power trip from him!"

Then her face takes on a serious expression. "I asked him if I should move out."

Where the fuck did that come from?

"Wait, what? Why?" I find myself reaching for her other hand, wanting to hold her so she won't leave.

She sighs. "Because it's just so much drama for you guys."

"Lexi, love, no," I reply, almost begging, before I clear my throat and continue. "This is temporary, the drama. It's temporary. It will resolve one way or another."

"That's what Jeremiah said too," she responds, and thank fuck he was on the same page as me.

I have no response for her. My guts feel like they were just turned inside out. I just need her close to me.

"Come sleep with me tonight? I know you still won't feel great, but I need to hold you." I smile softly and brush a tendril of hair out of her face.

"Maybe," she says coyly and then laughs.

I think that's a yes. She's just flirting with me. I press a soft kiss to her forehead, and then someone knocks on her bedroom door.

She smiles. "It's Grand Central Station around here today." She looks from me to the door. "Come in."

Carter looks between us and says, "I figured you might be alone since Jeremiah is downstairs now."

Alexis smiles at him. "I'm sorry, Carter, I didn't mean to brush you off downstairs."

He sits on the bed next to her, our knees almost touching. "It's okay, princess. You good?"

"Yeah," she nods.

"She was asking Jeremiah for advice," I confide and look at Lexi.

She nods, so I continue. "She was asking him if she should move out because of all the drama."

Carter's face reflects exactly how I felt when she told me; he looks at her. "I hope he told you no."

"He did tell me no, and so did Ethan." She smiles.

"We'll be okay." Carter smiles at her. "We were friends for over twenty years before you; you won't break us."

I know he believes the words he just said, but I'm not as confident as he is.

"Give us a minute?" Carter asks, looking at me.

"Yeah, you're good." I stand and kiss Alexis softly on the forehead, then pat Carter on the shoulder. "I'll see you both at dinner. Let me know if you need anything."

* * *

CARTER

As soon as Ethan is gone, I look at Lex and find her hands.

"I'm sorry," I apologize. "I *am* sleep-deprived and on either an adrenaline high or an adrenaline crash. Seeing you upset amped me up. I didn't mean to snap at you."

She lets go of one of my hands and reaches up to cradle my jaw. "You're fine, Carter; I wasn't upset with you. I'm glad to know you're a little protective."

Fuck, she's perfect.

Continuing, she adds, "I was upset at the situation, Holden is upset at the situation, nobody is mad at each other. At least, I don't think."

"I think that's an accurate assessment." I smile at her and then take a deep breath, moving to the chair next to the bed so I can really face her.

Lex watches me silently, like she knows I want to say something important.

I pull her right hand with both of mine and kiss her knuckles, then hold her hand next to my jaw.

"Lex, princess, last night was scary." The lump in my throat surprises me as those words leave me, and I swallow. "I don't think anyone really told you, but I couldn't wake you up; Holden couldn't wake you up. You were so, so hot."

I kiss her knuckles again, and I feel the sting of tears in my eyes; I can't remember the last time I shed tears.

"Lex, I was terrified. If Holden hadn't been here—I don't know what I would have done, but I did confirm something last night in all that chaos." Pausing, I bring her knuckles to my lips again. "Lex, I love you. I love you with my whole heart, with every breath I take."

Suddenly, Lex surprises me by moving from the bed to my lap, wrapping her arms around my neck. I hold her close, the warmth of her presence calming the storm of emotions raging within me. In that moment, her physical closeness fills a void I didn't even know existed.

After a few moments, she pulls back and meets my gaze with unwavering sincerity. "I love you too, Carter." Her words wash over me like a wave, affirming everything I'm feeling.

40

ALEXIS

After Carter leaves me to shower and change for dinner, I text Ethan because I know, after that exchange, I need to give Carter time with me tonight. And this is where this whole unconventional relationship starts to feel like pressure—like guilt.

(Me) *Hey, I might have to raincheck tonight, but do you want to come snuggle with me now?*

(Ethan) *That sneaky ... yeah, I'll come snuggle with you*

(Me) *It's me, not him lol - What do you have going on tomorrow?*

(Ethan) *Nothing I can't get out of lol*

(Me) *Good - I'll steal you then too*

(Ethan) *You don't have to steal what is already yours*

And my heart melts inside my chest.

* * *

Dinner is a little quiet and a little awkward. Jeremiah and Shawn do a lot of talking, trying to fill in the conversation gaps. Everyone is pleasant, but it feels like there's an elephant in the room.

Letting Carter hold me all night soothes my soul and my body. His strong arms make me feel safe, loved, and secure, and he needed this too. He needed to hold me to know I am okay.

I know he'll let me go to Ethan without worrying, but otherwise, I don't know that he'll let me out of his sight anytime soon. Being in the basement with Holden almost drove him crazy; there were other factors there, but still.

"Good morning, beautiful," Carter whispers against my neck when we start to stir in the morning.

Turning to him, I make sure to meet his eyes before saying, "Good morning. I love you."

Carter kisses me gently and softly and then makes love to me slowly. It's the most sensual and loving we have ever been together, and I love him more for it.

* * *

In the shower, I realize that I am feeling much better, and Holden was likely right about it being something I ate, probably while I was out to lunch with Carrie.

The snow is now passable, so Carrie is coming over this afternoon. True to my word, after lunch, I drag Ethan to his room, and my plan is to stay there until dinner and then the next morning.

I am craving the physical closeness with him; I have been since before I got sick. He's my rock. I'm sure someday he'll say something wrong, do something wrong, somehow piss me off. But Carter is right about that; it hasn't happened yet. Emotionally, he is the perfect partner for me.

They both give me things I need, want, and crave. They're not competition for each other in my mind or my heart; they're just different.

After dinner, I find myself back in Ethan's arms.

"I'm glad you're feeling better," Ethan says after I snuggle up on his chest.

We're watching some action movie I've seen too many times, lying in his bed. His hand is brushing through my hair and down my back in patterns that send electricity down my spine and leave goosebumps on my flesh. I love to breathe in the smell of him while running my fingers through his chest hair.

"Me too; that was a rough couple of days."

"Hey, Lexi, I have a question," he says curiously.

"What's that?"

"You don't have to answer if you don't want to," he starts. "But when you did your Readers Digest version of your life story, you said you had been engaged twice. What happened with the first one?"

I pick up the remote, pause the movie, and swallow before leaning up to rest my chin on my hand across his chest. "Do you want to hear my whole tragic tale or just that one?"

"Let's start with that one," he answers empathetically, meeting my gaze and running his fingers through my hair.

I swallow again before answering. "He died, Ethan. We were twenty-three; it was three months before our wedding date."

"Fuck, Lexi, love, I'm so sorry." He brushes his knuckles across my cheekbone.

"It's been a while, but I did leave flowers on his grave before I moved out here." I shrug.

"You don't have to tell me more than you want to, but what

happened, and how is that only *part* of your tragic story?" Ethan's questioning voice is colored with concern and empathy.

I pour out my soul, my tragedies from high school on, my parents' not-so-helpful and even potentially illegal involvement, and my love life from then until Brody. There are tears and it does dawn on me as we talk into the wee hours of the morning that Ethan probably now knows me better than anyone else in the house.

Since I moved in, he's always felt like an emotional safe space, so it makes sense that now we'd be here. Carter is my physical safe space, but Ethan locks the things we share, the conversations we have in a vault. My relationship with Ethan sometimes feels more intimate than the one I have with Carter.

After he has heard so much of my life story and we're lying there, quiet, I trace patterns on his chest.

"Ethan?"

"Yes, love?"

I lean up on my elbow and look at him. Meeting his eyes, I am suddenly overwhelmed with emotion, and tears involuntarily fall on my cheeks.

"Lexi." He smiles softly, pulling me closer, before he wipes the tears from my cheeks. "What's wrong?"

I smile. "Nothing is wrong, Ethan; I just need you to know that I love you."

"Alexis." My name comes off his lips like a caress, maybe a plea. "I love you so much. I thought it might be too soon to tell you."

He presses a gentle kiss to my forehead and then studies me reverently. We talk a little while longer, expressing feelings and talking about the dynamics around our unconventional relationship, and Ethan even dives into legal and logistical things we might want to think about—always the protector.

When we're finally done talking, Ethan just holds me for the rest of the night. It's sweet and exactly what I need. I wake up in his arms as his alarm gradually rises in volume until it's annoyingly loud.

"Ethan," I laugh as he pulls me closer.

He groans and rolls away from me to turn off the alarm on his phone, then turns back to me. "Jeremiah, Carter, and I have a meeting in thirty minutes. Will you wait here for me?"

"Maybe," I say playfully.

"I'll make it worth it," he states suggestively with a wink.

"Well, when you put it like that," I reply and pull him to me for a kiss before he disappears into his bathroom.

I take my time alone in Ethan's room to call Georgia and update her.

"It sounds to me like you're lucky you had a doctor in the house," Georgia observes. "Maybe he'll be in more than just the house soon."

She laughs. Hard.

"Georgia!" I exclaim.

"Come on, you want that, and you know it," she asserts confidently.

I clear my throat. "In all seriousness, I told him it was an option, but I don't think he wants that, not with Carter and Ethan."

Georgia laughs again, "You're such a slut." She's joking; she doesn't mean it as an insult. "I'm happy you're happy, Lex; sometime I'll need to come out there and meet this harem of yours."

Now it's my turn to laugh. "It's not a harem, at least not yet." My voice substantially rises in pitch at the end of that statement, and then we're both laughing.

The bedroom door opens while I'm recovering from that bout of laughter, and it's not just Ethan coming back; it's Ethan and Carter. I can see the intention in their eyes.

"Hey, Georgia," I laugh. "I think I need to go. I'll talk to you later."

"Okay, have fun," she laughs. "Keep me posted." She pauses, laughing again. "Siren."

I hang up the phone and look at my men, the men who love me, and the hunger and lust in their eyes is all I need to know.

41

ALEXIS

"Well, hi," I greet them as they enter the room and Ethan turns and locks the door.

Carter smiles salaciously. "You feeling well enough for this?"

"I guess that depends on what you mean by 'this,'" I tease.

"Oh, I think you know," Ethan adds with a smile. "And I think you're good."

"She is a *good* girl," Carter agrees, his voice low and lascivious.

Fuck me.

That voice right there, and I'm already wet; he doesn't even have to touch me. They're both in business clothes, Ethan in a polo shirt, Carter in a long-sleeve, button-down, and both in slacks.

"I think you are far too overdressed for such talk," I say, biting my bottom lip.

Carter starts on the buttons on his cuffs while Ethan continues to just stare at me, eye-fucking me.

"I know you're not wearing much, but why don't you be a good girl and take it off?" Carter suggests, tipping his chin up.

Ethan pulls off his shirt and moves toward me, climbing on the bed on my right.

Cradling my jaw with his hand, he leans his mouth next to my ear and whispers, "We just want to show you how much we love you."

Electricity dances across my skin and down my spine. Then he finds my lips and kisses me deeply, and the combination of Carter's dirty words and Ethan's sweet ones ignites a fire in me.

As Ethan is kissing me, he hooks his fingers under the hem of my tank top and, breaking the kiss, pulls it over my head.

I don't even realize Carter moving, but I become aware of his presence on my left as his hand slides up from my side to my breast. As I turn to look at him, he captures my mouth with his while Ethan's lips find my neck under my ear.

I'm not sure if I've ever felt so wanted in my entire life.

Ethan's fingers move down my body, snagging the waistband of my shorts and thong, then his mouth leaves my skin, and he smoothly tugs them down off my feet. I catch him in my periphery, taking off his own pants while Carter continues to kiss me and play with one of my nipples with his fingers.

As Ethan moves back toward me, his hand sweeps up the inside of my leg, teasing the outer folds of my pussy.

"Fuck, Alexis, you're so wet," Ethan growls just before his mouth finds the hard peak of my other breast.

My hands find places to hold on to both of them as Carter's mouth drops down to my neck, and he hooks his right hand behind me. Deft fingers slide down my ass until they reach my wet and waiting pussy, cupping me from behind.

"Wet, she is," Carter groans. "Look at how much you want us, princess."

Carter dips two fingers inside me while Ethan works his fingers in my folds to my clit that is already throbbing and aching to be touched. I gasp as they both work my aching cunt with their fingers.

I don't know if they planned the action, but having both of their hands on me like this is so fucking erotic.

I feel the intensity of the building orgasm relatively quickly. As my hips rise, my pelvis trying to grind into them, both of them, Carter inserts a third finger. Moving his fingers up to the perfect spot, his ministrations on my inner walls while Ethan handles my clit with expertise is enough to undo me.

I moan as my head tips back and my back arches. Ethan's mouth leaves my nipple as he moves up to trace his tongue up my neck, his lips and teeth finding my earlobe. As my body convulses under and around them, Ethan's words find my ear.

"I love the way you come," he whispers.

As my body settles, I hear Carter's filthy mouth, "Fuck yeah, baby, such a good girl—come for us again."

Carter's fingers never leave me, but they do still completely momentarily. Ethan brings his fingers up to my mouth and slides them past my lips, letting the taste of my fluids coat my tongue. His mouth meets mine again, and he kisses me deeply as his hand travels back to my clit to resume his perfect, gratifying movements.

When my toes curl and my mouth falls away from Ethan's as I come undone again, Carter growls more praises, "Such a good fucking girl, so fucking needy, so fucking perfect."

Ethan's eyes meet mine, and he drops his mouth next to my ear again. "You're perfect, I love you," he whispers.

They both run their hands over the length of my body. Working in almost perfect unison, Ethan rolls to his back, pulling me with him, and Carter lets me go.

Carter's mouth finds my neck quickly, his voice raspy. "Straddle him, princess, fucking ride him. I want that fucking perfect ass."

As he finishes the sentence, his fingers run from my cunt back to his not-so-forbidden target, and I inhale sharply as he enters it with one finger. He laughs sinfully and then smacks my ass after he removes his finger.

Ethan's hands find my hips as I sit up on him, his hard length under the wet folds of my pussy. Leaning forward, I kiss him, tilting my hips down toward his belly and then sitting back up, sinking him inside me with a gasp from both of us.

One of Ethan's hands runs up to play with my nipples while the other stays gripping my hip. Gliding him in and out of me a few times while Carter moves behind me and trails his hand all over my ass and asscrack, I lean over Ethan, my mouth meeting his again.

I feel Carter circling his target with the tip of his cock. As he slowly pushes into me, and the euphoria, the dizzying high, washes over me, I let my face fall to the crook of Ethan's neck with a moan. His facial hair is familiar, tickling the side of my face.

"That's so fucking hot," Ethan whispers against my ear, his hands grazing up and down my back, occasionally gripping at my hair.

"I love your fucking tight ass," Carter groans.

I move my hips the most I can, and they both thrust into me; Carter's much harder because he has more room to move. Carter holds my hips and occasionally smacks my ass, drawing gasps out of me.

My mouth and teeth find Ethan's neck while my arms work to support some of my weight off of him.

"Princess, you're about to be full of me," Carter growls and then thrusts twice more before I feel him shake and throb, signaling his finish.

I feel, more than see Ethan nod at him, and as Carter moves, Ethan pushes me over so I'm on my back, and then he fucks me hard for a good minute before he finishes and then lays down next to me. Both of them kiss my sweat-kissed skin and run their hands over my body in the aftermath of another intense escapade.

Ethan lies to my side, gently kissing my shoulder, while Carter is a little more aggressive, his lips and teeth on my neck. Eventually, I tell them it's bathroom time for me, and they release me to find my way to Ethan's bathroom.

I've learned, and I now take my clothes with me since they like to get dressed while I'm gone. In my own room, I keep extra clothes in the bathroom now because I like to be prepared, but I'm really comfortable in Ethan's giant bathroom as well. A quick whore bath, my clothes back on, a quick brush through my hair, and I'm ready to be back out in the bedroom.

They're creatures of habit, alright. Carter is already fully dressed, casually leaning against the back of the loveseat near the end of Ethan's bed. Meanwhile, Ethan is in sweats and no shirt, lounging against the bed as they chat casually, exchanging smiles.

When they see me, Carter wraps an arm around me and kisses my temple before speaking softly in my ear. "I love you; I'll see you later."

I smile at him, and as soon as he leaves, Ethan grabs my hands and pulls me closer to him. Naturally, I lean my head into his chest and he hugs me closer to him.

"You good?" Ethan asks.

"Yeah," I reply, adding a small laugh. "Very."

He holds me for a while before I crane my neck back so I can see his face and say, "I love you, Ethan."

One of his strong hands moves up and brushes the loose hair off my cheek before cupping my face and saying, "I love you too, so fucking much."

Pressing a kiss to my forehead, he sighs and continues, "I never would have thought that this kind of relationship would be so fulfilling, but it is. You are amazing."

I chuckle softly and kiss him quickly. "How was your meeting with Jeremiah?"

"It was good." A big, genuine smile crosses his face as his arms move down, wrapping around me, resting his hands on the small of my back. "We got the investors."

"That is good news," I agree.

"Worth celebrating," he says with a wink, and his hands move up the ladder of my ribs.

"Ethan! And you call me needy," I laugh.

"Technically, this time that was Carter," he argues jokingly. "But no, not right now. I want you to myself, yes, but not right this minute. I did want to talk to you about something, though."

"Yeah?" I ask, my hands naturally splaying and then trailing up his chest to his broad shoulders.

"Yeah, Carter just told me, well us, me and Jeremiah, about Chicago." He smiles.

"What about Chicago? I didn't let him do anything in Chicago," I retort skeptically.

"About helicopter rides and your favorite pizza place in the world," he jokes, brushing the back of his knuckles along my jaw.

"Oh, yeah, that." I smirk, biting my bottom lip.

He raises his hand and pulls my lip down with his thumb, dislodging it from my teeth. "I want to take you somewhere, just you and me."

"Mmmm, that sounds fun." I smile and kiss him. "What are you thinking?"

"I'm thinking maybe Maldives in June for my birthday." He winks at me.

"Um, that is definitely a step above a business trip with some flare to Chicago," I laugh.

"It's not really a competition," he laughs. "I just want some quality time with just you, but really anywhere with a beach. I like it there because we can have our own little private bungalow right on the water. We get the ocean without so much sand," he laughs.

"You want to spend your birthday with just me?" I grin. "I thought that would be one of those crazy parties around here."

Ethan kisses me softly. "Sometimes, but this time, I just want you. You have a passport, right?"

"I do. I've barely used it, but I have one." I smile.

"Okay, well, I'll let Jeremiah know so you don't get fired." He laughs a little harder this time.

"He wouldn't fire me." I wrinkle my nose.

"No, I don't think he would." He smiles and gently kisses me.

"Ethan?" I question flirtatiously, trailing a finger down his chest.

"Alexis," he laughs.

"Is there a reason why when it's the three of us, you both always take the same, um, spots?" I laugh, and I feel the blush burning my cheeks.

"Oh," he says, his voice turning lascivious and teasing. "You want us to switch?"

"Not necessarily; I just didn't know if there was a reason." I shrug, and Ethan laughs.

"Carter loves your ass, I love your face," he teases, shrugging with a laugh.

My jaw drops for a second and then snaps shut; his knuckles find my chin, bringing my eyes up to his. "And because of your rules, this way, I usually get to keep you for round two."

"Ethan Hoffman," I exclaim with false surprise. "Now who is sneaky?"

"It's not sneaky," he laughs. "I get what I want, and so does Carter."

42

SHAWN

I'm taking advantage of the surround sound in the theater room to watch the "Independence Day" movies. Almost nobody uses the room, but the sound in here is unbeatable compared to the rest of the house.

The first movie has only been playing for about ten minutes when the door cracks open and the hallway light floods the room. I turn, and I'm stunned to find Alexis, appearing to be clad in only a towel.

"Hey," she says softly, "I'm sorry. I thought I heard 'Independence Day.' I was just checking."

I pause the movie. "Yeah, they're on regular television, but I'm not watching on television because, you know, commercials, but it inspired me."

She lets out a small laugh. "Okay, well, maybe I'll join you." She pauses, looking down. "After I put on clothes, of course."

"Of course," I smirk and agree. "This one barely started; I can restart it."

"Okay." She wrinkles her nose. "Give me like fifteen minutes?"

"Sure, were you in the steam room?" I laugh.

"Yeah, I thought it might help me feel better after being so sick, and I am wearing a bikini, so I'm not naked under here, but I'll be back with more clothes," she jokes.

Fuck, if spending time with Alexis watching a movie in the dark and private theater room isn't close to a dream come true. I have no qualms with restarting the first movie to have her come watch it with me.

Ten minutes later, Allie, the little cupcake, is back. She's wearing sweats and a crop tank, and she still has wet hair.

"Are you ready?" I ask as she curls her legs under her in the recliner, which has a console like mine.

"Yes, without the oops," she says. Seriously, can there be a more perfect woman?

Five hours and a lot of joking and laughter later, the movies are finished, and it's time for dinner. I offer her my hand to help her stand up, and when she stands, she's standing so close to me that her breasts brush my chest when she breathes.

I stand there like the socially awkward idiot I am and just hold her hand and look at her. My mouth wants hers; my body wants hers.

Fuck, she is a siren.

She bites her bottom lip, and she doesn't move. I don't know how to read that; I don't know what to do with her.

I clear my throat. "I guess we should get to dinner."

She smiles. "Yeah, this was fun though, Shawn; we should do it again."

Fuck, please, yes, let's do it again.

"We should," I respond.

* * *

CARTER

"Daddy, are you going to buy me a dress?" Ana asks, handing me the flyer for the father daughter dance at her school.

"Of course, Ana," I answer her. "What color dress do you want?"

"Purple," she exclaims excitedly.

I look at Lex and ask, "Want to go dress shopping with us?"

"I would love to," she answers with a big grin for Ana; she looks at the flyer to see when it is. "You want me to do your hair too?"

"Yes, make me look pretty like you," Ana answers and I think both mine and Lex's hearts melt.

"You are so much prettier than me, Ana," Alexis says. "But we will do your hair, and you'll be the prettiest girl there. But more importantly, you know what you'll be?"

"What?" Ana asks.

"You'll be the most loved girl there *and* the one with the best daddy." Alexis beams. Ana answers with a huge, beaming grin of her own and then hugs Alexis tight.

I love this woman more every single fucking day.

The next day, Lex has Ana sitting on the kitchen island, running a curling iron through her hair. Ana's chestnut-brown locks fall in gentle waves where Lex has already curled them.

Ana convinced her to paint her nails, too, so she has cute little lavender nails to go with the frilly princess dress we bought this morning. Right now, Ana is only in leggings and a T-shirt, but Lex insists this is normal and that doing your hair before you get dressed is the way of women.

Once she is done with her hair, Alexis takes Ana into the downstairs bathroom, and they put on her dress, tights, and shoes. Then

Ana comes out like she is walking down a runway, and all of us cheer and tell her how pretty she is.

Holden is the only one not there because he is at the hospital, but otherwise, she gets all of us. After I finish tying my tie, Alexis insists on taking pictures. Honestly, I don't mind.

All of them wave us off as we drive off to the dance. I promised Ana ice cream after, so it's like our own little daddy and daughter date.

* * *

ETHAN

Since Carter is on his date night with Ana, I decide to take Lexi out. Dinner and a movie seem simple, but we haven't done anything together outside of the house, so it's huge, really.

I let her pick the restaurant, and she finds a chain steakhouse, but not one she had in Maryland. Jeremiah's assistant apparently recommended it. Then I look at what is out for movies and choose a romantic comedy. Even though that's not usually my first choice, I think it'll make her happy, and it is a date, after all.

In general, I don't date. My relationships with most women have been pretty casual, and because I have no desire to get married or have children, many women don't stick around. But Lexi is okay with it and our unconventional relationship makes it even more okay.

Jeremiah and I feel a lot the same about relationships. We both like the company of women, especially specific women, but we don't want to feel tied down. Jeremiah is probably a little more like that than I am, but we're pretty similar in that regard.

Even though it has only been a short time, I've already taken proactive steps to ensure that Lexi is safeguarded in much the same way a marriage would provide protection. That's all just paperwork, making sure that if something happens to me, all my roommates and her are taken care of.

It's not that I want other women; I don't. I just don't want to feel that accountable for every second of my day feeling I've had in previous relationships. But this, this beautiful woman sitting across from me at this nice restaurant, this I *do* want.

Alexis and I have had many deep conversations in the last few weeks. Our lives have so many parallels, even though the details are different. She understands me in ways I don't think anyone else ever has, even Carter, who lived with me and my weird familial life from the time he was thirteen.

If it weren't for Carter and the unconventional dynamic we share, I believe I could pursue a more traditional relationship with Lexi. But as things stand, I find myself feeling surprisingly grateful for the flexibility our arrangement provides. With Carter in the picture, I can easily hand off the reins to him when I need some space. I can enjoy intimacy with Lexi without the weight of guilt or obligation to stay by her side all night every time.

It's not that I don't cherish our time together; quite the contrary, really. However, being raised as an only child by nannies, I've grown accustomed to and even relish my alone time in ways that may seem peculiar to others. I crave and require that space to recharge and maintain my sense of autonomy.

Carter and I have plans when I get Lexi home tonight, which is also exciting. Sometimes, I want to show her the texts we share, how much we talk about her, how much we talk to each other about fantasies, and what we want to do with her and to her.

I'm sure Carter, like me, has his own personal desires he keeps to himself, to act on himself, but honestly, I never expected to like that part of this relationship so much. I figured it would be awkward, weird, and maybe make me a little jealous, but it is the exact opposite of that. The things we do together, the things Carter does with her before or after me, it all just makes me want her more.

* * *

JEREMIAH

Curiosity gets the best of me when Carter tells us he and Ethan are taking over the bedroom at the far end of the hall, across from the laundry room. It's Ethan's house, so if Ethan is a part of it, I certainly can't veto it, but as he carries boxes in there, I feel like I have to find out what is going on.

When I step out of the laundry room and find the door ajar, Carter's look is salacious, and he has a shit-eating grin plastered on his face. My jaw drops.

"What are you two doing?" I ask with a laugh.

"Pleasing our girl," Carter answers. "It's all stuff one or the other of us have talked to her about."

"This is some shit straight out of 'Fifty Shades,'" I say, taking another step into the room.

"Not yet, but we might get there." Carter smiles. "This shit is expensive."

"I'm sure it is," I reply, and just looking at what they have going on already, without Alexis even being in the room, makes my cock hard.

If this is what Alexis wants, even if it's only sometimes, I *want* her. I knew that already, but this steps things up to a whole different level for me. The word "sir" slipping off her tongue a while back runs through my mind, and I have to restrain the shiver that wants to go down my spine.

"You all are going to lock this room so people, Ana especially, don't just walk in whenever?"

"Yep, Ethan is on that; it'll be done by the end of the week." Carter smiles.

I take a deep breath in through my nose and blow it out of my mouth before shaking my head and leaving the room.

43

ALEXIS

Having a date night with Ethan is good for my soul. So much of our relationship has been in the bedroom, even the conversations, not that I mind that at all, but having more connection outside of the bedroom is nice, too. This is intentional time outside the bedroom, and I love him more for it.

Our emotional connection is strong. I don't even know how to describe it, but I feel like part of his soul lives inside me, and part of mine lives in him. He understands me so well, and I think I understand him just as well.

"Thank you," I say reaching over the console to rest my hand on his thigh as we're driving home. "This was nice."

Ethan smiles and rests his hand on top of mine, lacing our fingers together. "I have another surprise for you when we get home." He steals a glance at me before looking back at the road. "Or rather, *we* have a surprise for you."

His words, his tone, I have to clench my thighs, but I can feel the vibration, the ache, and the wetness already stirring between my thighs.

"Oh, you do, do you?" I tease.

"Yeah, and this one took some effort, so I hope you're happy." He smiles as he pulls into the garage.

"Effort?" I ask with a small chuckle.

"Yeah, effort." He smiles and winks at me.

When we walk into the kitchen, Carter is there. There's no sign of the other guys.

"Hey," I greet him, "how was your date with Ana?"

"It was good," he answers, pulling me into him and kissing me softly. "How was yours?" Carter looks between me and Ethan.

"It was nice, thanks. The movie was good—not the best, but it was nice," I reply to Carter.

It's undeniably a scenario that might raise a few eyebrows from the outside looking in. Walking in with Ethan after a date, only to be greeted by Carter asking about it and greeting me—kissing me—like I just am arriving home after work, could seem unusual to some. But for us, it's just another day in our unique dynamic.

"What did you tell her?" Carter asks, looking at Ethan but wrapping his arms around my waist and pulling my back into his chest.

"Nothing, except there's a surprise," Ethan says and he brushes his knuckles across my cheek.

Fuck.

I am so turned on right now. I'm pressed up against Carter, and Ethan is inches from me. I can feel my panties getting wetter by the second.

I clear my throat. "You also told me it took effort," I laugh.

Carter leans his mouth down to my ear. "Oh, it did. It took a lot of effort and money." He pauses. "But *you* are worth all of it."

His breath on my ear and neck sets my nerves on fire, igniting in white hot flames that travel through my entire body, settling in all my erogenous zones.

"We just want to spoil you," Ethan adds, just above a whisper, as his thumb pulls my bottom lip out from under my teeth—I didn't even realize I was biting it.

Carter then speaks, his voice low. "We thought about blindfolding you so you didn't know what was coming, but I think it might be hotter to show it to you first."

"First?" My voice is barely audible.

Ethan smiles, his expression a little evil and then his voice is dripping with sin. "First—then we'll blindfold you."

I find myself grateful to have Carter's arms around me because my knees start to weaken.

"Lexi, love, normally you turn nice and pink when you're turned on, but you are very pale right now. I think," Ethan's eyes travel down my body, "all your blood went somewhere else."

Holy shit.

"Let's go upstairs," Carter quietly orders, pulling on the belt loops of my jeans.

As Carter lets go and turns around, Ethan loops his hand in my hair and kisses me deeply before turning me, and I follow up Carter up the stairs. I'm very confused when he turns left.

"Shhhh," Carter whispers. "Ana is sleeping."

"Where are we going?" I quietly giggle.

"Maybe to heaven, maybe to hell," Carter teases in a whisper.

We get to the end of the hall, and Ethan pulls me back into him, my back flush with his chest, as Carter opens the last door on the right, across from the laundry room. My heart's palpitations are hard to ignore, and I feel my breathing growing ragged already.

"Ready, princess?" Carter whispers and then reaches for my hand.

I don't know what I was thinking, but what I walk into is not it. I've been in this room before, once anyway. I hesitate a few steps into the room and Ethan is quickly behind me. He wraps an arm around my waist and moves me forward enough to shut and lock the door behind us.

Holy fuck, these guys.

"What did you do?" I ask, and I'm sure my eyes look like golf balls.

"We created a little fun room. We figured we'd call it a blue room since a red room is too cliche, and blue is your favorite color," Carter rasps with pride. As Ethan moves me forward, they sandwich me quickly.

My eyes are still taking everything in. There is *a lot* of blue.

The bed that was covered in the same bedding mine had when I moved in is now covered in blue satin, maybe silk—I don't know. The headboard has been changed out, and rings are attached to it—rings to connect rope, cuffs, and other things.

A rack on the wall to the right of the bed is adorned with canes, crops, and floggers—all soft, basic ones. These are things I've talked to them individually about and that they have individually and gradually questioned me about.

"Give me a second," I say and step out from between them, looking around and taking everything in.

My eyes keep moving, and I turn; on the wall behind me is another rack with cuffs—soft, suede, and leather cuffs—no metal, all with different clips and attachments for different purposes.

I walk along them and run my fingers over them and then over the items on the other racks. Pausing, I feel the falls of the floggers, and they're suede and soft. My cunt is literally vibrating; my clit has a pulse of its own.

I cross my arms under my breasts and continue. I refuse to look back at them, but I can feel their eyes on me.

There is a coil of soft red rope looped over one of the bed posts, I reach up and feel that and then run my hand along the sheet on the bed. Only then do I note the metal rings about every two feet at the base of the mattress, and I assume they go all the way around.

On the wall by the bathroom, blindfolds and chokers hang from hooks. And there are drawers underneath. For the first time, I steal a look at Carter, and he nods as I reach for the drawer. Slowly pulling it open, I see nipple clamps and vibrators. I bite my lip and turn toward them.

"You did this together?" I ask, my arms, again, crossed under my breasts.

"We did," Ethan says, and I laugh, eliciting a question from him. "What?"

"That's exactly what you said, in that exact tone, the first time we were together, and I asked if you two had talked." I smile and bite my lip. "Did I miss anything?"

I watch as both their eyes look above me. My eyes follow theirs.

Fuck me.

There is a suspension bar above my head. They can cuff me to the mother fucking ceiling.

"We only have one question for you," Carter says, walking toward me, but then past me, grabbing a blindfold.

"What's that?" I ask, looking at Ethan and then back to Carter.

"What's your safe word?" Ethan asks.

I think for about half a second. "Purple." I shrug.

The corner of Ethan's mouth curves up.

"What did you think it would be?" I ask. "Something more exciting?"

"I like purple," Carter rasps from behind me. "It's easy."

I see Ethan look over my shoulder at Carter, and then he hooks his fingers under the hem of my shirt. He quickly has it over my head and on the floor, and just as fast, Carter has a blindfold on me.

Now, I don't really know who the hands touching me belong to. I will know their voices, but hands, that's harder.

The excitement coursing through me is almost enough to make me come before they do anything else. I am so turned on. I had told them both that I love being blindfolded, not knowing what was going to happen to me, being completely out of control—at their mercy.

I know they will enjoy this, but I will enjoy it just as much. They listened to me—both of them. I talked about how I didn't like metal cuffs, just leather and fabric ones with Carter, and how I liked shorter suede floggers and soft leather crops with Ethan. They both asked how I knew and what experiences I had in the past.

The story of Jake, my college boyfriend and first fiancé, was a chapter I hadn't shared with Carter and I still didn't share everything. Ethan already knew, though. There was something about it that intrigued Jake, and somehow, I found myself drawn into the allure of it, too. Surrendering control and allowing someone else to take the reins became a journey of self-discovery for me.

Letting go of that control was surprisingly liberating. It's hard to explain to those who haven't experienced it, but there's a certain healing quality in being at the mercy of another's touch. It's like shedding layers of stress and inhibition, opening yourself up to a flood of sensations and pleasures that you wouldn't have known otherwise.

The rush of adrenaline, the surge of oxytocin, dopamine, serotonin, and the release of endorphins—it's like a cocktail of happiness coursing through my veins. A natural high that leaves me feeling alive and invigorated.

But it's not just about the physical sensations; it's also about the dynamics at play. There's something undeniably powerful about witnessing the dominant masculinity of the men who pleasure me. The way they exude confidence and control, the surge of hormones and pheromones—it's intoxicating.

Knowing that I've willingly placed myself in their hands,

allowing them to dictate the course of our encounter, adds another layer of intensity. It's a dance of dominance and submission, with my life quite literally in their hands. And seeing how they rise to the occasion, embracing their role with a primal energy, is a sight to behold.

In the end, it's a symbiotic relationship, a delicate balance of giving and receiving pleasure. And I can't help but marvel at how it brings out the best in some men, tapping into their pure masculinity and primal instincts—unleashing a raw, unbridled passion that leaves me craving more.

My bra comes off quickly, and while one of them works on my jeans and shoes, the other grabs my arms and buckles leather cuffs on each wrist, but they're not attached to each other, at least not yet.

"Princess," Carter purrs in my ear. "Since this is the first time in this little blue room we made, do you want to be cuffed to the ceiling or the bed?"

I don't answer; I'm considering how to respond. Then I recognize it must be Ethan's hands hooking in the waistband of my panties and pulling them down since Carter's are clearly the ones on my shoulders.

There's a sharp smack on my ass, and I gasp. "Answer me," Carter groans, humor in his voice.

"The ceiling," I manage to rasp out.

Each of them grabs a wrist, and in seconds, my hands are hooked above my head, about shoulder-width apart from each other. Now I'm blindfolded, bound, and I have completely surrendered to their will.

44

ALEXIS

I realize quickly that I may have missed something. Hands move down both sides of my body, all the way to my ankles, leaving goose-bumps and electricity in their wake. Quickly, straps bind around my ankles, too, and then I feel the pressure and hear the click of the leg spreader.

Fuck, where were they hiding that?

"You okay, Lexi?" Ethan asks.

"Yeah," I rasp.

It's interesting how different Ethan and Carter's reactions can be. Ethan, with his gentle demeanor and deep emotional connection, is likely to be more worried about me. His caring nature and our strong emotional bond mean that he's attuned to my feelings and well-being in a way that few others are.

On the other hand, Carter's response is driven by his strong physical connection to me. He trusts his instincts to read my re-actions and gauge how I'm feeling. I think he also fully trusts my ability to use a safe word if I need to. I had already told both of them I refuse to be gagged and blindfolded at the same time. It's one or the other, and I prefer the blindfold.

The two of them working together reminds me of the unique dynamics between us.

I feel like everything I hear is exaggerated in anticipation. They leave me, I don't feel their presence close to me for a minute, and then quickly, there's a *snap* on my ass from a crop. I gasp, and the crop grazes over my skin on my ass and up my back before disappearing quickly and landing on my other ass cheek.

I try to pull my thighs together to ease the ache of my pussy, but I can't.

Fucking leg spreader.

There's going to be some edging, but hopefully, there will also be orgasms that I can't stop. It's also possible one of them might have to carry me out of this room—if not tonight, at some point.

Then I feel the falls of the flogger grazing the front and then inside of my thighs, all the way up to my breasts, and then softly hitting my belly. Followed by the crop to my ass. The falls grazing against my skin cause fire and ice to flow through my veins, turning me on impossibly more.

They're circling me; the flogger drags across my hip, and then with a *hiss, snap*, the flogger hits me harder on the ass. I gasp and jump; the crop has made its way around to the front of my body, grazing up my ribs, tickling me, and electrifying me at the same time. There's a quick snap to my breast, just above my nipple, and with that, I'm pretty confident that Carter has the crop and Ethan has the flogger.

The flogger moves up the inside of my thighs from behind, the handle teasing the entrance of my extremely wet cunt. As the flogger trails up my back, the falls tickle my ass crack and then quickly *hiss, snap*, the falls smack my ass cheek.

"Fuck," I moan.

"You like that, princess?"

"Yes," I rasp, and the flogger hits my ass again while the crop hits just below my belly button.

I hear Ethan inhale loudly through his nose, and fuck, him getting off on this and not shying away from it makes me even wetter. *Hiss, snap,* the flogger hits my ass again. I hear movement off to my left, the drawer, and then the buzzing of a vibrator.

Holy fuck.

Neither of them has ever used any toys with me; my clit starts throbbing in response to the noise of the vibration. I'm thinking about that when the flogger quickly trails up my ass again and then *hiss, snap,* smacks me hard. My head tilts back as I moan, and my wrists pull against the cuffs.

A strong hand moves up my arm and around my throat but doesn't stop. Moving up my jaw, a thumb crosses my lips.

"Suck, baby," Ethan orders, and I do.

I lick and lightly bite, but then I suck.

Hiss, snap, the flogger hits my ass again as fingers separate the wet folds of my pussy.

"Fuuucck," Carter growls. "You're so wet."

The vibrator slides between my folds, replacing his fingers, and I jerk against the cuffs. The hand pulls away from my face, around my shoulder blade, and back around my side to find a hard nipple to play with.

"You're not going anywhere," Carter whispers inches from my face.

He pinches my chin and then takes my mouth with his.

His mouth is on mine.

Vibrator on my clit.

Fingers on my nipple.

Hiss, snap, the flogger as hits my ass again, and I come completely undone.

My head tips back, and I pull against the cuffs on both my wrists and ankles.

"Geezus fucking christ," Carter groans as I come, and the gush of fluid comes from me. "Such a good fucking girl."

The touch of his fingers on the inside of my knee, sliding up the fluid that is coating my thigh from my knees to my cunt, causes me to moan.

The vibrator still in place, Carter's fingers, coated in the fluid that just came from me, find my mouth, and I clean them for him with my tongue. The taste of my own arousal turns me on even more.

I hear the rustling of clothes, and then I feel a change of hands on the vibrator, but my body is already working its way to another orgasm. I grind into the vibrator the best I can, and I hear Carter laugh a little maniacally.

"So fucking needy and so fucking wet," Carter rasps.

I feel the flogger run up the inside of my thighs again and *hiss, snap*, my ass feels the falls, and, again, it pushes me over the edge. My body convulsing and pulling. My cunt desperately wanting to be filled, to have something to convulse around.

"Fuck," I whimper.

"What do you want, love?" Ethan asks, his mouth inches from my ear.

I breathe hard. "I need—I need to be filled," I manage to rasp.

The vibrator changes hands again, but it's still pressed hard against my clit; my body wants more and wants it to stop at the same time.

It's so good and too much all at the same time.

Fingers slide down my ass to my taint and then slide to my opening. As those fingers enter me, I gasp loudly.

"Fuck." The word slips from my lips, and it's guttural and pleading.

The vibrator disappears, and I feel both relieved and disappointed.

The fingers inside me keep working. I feel Ethan's facial hair against the crook of my neck as his mouth delicately finds the sweet spot under my ear.

Carter's hands are at my ankles, undoing the buckles attaching me to the leg spreader. Once he has them both off, his strong hands are on my ass, and he lifts me.

"You're gonna want to hold on to the bar, baby," Carter whispers against my neck.

I listen, and when he lifts me, I grab the bar above my head and wrap my legs around him. He wastes no time impaling me on his cock. I take some of the weight with my hands, but then I feel Ethan behind me.

His fingers, well lubricated, run over my rear entrance, and then he enters me slowly. It's the first time he has taken my ass, and it's total ecstasy.

He grunts hard as he pushes all the way in. I feel so full and so wanted. I roll my head back into his shoulder while Carter fucks my pussy.

Ethan wraps one arm around my waist, and the other moves up the other side of my body and finds my throat. He holds me stable, so I'm not swinging from the bar, while Carter holds most of my weight, and they both fuck me relentlessly.

As my moans get louder, Ethan's hand around my throat constricts until I can't moan anymore. I start to see stars behind the blindfold, and all I feel is euphoria while another orgasm starts building. My thighs tighten around Carter, and he comes almost at the exact same time as me, with Ethan only seconds behind. I milk them both as they fill me with their cum, and I feel both depleted and energized at the same time.

My body is completely sated.

Ethan holds me around the waist while Carter unwraps me from around his waist. My feet gently hit the ground.

The blindfold slides up my face, and I immediately am looking into Carter's eyes.

"You're such a good, dirty, fucking girl," he says and kisses me hard before reaching up and unhooking my hands.

I hold them out to him, and he unbuckles the cuffs. Carter embraces that dominant side of him while Ethan is already into an aftercare mode.

His arms are still supporting me, and his fingers are gentle. They move across my skin, full of soft caresses and gentle touches and all the subtle signs to let me know that just because we all like it rough doesn't mean that he doesn't love me or care about me.

As soon as my hands are completely free, I give Carter my back so I can face Ethan, and I kiss him deeply. I will take his aftercare, but I need him to know I'm okay.

After we kiss, I look into his eyes, having a silent conversation to assure him that I really am alright. Eventually, I make it to the bathroom, and I hear them picking stuff up in the room. I laugh to myself, thinking this is just another reason it's nice that all the bedrooms have their own bathrooms.

When I come back out, they're both dressed from the waist down. I'm still very naked.

"You good, princess?" Carter smiles.

"Yeah, I'm good." I smile back.

Carter moves toward me and wraps his arm around my waist, pulling me close to him, my naked breasts skin to skin with his chest. He kisses me deeply.

"I hope you like your surprise." He smacks my ass.

I laugh and sniffle. He casts a look back at Ethan and leaves. Apparently, Ethan gets to keep me tonight.

Feeling vulnerable, standing there naked, which I know is silly with everything that just happened, I quickly make my way to Ethan so at least I'll be pressed against him. He doesn't let me bury myself in him though, not the way I want to.

Ethan's knuckles find the bottom of my chin and tilt my head up so I meet his eyes. Then he cups my face, gliding his thumb over my cheekbone.

"That was really fucking hot, Lexi; you sure you're good?"

"I am *so* good," I reassure him.

Snickering, he kisses my lips before he pulls me close to him.

After a long moment of holding me, he hands me his T-shirt. "This and your underwear should be fine to make it to my room."

"Look, you got both parts tonight," I tease him. "You got my ass and you get to keep me."

He laughs. "Yeah, well, he has Ana, and I *know* I want to sleep with you in my fucking arms tonight."

"I'm okay with that." I smile and kiss him.

45

SHAWN

As April fades into memory, the warmth of spring breathes new life into everything around here. Ethan's gearing up to unveil the pool, Jeremiah's sorting out our company softball schedule, and we're already mapping out plans for our epic 4th of July bash.

But in the middle of all the excitement, there's another important day looming on the horizon this week, at least for me. So, when we all happen to gather in the kitchen for our morning coffee, I decide to broach the subject.

"So, Allie," I begin, a mischievous glint in my eye. "Do you know what important day is at the end of this week?"

Jeremiah groans dramatically, his hand sweeping over his face in mock exasperation.

"I think this is a trick question," she says, wrinkling her nose in playful suspicion. "Because you probably expect me to say Cinco de Mayo, but what you *want* me to say is Star Wars Day."

The other guys burst into laughter, but I can't help but gaze at her, utterly smitten. Because, damn it, she's perfect.

"There you go, melting his little nerd heart again," Jeremiah teases, earning a playful swat from Allie.

She smiles at me over her coffee cup, and my heart skips a beat.

"Well," I say, trying to regain my composure. "Who's up for the marathon?"

Allie answers eagerly, her eyes sparkling, "I am."

Those two words fill me with an indescribable happiness.

"*But*," she almost sings, "what order are you going in? And are you including the extra movies?"

"Careful, you might give him an attack, heart, panic, something," Jeremiah cautions her.

"I'll watch some of them, but no Jar Jar," Carter interjects.

"I like Jar Jar," Allie pushes back, earning a chuckle from Ethan.

I focus on Allie. "Release order, I think, and just the nine."

She nods, then turns to Carter. "So you'll watch the first three? Four, five, and six?"

"Probably," he sighs. "But I'll have Ana, so we'll see."

"What about the rest of you?" Allie asks.

"I'll be at the hospital," Holden answers quickly.

Jeremiah and Ethan exchange a look, and Ethan speaks up. "Jer and I like the movies, but we've seen them so many times, I don't know if we need to see them again."

"Blasphemy," Allie jokes.

"We'll see." Ethan smiles at her before cupping her chin and kissing her gently on the forehead.

I'm still adjusting to the PDA from Ethan. I have to remind myself that Carter and he are okay with it. Holden seems to be handling it surprisingly well these days. I don't know how much he needs to steel himself, but he's coping better than expected.

"Alright," I say, turning to Allie. "I guess you and I plan it, and if the others want to join, they can."

"How much planning are we talking about?" Allie leans over the island, inadvertently putting her perfect tits on display.

"Times and snacks, really," I repeat with a shrug.

Allie gives me a speculative look. "Well, the total runtime of the nine movies is just about twenty hours. Are you sure you want to do it all at once?"

Jeremiah's eyebrows shoot up. "How the fuck do you know that off the top of your head?"

"ADHD superpower," she says with a smile. "I remember relatively useless details about a lot of things."

Jeremiah shakes his head, chuckling. "We need to put that to good use with your job."

"Oh, I do." Allie grins mischievously.

I want to redirect her attention to our plans. "What if we do four, five, and six on Friday night and then the rest on Saturday?"

Carter chimes in, "What if you do it chronologically and watch one, two, and three on Friday night? None of the rest of us care about those, and then the good ones on Saturday. Maybe I can convince Ana to watch a couple."

"That works too," I agree.

"Ana would probably like Jar Jar, but those Senate scenes are boring." Allie wrinkles her nose.

Laughter fills the kitchen, and I nod, "Okay, we'll do it Carter's way."

* * *

It's May third, and Allie and I agreed to start the movies around four in the afternoon. By midnight, we'll have watched the first three, with breaks for snacks and such.

Armed with popcorn and caffeinated beverages, we settle into

318 ~ MAELANA NIGHTINGALE

the middle of the three rows of recliners, the fold-down console with cup holders between us.

Allie is wearing leggings that hug her curves just right. I can't help but notice she's wearing a thong paired with one of those cute little crop tank tops that showcase her flat stomach and her pushed-up tits. She brought down a pink, fuzzy blanket that at least covers a lot of her most of the time. But during the first two movies, she spends a lot of time leaning towards me over the console, her legs tucked under her opposite me. It's hard for my eyes not to be drawn to her perfect cleavage whenever she leans in like that.

Somehow, a conversation about Anakin and Padme during the credits of episode two segues into a discussion about Allie's relationship with Ethan and Carter. I start asking her some logistical questions, and she's surprisingly open and not hesitant at all about answering me.

In that moment, in that conversation, I'm not sure what exactly it is, but something emboldens me.

"Allie, Alexis, what if," I start, feeling my throat tighten, but she just looks at me expectantly. "What if I wanted in on that?"

I hold my breath, waiting for her response. She looks away, up at the screen. Is she ignoring me or did she not understand the question? The weight of the moment feels suffocating. It took so much damn build-up to ask, and I almost instantly regret it.

Then, she clears her throat and subtly shifts her drink and the popcorn bowl to the other side of her. I'm utterly lost—what is she doing?

Seemingly out of nowhere and not on topic, she asks, "Does your little nerd heart like 'The Big Bang Theory?'"

I snicker a little, relieved by the lightness of the subject but still confused. "Like the television show or the actual theory?" I inquire.

She giggles, and it eases the tension I'm feeling, "The television show."

"Yeah," I answer. "I'm a fan."

I'm still puzzled about where she's taking this conversation.

"Do you remember the episode about Schrödinger's cat? When Leonard and Penny are thinking about dating?" she asks.

Fuck me, now I know where she's going with this.

I swallow hard, trying to steady my nerves. "Uh, yeah. When they kiss to see if there's any chemistry before they go out?"

I glance at her, but she doesn't respond. This moment feels like a tipping point—she could either break my heart or make me extremely happy.

Without a word, she picks up my drink and, reaching across me, moves it over to the console on my other side. Then, she flips up the console between us. Nerves surge through me, my hands clammy, butterflies fluttering in my stomach, and my heart thundering against my ribs.

I half-expect her to kiss me based on the reference, but what happens next catches me completely off guard. After she flips up the console, she doesn't just kiss me. She moves quickly, and suddenly, she's straddling me.

Her hands find the sides of my face, and her lips are on mine before I can fully register what's happening. At first, I freeze, stunned by the suddenness of it all. But then, I gather my wits and kiss her back, my hands finding her hips instinctively, pulling her closer.

She's hovering above me, likely intentionally, so she is not grinding on me; she can't feel my suddenly rock-hard dick.

The kiss lingers, but it feels like it's over too soon when she leans back and asks, "Is the cat alive?"

My voice is raspy as I reply, "It is for me. You?"

"Yes," she whispers, ghosting her lips across mine before kissing me again, deeper this time.

My hands continue to explore her body, keeping it PG but reveling in the sensation of her back, rib cage, thighs, and arms.

Eventually, she breaks the kiss and rests her forehead against mine. Her words are quiet but steady. "We'll need to have a conversation with Carter and Ethan," she says softly, planting another gentle kiss on my lips. "But if you want in, I'm good with that."

She kisses me deeply once more, and my hand instinctively weaves into her hair, relishing the softness between my fingers. Her lips are addictive.

As the opening for episode three starts, she dismounts me, but she doesn't put the console back down between us. Instead, she leans into me, interlacing her fingers with mine.

I feel like I'm riding a wave of chemicals, swept up in the exhilaration of the moment.

Later, during a quieter scene, I seize the opportunity to ask Allie about the conversation she mentioned having with Carter and Ethan.

"They have expectations. That's the best word for it, I guess. And obviously, they need to know," she explains. "They honestly talk more to each other about logistics and stuff than they talk to me. Not that I don't have a say or choice or whatever, but they make sure they're not stepping on each other's toes or making each other upset."

Her words sink in, and it all starts to make sense. From what I've observed around the house, Carter and Ethan do seem to have grown closer, yet they also give each other space and time with Allie. It's a delicate balance that I'm sure requires communication and openness. Any hint of jealousy could spark drama.

"It's probably best if you have that conversation with them." She hesitates slightly. "They had it with each other before Ethan and me, and honestly, Ethan had the conversation with Holden when he was so upset back after I was sick. It wasn't something he thought he could do, but I do think it's best for you to talk to them."

I squeeze her hand in understanding, my mind already swirling with thoughts. When the last movie of the night comes to an end, Alexis kisses me on the cheek before heading upstairs. That night and into the next day, I find myself lost in contemplation, grappling with the choices and conversations that lie ahead.

46

ALEXIS

Kissing Shawn is electrifying. I could feel the chemistry between us, but it was uncharted territory in terms of physical intimacy. I know Carter and Ethan will be understanding as long as Shawn respects their boundaries—boundaries that I will let them discuss with him, knowing they're mainly focused on protecting our relationships and my well-being.

But I have to tell Georgia because I can't keep it to myself.

> (Me) *I kissed Shawn lol*
>
> (Georgia) *What? Dish*
>
> (Me) *He asked if he could be in and I honestly wasn't sure about the chemistry, so I pulled the Schrödinger's Cat thing on him*
>
> (Georgia) *Such a vixen - and is the cat alive?*
>
> (Me) *Very much so - he's going to talk to Carter and Ethan*

(Georgia) *Honestly, from everything you have told me I didn't think he'd be next lol*

(Me) *Who did you think would be?*

(Georgia) *Holden, hands down*

(Me) *I would love for that to happen, but I don't think it will*

(Georgia) *Don't count him out yet*

(Georgia) *Also, I'm pretty sure that if you give Carrie what she wants, Jeremiah will be yours too lol*

(Me) *Georgia!*

(Georgia) *Seriously, once he gets a taste of you (both literally and figuratively) he's not going to be able to let you go*

(Me) *You're ridiculous*

(Georgia) *I think they're good for you - all of them*

(Me) *They are, but it is a lot lol*

(Georgia) *Who would have thought that little Sexy Lexi would have a harem*

(Me) **facepalm emoji* I'm done talking to you now*

(Georgia) *for now - love you bitch*

(Me) *love you too*

The next morning, Ethan joins Shawn and me for episodes four and five of our show. I manage to persuade Ana to join us for episode six, promising her a glimpse of the Ewoks, which she ends up loving. Of course, Carter accompanies her.

As I settle between Ethan and Ana, with Carter on her other side and Shawn beside Ethan, I can't help but feel a small twinge of concern for Shawn. Ethan's touches remain subtle, as always when Ana is around, but they're noticeable.

Carter and I have talked about explaining our dynamic to Ana, but he's apprehensive about how her mom will react. For Ana's sake, it's simpler if I'm just his girlfriend in their eyes, at least for now. We both know that, eventually, Ana will need to understand, but perhaps she should be a bit older to fully grasp the complexities of our situation.

After episode six, Carter, Ethan, and Ana depart, leaving just Shawn and me to finish the last three movies. Ana will be heading back to her mom's tonight, so I give her plenty of big hugs. Ethan kisses the top of my head, while Carter hints not so subtly that he wants me in his bed tonight with a wink.

"After we're done with the movies, I need to run to the store for a few things, but then, yes," I tell Carter with a smile.

Once again, it's just Shawn and me, watching the final movies. I know some people would consider it blasphemy, but they're my favorite. Maybe it's just nostalgia, with them released later in my life, but they are.

"The three of you really do have it all figured out, don't you?" Shawn remarks, laughing a little.

"We do," I nod, catching his gaze, "Are you having second thoughts?"

"No," he shakes his head, smiling. "Just trying to figure out when and how to have this conversation."

Mid-action scene, I look at him, and I'm drawn to him. Suddenly, I'm straddling his lap again, our lips locking in fiery passion.

"Allie," he cautions against my lips as my hips move against his, intentionally this time, offering encouragement to at least have the conversation.

Breaking the kiss, I ask him, "Do you want me to ask them to talk to you?"

He studies my face, his thumb gently tracing my cheekbone. "No —maybe. I'll talk to them tomorrow."

"Okay," I say, kissing him softly. "Just let me know, or if you change your mind."

"I'm not changing my mind, cupcake," he assures me, playfully smacking my ass, eliciting a laugh from me. "Just finding my words and timing."

I kiss him again. "Okay, just let me know if you need my help."

"I will," he says, rolling his hips into mine, a mischievous glint in his eyes.

After a few more minutes of kissing, I settle next to Shawn to continue watching the movies. I manage to mostly behave myself for the rest of the time.

We finish all the movies by around nine o'clock, and I text Carter before I head to the store.

> (Me) *Hey, I'm going to run to the store for a few things for Cinco de Mayo tomorrow, then I'll find you*
>
> (Carter) *Okay, wake me up if I don't wake up when you get your sexy ass in my bed*
>
> (Me) *But you're so cute when you're sleeping*
>
> (Carter) *lol - just wake me up, I need you*
>
> (Me) *Soooo needy*
>
> (Carter) *Maybe*
>
> (Me) *Maybe I should make you wait longer*
>
> (Carter) *Woman - I'll chain you to my bed if I need to*
>
> (Me) *Don't threaten me with a good time*
>
> (Carter) *Don't joke about something I'm very willing to do*
>
> (Me) *Now you're just turning me on*
>
> (Carter) *Good, now go, so you can hurry home*

Walking out into the night, it's a little chilly for May and drizzling. I still don't get a garage space even though my car is more expensive than all of theirs, except Ethan's coupe, but I don't really mind.

I promised the guys I'd make margarita cupcakes for our small gathering tomorrow, but I forgot to put the ingredients on the shopping list. Luckily, our normal grocery store is only a few blocks away, and open twenty-four hours.

47

HOLDEN

I hate thinking the word—and I don't say it out loud—but the ICU is *quiet* tonight. A stark departure from the usual cacophony of beeping machines and bustling staff. With only half our beds occupied and the patients all relatively stable, I find myself with a rare window to delve into chart reviews alongside the first-year residents.

We meticulously dissect the histories and treatment plans of our current patients, and when we're done, we see the notifications that we will be admitting two additional patients sometime tonight. Normally, we'd wait for the emergency room or the operating room to call up a report before we look through the charts, but we have time tonight, so I seize the opportunity to guide one of our novices, Malarie Stone, through the planning process for admitting new patients, proactively planning and thinking about what they might need.

"Malarie," I say, my tone gentle yet firm. "How about you take the lead on our next two admissions? It'll be good practice for you."

"Which patient should I go with first?" Malarie asks.

"One is an ER admit, and one is an OR admit, right?" I ask her, trying to feed her a hint.

She pauses, processing the hint before her face brightens with understanding. "ER first, right?" she confirms, seeking validation.

I offer a subtle nod of agreement. "And why do you think that is?" I prompt, eager to gauge her analytical skills.

"They'll arrive here sooner than the OR patient," another resident chimes in, their voice echoing my unspoken sentiment.

"Statistically speaking," I interject, underscoring their rationale with academic precision.

The first patient Malarie reads off is a severe pneumonia. "Seventy-two-year-old male, persistent cough for at least three weeks; oxygen sat 84% room air, 92% on 3 liters per minute, tachy and hypotensive, nausea and vomiting started this afternoon."

"What will we need to do for them?" I ask

Another resident answers, "The patient likely will need a vent, there is potential for a cytokine storm, and we need to get the inflammation down."

Malarie verbalizes a more detailed plan like a champ, discussing medications and interventions to get the inflammation down.

"Excellent job," I commend, a sense of pride swelling within me at her progress. "Now, let's turn our attention to the OR admission, shall we?"

Malarie reads the synopsis, "Twenty-nine-year-old female, driver in an MVA with trauma from a side impact to the driver's side, negative EtOH and rec drugs, traumatic brain injury of undetermined severity at this time, unconscious but vital signs stable on EMS arrival, left fractured ulna and radius, will likely require surgery after ortho consult, will be in the surgical suite for splenic injury and exploratory laparoscopy for other potential internal bleeding." She gets through all of that, reading it like it's a textbook.

"So, Dr. Stone, what do you anticipate this incoming patient will require upon arrival on the unit?" I inquire, directing my attention solely towards her and waving off the other residents for the moment.

Malarie doesn't miss a beat this time, her response poised and confident. "Likely medication-induced sedation and ventilation, stabilization of the fracture pending orthopedic intervention, along with close monitoring of the traumatic brain injury and potential internal bleeding," she articulates, her words a testament to her growing confidence.

A smile tugs at my lips as I nod in approval. "Excellent assessment," I commend, acknowledging her observations. "We'll need to await further information from general surgery and neurology before finalizing the treatment plan, but you're certainly on the right track."

"I do have a question," Malarie says; I raise my eyebrows, prompting her to continue. "How do we check if they've started surgery?"

I move around the physician's station to demonstrate on the screen how to navigate to the relevant information. Then, as I glance at the patient's name, my heart sinks into my stomach, and I'm sure they all watch as the blood drains from my face.

Alexis.

"Move," I snap at Malarie, urgency lacing my tone.

Despite my abruptness, I quickly show her how to access the information. I need it for myself, too. I locate the operating room and identify the surgeon. Turning to one of the third-year residents, Danny Cartwright, I struggle to keep myself composed.

"The unit is yours. I have my pager and my phone," I manage to say, my throat tight with anxiety.

As I walk away, a barrage of questions flood my back. Ignoring them, I dial the chief surgical resident's number. He answers on the second ring.

330 - MAELANA NIGHTINGALE

"What's up, Holden?" Kevin's voice sounds cheerful.

Skipping the pleasantries, I get straight to the point. "You're going in on this MVA? Alexis Branthwaite?"

"I am," he confirms.

"Let me scrub in. I won't get in the way." I say it like it's an order, not a request.

"What's going on, Holden? This isn't a super interesting case," Kevin questions.

"I know her. She lives with me." I pause, my emotions on the edge. "Just please, Kevin."

"You know there are some ethical issues here, Hold," he sighs.

"I do. I'll stay out of the way. I just need to know what's happening with her." I feel like I'm about to break as the line goes silent.

"Fine, but if I tell you to leave, *you leave.* And you don't let anyone else in the room know your connection," he says firmly.

"Thank you. I'm getting on the elevator now."

As soon as I get to the surgical floor, I dial Jeremiah. I can't have this conversation with Ethan or Carter. They're going to need each other and him.

It's midnight, and I'm hoping Jeremiah has his phone on. He didn't answer the first time, so I try again two times, hoping to break through his do-not-disturb.

Please answer. I do not want to have to call Ethan.

"Holden, it's the middle of the night," Jeremiah scolds when he answers.

Thank fuck.

"Jer, this is important. I need you to stay calm. I need you to keep everyone else calm because I don't have a ton of time or information right now." My voice is clear but fast. I am trying to turn on my business mode.

"What the fuck is going on, Holden?"

"Alexis was in a car accident, a bad one. They're prepping her for surgery, and they're letting me scrub in, so I'll be in the operating room—"

Jeremiah interrupts me, "Holden, I am going to need more than that before I go to Carter and Ethan."

"I know, let me finish," and then I recite off what I know. "It was a side impact accident to the driver's side; that usually means that they were t-boned, but not always. She was unconscious at the scene when the ambulance got there, but her vital signs were and are stable. They're still determining the severity of the traumatic brain injury, but she definitely has one. She has a broken arm that will need surgery, but it's not the priority, and they have to wait for the swelling to go down—"

"Geezus, Hold," Jeremiah interrupts me again.

"I'm not done, Jer." I swallow. "The surgery they're prepping her for now is both exploratory, looking for the cause of internal bleeding they know she has and repairing or removing her spleen."

"I don't know that I'm going to remember all that, Holden," Jeremiah sighs, and his voice cracks.

"I'll text you too, but I'm going into the OR and will be unavailable for a while. I know they'll want to, but there wouldn't be much point in coming now, and they won't give them any information anyway. She'll be in surgery for a few hours, and then she'll be in post-op. Eventually, she'll make it to my ICU, and she will be on a ventilator for a day or two, hopefully not longer." I have finally found my way into business mode. "I will call you as soon as she's out of surgery—hold on, Jer," I request as Kevin approaches me.

"We're starting in less than ten minutes," Kevin says. "She has a Maryland license, and her emergency contacts are her parents and a brother, all of them in Maryland; the ER already called them. You sure she is who you think she is?"

"Positive," I answer. "Even more so after that."

Kevin nods at me and squeezes my arm as he heads to scrub in.

"You hear that, Jer?"

"I did," he sighs. "So her parents know, and they'll be considered next of kin for information and such."

"Yes, but you have me." I pause. "Please keep Ethan and Carter calm. I'll call you as soon as I can."

I quickly text Jeremiah, relaying as much information as I can, before preparing myself to enter the operating room. Kevin nods at me as I step inside. My heart races in my chest, palpitations almost drowning out the sound of my own thoughts.

Seeing Alexis lying on the table in the cold, sterile room seizes the air in my lungs. I steel myself, knowing that any display of emotion will prompt Kevin to make me leave—as he should. At that point, I'd be a distraction, a danger to her, and I don't want that.

There's no visible blood; I can only see the faint traces of airbag burns. She looks just as beautiful as ever, like a sleeping angel. As someone who cares deeply for her, I find relief in her appearance. But as a doctor, I know it only makes things worse because almost all her injuries are internal.

If only she just needed stitches or staples. Even the broken arm is manageable.

Once safety checks are completed and anesthesia gives the go-ahead, they begin the procedure. They intubate her, then start the incisions.

I know I had to be here; I couldn't not be here.

But I also know that I am not okay.

48

CARTER

As Jeremiah, Shawn, and Ethan stand before me at my bedroom door, their presence in the middle of the night sends a wave of dread crashing over me. I know, I just know something is very wrong.

Alexis isn't home yet; she'd be in my bed if she were. It's all fueling a growing sense of anxiety that threatens to overwhelm me.

I can see it written plain as day on Jeremiah's face—the gravity of the situation, the weight of the news he has to deliver. With a sinking feeling in the pit of my stomach, I shoot him a warning look, my voice trembling with desperation.

"Jer, what the fuck happened?" I demand, my words laced with fear and urgency.

"Let's go downstairs," Jeremiah instructs, his tone clipped and businesslike—his boardroom persona. "I'll tell you what I know."

Ethan's eyes spark with understanding, discovering Lex isn't with me, the gravity of the situation sinking in. And in that moment, I know he realizes as well something is very, very wrong.

As we gather in the main sitting area, the tension in the air is palpable. Each of us is grappling with our own fears and anxieties. Our body language speaks volumes, revealing the anticipated turmoil within each of us.

Ethan sits on the very edge of the couch, his posture tense, knees wide apart, elbows resting on his thighs as he buries his face in his hands. It's clear that he's struggling to contain his emotions, the anticipation of the weight of the situation bearing down on him.

Shawn, typically composed and reserved, displays subtle signs of anxiety. Though outwardly calm, the nervous ticks betray his facade. He absentmindedly picks at the cuticle on his thumb with his index finger, the inside of his cheek caught between his teeth—an outward manifestation of the internal emotions he's experiencing.

As for me, I can't bring myself to sit down. Arms crossed tightly, I pace back and forth behind the couch, the nervous energy coursing through me is too overwhelming to remain still.

Jeremiah, our current, involuntary anchor in this storm, takes a seat on the coffee table, facing us with a mixture of concern and determination. He tries to strike a delicate balance between closeness and giving us space to process. He fortifies himself as his knees fall wide apart, one bouncing anxiously under his elbow. He takes a deep breath and begins to speak.

"Holden called me from the hospital," Jeremiah begins, his voice strained with emotion. "I don't have a ton of information; he was rushed. But Alexis was in a car accident, a bad one. She's at his hospital."

As Jeremiah delivers the news, my heart feels like it's lodged in my throat, each word he utters sending shockwaves through me. I need him to get on with it, to rip off the bandaid and reveal the extent of the damage, hoping against hope that the anticipation is worse than the reality.

"Holden texted me so I would remember more information for you than I probably would have from talking to him," Jeremiah continues, his voice cracking slightly. "But he's in the operating room with her now."

Ethan's head snaps up, his expression a mix of disbelief and anguish, while I stop pacing, my entire being focused on Jeremiah's next words.

"Holden said it sounds like she was t-boned on the driver's side," Jeremiah continues, his voice heavy with his own anxiety. "She was unconscious when the ambulance got there and hadn't regained consciousness yet."

Ethan's head drops back into his hands, and I feel a surge of frustration and helplessness wash over me. Without thinking, I kick the back of the couch and resume pacing, the nervous energy within me threatening to consume me entirely.

"Before I read through this," Jeremiah pauses, looking at us with a mixture of empathy and apprehension. "I want you to know that nothing he said made it sound like she won't be okay. It's just going to be rough for a few days."

My breath catches in my chest, and I freeze, all my senses honed in on Jeremiah's words. He pulls out his phone, preparing to relay the details Holden had sent him. My heart sinks further with each passing moment, the reality of the situation settling in my soul.

As Jeremiah continues to relay the details of Holden's message, each piece of information, each injury, feels like a weight pressing down on me, threatening to suffocate me with its gravity. My chest tightens, and a wave of panic washes over me, threatening to engulf me entirely. My breathing becomes shallow and erratic, my heart pounds hard in my chest as the reality of Alexis's condition sinks in.

Every word from Jeremiah feels like a hammer to my senses, driving home the severity of the situation. I fight to keep the panic at bay, but it's a losing battle as fear and helplessness grip me tightly. I'm teetering on the edge of a full-blown panic attack, and I'm not sure how much longer I can hold it together. All I can do is cling to the hope that Alexis will be okay, feeling that with every fiber of my being.

"Did he say how long she'd be in surgery?" Ethan asks.

"He said a few hours; it probably depends on what they find," Jeremiah says empathetically. "There's something else you guys should probably know. Her parents were listed as an emergency contact attached to her driver's license. The emergency room was able to reach them, so the hospital probably won't give us much information. Obviously Holden will help there and he can probably bend some rules, but you need to know that."

Ethan starts laughing, and I want to fucking punch him. I realize he is slaphappy, but, fuck.

"What the fuck, Ethan?" I snap, unable to contain my frustration.

He rubs his face wearily, his laughter fading into a solemn expression as he steeples his fingers in front of his face. "Her parents have no say over anything, and we need to go to the hospital," he explains calmly. "I have a signed and notarized medical power of attorney for her."

His words hang heavy in the air, and it takes a moment for them to sink in. Three pairs of eyes fix on him, a mixture of surprise and realization dawning on us all.

"When?" I manage to choke out, my mind reeling with the implications of Ethan's revelation.

"About a month ago, after the fever," Ethan replies with a nonchalant shrug. "You know we share parent trauma. Holden is my medical power of attorney because I don't want my parents to have any say if I were in a similar situation. She thought it both served that purpose and logistically made more sense because her parents are seventeen hundred miles away."

As the weight of Ethan's words settles over us, I find myself grappling with a mix of emotions. While part of me is frustrated that I wasn't aware of this, another part is deeply grateful for Ethan's foresight and thoroughness. His anxious planning may be what we desperately need right now.

* * *

Jeremiah texts Holden to inform him about the power of attorney and that we're heading to the hospital. Despite Holden's initial reluctance, Jeremiah wasn't about to stop us.

As we approach the surgical waiting area, we're taken aback when we spot Brody. Ethan wastes no time in confronting him.

"What the fuck are you doing here?" Ethan's tone is sharp.

Brody actually looks genuinely concerned, which only fuels my anger. "Her parents called me. Apparently, she never told them she broke off the engagement," he explains.

"I hope you set that straight," Ethan retorts.

Brody nods his head. "I hadn't talked to her since the day she came to pick up her stuff. I didn't know where she was living, what she was doing, or anything else. I figured someone needed to be here, so I came."

"Well, you can leave now," I interject firmly.

"I need to tell her parents something," Brody insists.

"You have their number?" Ethan questions. "I will update them."

"I do, but they're on a plane on their way here," Brody replies, his voice subdued.

"Brody, just give me their numbers. You need to go. Give me yours, too, and I'll let you know if anything significant happens," Ethan concedes.

Brody reluctantly agrees, and Ethan takes charge, texting Lex's parents to inform them that he's her medical power of attorney and to notify him upon landing in Denver. If anyone knows how to handle distant parents, it's Ethan, so I trust him to handle it.

Lex's parents are about to receive a lot of unexpected information in addition to updates on their daughter's condition. I can't help but feel conflicted about Lex keeping them in the dark about Brody.

It has only been about twenty minutes when we receive two back-to-back texts in the group from Holden.

(Holden) *Ethan is a fucking genius for the power of attorney*
(Holden) *They're moving her to post-op, it went well, the surgeon and I will be out there in a few minutes*

I think we all let out a collective sigh of relief. When Holden emerges, I barely recognize him. He's still wearing a surgical cap, his mask hanging off his face. Of course, we all know he's a doctor, but we've never seen him in this capacity before.

He looks exhausted—worn out—as if he's not faring much better than any of us. He introduces us to the surgeon and allows him to do most of the talking about the surgery.

"Hey, this is Dr. Maxwell, Kevin," Holden introduces, gesturing towards him. "He's the chief resident of surgery. Kev, these are Carter, Ethan, Jeremiah, and Shawn—all my roommates, and Ethan is her MPOA."

"Okay," Dr. Maxwell begins. "The surgery went well. We knew from emergency scans that there was damage to her spleen from a broken rib, but it was minimal, and we were able to stop the bleeding—repair it, so we didn't have to remove it. We used laparoscopic cameras to explore for a while, ensuring there were no other sources of bleeding or potential infection." He pauses, looking at Holden. "From the general surgery side, she's clear. She should make a full recovery. However, she still has some other issues that neurology and ortho need to address."

The two doctors exchange a nod before Dr. Maxwell turns back to us. "Let Holden know if you all need anything else from me."

Once he's gone and the doors close behind him, Holden sinks into a chair across from us, running his hand over his face in exhaustion.

He takes a deep breath and then proceeds. "She'll be in the ICU—*my* ICU—in about thirty minutes. I need to prepare you all before you go see her," Holden announces, his tone serious.

My breath catches in my chest; that doesn't sound good at all. Ethan's head drops back into his hands.

"It will look scary," Holden continues, his voice steady as he delivers a speech he's clearly given before. "It will look worse than it is. She's going to have *a lot* of wires and tubes attached to her. There will be a lot of machines and monitors beeping and making noise in the room. She has small, superficial burns on her face from the air-bags and bruising on her left side and arm from the broken arm and ribs, but otherwise, from the outside, she looks okay. She looks like her. Kevin only had to make three very small incisions in the OR.

"The scary part now is the head injury; from scans, it doesn't look awful, but they're going to do more tests, an electroencephalogram —an EEG—almost as soon as she gets to the unit. After that, neuro will want us to let her brain rest, so they'll administer drugs to slow down her brain activity, to aid in the healing process." Holden pauses, looking at each one of us before continuing.

"Because of that, she'll be kept in a medically induced coma for twenty-four to forty-eight hours, hopefully not longer, and she'll be on a ventilator. You should know, though, that she *can* breathe on her own. She was just heavily sedated for surgery, and she'll remain that way for the brain rest. She'll need the support of the ventilator."

He gives us a moment to respond, but none of us do. Then, he swallows hard. "It is widely believed they can hear you talking to them and feel you touching them, even though they won't remember it. The ICU has a visitor limitation of two people at a time. I might be able to pull some favors on that, but not tonight. I need to wait until the right people are here."

Then he adds, almost as an afterthought, "I won't be making any medical decisions for her. I'll consult, and I'll know what's happening, but ethically and responsibly, I can't actually put in any orders or make any decisions unless there aren't any other options. What else do you need to know right now?"

"More than you can tell us," I scoff; Holden nods in understanding.

"I'm not sure we know what to ask," Ethan adds.

"I'm going to go back to the unit. I pretty much abandoned them when I saw her name," Holden admits, his voice tinged with guilt. "As soon as she's ready for visitors, I'll text you. They're probably moving her now, but the nurses and respiratory therapist will need some time to get her settled."

When Holden stands, we all stand, too. Ethan moves first, embracing Holden with gratitude, and then I follow suit. Shawn and Jeremiah do the same, but theirs feels more comforting of Holden, especially Jeremiah. After Holden retreats behind closed doors, we all sink back into our seats, quietly processing the weight of the news.

49

ETHAN

This feels like a nightmare. Holden and Dr. Maxwell were re-assuring, but until she wakes up, I don't think any of us will be okay, not even Jeremiah and Shawn.

Holden has only been gone for about fifteen minutes when a nurse comes to the waiting room. She's probably in her mid-forties, wearing navy blue scrubs, about six inches shorter than me, with dark hair and eyes.

She smiles softly. "One of you Ethan Hoffman?"

"That would be me," I say, standing.

"My name is Claire," she introduces herself. "I'm one of the charge nurses for the ICU. Dr. Ashford, Holden, sent me for you. I'm going to take you all up to the ICU waiting area, and then I can take two of you back to see her, okay?"

I nod, and the other three stand. She takes us through restricted doors, and I find myself questioning if this is normal or if it's because we're getting special treatment from Holden. After a short walk and elevator ride, we arrive in a nice waiting room, nicer than the surgical one.

Claire points out the beverage station and the vending machines. She tells us she can get us blankets, phone chargers, or whatever we need. Then she turns to me.

"Okay, I can take two of you." She follows my gaze as I look at Carter and gesture with my head.

Then I turn to Jeremiah. "One of us will be out to let you go back relatively soon."

"Take your time," Jeremiah replies. "You two being back there is most important."

I'm grateful for his generosity, but he and Shawn will need to see her, too. Taking a deep breath, I walk through the ICU doors as Claire scans them open with her badge. The area is large. It appears there are rooms all around the outside of the floor, with glass walls and doors facing a nurse and doctor area that takes up the middle of the large space.

We walk by Holden, and he nods to us. He's talking to another doctor at a counter in the middle. Maybe he wants to keep this private for us, or he doesn't want to see our reaction or explain anything more to us. I don't know, but he lets Claire lead us to room fourteen, to our girl.

The tension coming off of Carter is palpable; he is making me more anxious, but I'm not going to tell him that. When Claire leads us into the room, I'm grateful for Holden's prep because I don't think either of us understood how many wires and tubes or machines there would be.

There's another woman in gray scrubs adjusting tubes and machines near Lexi's face. Her beautiful face. Holden was right; she looks mostly unmarked, but there are tubes in her nose and mouth and tape holding them there. She has a cap on, covering all her gorgeous hair.

Claire senses our trepidation. "This is Max, the respiratory ther-apist. She is just double-checking the ventilator. They set it up in post-op." She pauses, and Max turns and smiles at us.

Claire continues, "I know it's a lot, but most of it is monitor-ing." She points out each machine as she talks about them. "Only the infusion pump, feeding pump, and ventilator are actually doing something for her or to her right now; everything else is just moni-toring. I'm sure you were told, but the ventilator is just because she is sedated; it's not true life support."

Max turns and nods at us, agreeing with Claire, as Holden and another doctor come into the room.

Holden addresses Max first, "We good, Max?"

"Yeah, she's good. I know we're waiting on neuro for full sedation, but she'll wean fast at the end. She's breathing over the vent, trying to maintain about twenty on her own." Both Holden and the other doctor nod at her; Carter and I look at each other. They're speaking a completely foreign language.

I expect Holden to explain, but Max does. "Sorry." She smiles. "The vent maintains her at fifteen breaths per minute. She's over-breathing the vent, breathing on her own at about twenty breaths per minute. That's good because it means when neuro decides to pull the sedation, she *should* be able to be pulled off the ventilator quickly. She doesn't need the ventilator right now, but after neuro is done, they'll sedate her more, so we're leaving it in place."

So much information, too much information.

I nod.

The doctor who came in with Holden interjects, "Speaking of which," he looks between Holden and Claire, "EEG will be here shortly, and they ordered an ICP."

I don't miss Holden's body language shift on that news. He swal-lows, but then he turns to us. "You won't want to be here for that, the ICP placement. It's not a big deal, but they need to put in a wire to monitor the pressure from her brain."

"So why don't we want to be here for that?" Carter asks.

Claire gently touches his arm. "They have to drill a hole in her skull."

I feel like I'm going to vomit.

Claire then continues, "Most family members and friends don't want to be here. It's safe; we do them all the time. Half the patients on the unit have one; you'll just want to step out for a few minutes while they place it."

"But," Holden interjects, "they'll do the EEG first, so it'll be a bit." He looks between Carter and me and then adds, "This is Dr. Cartwright. He's a third-year resident. He will probably be chief when I graduate residency next month. I trust him implicitly. Until the end of our shift, he'll be in charge of Alexis's care, with help from the attending if needed."

"If you're friends with Holden, you can call me Danny," Dr. Cartwright, Danny, says and reaches to shake my hand. Then he continues, "We're pretty confident she's going to be completely okay; she just needs to recover from a lot of trauma."

Danny looks at Holden. "Did you see the MVA report? I don't think you did because it came in while she was in the middle of surgery."

Holden shakes his head no, and Danny continues, glancing between all of us, including Claire, "Estimated speed of impact was forty-two miles per hour; the other driver was intoxicated, at fault, and in far worse shape than she is. They were both high-impact traumas so they split them and took him downtown. The paramedic told the emergency room physician that her car's safety features did everything they were supposed to do."

Carter snorts and lets out a humorless chuckle. "Fucking Audi, thank god that money goes to more than show." Then he looks at me. "She's going to need a lawyer."

I nod in agreement, but it's definitely not my priority right now. I do accept Carter's coping mechanisms will be different from mine.

I know we're getting different treatment because of Holden, which is both better and worse. I can't imagine that the conversations would be this casual normally, but who knows.

Claire then adopts a more typical nursing demeanor. "You guys can sit down."

She gestures toward Max and pushes a chair in her direction. The two of them place the chairs on either side of the bed.

"She can hear you; she may not remember when she wakes up, but she can hear you and feel you if you hold her hand." She pauses. "EEG should be able to work around you, but they're not here yet. If you need anything, just press this button right here." She points to a button on the bed. "Otherwise don't touch any buttons." She smiles softly.

I glance at Holden, and he nods before we both find the chairs on the sides of her bed.

Holden warns softly, "Just be a little careful, Ethan; that's her broken arm side; it's splinted. You can hold her hand; just don't jostle her. They'll probably do that surgery tomorrow as long as neuro says it's okay."

As I nod in response to Holden's guidance, I'm acutely aware of the situation's weight bearing down on me. Despite the reassurances we've received so far, fear and uncertainty gnaw at the edges of my consciousness, threatening to overwhelm me.

With each passing moment, the realization sinks in more that Alexis's very life hangs in the balance, and my heart fucking breaks with a profound sense of helplessness. I try to cling to the hope given by the words of the medical staff, but doubt looms in the recesses of my mind. The anguish of seeing her lying helpless in that hospital bed threatens to consume me whole. My heart lies fucking shattered alongside her, the depth of my love for her never seeming so clear.

An alarm starts in the hallway, they call some kind of code in the ICU, and they all leave us. Holden, Claire, Danny, and Max, they all go, and then it's just Carter, Alexis, and me.

I gently wrap my fingers around hers and run my thumb over the back of her hand. I feel like I'm going to break her, but I can't not touch her.

My heart feels so fucking broken.

50

ETHAN

It has been a long few hours, but they just let us back in the room after placing the pressure monitor for her brain. Holden tells us the EEG was promising, that she probably just needs rest, and then we're alone again, just the three of us.

Looking at Carter, I inquire about his well-being, "You doing okay, man?"

"No," he lightly scoffs. "I'll be a lot better when she wakes up."

"Me too," I agree and run my hand through my thick hair; looking around at the machines, it feels surreal.

I just want to hold her, climb into the bed with her, and feel her softness against me.

My thoughts are interrupted by my phone buzzing. I pull it out of my pocket and look at it. It's Lexi's father. I hold up my phone to Carter; he nods, and I step out of the room. Taking a deep breath, I steel myself for this conversation.

"This is Ethan," I answer the phone tiredly but in a business tone.

"Ethan, hi. This is Alexander Branthwaite, Lexi's father." He is also in business mode.

"Hey, it's nice to meet you over the phone, anyway. The doctors aren't here right now, but I can tell you what I know," I start.

"Please," he says. "Let me get this on speaker so her mom can hear too," and I exhale, grateful we're not getting into the non-medical stuff yet.

"Okay, go ahead."

I take a deep breath and explain most of what I know.

I hear a woman's voice; it must be her mom. "Is she on a vent?"

"She is, but," I pause, "I'm sorry, I'm not medical, and I know you both are; they told us she was breathing over it, but she'll need to stay on it during sedation. They said she would come off quickly when they pull the sedation."

"That sounds right," the woman says. "I'm Carol, Lexi's mom, by the way."

"Ethan," I introduce myself. "It's nice to meet you."

"Ethan," Alexander comes on more clearly, and I'm relatively, but not completely sure I'm off speakerphone. "I—Alexis—" He clears his throat. "Alexis and I, Alexis and her mom, we haven't always had the best relationship. I need you to know that I'm not surprised we haven't heard big news in her life, but if you can update us. We thought she was still engaged to Brody. I just don't want to be blindsided."

He sounds so incredibly apologetic and sincere, his words filled with regret and sincerity. But life-and-death situations can do that to a person sometimes.

"A lot of what you need or want to know, she will need to choose to tell you," I state. "But I will give you the big picture."

"That's fine, thank you," Alexander agrees.

"Okay," I start to explain. "We hosted a Super Bowl party at our house, and Brody was caught completely red-handed at that party cheating on Lexi with one of my roommates' girlfriends. She had no place to go, all she had was Brody, so we gave her one of our guest rooms, and she has been living there ever since."

"Since February?" he asks, almost in shock.

"Yes, since February," I confirm.

"Well, thank you for giving her a roof over her head," he hedges, "Do you know, can you tell me if she found a job out there?"

"She did. She's the director of marketing for a software company." I hesitate, wondering if I should divulge more. "There's a lot more to all of that, but I think she should be the one to tell you."

"Okay, I understand," he says. "We're waiting for our rental car, but we'll be at the hospital sometime in the next few hours."

"Alright." I swallow. "One other thing you should know is that one of the doctors here in the ICU, the chief resident intensivist actually, is also one of our roommates. He knows Alexis well, so he's not putting in any orders for her, but he is involved."

"That is good to know, and probably good for Lex, too. Thank you."

We say pleasant goodbyes, and I go back into her room.

"That her parents?" Carter asks softly.

I nod, "It went okay. Her dad seems concerned and regretful. They'll be here soon, so we'll see."

Carter agrees. "This is all so crazy," he admits.

"I know, Carter. My brain and emotions are in overdrive, for sure," I admit and gently graze my thumb over the back of Lexi's hand.

* * *

SHAWN

This sucks so fucking much. I'm sitting here, biting my tongue, unable to spill a word about Allie and me, about the conversations we had, and the ones I planned to have with Ethan and Carter. It's like walking a tightrope, trying not to overstep boundaries, especially not now.

I'm worried about her.

I'm worried she won't remember.

Fuck.

We've been in the dark out here in the waiting room, barely a peep beyond a few text messages. I keep hoping Jeremiah will push to see her, but he won't, even though, deep down, I know he's craving just a glimpse of her, too.

Then the door swings open, and Ethan strides in.

"I'm going to wait for her parents if one of you wants to go back," he announces, his voice heavy.

Jeremiah and I share a glance. He nods, silently urging me to go.

"I can meet the parents too," Jeremiah suggests, and he doesn't have to tell me twice.

* * *

HOLDEN

SIX DAYS LATER

I've practically taken up residence in her room. I haven't set foot at home, surviving on cafeteria food and swapping out surgical scrubs while showering in the locker room.

The director of intensive care made an exception for us, allowing four visitors at a time, not counting me. Alexis's dad has been a regular presence, while her mom comes by less often. Carter keeps me company during the day but retreats home at night for a few hours of rest. Ethan's practically glued to her side, though he occasionally slips away for a quick shower and change of clothes. Jeremiah and Shawn have been pulling shifts, ensuring there's always someone with her.

But right now, it's just me. Ethan's off for a shower, Jeremiah's heading home, and Shawn and Carter are on their way here. I haven't seen her parents yet today.

My doctor brain is in overdrive, running through statistics, fueling my worry. It's been four days since she came off medical sedation and the ventilator.

Everything is stable.

All the tests indicate she should wake up on her own—correction, she should have already woken up on her own—but here I sit beside her bed, watching her sleep.

Alexis is in a genuine coma, not one we induced, and she's been unconscious since the accident. Her brain function, intracranial pressure, labs, vital signs—they're all normal. She just won't wake up.

Last night, Danny attempted to rouse her using external and pharmaceutical methods. I think Ethan was traumatized, and I believe that's why he had to leave early this morning.

She's beautiful.

Even with the small feeding tube in her nose, which is the only thing remaining on her face now, she's beautiful.

Claire did me a favor and made sure they washed Alexis's hair during her bed bath earlier. She's my angel, my beautiful, sleeping angel.

I'm so tired.

So, so tired.

My elbows on her bed, one hand on hers, I rest my head in my other hand and let my eyes close.

EPILOGUE

ALEXIS

I inhale deeply through my nose as the sensation of falling jerks my body awake, reminiscent of those moments in class when I'd nod off and suddenly startle awake.

Making an effort to open my heavy eyelids, I can barely open them, and everything is blurry through the slits. I try to lick my lips; my mouth is parched, and my lips and tongue are so dry. I want—no need—ice water so much right now.

And my nose itches relentlessly.

There's a comforting presence beside me, someone holding my right hand. I try to move my left hand to rub my eyes, but it refuses to obey. Faintly wiggling my toes, I sense the rough texture of cheap sheets and something wrapped around both of my calves.

Groggy and disoriented, I struggle to piece together where I am and what's happening.

A muffled announcement over a loudspeaker catches my attention, calling for a doctor to the emergency room.

Emergency room?

I'm in a hospital.

My brain suddenly flashes back to the last thing I remember—the sound of crunching metal, shattering glass, and searing pain. Sirens blaring, then darkness.

I close my eyes tight and try to open them a couple of times, and on the third time, they open more, and I'm finally able to look around the room.

There are so many machines. With a surge of panic, I realize I'm in the intensive care unit, surrounded by machines and monitors. The gravity of my situation sinks in, and I fight to keep from panicking amid the flood of memories of Jake, of car accidents—of death.

You're awake, Alexis; you're not going to die here. You're awake.

As my vision focuses even more, I look down at my left arm that I can't move and it is in a cast, lightly tied to the bed rail. My eyes gaze a path across my body to my other hand, covered gently by someone else's hand.

Sandy blonde hair, blue surgical scrubs, and a white lab coat hanging over the back of the chair.

Holden?

As I gently pull my fingers out from under his, I attempt to speak but only manage a hoarse whisper; he doesn't hear the effort. When I reach out to run my weak fingers through his hair, he twitches, and I can't help but smile at the reaction.

I repeat the action and then play with the hair on the nape of his neck.

Startling, he lifts his head and looks at me.

"Alexis?" he utters, his voice filled with astonishment.

I reach for his face, cupping his jaw, feeling the short beard that has grown since I last saw him. My thumb moves over his cheek.

"Oh my—thank fucking god," he exhales, his already bloodshot eyes brimming with tears before he gently embraces me.

When he pulls back and strokes my hair, there are tears on his cheeks. I reach up and wipe them with my good hand.

"Hi," I barely whisper.

"Angel," he murmurs, grabbing my hand and pressing a kiss to my knuckles.

He then reaches for his phone, quickly sending a text before returning his full attention to me.

As he meets my gaze with his piercing blue eyes, reassurance fills his words. "You're gonna be okay," he laughs softly. "*We* are all traumatized, but you're going to be okay."

I squeeze his hand and smile softly. I wonder where the rest of them are, but I know he sent a text, and my voice isn't really working. I have so many questions.

Someone is pulling back the curtain, and both Holden and I turn.

I feel a mixture of surprise and apprehension as I see my parents walking toward me. Squeezing Holden's hand tighter, I brace myself for the inevitable drama to come.

TO BE CONTINUED

Milton Keynes UK
Ingram Content Group UK Ltd.
UKHW051450140724
445326UK00013BA/484